W9-ACL-370

WITHDRAWN

THE MUDLARK

The Mudlark

BY

THEODORE BONNET

GARDEN CITY, N. Y.

Doubleday & Company, Inc.

1949

CARL A. RUDISILL
LIBRARY
LENOIR RHYNE COLLEGE

With the exception of actual historical person-
ages identified as such, the characters are entirely
the product of the author's imagination.

COPYRIGHT, 1949, BY THEODORE BONNET

ALL RIGHTS RESERVED

PRINTED IN THE UNITED STATES

BY

H. WOLFF, NEW YORK

To L. W. B.

Lines of Goethe's *Mignon* in Chapter 14 are from the English rendering by George L. Hanlin. Used by permission.

THE MUDLARK

1

Wheeler, or the Ha'penny Bit, as
his countrymen ever after were to speak of him, makes his entrance
into history at the fall of a November evening in the thirty-ninth
year of Victoria's reign, and stands in front of Windsor Castle in a
thick Thames fog. A sentry of Her Majesty's Grenadier Guards sees
him loom up vaguely against the grey world outside King Henry
the Eighth's Gateway on Castle Hill and heave to on the black
paving stones for a moment, looking in. . . .

Or that is the scene as you find it in history—but who ever heard
of a sentry of the Royal Household Guards dropping his eyes to
look at so thoroughly inconsequential an object? Really, the scene
is more plausible the other way round: not the sentry looking at
Wheeler, but Wheeler looking at the sentry, standing within an inch
of him, too, and leaning backward in the shadow of the overwhelm-
ing bearskin cap to peer up the column of buttons at a face as rigid
and careless of the weather as the face of the Iron Duke himself in

front of the Royal Exchange; because that is the way small boys always inspect the guard at Windsor Castle.

Wheeler was a grotesque urchin no higher than a Grenadier's belt buckle, and he was swaddled in a grown man's castoff coat that hung clear down to the tops of his shoes. Round the hems the coat was all caked with mud, a mark not of his character, however, but of his calling; and it had long since parted from its buttons. When he had no rope yarn for a jury rig, it would belly out in any wind, considerably impeding his progress and causing him to appear at a distance rather like a little catboat taken aback in the luff. And he wore a faded green cap pulled down over a tawny clump that crested over his ears and, round his neck, a grimy rag of storm canvas to keep out the damp.

But you can't always tell a man by his clothes, nor a boy either, and Wheeler had been better served by Nature than by tailors. If he was undersize and thin and had the London pallor, one couldn't blame Nature for those things: in the circumstances, one would do better to look on the bright side and observe that she must have given him an auspicious start to enable him to carry on as well as he had. For he was vigorous, agile, and erect; his face, with its thumb heel of a nose, gave no promise of beauty, but it guaranteed intelligence; and his eyes were extraordinary. It wasn't their size, which was large, nor their colour, which was deep brown; it was the light in them, an arresting, amusing light, as of some enormous surprise, which constantly leaped up in them, and which somehow lingered when other emotions were visible in them as well, so that even his saddest looks held an element of wonder. And that light gives us a clue to his character.

It helps to explain, to begin with, why he was easily the best audience to be found on his reach of the river, which extended properly from the East India Docks to the Pool. Seamen were charmed by it, and were encouraged to pour forth so freely of their wisdom that they must be counted as having supplied, up until this evening, the

major part of his education. It was thanks to them that he knew of
Drake, Nelson, and Forty Fathoms 'Ammersmith, Foochow and
Sydney and Java Head, which is to say some history and geography,
and even a bit about the Bible, though in biblical matters he was by
way of being a heretic, having been ably persuaded that no fish
could swallow a bloke. Captains, seeing the way Wheeler looked
at their ships alongside the jetties, took on the stance of admirals, or
else began behaving more like bos'ns, each according to his nature.
Policemen, gazed upon by him, felt keenly the weight of their public
responsibilities, and said, "Nah, then, push along there," to suspicious characters they might otherwise have overlooked entirely. But
guzzlers and their jollies were disposed to fling the back of a hand
at him, or snarl and turn away.

The authorities never quite understood how he happened on this
fateful evening to be in Windsor Town in the first place, so far up-
river from his native habitat; but then the authorities never quite
understand anything. He was habitually a rover. His mother, a barmaid at the Waterman's Arms, had died of typhus while he was still
in arms, and if he had a father, he was unaware of the fact, as probably was the father himself. His mother proudly used to ascribe him
to a chief officer, but never could remember the man's name, nor
even that of his ship, a tragedy that lost something when one reflected
that she was in exactly the same dilemma regarding the paternity of
her other two children. (Or that was what she gave you to understand if you pressed her, but to tell the truth, it was doubted by those
who knew her best. Not her way, it wasn't, to be throwing a thing
like that up to a man, they said: that sort, she was—poor Nan!)
And Wheeler's two brothers had vanished as utterly as their fathers
before them.

In those days, when half the children of the East End ran foot-
loose in the streets and compulsory education had not yet caught up
with them, cases like theirs were common. The eldest, seldom at home
from the age of six, had gone on his own at eight: he had been vari-

ously reported from time to time—once as a crossing sweeper cadging tips from passers-by, again as a mendicant shoeblack, then as having been seen in the company of a buzzer in Hampstead Heath, and finally as having shipped off to sea. And the other brother had somehow come under the protection of a beggarwoman of the Ratcliffe Highway, who had found him useful in her business, till on an evil day they happened to be passing a brewery at the exact instant the vats burst and, being swept into a cellar, were drowned in an ocean of beer. This left the third of Nan's children the sole charge of a bachelor uncle, a Thames bargeman; and the boy being anyhow, as it were, the issue of a union of the sea and the shore, he naturally gravitated to the river, in which he was soon wading with the swarms of mudlarks young and old that daily salvaged the leavings of the tides from Woolwich to Vauxhall Bridge. Lumps of coal, pieces of iron and rope, bones and nails were his haul, with which he turned a few pennies at the shops; and he aspired someday to be as 'Ooker Morgan, the dredger, of whom it was told on Blackwall Stairs that he had grown rich from the pockets of drowned people alone. And if as time went on his uncle did not send him to school under the Act, which would have taken a bit of tin, neither did he put him out to work his passage, though he often talked of doing so and lately had approached a master sweep about it.

"Getting on for ten, 'e is," said he, exaggerating two full years to the best of his recollection; "time a boy learned a tride. Wot would yer say he'd bring, now, all ad walorem and no inchmaree, eh? Wouldn't yer say all-found and a bit of a charter fee, now?"

"Me?" uncomfortably inquired the sweep, who was of the knulling or door-knocking variety, and therefore, as he well knew, not entirely above suspicion as to ethics. "Wot's it got to do with me, I'd like to know?"

"Aow, come off!" laughed the bargeman. "You're a man o' business, ain't yer?"

The other eyed him distrustfully. "A man o' lawful business, I am. And if it's climbing boys you 'ave in mind, we've no more use fer 'em in the respectable chimney line. The law don't 'old with no more chummies, not these days it don't."

"The law! And did anyone 'ear me say you'd 'ave the lad for a chummy—I arsk you. Not likely they did! 'Ow would I know wot you'd be 'aving 'im for? All I says is, you'd find 'im 'andy and willing for wotever you'd put 'im to, see?" He nudged the man of business playfully. "An' *small for 'is aige.*"

But if this eased the knuller's mind on one point, he was still skeptical, and shook his sooty head into his mug of ale. " 'Appen 'e's right enough nah," he said, out of a cynicism born of experience, "but I knows these lads. They gets bigger!"

"Bigger!" snorted the uncle. "Not this lad 'ere. 'E was the runt o' the litter. Nigh onter ten 'e is, and not a 'and 'igher nor 'e were at five. Reg'lar certyfied little 'Op-o'-me-Thumb, that's wot 'e is. 'E'll not get any bigger."

So it finally was agreed that the sweep should see the candidate in person and judge for himself; but the bargeman, being given to procrastination in most things, hadn't yet got round to producing his nephew for the inspection, and perhaps he never would. He was a careless man, but amiable, even in his cups, and although it could not be said that he was both father and mother to his ward, at least he had made the sacrifice of moving ashore from his barge and taking a room over a Chinese establishment in Dolphin Lane in order to provide the boy with what he deemed "a proper 'ome."

Home it was, in the sense that Wheeler often slept there, ate there when his uncle had remembered to supply food to eat, and used it as a base for the operations of his exploratory existence; but from observation of the world around him, he knew that there was something missing. On nights when his uncle was away on his barge, or detained by his mates at the local, an intense loneliness would creep over Wheeler, possibly heightened by the fact that he was hungrier than usual, and he would go forth to the back door of the Waterman's Arms, where for his dead mother's sake they might give him a muffin, or perhaps he would receive an exotic handout from the kindly Oriental merchant belowstairs, who drove a brisk trade in bird's nests, opium, and bhang. And then, lingering under the gas lamp at the corner, he would watch the street fill up with merry-makers, or go and peer in at the doors of pubs, till someone came and shooed him off; and then he would put his back to the river and set out for foreign parts.

The first of these nocturnal expeditions had begun aimlessly enough, merely from being at a loss with himself; but thus it had happened that in more respectable quarters of London he had come upon the outsides of real homes, with clean curtains in cheerfully lighted windows, through which, occasionally, pleasant laughter floated, or the soft muffled music of a piano. And he would hang about the steps, listening, or, when no one was coming along the street, climb up to a window where the people had forgotten to draw the blind, and peer in. Sometimes there would be a man enthroned in an armchair, and a woman in a smaller one at the other side of the fire, sewing, or seated at the polished instrument from which the music came, and sometimes children no older than himself, but scrubbed clean and finely dressed, looking at picture books on the sofa, or playing on the floor. And all this struck him as very admirable and attractive. And it was how he knew that he had betters.

The deeper he ventured into London, the more he saw that was interesting, and the deeper it drew him, till the time came when he stayed away from home for days, foraging for his food in dustbins, or filching it when he could from street stalls, and sleeping in doorways, freezing cold. He liked to see all the carriages in Piccadilly, the toffs and street performers in Covent Garden, and he would follow a dancing bear for an hour. He often reviewed the troops in front of Buckingham Palace, St. James's, and the Horse Guards, attended the concerts of hurdy-gurdy men and strolling German bands. He revelled in the gay atmosphere outside music halls, taverns, and oyster rooms; and, floating luxuriously on the evening tide, would attach himself unnoticed to a likely couple in the Strand, pretending it to be a threesome, till the other two turned off and he found himself again alone. He had penetrated Belgravia, Rotten Row, and Grosvenor Square, visited Clerkenwell and Camberwell, Hackney and Hatcham, Chelsea, Clapham, and Notting Hill, and in sum, no doubt, had seen more of the *outside* of London already than most Londoners ever see. For the rest of the world, he had been all the way to Gravesend on his uncle's barge, had called at Grays Thurrock and looked in at the caves, and indeed had seen Windsor Castle before, but only from the river on a haul to Oxford.

"There she stands," Bill Grams had said, throwing out both arms to frame the rosy pile between them in the sunset—"the pilot'ouse o' the ruddy world! Mark you, matey, 'ere's the old world a-rolling through spice at thousands o' knots, and up there's all them stars and 'Alley comets a-coming at us faster yet; and why don't they ram us, why don't they up and stove us in?" Bill Grams, it was believed, usually had a drop of gin stowed somewhere aboard. " 'Cause up there's an 'and on the wheel wot keeps a sife course, that's why—the 'and of 'Er Majesty the Queen! And when one o' them big foreign stars up there comes too close for sifety, wot 'appens? Why, she leans outer that pilot'ouse and 'ollers, ' 'Ere, you, sheer off!' And you yjer, it sheers!"

"I *yjer!*" Wheeler agreed with enthusiasm, for he was convinced that it had better.

Of course he had heard other reports of the Queen at Windsor that were not so flattering as Bill Grams's. "Shuts 'erself up in 'er carstle like a blinking nun, she does!" This from a patron of the Waterman's Arms. "No more good to England these d'ys than 'Enry the Eyth. 'E's shut up in Windsor Carstle, too, mind: shut up tight in a blooming vault o' St. George's, that's wot—'im and Jine Symour. Not proper for the Widder yet, eh? Let 'er wait 'er turn!"

But the loyalty of Wheeler to his Sovereign remained unshaken. The Mother of England, his uncle said she was, and it disconcerted Wheeler to hear anyone speak ill of her. He thought about her sometimes, and always stopped to look at her pictures, and he liked to hear his uncle tell about the time he had seen her. Only once had his uncle seen her, and then he had not been much older than Wheeler was now: the day she had ridden out in her carriage with the Prince Consort to open the Great Exhibition at the Crystal Palace; but he was not likely to forget it.

"Great d'y for England that was; aye, a great d'y for London. Arf the world was in London that d'y, come to be'old the glories of English Tride. You never seen such a 'olid'y, and belike you never will. Crowned 'eads? The streets was awash with 'em. 'Specially 'Indoos; 'undreds of 'Indoos; and Roosian jukes and Chiny mandarins and American millionaires. Right at 'Ide Park Corner, that's where I was, squeeged in like a little 'erring; and when the Queen's carriage hove in sight, my guv'nor give me a leg up so as I could 'ave a look at 'er; and I could see 'er pline as I see you. Oh, she was royalty, right enough; royalty to 'er fingertips, I lay my life, and a proper little lydy in all respects. 'Andsome, too, she was then, for all she was only a little bit of a queen; a-smiling and a-nodding 'er 'ead right pleasant; and we all cheered as she went by. . . ."

But it wasn't many saw the Queen any more, his uncle said, she being all the time in her mourning. And looking up tonight at her castle, Wheeler wondered which part that might be in.

The pilothouse of the ruddy world; the Queen in her mourning, and Henry the Eighth down in St. George's Chapel with Jane Seymour; less imaginative minds than Wheeler's have been stirred by Windsor Castle. It is the Great Cairn of the English dynasties, founded by the Conqueror and shaped stone on stone by the sovereigns after him, a vast enclosure of architectural anachronisms high and low, of towers and pinnacles, gardens and courtyards, sprawling above the river like a walled city into which the Middle Ages have withdrawn in full harness and shut themselves up for ever. This is the gate King Harry built; within are the quarters of the Military Knights, built by Bloody Mary; and the Horseshoe Cloisters, by Edward Fourth, lately redone by Victoria, whom God preserve. And there, dominating the crowded close that is called the Lower Ward, is St. George's Chapel—cathedral is a word that would suit it better, and in fact it is the cathedral of the Knights of the Garter, whose prelate is the Bishop of Winchester, and whose banners overhang its stalls. Its history is so long and complex only a scholar could tell it all, but they do say the place was old already when Dan Chaucer took it in hand for repairing, and that not far from where the eighth Henry is entombed beneath its choir, the sixth lies, murdered in the Tower of London; likewise the fourth Edward and his queen; and Charles the First, with his head reverently put back again. And if we were to go into Windsor Great Park, we should see, lining the Long Walk, the elms that they say were planted by Charles the Second. But the jackdaws in the Round Tower have been there since Edward Third's time. Edward of Windsor he was called, for in this castle he was born; and here his son, the Black Prince, was married to the Maid of Kent; and his wife, Philippa, died. Here King John of France was held for ransom after Poitiers, and George the Third was shut when he went mad; and it was in one of these towers that another royal prisoner, he that was to be James First of Scotland, looked down from a window and fell in love with Jane of Beaufort, walking in the garden. And the Lion Heart rode out to the Crusade from here, and his brother John to sign the Magna Charta at Runnymede. This is the manor house of the whole entailed estate of England; alluvium of eight hundred years of the flowing English river. But what are eight centuries to the immemorial and mysterious history of the boy standing under its battlements in the fog? By your leave, his forbears built the first London Bridge, for all anyone knows; fought Caesar at Verulamium, and were begat of women whose fathers had held this land since the cliffs of Dover were downs at Calais and the Thames flowed into the Rhine.

He left King Henry's gate, and, clambering up on the high sloping lawn that covers the old castle ditch, slowly followed the curtain walls up the hill, now and then intimately touching the stones with his hands, until he came to the place where the lawn ends, and, climbing down, he found himself close to another gate. Outer St. George's Gate this was, a pair of stone pillars in an iron fence. Two more sentries rigidly faced each other in front of it. Neither of them noticed Wheeler. After all, it wasn't as if anyone were expecting an assault upon Windsor Castle: nothing like that had happened in centuries. Then, of course, it was foggy. And Wheeler, a bit startled at having come upon them so suddenly, drew quickly back behind the sentry box, so that there was only an instant when he might have been visible to them in any case.

This brought him up against the iron fence. Naturally he seized two of the upright palings in his fists, the better to peer in between them; and then the thing happened that put all the folly into his head. The fence yielded to his pull! For just at that point there is a pedestrian gate in that fence, and by some shameful carelessness (or conjunction of stars) *it wasn't locked!*

Wheeler froze as stiff as the Grenadiers. Did they know he was here? They must have heard him. But almost a minute passed and nothing happened. Holding his breath, he drew the gate an inch toward him. It came on oiled hinges. He drew it wider, just wide enough for his chest, and held it there. From somewhere came the noise of a horse pulling a trap over the cobbles. It faded into the dusk. Wheeler dared to look round. No one; nothing but the fog. That was when he slipped through. Then he had dropped to all fours, and was creeping stealthily forward, an obscure object resembling an old-clothes bundle propelled by unseen mice.

But it wasn't going to be so simple as that. He was only just launched upon one of the most improbable of all routes for stealing into the castle, a route that any professional cracksman would have shunned. When one considers how he finally made it, one can only marvel at the humour of a Fate that would conspire so elaborately to help him. There was still the inner gate to pass, a pointed archway in a high, crenellated wall of stout heathstone that stretched across his path between two formidable towers, and it was flanked by two more guards. Because of the thickness of the weather, he didn't discover this barrier until he was almost upon it: then he knew that he was boxed in; he was on the very point of turning back when Fate commenced her ingenious machinations to detain him. There was a grinding of heavy hoofs and wheels on gravel; two great dray horses thrust their heads through the murk of the gateway arch and came straight at him.

"Halt!" a voice commanded them, but they didn't halt.

Wheeler leaped to one side just in time to avoid being trampled. Frightened at this unexpected movement under hoof, one of the animals reared up and plunged against the other. The driver of the lorry in their wake cursed and pulled at the reins. A guard from the gate came running up behind the second horse, exploding "Halt! Halt!" like a Gatling gun, at which that horse reared too. The guard tried to catch its bridle, the horse plunged, and the man went sprawling.

"Blarst yer!" roared the driver. He was a big, stout fellow whose broad face was smeared with damp coal dust, and in his rage he was jerking the reins this way and that, in a manner that only excited his team the more. "Bloody lobsters! Wot 'ave yer done to me 'orses! I'll 'ave the bloody law on yer if they breaks a leg!"

But now the second guard, having seen his mate go down, appeared on the other side of the conveyance shouting that the driver would get his bellyful of law if he didn't clear out of this with his bloody horses and his bloody coal lorry too, and why hadn't he halted at the gate as he'd been told? Thus, for an instant, Wheeler, who by this time would have been as glad of a chance to get out of the castle as in, was offered one clear avenue of escape from the immediate danger of discovery, and he took it. He crawled as fast as he could crawl, straight through the unguarded inner gate that gave upon the Great Courtyard of the Upper Ward, dug in behind the equestrian statue of Charles the Second, and for the moment was safe in the very heart of Windsor Castle.

What happened to the coalman and his dray he never knew, nor did history stop to make a note of it. Having materialized in the emergency like a fairy godmother's coach-and-six, doubtless they were as efficiently dismissed again as soon as Wheeler had no further need of them. The uproar ceased: silence, like a routed jackdaw, returned to the castle and folded its wings. The vaporous evening dissolved the great weight of Windsor into a vision of Camelot, quite as a romantic artist, a Turner, might have presented it to him, softening the contours of the walls, blending towers into air, and transmuting the lights at the casements into glowing daubs of gold. Dimly, as for centuries at every hour of night, a voice broke the stillness announcing the time: seven o'clock, it said, and innocently assured everyone that all was well.

The marauder came out from behind King Charles and began to crawl across the gravelled courtyard. He was bearing diagonally for the great pile of the State Apartments on his left, and had covered about a quarter of the distance when, turning his head to keep watch upon the right as well, he was brought up all standing by the sight that met his eyes; he whirled to face it, pressed himself close to the ground, and lay doggo. At an upper window was a man in a scarlet coat, not a coat such as the sentries wore, but more splendid, and on his head was a white wig. But he had only come to draw the blind, and directly it shut him from view. This was at once a relief and a disappointment to Wheeler, who remained for a full minute stationary, torn between caution and curiosity, half hoping that the man would present himself for further inspection at one of the other windows, if only to draw the blind there too, for the coat and wig clothed him in grandeur and his being inside the castle invested him with all the possibilities of a lord chamberlain. But the scarlet figure appeared not again. And the Imp or Spirit that had got Wheeler this far was growing unmanageably impatient.

Returning to business, Wheeler swung round on his knees in the dark to regain his course, and, pitching forward with his hands, alighted upon nothing—nothing, that is, but air, which was where he had expected the ground to be; he disappeared as suddenly as if the courtyard had swallowed him, which, in the only practicable sense of the expression, it had. Wheeler was sliding headlong into the earth, his astonished hands still thrust out in front of him, a screech locked tight in his throat. He struck bottom with a crash, tumbled head over heels, and the shock, releasing his vocal cords, also knocked the wind out of him, so that instead of a screech he emitted only three emphatic grunts in the process of coming upright upon his posterior amid swirling clouds of black.

It wasn't a dungeon: it was a clean, well-lighted tunnel. Down the middle ran a narrow railway track, upon the track stood a little car filled with coal, and it was upon this coal that Wheeler was sitting. For the Great Courtyard of Windsor Castle is pierced in several places by coalholes, which, when not in use, are supposed to be covered with iron lids, and the lids gravelled over, but the careless coalman just departed had left one of these pitfalls open, and down it Wheeler had plunged into one of the passageways of the utilitarian labyrinth known as Underground Windsor. It was a passage dating not from William the Conqueror, but from Albert the Good, who might as aptly have been agnominated the Efficient. There even was a sensible little guide sign with an arrow.

But dungeon or no, Jonah arriving in the whale could not have been more appalled at the surroundings than Wheeler was; and perceiving overhead the gaping maw that had swallowed him, he sprang to the task of heaving himself out of it again instantly. But the coal chute was steep, polished by the avalanches of years, and sprinkled with a fine dust; his knees slipped out from under him, or his coat got in the way, and his grip on the thin sides failed; three times he slid back to the bottom. Then he heard sounds in the tunnel. He listened. A low laugh, hollow, as in a tomb; someone talking; and then—unmistakably—approaching feet. He scrambled to the ground, retreated in the opposite direction, and hid behind a turn of the passage.

Two grimy navvies hove into view, thick-chested, slope-shouldered, swinging their long, toil-warped arms like a couple of orangoutangs.

"It ain't as if yer'd been to sea like wot I 'ave, 'Arry," one was saying. "Ah, that'd change yer mind quick enough, that would. But ignorance is bliss every time, I s'y, and if a bit of English fluff contents yer, where's the 'arm?"

"Hear, 'ear," jeered the other. "You and yer blinkin' Eyetalians! 'Op it and lend a 'and 'ere. I want me supper, if you don't."

"Right you are, then, but you needn't get yer back up. It's like I s'y—all a matter o' where yer been an' wot yer seen. Easy does it; 'ere we go."

He watched them wheel the car down the tunnel, round a corner, and out of sight. Then he went and stood where the car had stood, and looked forlornly up at the coalhole in the roof. It now was hopelessly out of reach. Panic seized him. He felt himself trapped in this treacherous hole; it flashed upon him that he would be hunted down its length and taken, then that he might be left here to die—shut up in Windsor Castle for ever, he and Henry the Eighth! Desperately he determined to brave a bit of exploration in search of another exit.

He could not read the sign, but had been born with the confidence of all honest citizens in arrows, and noting that the direction recommended by this one went opposite to that taken by the navvies, he followed its advice, walking as quietly as possible and with an eye out for trouble.

It was a broad passage of whitewashed stone. The floor was

flagged and swept clean, the roof at first low and gently rounded, but at a little distance vaulted into a fine Gothic arch, as if at this point the modern burrow joined a medieval one, and from here on the flags looked older, worn as by a procession of servants passing over with the centuries. Gas jets, spaced at reasonable intervals, burned low, bluely, and flickered a little. He passed platoons of stout oaken doors, each presenting to him a polished brass plate with a number surmounted by a crown. All were locked. Once the passage intersected another, but a second arrow pointed him on; then the passage turned, and abruptly it stopped. It stopped dead at a narrow, winding staircase dimly lighted by an oil lamp hanging by a rusty chain; and, taken by surprise, Wheeler stopped short of it. Clearly the staircase wasn't a way out; it would only lead him up into the castle. Yet even as he hung back, he remembered that it was the castle he had come to see, and as nothing further occurred to alarm him, he commenced to waver in his mind between escape and his original intention. He approached the staircase warily, laid his hand on the heavy, blackened newel post, and stopped again, looking up, large-eyed, listening. There wasn't a movement, not a sound. A little thrill passed over him, half of fear, half of downright relish in his unobserved proximity to the world abovestairs. His throat was dry. "Lawks!" he whispered, and swallowed hard. He took a grip on his courage and began cautiously to climb his Beanstalk.

2

There really was such a boy as this. What he did in the Queen's house that night stirred all Britain at the time, and so puzzled it as to move the people in charge to amass a power of official reports on the case, which you may read for yourself if you choose. But it must be admitted that in pursuing their inquiry the authorities held to a straight, businesslike road that of course didn't lead anywhere, and never bothered to explore a single one of the devious little bypaths that did. Consequently the historians have entirely missed the point of the boy; his very character has eluded them, and they understand neither what he did nor what came of it in circles widening far out from the ignominious coal-hole down which he slid into the Wonderland of Britannic Majesty. For as with many another piece of inner lore from every time and reign, much of the story of Wheeler is preserved only among the vanishing hereditary servants of the Royal Household, to be handed down discriminatingly in the Servants' Hall after hours, and only there, at the expense of considerable pains and guile, might you be able to hear it told.

As to the historians, with their versions of things culled from newspapers, books, and old manuscripts, their conflicting sources, their queer mixed habits of scientific analysis, respectable reticence, and mere loose talk, they are notoriously misleading on occasion, and the earnest student will do well not to believe all he reads in books of theirs. They are fond of referring to Victoria's reign as an era of peace and prosperity in Britain; after which the student may find it confusing to read their accounts of the "Hungry Forties," which were distinguished mainly by famine, a wrathful insurrection of the poor, the First Afghan War, the Sikh affair, and the brutelike drudgery and brutal beating of small children of both sexes in coal mines and cotton mills; of the stinking, jam-packed slums that were sinks of misery and degradation until the century's close; of the Crimean War, the Indian Mutiny, the commercial panic and bread riots of the fifties; of the Fenian outrages of the sixties, the Kaffir War, the Zulu War, the Second Afghan War, the Ashantee Expedition, and the final collapse of English agriculture in the seventies; of Majuba, Khartoum, the Dockers' Strike, the plight of the girls in the match factories, and the bayonets fixed against an army of jobless men in Trafalgar Square in the eighties; finally, of Kitchener's two-year campaign in the Soudan, and that most conspicuous event of the *fin de siècle*, the Boer War. Peace and prosperity they call it.

What the historians mean is that in Victoria's time Britain never felt her security seriously threatened from abroad, but attained to a new pinnacle of power in the world, broadened her empire, extended her trade, increased on a vast scale her capital goods and means of production, developed her resources, raised up a new breed of wealthy, enterprising sons, and, at the end, had improved the general standard of living to a degree not dreamt of by practical men at the reign's beginning. But the process was attended by violent dislocations and convulsions. Britain was changing rapidly from an agricultural nation to an industrial one, so rapidly that she scarcely grasped the significance of what was happening, and her confused attempts at adjustment to the strange new order continually defeated themselves at first in monstrous blunders conscientiously committed in the name of a social philosophy which, while it enabled the rich to grow richer, rendered the poor yet poorer, the vitality of the race weaker, and evoked ominous rumblings that rattled the windows of Westminster like a rising wind, till at last it gave way in the full gale of new age and had to be thrown in tatters onto the same heap with feudalism and oligarchy, rapiers and perukes, the crossbow and the cottage loom. Peace nothing. It was an era of civil war. And as for the prosperity that came with the latter part of the reign, it could be shown as late as the nineties that the needy of London still comprised thirty per cent of the population. It was a time of portentous comets and meteors; it saw the beginning of the end of an ancient stewardship, a reckoning of accounts outstanding since the days of villeinage. And at a moment in this greatest of British revolutions, the singular unit of humanity with whom we have to deal is climbing the stairs of Windsor Castle.

The portcullises of privilege and patronage already have been breached, and those who a few years ago stood for repression now give ground before the inevitable. The working men of the towns have been given the vote, if as yet the miners and farm labourers have not; the universities and the Civil Service have been thrown open to all; the system of commission purchase in the Army has been abolished; law and the courts of law are in process of reform, while with one hand the protection of the Constitution has been extended to trades-unions and taken away with the other. Parson Malthus is in his grave, and after him is dying hard the doctrine of devil-take-the-hindmost; and so such matters as public health, education, and the condition of the poor now are generally conceded to be some concern of government, though how much of a concern is still a question. Adam Smith has been dust these many years, but the principle of laissez-faire, which he imported, expounded, and enshrined, lives after him and flourishes. Neither is old Jeremy Bentham to be seen abroad any more, leaning on the stick he called Dapple, his bright eyes probing into the value of everything; but wherever stands a British institution, men ask themselves the question he drummed into them: What is the use of it? And now, in a strange new democratic spirit he never intended, his inflexible logic is turned against the Throne itself. For this is the Age of Reason. The cold wind of Darwinism blows through the churches. It is the Age of Doubt, of New Directions. In the general clamour for change, few remember Cromwell's warning, None goes so far as he who knows not whither he is going; nor reflect with Disraeli that if they pull down the masonry of her greatness, England cannot begin again.

It is the Age of Progress. Slag heaps blacken the Welsh countryside, furnaces like the watch fires of armies redden the night sky of the Potteries, steam boilers drive the mills of Lancashire, ships from every corner of the seas crowd for room on Thames and Mersey, and smoke hangs thick over a very grimy London. It is the Age of Acquisitiveness, expressing itself in ugly villas and cluttered drawing rooms; of Large Families, Eminent Respectability, Enormous Dinners—and of Mudlarks, Rookeries, and Malnutrition. It is the Age of the Railway, the Steamship, the Telegraph; the tempo of life quickens and competition has become a deadly game. Venturing into the City, which he seldom does any more, an old buck in the blue coat and brass buttons of William Fourth's time disdainfully pushes his way through crowds all in sober black, distastefully notes the hard faces, the cold, inward eyes; and over the tea in Upper Brook Street, his dame deplores the modern introduction of money into polite conversation. But this is the Age of Money. It is also the Age of Vision, of Opportunity, of Expansion. At Oxford, Ruskin lectures on the Nobility of Empire, while among the fascinated undergraduates sits young Cecil Rhodes. Refuse litters the floor of the British Museum and dust gathers on the Elgin marbles. . . .

To hover in the outer darkness of a future century and look down upon the limelit "turn" of the Past on such a stage as England can be an instructive pastime, nor in this case might it be altogether a distraction either, for boys no less than men should be observed in relation to the world around them, and this is a study of a boy named Wheeler. Were the evening longer, it might be worth while even to review some things that happened before the boy was born—to begin with the time of the longbow in the Welsh marches and the sword at Runnymede, and coming forward to Wat Tyler, Thomas More, John Bunyan, William Cobbett, and the rest, follow the fortunes of his estate in chancery before he came along to claim it; but none of that is part of this story as they tell it in the Servants' Hall, and why go yawing about in Time to explore such recent history anyway? The earth is reckoned to be some two or three billion years of age, and in our own day, says H. G. Wells, there exist certain mudfish which enable us to understand quite clearly how the vertebrated animal first came out of the ooze.

3

It was coming on to be the kind of night on which it once was commonly believed that the horned figure of Herne the Hunter prowled the Park, and on which sentries still thought they saw Anne Boleyn ascending to her bower in the Dean's Cloister. In that fog, the castle seemed a place where the living only trespassed, and only the dead belonged. The towers hung aloof and mournful, as if in reverie upon their Iliad. The darkness palpably brushed the cheek, and felt of cold sweat. Without half trying, one might fancy Tudors and Stuarts, Yorkists and Lancastrians, Plantagenets and Normans silently intermingling there, each upon a separate dead world's business, and all keeping watch upon the trespassers; so that tonight the porter of the Round Tower might hasten his steps a bit as he passed by the armour of King David of Scotland, and a page, going down a lonely corridor, shun the gallery where it was said that still, when the mood was on her, Elizabeth walked.

But from the tales of Windsor's ghosts, its living tenants had at least some comfort in numbers, for in the twelve acres of buildings girded round by its walls dwelt some two thousand persons with bodies. There were officers of the castle and of the Garter, equerries and ladies- and gentlemen-in-waiting, Military Knights and Royal Guardsmen, canons and choristers of St. George's, custodians and antiquarians, secretaries and clerks, and sufficient domestic servants alone to have destroyed a besieging army with boiling soup from the battlements. There were master cooks, assistant cooks, roasting cooks, and bakers, all seneschalled by a lordly chef at nearly seven hundred a year, and there were footmen and stewards, housekeepers and butlers, storekeepers and pantrymen, kitchenmaids and chambermaids, sempstresses and valets, laundresses and table deckers, gardeners and greenhousemen, not to mention apprentices in almost every line, nor the coachmen and postillions, grooms and farriers from the Stables, nor the lads from the Kennels either. So you may imagine what a busy place it was, and perhaps something of the bickering and gossip, dalliance and intrigue, dreaming and weeping that still went on in it.

As Wheeler was creeping nervously up from the cellars, the royal stag whose head presided over the prodigious vaulted kitchen was looking down upon a sight that would have entranced the boy, could he have beheld it: a regular concourse of beef joints and saddles of mutton turning and crackling on their spits, six rows of them before each of two great roasting ovens; whole fowl sizzling in front of an open fire; multitudes of whacking copper potfuls steaming on four enormous ranges; clouds of white-clad cooks turning and basting, sniffing and tasting, seasoning and stirring, while perspiring stokers fed the roaring flames, and maids and potboys went every which way, and yeomen of the pantry bore in the gleaming platters, tureens, chafing dishes, sauceboats, and trays on which the mighty dinner was to be served, and gusts of heathen incense arose to the timbered dome. Of course this was only the *main* kitchen. In another the potatoes and greens were cooking, while in another yet a boy might have gazed upon a vista of cranberry tarts and seen a pastry-man thrust a ladle as tall as a trident into an ocean of chocolate that soon would inundate a continent of cake. A stranger might have thought they expected Gog and Magog in to dine; but this was quite the usual dinner in Windsor Castle, and as for guests, there was only Mr. Disraeli.

Mr. Disraeli, at a royal invitation solicited by himself, had come to stay the night. He had been shown to the customary chambers in the Lancaster Tower, and had not yet finished dressing for dinner when three peremptory knocks from the hall sounded at the door of his sitting room; such peremptory knocks that his secretary, Mr. Darcy Hammond, a tall, fair young man of a usually amiable temper, deliberately kept the knocker waiting a moment. But this only brought three more knocks more peremptory than the last. Hammond opened. He found himself confronted by a burly Highlander in full regalia, who looked him sternly in the eye.

"He's to come alang now," commanded the visitor in a kind of low roar.

In that outlandish costume (for all that Hammond was able to recognize the royal Stuart tartan) and with his red-bearded face and lowering brows, he looked less like a servant sent to conduct the Prime Minister to the Queen than like some outlaw from the craggy wilds come to carry him off to his fate, an impression only height-ened by an address as blunt as his fist; and Hammond, being accustomed to more deference towards the Chief of the great Conservative Party, bristled. Not so the Chief. He, having heard and recognized the roar from the bedroom, emerged at once, and called out, "Come in, Mr. Brown," in a tone that bespoke a certain deference on his own part; but what confused the secretary even more was the fact that the Chief was in his waistcoat. This was not at all like the fastidious Mr. Disraeli, who appeared quite casual about it notwith-standing.

"As you see, I'm behindhand with my toilet as usual," he remarked cheerfully. "A dawdler, Mr. Brown. If you had arrived two minutes sooner, I'd have been caught at my worst disadvantage since the day of my maiden speech."

The Scot had lumbered into the room without so much as another glance at the secretary. He grinned hairily.

"She'll no' mind bidin' till ye've made yersel' presentable."

The secretary shuddered. *She!* All Britain shuddered at the insolence of this outrageous hillman—for Hammond knew him now. It was the barbarian John Brown, the Queen's gillie, a preposterous royal favourite who by common knowledge stopped the mouths of peers when it suited him, and spanked the royal grandchildren. John Brown was notorious. There was a story current that once, in the Queen's presence, and in a roomful of lords and ladies, the presumptuous oaf actually had proposed a toast to her—and by God, she had submitted to it! (By God, they had jolly well drunk it, too!) On another occasion, he had dared criticize Her Majesty's frock —"What are ye daeing wi' that auld black dress on ye again? It's green-mouldit"—and damned if she hadn't gone and changed it to please him! And this great bullyragging lout from the Balmoral stables had the insupportable effrontery at times, they said, to address the Queen of the United Kingdom as *Woman!* It was said he drank, too. Whisky! Worse, that he was sometimes under its influence while attending her. Once he had been so drunk in her presence that he had fallen to the floor. And what had the Queen said? Why, she had remarked to the nearest duke that she believed she *had* felt a slight earthquake. God only knew why she put up with him. And now here was the Prime Minister treating him with an easy cordiality, even with regard.

Disraeli's secretary, nonetheless, understood more than his valet, who, having followed the great man in from the bedchamber, now was fussing with his collar. Being also more or less familiar with the general gossip concerning John Brown, who was said to constitute an embarrassment to the Government and a disgrace to the Crown, the valet was astonished to observe that Mr. Disraeli appeared delighted to see the old airedale. The usually drooping lids of the Prime Minister had lifted, the graven standstone features had arranged themselves in a smile, and he was saying, "Bear with me, then; I'll only be another moment"—really as if apologizing to the brute.

The valet was a very good valet, the secretary an excellent secretary; and Mr. Disraeli was the Queen's favourite prime minister since Melbourne.

Mr. Brown watched the dressing of the spare and emaciated old statesman with a whimsical eye. "Ah, now," he said, "if I'd just come i' time to hae a look at ye standing up i' yer shanks."

"Shanks?" Disraeli repeated, a bit startled. "But my shanks are a Party secret, Mr. Brown. Dear me. *The Times*, you know, has circulated the fiction that I'm the Sphinx of British politics, and as was so long the case with the Great Sphinx of Egypt, it is not generally supposed that I have any shanks. In confidence, I have, and am as vulnerable in them as Achilles was in the heel."

"Aye," chuckled the savage, "I ken it's a blessing they dinna wear kilts in Parliament."

The withered dandy of a vanished London smiled a trifle wanly, conceded the blessing, and changed the subject. "Before we go in to the Queen, Mr. Brown, tell me, how is Her Majesty's health? I don't mean what her doctors say, I want your own opinion."

"And I'll gie it ye," forthrightly answered Mr. Brown, as if prime ministers only naturally asked his opinion every day in the week. "She looks well enough, ye may think, but she wurrks too harrd. Up till past midnight she is, scribbling awa' at her desk and abusing her een at thae bills ye keep firing at the puir wumman, till what wi' the rest of it, it's a wunner she's the strength left to hauld her head up."

"I know," nodded Disraeli, who knew only too well and would have been better pleased if the Queen would spare her eyes and leave the bills to her ministers. "The Queen will look after her people though it kills her. Oh, the rest of us may potter about at the details, but the main burden she takes on herself and her doctors can't persuade her to lay aside a bit of it. That's where you come in, Mr. Brown; it's to you alone that a grateful nation must trust the real care of the Queen."

Mr. Brown nodded, scratching his beard. "Aye," he agreed, Mr. Disraeli being the only minister he ever agreed with. "I do as I think best for her. But it's a struggle at times. Would ye believe it, she can be as stubborn as Auld Hoofie when she's minded."

The secretary gasped.

"Her Majesty's health," pursued Disraeli, by no means aimlessly, "must never be endangered by overwork. She could not be persuaded to sacrifice her duty to her welfare, of course, but I think there are duties of which she might conscientiously avail herself with benefit to her health." And he approached a little nearer the intelligence which he hoped Mr. Brown would give him: "She needs change, fresh air, relaxation. Don't you think so, Mr. Brown?"

"Aye."

"Does she show any inclination to go about a bit?"

"She gaes ower to Frogmore and maybe tarries in the yard."

"Is that all?"

"Oh, now, we gang walking at Balmoral. She's fond o' that, and will stop to gab wi' the cottagers and tak' a drap wi' 'em maybe."

"Excellent. But——" Mr. Disraeli paused. "A drop, Mr. Brown?"

"A wee whitter, man! It does her good for the plain sociability."

The secretary winced.

"Ah," said Disraeli vaguely. He had not yet learned what he wished to know about the Queen's temper, nor, he felt, had he yet primed the honest mind of John Brown quite as it might be primed for valuable assistance later; but he did not return to his line of questioning. To do so might be to court the danger of seeming to insist, and insistence was a gaucherie that Mr. Disraeli would rather have died than be suspected of. "Well, Her Majesty's in good hands, Mr. Brown—of that I'm sure." He slipped into his tail coat. "And we'll keep her waiting no longer. After you, Mr. Brown."

"Aye."

And the Prime Minister followed the brawny gillie out of the room, leaving secretary and valet wondering what England could be coming to.

Down the corridor in silence strode the Highlander, his sporran swinging ahead of him like a claymore clearing the road, behind him the great Tory, leaning on his stick, his face returned to its settled cast, as of the Masque of the Wisdom of Sorrow, cut into deep lines as if by the winds of centuries. The fine black hair that women had so admired in his youth was, save to a woman's eye, black still, and in the middle of his forehead yet hung a single black ringlet of the many that once had framed the face of a Byron, a face which, with the short, straight tuft of hair that lately had appeared at the point of the chin, was more reminiscent of a Pharaoh's now. Down the grand, exquisitely vulgar corridor that was a gallery of treasure and art, arrogance and mortality, between ranks of great faces and noble heads, a pathway of glory leading to the Queen. And as he walked, this one-time upstart, drawing-room poseur, and gadfly of office, whose impudence had made Lord Melbourne smile when long ago he had set his sights on Downing Street; this writer of novels and playwright of his own destiny, this cynical old romantic whom England once had scorned for his ridiculous ambition, and once had called a mountebank and now called a wizard—he preened himself upon the consummating touch of a lifelong artistry that he felt to be implicit now in his presence upon this supernal promenade. His face remained cold, inert, betraying nothing, but that had become part of the role. Behind the mask of the actor, the dramatist smiled, gratified at this scene which to him gave clarity and meaning to the whole tempestuous play. But it was a little sadly that he smiled, mindful of the devoted Mary Anne, his wife, no longer alive to share his triumph, and of the beloved, ever-admiring Sa, his sister, who had not lived to see it. They were the ones he had played to; and he thought, "But I have lost my audience!" Down the Grand Corridor into the Royal Apartments, and past the Anteroom beyond which his rival, Mr. Gladstone, had never got. Not since Melbourne had the Queen received a minister in her Private Sitting Room, but it was through this door that her gillie now conducted the old Jew Benjamin Disraeli, the wreck of an incorrigible Childe Harold limping into heaven.

It was a high, almost square room, its walls covered in crimson silk, its floor by a crimson carpet, its ceiling an elaborate canopy of gold from which hung chandeliers of burnished silver decked with tall wax candles. It had a great oriel window at one end, at the other a graceful mantelpiece of white marble, carved and decorated in ormolu, and above the mantel a mirror reaching almost to the moulding. It was an overstuffed room, looking altogether preoccupied with itself; it was at once magnificent and cosy, pompous and sentimental, completely honest and curiously banal, and somehow it was just like the letters its royal occupant dispatched from it, being mainly in italics. Round its silken walls rose tier upon tier of oils and water-colours heavily framed in gold; a ponderous Empire clock ticked precisely in the middle of the mantel, with tall candelabra, military bronzes, and fat Chinese vases weighing and balancing one another to either side of it; and the floor space of this retreat of solitary grandeur was as crowded as Piccadilly. There were couches and chairs in profusion; tables littered with photographs, albums and illustrated catalogues of the royal collections; glass cabinets, full of figurines; a grand piano, platforming disciplined ranks of pictures, statuettes, souvenirs; and over by the window, looking out upon the lush reaches of the Great Park where as a bride she had ridden with young Prince Albert, was the Queen's sturdy desk, itself a platform for an array of photographs, miniatures, what not. And the windows of this room were set off by draperies of heavy crimson damask and had diaphanous blinds woven with the insignia and motto of the

Garter; a motto, indeed, that confronted one rather challengingly here, under the circumstances: *"Honi soit qui mal y pense,"* it said—"Shame upon him who thinks evil of it." The place was like a museum—but of course it was one, a museum of her life. Everywhere one looked was some dear face or figure, or the memento of some bright day out of her past, like a pressed leaf under glass, as if she had tried to stay the past round about her here till the time came when she and it might go off together hand in hand; but principally one saw the enshrined image of Albert.

And here tonight she waited for Disraeli—Victoria of England, a doughty little widow somewhere in her fifties, with greying hair severely parted in the middle, haughty, red-rimmed eyes, and a small, wilful mouth. Wrapped in her weeds, upright upon a many-cushioned couch of crimson silk before a timid-looking bamboo table in front of the fire, she sat surrounded by her ikons and amulets and by her symbols of the transience of the lords of the earth, and she was sedately playing patience.

"A fiery little devil," the American Minister, James Buchanan, had called her once; to which the great Sir Robert Peel might have added that it didn't do to cross her either, for time was when she had kept him from the Treasury Bench for meddling in the choice of her Ladies of the Bedchamber. The austere Sir Robert had used to fidget in front of her, the supremely self-confident Mr. Gladstone was distressed and made uneasy by her coldness, and the arrogant Prince Bismarck himself, when in after years she would grant him audience, would perspire under her gaze, and exclaim afterwards, "God! There is a woman!" But two men there were in the world who could handle her, and they came in together.

"Mr. Disraeli, Mum," announced Mr. Brown; and as her gillie closed the door behind them, up went the courtly minister to the couch, then down upon one creaking knee to kiss the plump little hand that she held out to him, beaming.

"God save our Gracious Queen!" he said in a reverential and at the same time almost intimate whisper.

"It's always so good to see you, Mr. Disraeli!" said Queen Victoria, and she almost glowed as she said it. "Do get up; I'm told your gout has been troubling you again. I'm sorry you had to come so far when you're not well. There, I see it does trouble you. You shall have a chair!"

Disraeli could not help but remember the story of what she had said to Lord Derby when that Prime Minister had stood before her faint with illness: "We regret that etiquette does not permit us to ask you to be seated." He might also have reflected that since he, a guest in the castle, now was being received informally in the Sitting Room, perhaps she did not consider this in the strict sense an audience. All the same, a chair from Victoria was like the Garter from one of her predecessors; and this thought occurring to Mr. Disraeli, he was artist enough to know how to bring it to life.

"A gracious warrant from a clement mistress, Ma'am," he said, rising. "But it's most difficult for an old dog to learn new tricks. Were I to sit in the presence of my Sovereign, I should be as uncomfortable as I should be with my hat on, even had I the royal warrant for that. So I ask Your Majesty's indulgence that for the sake of his spiritual comfort the old dog be permitted to stand."

Thus was a bit of Christian charity transformed into the Order of the Chair, and he made a mental note to mention the offer of his investiture when next he dropped in at the Carlton Club.

As for Victoria, the alchemic mind of this Cagliostro of courtiers, bringing the sheen of glamour out of the commonplace, touching all with romance, turning her world into a place of chivalry and the Divine Right of Queens, always delighted her; and besides, she understood his reluctance perfectly.

"Oh . . . well! Do at least put your back to the fire and warm yourself; I know men enjoy that so! The dear Prince always did it."

"So he did, and dignified the practice by its adoption," agreed the

— 32 —

artist, who had never seen the Prince do it in his life, nor even heard of it before; and he backed himself up to the crackling beech logs, hands behind him, as nearly as he could imagine the Prince doing it. "What kindnesses you show me, Madam! Sometimes, you know, I rather feel it my duty to warn you that it may be dangerous."

"Dangerous, Mr. Disraeli?"

"Most dangerous, Ma'am. I have known it ever since the first time my Sovereign sent me posies from Balmoral, picked by her own fair hand. Snowdrops, they were, and I confess that at a banquet that evening, seated next a beribboned earl, I presumed to wear a little bunch of 'em on my coat, and to boast that I, too, had received a royal decoration—sent by a Faery Queen. And then, too late, I remembered that faery gifts often turn the heads of those who receive them. Doesn't my royal faery think that likely to happen to her minister?"

He often called her his royal faery: it was the kind of liberty that no one but Benjamin Disraeli would have dared to take with her; in fact, it was the kind of description that would have occurred to no one else. And Victoria, laughing, almost blushed. "What an amusing man you are, Mr. Disraeli!" she said prettily.

Disraeli ever admitted that he flattered all women, and once had been heard to remark that where royalty was concerned it ought to be laid on with a trowel. Extravagant he was, but he was *cum laude* in his school, the drawing rooms of fashionable London where he had matriculated in his youth—a school where more battles have been won for England than on those playing fields of Eton. He had also been heard to acknowledge that it was lucky for him England had a queen instead of a king; and, classicist that he was, with a feeling for the natural progression of things, he was not unaware that his successes in the Sitting Room of Victoria went all the way back to lessons learned in the salons of Fanny Londonderry, Caroline Norton, and the notorious Lady Blessington. There he had mastered the strategy that Mr. Gladstone would never learn (or approve):

Woo the woman if you would win the queen. "He always addresses me," Queen Victoria had complained of the lately incumbent Mr. Gladstone, "as if I were a public meeting!" But Mr. Disraeli, while careful never to overstep himself, spoke to her almost as if she were his secret love. He gave homage the air of courtship, feeding pride and vanity together; and she found him charming. He protested that he lived and worked only for her, and seemed to strew her path with roses. In state matters, Mr. Gladstone had made everything that he tried to explain to her sound so horribly complicated! Mr. Disraeli made it all so simple! He could explain a bill with an anecdote, policy with an aphorism, a person with a *mot*. He was both loyal and attentive, appreciative and sympathetic, wise and witty. And she felt that she had found a friend.

Ever since the day Britain first had turned and bent the knee to her, a sheltered girl of eighteen, Victoria had played the Queen so regally that she had fairly succeeded in effacing the woman from the view of all but Albert, whom the woman loved; and then, bereft of him, all her children in awe of her, and all but one gone off to live in other palaces, she had found herself very much alone in her tower, on the brink of growing old. She had clung to John Brown, a wistful link with the old times at Balmoral, when there had been gaiety, parties with pipers in the hall, the gayest of rides and expeditions, and Albert climbing up to place the last stone upon their very own cairn! Only John Brown—and now the delightful Mr. Disraeli! She felt he understood her, as indeed he did. And for all his flattery and guile, it could be argued that in his own way he worshipped her, just as it may be shown that a cynic often is the worst kind of romantic— or the best. He had always preferred the company of women, craved the company of great ones; and in gratitude for this votive compliment, women had undertaken his education and the management of his career. They had handed him along one to another. And now he had come to the Queen. He had always idealized imperial England, of which she was the symbol; he had dreamt of splendour and power, and these she personified like a goddess. So perhaps it wasn't he that flattered her so much as she that flattered him. And then he was old, almost seventy, a childless widower, even more lonely than she. In the end, they found pleasure in each other's company for much the same reasons.

But this evening there was an undercurrent. Victoria had the intuitive kind of feeling that her First Minister had come personally to inform her that at last she was to be declared Empress of India! It was a wish that she had set heart and will upon. Disraeli, at first, for all his imperialistic leanings, had seemed rather bowled over by the idea, but once he had got used to it he had waxed properly enthusiastic and promised to see what could be done. There had been, however, some unreasonable delay. He had explained that there was some republican nonsense in the air just at present. Besides, he had said, she knew how the English were—so stolidly set against change, always saying that what had been good enough for their fathers was good enough for them. It wouldn't do to tell them suddenly that they had an Empress. First, they would have to be made used to the idea. He had said that he was merely awaiting the opportune moment for mentioning it. And nothing had happened. Really, she had almost begun to lose patience with the man: she had been obliged to insist. Why shouldn't she be Empress of India if she wished? Only three days before she had dispatched him a firm memorandum on the subject. And now, no doubt, she was to have her answer. Or why else should he have requested an audience and come running here from London in the midst of all this trouble about the Trades Unions Question and the Criminal Law Amendment Act that had been botched so badly by that Mr. Gladstone? (And of course the answer would be *Yes*, or he wouldn't have dared come!)

But the opportune moment was not yet. The Prime Minister, to be sure, was aware that the touchy subject could not very well be avoided this evening, but it wasn't India that had brought him to Windsor this time—it was only Manchester; and he feared that his real errand might prove even more touchy than the other business. For how was he to tell her that she must emerge from the reclusion of her sacred grief (which had lasted now some fourteen years) in order to loose the unutterable vulgarity of the Manchester Exhibition of Scientific Industry? Not that Manchester was that important, or Scientific Industry either; it was the popular prestige of the Queen herself that was at stake. Britain had grown resentful of her protracted mourning. The merchants were openly hostile. Some, complaining of what they termed her neglect of her duty to Trade, were publicly questioning the wisdom of having a Sovereign at all; they were always reckoning up the cost of maintaining the Royal House, and offering suggestions as to how the same amount of money might be spent to greater advantage elsewhere. Some republican rascal had gone to the length of posting "To Let" placards on Buckingham Palace, to the huge amusement of the multitude. And all this was becoming painfully embarrassing to the Government—to the Conservative Party, that was, which had only just come back into power and now found itself in the anomalous position of trying to maintain the balance of the country's ancient institutions upon a platform of economy, encouragement of trade, and progressive social reform. The Government must strengthen its position at once, which of course meant that the institutions must do their share, most particularly the Throne. Manchester offered an excellent opportunity to rally the manufacturers and merchants back round the Royal Standard, a consummation devoutly to be wished. But how to get the Queen to Manchester? True, the Exhibition wasn't until spring, but the city was already pressing for an answer to its invitation because it happened just now to have a fine political club. And this was the problem that Mr. Disraeli was pondering at the back of his Oriental mind, even as he bandied trivialities, loath to be brought to the point.

But the Queen could wait no longer. To the watchful Mr. Brown she made a little gesture indicating the patience table, which he instantly removed (being careful to leave the cards exactly as they were); then, smoothing her black velvet lap with hands that might otherwise have fluttered, she smilingly gave Disraeli to understand that she was ready for business. "For I know," she said, "that you haven't come all this way just to see an old woman."

"Indeed I haven't, Ma'am!" readily agreed the practiced gallant. "I have come to see the most fascinating woman in England, in her enchanted tower. But I will admit that lest the lady accuse me of idle doting, I did prepare some slight excuse."

"Aha! Then we shall hear it and judge whether the excuse be suitable. What is it?" she asked eagerly.

Disraeli leaned forward and in a dramatic whisper gave her what was only an excuse indeed; but he was far too clever to have made it a slight one.

"It has come to my ears, Madam—only privately, I am bound to add—that the Khedive of Egypt is in financial straits!"

"The Khedive of Egypt!" Victoria was disappointed and a little annoyed. "Well! We regret to hear it, of course, but it probably serves him right! None of those Eastern princes has the least sense of economy."

"Ah, fortunately not, in this case, Your Majesty. The Khedive finds it necessary to dispose of his shares in the Canal."

The Queen's eyes flashed. "The Suez Canal?"

"The same, Ma'am. It will take four millions to secure 'em."

"Four million pounds! Gracious! Do you think them worth it?"

"I think it a windfall. Consider what it would do for the Empire."

"H'm . . ." pondered the Queen, compressing her mouth, instantly the woman of affairs.

"The French, Ma'am——"

"Four million pounds!" mused the thrifty lady.

"I count on Rothschild's—the only firm that could manage it."

"H'm . . ."

"Prussia——"

"Prussia!" She thought a moment. "You know, the Prince always said that Prussia's interests and ours went side by side. He said that if Germany were united under Prussia, her influence joined to ours would bring about a Golden Age."

"What a glorious vision! Indeed, I have long studied the policies and ideas of his Royal Highness. But times have changed. Do you know, Your Majesty, what I believe he would say now, if he were here to guide us? That Bismarck, with his warlike ambitions, has destroyed the image of true German greatness; that he is another Bony, and must be checked before it is too late! And how the Prince would have risen in royal wrath, could he have lived to hear of what Bismarck said only a few weeks ago!"

"What did he say?"

The Prime Minister appeared to hesitate. "I regret to inform Your Majesty that according to recent intelligences received by the Foreign Office, he said that Britain had ceased to be a power in European politics."

Victoria stiffened. "Prince Bismarck said that!" Her head was back, her small chin raised. "Impudence! Oh, that man!" she said. "That cheeky man!"

"So he is, Ma'am. And yet"—Disraeli smiled—"somehow it amuses me. I reflect that Prince Bismarck is not the first foreigner to think that about us, nor probably the last. And there are times when it is well for all our enemies to think it, for that makes us all the more formidable. It will be an expensive lesson to Prince Bismarck when he wakes up to find us stronger than ever in the Mediterranean, and bestriding the route to the East."

"Ha!" said Victoria triumphantly.

Disraeli waited a moment to allow the point to sink in. "Through Suez, dear Lady, lies our Path of Empire. Secure the Canal and you secure India! And what better way to serve notice of the fact upon the world than by hailing our Britannic Sovereign—Empress of India!"

Victoria, upright and motionless, peered keenly right through the Empire clock on the mantel. It clucked thoughtfully. She thrust out her lips. "Buy out the Khedive! We most thoroughly approve!"

Which was exactly what the British Government had determined to do.

4

The man in the scarlet coat, whom Wheeler saw drawing the blind a while ago, was nothing so grand as a lord chamberlain, but he was nothing less than the Sergeant Footman of the castle, and it wasn't every evening that he went about drawing blinds. He probably had an assistant just for that, the same as he had one who did nothing else in the world but lay the fires, and another who only lighted them, and if he didn't have a Royal Blind Drawer too, it could only have been that he didn't care for one, having enough assistants to worry him already.

Mr. Naseby was an important officer in Windsor Castle, and he looked it, a round and imposing man with a big red face to go with the coat and rusty brows as thick as Spanish moss and a head under his white wig that was like a glowing coal. But the responsibilities of his position weighed upon him heavily. It was not the big things that worried him—he could do for any of them in a minute; it was the multitude of little things, for Mr. Naseby, as he admitted to himself, had no head for details. Large affairs were his métier, and he really didn't see why a sergeant footman had to be bothered with anything else. But there was the Master of the Household for you, a fussy man to whom details were everything, and he had spies. Mr. Naseby regretted the impecunious habits of his youth and longed for the time when he should have enough put aside to go and keep a cosy inn near Sunningdale and have an assistant who should do nothing else but look after the little things.

Tonight he was more on edge than usual. This afternoon the Master of the Household had given him a regular wigging about one of the underfootmen who had taken a drop too much and been found asleep on the stairs; and now here was the Prime Minister in for dinner, admittedly a small affair but one from which a dozen disasters might arise. So it was purely out of edginess that Mr. Naseby, on the prowl for little things before the dinner party should begin, had personally drawn the blind; and then he went rolling down the crimson carpet of the Grand Corridor toward the Private Dining Room.

The Royal Apartments had been a lonely section of the castle for years. No doubt there had been high goings-on here in the time of the Georges, Mr. Naseby often thought; no doubt his father, old Mr. Tobias, as he was now referred to by those tottering members of the staff that had served under him, had seen a thing or two in King William's time; and although Her Majesty had calmed things down a good bit when she came, even Mr. Naseby the Younger could remember life and warmth and gaiety here—in the Prince's day, when their present Royal Highnesses were children. Not that any of that had been anything, nor had Mr. Naseby ever said what in his opinion *was* anything. He only said, in a knowing way, that a royal palace ought to have more of an *air*. He was a man to brood about such deficiencies of the age. Like his father and grandfather before him, he had been, as one might have said, born to a position of considerable distinction in his world, but where was the good of it?

Royalty wasn't what it had been. Mr. Naseby had been born too late.

In the door of the dining room, he brought himself up with a snort, glaring at Noonan, whom he had caught kneeling over a pail of water on the floor.

"What's this, what's this! Mopping the floor at this hour?"

Noonan looked up at him with frightened eyes. "It's only that a bit o' water got sloshed on it, sir," she said.

"Water, my girl? Water?" It was as if she had said acid. "How did that happen?"

"I'm sure I don't know, sir."

"Carelessness, that's what. Carelessness. Eh? Well, then, slosh it up again, slosh it up again," directed Mr. Naseby, himself sloshing the air with an illustrative hand, and he began rolling slowly round the room on a tour of inspection.

The table this evening had been laid for only four—the Queen, the Prime Minister, the Queen's Private Secretary, and a Maid of Honour, the Princess Beatrice being away on a visit to Sandringham and the Lady-in-Waiting ill. In the rather dim light of a candelabrum and the capricious flames of the two fireplaces (for the central chandelier as yet was dark) Mr. Naseby peered anxiously at everything. His eye was caught by the pair of saltcellars, gifts of the eminent Mr. Brown, which the Queen would not dine without. He reached over and moved them conspicuously near the royal place, and nodded with satisfaction like a man who has pulled off something good at chess. Then he heaved himself over to the sideboard and seemed to be making passes with his hands. These nervous exertions caused his gills to begin throbbing like a salmon's, and he was puffing a bit as he rolled out of the room again on his rounds.

Noonan sloshed on. She was a woman who couldn't have reached forty yet, and who might not have been more than thirty, a small woman with mouse-coloured hair and forearms reddened by hot water, and we shouldn't now be giving her a second glance but for the fact that as Mr. Naseby's footsteps die away in the corridor she has raised her head furtively to look around. Noonan is a scullery maid; there are rules which ordinarily confine such drones to the lower regions of this well-kept hive; she has never before penetrated to the precincts of the Queen. She is looking at the lace tablecloth, the gleaming silver and crystal, the fine, blue-bordered Minton china service with the letters V. R. in raised gold, at the paintings and tapestries on the oak-panelled walls, and she seems to be trying to take in everything at once. Her eyes shine. Black eyes she has, which seem strange in that face and suggest perhaps a touch of the Armada. No, she cannot be thirty yet. Her bosom, rising and falling gently as she kneels there with her bit of rag in her hand, asserts through her shapeless blouse its own firm contours; her slightly parted lips are full and passionately curved.

Suddenly she stiffens—and stares.

It is to her credit, a testimonial to her strength of character, that in this moment she neither cries out nor crosses herself, for in the doorway has appeared what the guilty woman takes in the uncertain light to be a man's empty coat standing upright without any means of support, and unaccountably surmounted by a cap. From less curious optical illusions in Windsor Castle doubtless has grown many a bogle to affright all hands afterwards in the Servants' Hall—though who indeed is to say which of them was illusory at all?

When upon closer inspection she perceives the nature of this phenomenon to be a boy, she only continues to stare. The boy also stares, but not at Noonan. He has not even noticed her, since she is partly shut off from his view by the table, and his eyes anyway are fast upon other objects which he might reasonably be expected to notice first. Wheeler has entered upon tiptoe, but, having come all at once upon the glory of this royal table laid for dinner, has been pushed back on his heels again by the impact of it, and there he stands, motionless, elbows still slightly raised behind him, as one carries elbows when on tiptoe, eyes like two full moons. . . .

In another quarter of that swarming castle, had it not been for the extreme illogic of his attire and the quantity of coal dust on his face, Noonan might have taken him for granted, but of course in the Queen's dining room he could not have been more obviously extraneous had he been fish and chips, and it was plain to her that his presence boded trouble. He might, she supposed, be some new potboy that had stolen up from the kitchen, but he didn't look it; more probably he was some tradesman's lad, brazenly inquisitive.

The elbows slowly lowered. One foot suffered itself to be drawn forward. He was a victim of hypnosis and obediently approaching the table. Arriving at it, he stopped; one hand came out and received from it a sugar-coated almond.

"Here, now!" Noonan cried, springing up, and she seized him.

Wheeler whirled and jerked away; she made a lunge and recaptured him; he kicked at her viciously and thrashed; her right fist was clamped onto his left arm, and now with her left hand she managed to catch his right one that had purloined the Queen's almond.

"Drop that! Drop it, I'm saying!"

But he held fast to it, pitching and squirming with all his might, and in the midst of this silent battle a shaming thought struck Noonan, who had the Great Potato Famine in her soul:

"Is it hungry you are?"

He fought on without answering, and seeing that this sort of thing was getting her nowhere, Noonan resolutely bore him to the floor and sat on him. Wheeler, by all the laws of the London streets that he came from, was beaten, but he did not give in gracefully. He turned his face from her and kept his eyes screwed tightly shut so she shouldn't see into them and perhaps so that in this desperate predicament, furiously humiliated as he was, he shouldn't be unmanly.

"There, I'm not meaning to hurt you," Noonan panted, a little too grimly.

But by no word did he recognize her existence, though she saw his lip quiver.

"Are you famishing, tell me. But you know well enough this is no place for you to come thieving. And who are you at all? Do you hear me? . . . Has the cat got your tongue? . . . But you've no hurt to fear from me; it's only Noonan," she assured him, still sitting on him.

In that ridiculous position, he made her feel sorry for him and rather ashamed of herself, and anyway, now that she had him, she hadn't a notion what to do with him. She studied the situation. "Sure, it's no peeler I am," she said, as much for her own information as for his, and after asking herself what she was doing sitting on him then, she sighed, gave his shoulder a rough pat, and with a rolling motion transferred herself to the carpet, sitting on her legs.

"Have your sweet if you want it, then," she grudged him.

Wheeler sat up but kept his head down and his eyes on the floor and his underlip thrust out to show that he conceded nothing. He, too, was at a loss, and decidedly uncomfortable, but in token of his defiance and for want for anything better to do just then, he put the prize of battle into his mouth and began to chew it. He looked ludicrous enough to make Noonan smile.

"And there's more on the table——" But even as she made this generous offer she saw the folly of it and quickly added: "But you'll not take another one of them if you know what's good for you; Herself's own dinner it is and you'll get into trouble if they catch you."

A sound startled them both. Noonan rose swiftly. "Whisht! Somebody's coming," she said, and altogether inconsistently appointed herself his protector. "Hide yourself, quick!" She pulled him to his feet, looking about frantically. "Here!" And she pushed him behind the heavy crimson hangings by the window. Then, flustered, one hand gone to her disarranged hair, the unreasonable woman turned to face the newcomer.

It was only Slattery. He was the candlelighter of these apartments, a tall, thin, black-haired young man with intense blue eyes, a pinched nose, and lips habitually pursed as if in constant exasperation at everything the eyes saw or the nose had scent of, and he carried in his hands the symbols of his office, a lighted lamp (which seemed to suit him as one had Diogenes) and a long taper. He looked at Noonan in surprise.

"What might you be doing in this room?"

"And what affair o' yours is that, I'd like to know?" she flung at him out of an hostility born of her own discomfiture, her two feet firmly planted between him and the window.

Slattery's eyebrows arched sarcastically. "Oh, Miss High and Mighty, is it? Excuse *me*. It's no affair o' mine at all, but it might be one o' Mr. Naseby's now, if he should be finding you here."

"Fa! He's after doing that already. Wasn't I sent here to clean, and Mrs. Beebe ailing in her bed?"

"Ah, so that's the way of it. Excuse *me*," Slattery repeated, and elaborately bowed from the hips. "And I suppose you've no objection if I only light the candles, now?"

Noonan ignored this sarcasm. She walked past him, knelt down by her pail, and resumed mopping the floor with her rag, hoping to be rid of him the sooner. Slattery gazed at her. A fine figure of a woman, he thought, but the nature of a zebra.

He went to the table and prepared to light the chandelier above it. Noonan, watching him under her brows, saw him ignite the taper with the lamp that he carried, and start at each of the candlewicks a graceful flame that twinkled among the crystal baubles of the fixture and shone on the silver beneath. Slattery was taking his time. He was relishing every detail of the ritual that he went through every evening in exactly the same way, and the lights that he lit gleamed not half so brightly on silver or crystal as they did in his eye. Slattery was not the man to conceive of his function lightly. A chandelier in full bloom was a beautiful thing, and the castle at its best by candle-light: in his world, it was as if he went about every evening with a

wand and brought out the stars. He finished and stood looking up at
the miniature conflagration admiringly. Then he did a strange thing.
Slowly he lowered the burning taper till it was just opposite the overhang of the fine lace table cover, and began moving the flame closer
and closer until it was almost but not quite touching, so that it
seemed the heat must start the lace in a moment.

"Slattery!" Noonan screamed at him. "Would you burn us all up,
man!"

Slattery sighed and withdrew his torch. But he had known quite
well that she was watching him, and had achieved precisely the effect
upon her he desired. He said gently, "I was practising only."

"Practising!" echoed Noonan. "Well, the saints preserve us, is it
mad the looney is entirely?"

"Ah, Noonan," Slattery said, nothing daunted, cocking his head
to consider the matter. " 'Twould be a job would warm many a poor
cold heart this night." He seemed to muse upon this thought, a poeti-
cal look to the very angle of his head, and then, receiving no encouragement to enlarge upon his theme, he took two steps to Noonan's
side, bent down, and whispered: "Do you take me meaning,
Noonan?"

"Meaning, is it? Faith, you're daft surely, or drunk again."

"Sanity itself I am, and devil a drop in me! But it's a thick skull
you have or there'd be no call for plainer words than I'm after saying
this minute, and you from me own land, God help her."

She looked at him in blank astonishment as comprehension over-
took her, and then, to his consternation, sat back on her heels and
laughed. "So you'd think to burn down Windsor Castle and be
striking a blow for Ireland, would you? Well, Holy Mother o' God!
And wouldn't you look fine hanging from a gibbet!"

"It's no joking matter! Many a good man's risked his neck in an
English noose for Ireland's sake."

"And don't I know that? And what did it bring Ireland but more
pain and sorra, will you tell me?"

"Pain and sorra! Do you not mind Drogheda in Cromwell's time when they butchered the men and despoiled the poor women?"

"I do, and Limerick too. And well I mind what it was brought the Butcher to Ireland in the first place was Rory O'Moore and them hotheads running wild in the North."

"Running wild? And why wouldn't they? What kind of a man was it would twiddle his thumbs in the Plantation? And the same in these times? It's a woman's power o' reason you have, and that's the same as no reason at all; but it's a shameful thing for you to be taking England's part against Ireland."

Noonan rose straight up on her knees with her fists doubled up on her hipbones. "Would you listen to that, now! As if the women of Ireland didn't mind the Droghedas and the Limericks better than the men, me bold little rapparee! Isn't it themselves knows the trouble comes o' killing and burning and the like, and no hope but defeat in the end? My soul from the devil! Take yourself out o' this and leave me in peace, you the poor fool talks o' burning down Windsor Castle by his lee lone."

"By me lee lone? Did I say by me lee lone? Did Brian Boru cast the Danish from Ireland by his lee lonesome either?"

Noonan went all of a sudden grave, even a shade pale. She searched his eyes and asked in a confessional voice: "Tell me straight out, Slattery, is it them Fenians you're in with?"

This direct leading question apparently caught Slattery in something more than he had intended. He pulled in his jutting chin so quickly it seemed he must have burned it over his lamp. For indeed to be suspected a Fenian was a frightening thing; but it was a flattering too, and he was not one to sacrifice a good effect if he could safely help it. In the end he summoned his courage and stood forth squarely between the yes and the no: "And if it was, would I break me sacred oath and tell it, do you think? Would I jump up now and be noising it in Gath and the streets of Ascalon itself any more than if it wasn't? Sure and that's a hanging word any place these times and I've not even heard you say it."

She scrutinized him uncertainly, a scornful smile hesitating on her lips. "Go on with you!" she said then. "You'd burn no castle in a hundred years."

Stung by this aspersion upon his character, he lashed out: "Wouldn't I! A great lot you know about the man you're talking to."

She leaned back on her heels again, narrowed her eyes at him, and folded her arms. "All right," she challenged, "burn this one down then, me boyo, and let me see you do it."

"Oho! Is it now you want me to do it?"

"It is, then."

"Oho! There's the woman of it, now. Wouldn't I be the fool of a man to go setting me plans in motion before the time was ripe?"

"Plans!" she scoffed. "What kind of plans, I'd like to know?"

"Plans I'll not be trusting to any female woman, you may be sure. But this much I'll tell you, and no more: that I could have Windsor Castle a blazing pyre in less time than it takes to blow your nose! Only watch this now!" He stepped quickly over to the table and once more held the taper flame in dangerous proximity to the lace. "A bit here, you see"—he sprang over to the window draperies—"a bit more here, now——"

Noonan screaked; she scrambled to her feet, flew between the aspiring arsonist and his tinder, and commanded: "That'll be all, Slattery!"

This action in itself might have been enough to arouse the candle-lighter's suspicions, but there was something else besides, and it distracted him. Those draperies had moved! Reconnoitering them cautiously, he perceived the point of a boot protruding beneath their folds; he retreated two steps in alarm, and asked Noonan hoarsely: "Who—who is it behind there?"

"Behind where, at all?"

Slattery pointed a bony forefinger.

"Go on with you and don't be nosing into things you've no concern with."

"There's a man in it! By the powers, I believe you're after hiding him there this long time!" And emboldened by the fact that the intruder hadn't pounced out to strike him dead on the spot but evidently chose to remain behind the double shield of the drapes and a woman's skirt, Slattery bounded to the sideboard, exchanged the lamp for a carving knife, and bounded back again. "Come out of that now or I'll dragoon you hangings and all!"

"You'll not!" cried Noonan, pushing in front of him, and, being a practical woman, saved the situation by reaching into the hiding place and drawing forth to her side the extraordinary figure of Wheeler.

Slattery was spiritually disarmed on the instant. His sword arm fell to his side. "Glory be to God! Now what might that be?"

"Ask me no questions and I'll tell you no lies."

Slattery looked at Wheeler and Wheeler looked at Slattery, and undoubtedly Wheeler would have run for it but for the protecting arm on his shoulder that seemed to give him haven. He was terrified; but knowing well the first primitive law of battle, he tried desperately to conceal the fact and kept his underlip out where it belonged, which was the same as having one's flag up for a fight or a parley.

"What, is it your own brat, then?"

An unfortunate question. Eyes ablaze, she struck him such a blow across the mouth that he reeled back and the knife fell to the floor.

"Devil take you!" he said. " 'Twas no such way I was asking."

"Then you'd best mind your tongue, Mr. Slattery."

"You've a heavy hand, woman, and a hasty temper, and yourself would do better to mind the both of them."

"Be off with you then and leave the lad be."

But of course Slattery could not with any grace retire from the field so soon after the ignominious rebuff he had just suffered, and he snarled from a safe distance: "Oh, we're very high and mighty, we are, but what do you think will Mr. Naseby do when he finds out you're harbouring vipers in his bosom?"

"Mind your tongue, I'm saying, or it's worse than the last you'll be getting for calling the poor lad a name the like o' that! *And,*" she added, raising her chin pugnaciously, "if I was you, me bucko, I'd not be carrying tales to Mr. Naseby about this lad here, and he knowing a tale or two about yourself, Mr. Burn-me-down-castles; for isn't he after taking in every hanging word that came out of your mouth a moment since?"

Slattery had not thought of this. He shot a sidelong glance at Wheeler, but the boy's face under all that coal dust was inscrutable.

"So it's blackmail, is it?" he said at last.

The terrible word was received in silence, and Slattery took this to mean that he had scored.

"Blackmail it is!" he emphasized. "And from one o' me own kith and kin, as you might say, in a manner o' speaking!"

As a matter of fact, Noonan wasn't clear on what was blackmail, nor indeed on what blackmail was, nor in either case did she propose to give him the advantage of letting him tell her; but her happy feminine instinct for a tight corner did not desert her. "If the shoe fits," she said, complacently clasping her hands across her apron, "you may wear it, I'm sure."

"Me, is it? Me? Now in the name o' God——" But he saw that he had somehow got into a blind alley, and he slid to a halt. "As if," he said, feeling his way, "as if I'd be the one would carry tales about the lad here anyhow."

"Oh, wouldn't you now!" said Noonan with fine irony.

Slattery beat a masterly retreat. "Oho! So that's what you're thinking, is it?" He raised his eyebrows and struck a purely conversational stance. "And how would I be the one to do that, pray? I'm asking you, would I be the one to care who was behind the hangings o' Windsor Castle if it was a burglar itself? And look now, if he was to steal the Royal Crown and Sceptre even, would I lift me little finger"—he artfully displayed the little finger—"would I lift me little finger that much, do you think, to be stopping him?" He chuckled scornfully. "Use the brains God gave you, woman. Amn't I just after talking the other way, entirely? Faith, I do believe I wouldn't lift me little finger," he finished, "if somebody was to burn the place down!"

It was a persuasive argument, and Noonan was not the girl to find holes in it. The angry frown on her face had changed to a look of confusion, for only a moment ago she had thought she had him, and now it seemed it was he that had her. It was the second time this evening that Noonan had been robbed of victory by a male.

"Well, now——" She hesitated.

" 'Twas all I was wondering," Slattery assured her, "what was the little frainey doing here?"

"Well, to tell you the God's own truth, Slattery, I was wondering the same thing myself." She held Wheeler at arm's length and surveyed him curiously. "What is it you are doing here, alanna?"

Wheeler scuffed one shoe against the other in embarrassment.

"Ah, come now," Noonan coaxed, "there's none here will harm you."

"There's not, surely," abetted Slattery in stroking tones.

"Arr," Wheeler said aggrievedly to the floor. "I falled in 'ere—straight down the 'ole."

"What's that you say?" puzzled Slattery.

"Sure," said Noonan, "I thought he said he fell in."

"Fell in, is it? Well, that's the queer one. And what great wonder of a distant star or planet did he fall from, then? For I'm thinking it's true from this that Almighty God has other worlds we know not of."

"Whisht!" said Noonan suddenly. Again she heard footsteps, this time in the Grand Corridor. "Sacred Heart o' Jesus! Quickly!"

But Slattery had heard for himself, and now, oddly enough, it was he that was pushing Wheeler behind the hangings. "Hide now, and not a word out o' you. Whisht!"

He motioned Noonan back to her pail, achieved a silent gambado to the sideboard to retrieve his lamp, then another to the table, blew out as many candles on the chandelier as he could quench with one vigorous breath, ignited the taper and set about relighting the candles leisurely, giving first attention to the wicks that were smoking.

Thus did the candlelighter, though scarcely realizing what he was doing, ally himself with the scullery maid in Wheeler's behalf, and become, as they say in the courts of the law, an accessory after the fact. And so did Mr. Naseby, upon re-entering the room, discover nothing much amiss in it—only two servants busy at their tasks. But he was far from pleased.

"Here, here, on with it, you two! Hurry along. Why!" he exclaimed with a special frown at Noonan. "Are you trying to take the wax off that floor, girl?"

And she, looking down at where she had been mopping with her rag, was abashed to discover that the floor was quite as dry as a floor ought to be.

"I'm only just finished, sir," she said, rising with her pail in her hand, and she fled into the kitchen passage.

Mr. Naseby turned his attention to the candlelighter and waited impatiently till the last candle was lit. "Now, then, Lights, off with you! Off to the White Drawing Room; quick about it!"

"That I will, sir," answered the secret rebel meekly, and hied himself through the other door.

Tarrying nervously in the passage, Noonan heard the Sergeant Footman grunting and muttering to himself as with huge difficulty he stooped and recovered the carving knife from the floor. A moment later she was passed by four underfootmen bearing covered platters of food up from the kitchen below. And hardly had they entered the dining room when she heard their commander trumpeting the unthinkable:

"Look sharp! Her Majesty will be coming directly."

5

Victoria was a dutiful hostess, and at her infrequent dinner parties always did her best to keep the ball rolling.

When her guests were seated, she would turn to the gentleman on her right and ask him, for example, whether he had read the latest book, and on being informed that he had, or hadn't, would incline her head at him graciously, turn to the gentleman on her left, and give him equal opportunity to shine, this being the signal to everyone that conversation was in order and England expected every guest to do his duty. So, with a little assistance from the best wine cellar in the country, the party soon would find itself in full career, in a relative kind of way. Yet at intervals it did keep slowing down again, by reason of the fact that the Queen never allowed conversation to interfere with her dinner, while those of previous experience at her board took care not to do so either, knowing that as soon as Her

Majesty had done with a dish, that dish would be snatched in a trice from under the nose of every diner in the room.

Old Lord Bartington had been the only man ever known to complain of this arbitrary treatment from the House of Hanover. He had snapped at the footman, "Here, bring that back!" A dreadful hush had fallen, in the midst of which the footman stood as if paralysed, his eyes upon Mr. Naseby, who had turned green. The Queen alone remained calm. "His Lordship hasn't finished yet," she said quietly to the footman. "Put back his plate." And to this day, at his club, where his picture hangs above crossed swords in the dining room, old Bartington is pointed out to guests as the Simon de Montfort of roast beef.

But the little dinners with Mr. Disraeli were always freer and gayer, and the Maid of Honour was thankful for his presence this evening. She didn't much fancy being a Maid of Honour; she had become one only in obedience to a royal request to her family, and to please her mother, who was a friend of the Queen's, and because her father thought the training might "steady" her. Sometimes she found the going rather hard.

But Disraeli felt that he was in his true element.

Aloud he was tactfully admiring Richter's portrait of Her Majesty's newest daughter-in-law, the Duchess of Edinburgh, which hung on the wall, but privately he was more appreciative of the Minton china, not indeed because he thought it very grand, but because he affectionately conceived of it as the latest symbol of his own success, the symbolism lying in the fact that it *was* the Minton china, and neither the gold nor the silver plate, and might be taken to indicate that he was now regarded almost as one of the Family. Besides, Disraeli, taking a wafer from a bowl embossed with that golden *V. R.*, could feel as full of symbolism as the Archbishop of Canterbury raising the Chalice to his lips.

He was a man who lived in his own lyric imagination as much as in the world of fact, without ever confusing the two, but rather fusing them in such a way that each enriched the other; and to him the dinner too was a symbol. It was a recognition of his art, a regular testimonial banquet as it were; and considering the matter subjectively through the eyes of a man who had begun with so little and overcome so much, who cannot see that he was right? And the castle itself, of course, was a perfect symbol, one of the half-mystic kind from which he derived inspiration for his romantic politics, which he was able to rationalize quite as well as Mr. Gladstone could sanctify his own pragmatical ones. The castle was a kind of temple (though he never put it into such a word) presided over by the Spirit of England and haunted by all those ghosts holding title deeds in mortmain; and tonight he was dining not with one British Sovereign, but with many, all their courts around them, and in this great company felt that he belonged—he, the Prime Minister of the moment, the peer of a Wolsey, a Clarendon, a Pitt. He had a way of looking at things, this old man; and was it not all so indeed? Benjamin Disraeli, with only a few good years left in him—a foreigner, and alone—felt that he was dandled in the lap of the Ages and fed with a golden spoon. Ah, if only——

But of course he betrayed no hint of any of this, nor appeared in the least abstracted, nor forgot for a moment what he had come for; nor, having as keen an eye for what was present as he had for what was not, was he half so taken with Her Grace of Edinburgh as he was with the Maid of Honour herself, of whose beauty who had not heard? She was very grey and gay of eye, almost black of hair, with a peach-blossom look to her skin, and a figure whose wanton bloom mocked the deep blue decorum of her dress, and the Prime Minister silently agreed with those who held the Honourable Emily Prior to be the beat of both the Moncreiffe sisters, who were the most famous beauties of the day—barring, of course, some professional ones, who were not to be considered. Mr. Gladstone, on the other hand, had thought Miss Prior giddy, and this devastating judgment was wielded like a sword by the Moncreiffe Party against her. Well, she was young; but Disraeli rather imagined that, giddy or not, she kept a tight rein on herself in the presence of the Queen, who was said to be fond of her.

"It's always so nice," Her Majesty had said in reference to her Maid this evening, "to have lively young ones about!"

Disraeli was surprised to hear she thought so, but he himself was sure of it, and would have liked to pay his compliments to this lively young one in his best Georgian manner, did he not know that the Queen had a rule against talking across the table, and suspect that she would frown upon any frivolous byplay between her Prime Minister and her Maid of Honour, no matter where they were sitting. Disraeli confined his frivolities to the Queen, the Honourable Emily smiled, sparkled, and managed with barely a word to take a lively young part in the conversation, while General Sir Henry Ponsonby, the Queen's Secretary, listened with intelligence and expeditiously made off with his dinner.

Under the stimuli of the gay eyes and the tired, red-rimmed blue ones of the Queen, Disraeli was in top form; his table talk glittered with epigram in justice to his reputation for it, his droll comments upon figures and events of the day made the gay eyes dance and the tired ones brighten, and drew appreciative smiles from the general; so that, thanks to him, this little dinner of the Queen's promised to go off a deal better than most. Mr. Brown himself, a great flamboyant mass hovering protectively behind the Queen's chair, paid the conversation the compliment of following it, nodding or chuckling aloud when something struck his fancy, and now and then contributing a remark of his own—to the cold horror of the general, who would never get used to him. Even Mr. Naseby, much too watchful for little things to heed talk that he couldn't be held accountable for, was beginning to think well of matters as he stood at the Queen's elbow directing with his eyes the serving of the dessert by the four impeccable underfootmen, whose own eyes remained lowered the whole time so as not to run afoul of another royal regulation: the Queen could not bear to be looked at by the servants. Then, as if Fate were losing patience with a dinner that would go so well—something happened.

Out in the corridor, Slattery had been hanging about on tenter-hooks. A wiser man in his position, realizing that events as they stood now had gone beyond his power to alter, might have chosen for the time being to vanish into some remote corner of the castle; but Slattery, with his lively imagination warning him of the consequences to himself should Wheeler be taken in the Queen's presence and a confession wrung out of him, was of too nervous a temperament not to return to the scene of his crime. He had to know.

Somehow, as he stood listening at the portieres, he dropped his unlighted lamp; it thudded on the carpet, breaking its glass chimney, clattered onto the bare floor of the dining room, and Slattery bounded after it.

The wildly agitated figure that suddenly had leaped into the door-way could not help glancing at the Queen, and was turned at once into a pillar of ice by the imperial stare it encountered. There was an instant of silence, during which the Sergeant Footman wrestled against an attack of apoplexy. Then Slattery convulsed himself, scooped up the lamp, and was gone.

Victoria half turned to the unstrung Mr. Naseby and with an appearance of great severity said something that only Mr. Brown could overhear. The gillie groaned and bent down.

"Woman, woman," he said in a whisper heard everywhere in the room, "ye're growing stiffer and stiffer! Hae ye ne'er drappit anything yersel'?"

General Ponsonby turned purple, the Honourable Emily kept her eyes discreetly upon her plate, and the great diplomatist of the party diplomatically sipped his wine. But the Queen did not move. She sat with a petulant frown upon her face, and one could hear the clock tick. And presently she turned again to Mr. Naseby and said something else, then turned in the other direction towards Mr. Brown and snapped her head downward just once, as if to say "There!"—having, as it seemed, remitted some terrible punishment upon the candlelighter in deference to Mr. Brown's judgment.

"Why is it, Mr. Disraeli," she asked, "that Ireland sends us nothing but trouble?"

Disraeli appeared to choke on his food, but quickly recovered himself.

"Why, as to that, Madam," he made answer, "I should say that from time to time the same question must be put to their ministers by both God and the Devil."

Emily and the general laughed, but instantly saw their mistake: the Queen was not amused. The incident might be closed, but it had considerably annoyed her, and possibly Slattery had got himself pigeonholed in her mind with the villains in some more serious incidents that were not settled at all. Disraeli tried another tack.

"I remember," he said, "an Irish legend that I once heard somewhere. Your Majesty will recognize in it a curious likeness to the Greek myth of King Midas and Apollo; but this version is so characteristic of the Irish that I sometimes think it may contain a lesson to ourselves in administering the country. Will Your Majesty give me leave to tell it?"

Her Majesty inclined her head.

"Once upon a time, then, so the pretty story goes, there reigned in Ireland a king who had the ears of a horse——"

"A horse?" asked Queen Victoria.

"Exactly, Madam. Naturally the King was very sensitive about it, and so he went about at all times in a bronze helmet to conceal the deformity."

The Queen nodded with perfect comprehension of this expedient. "They say," she said, "that the late King of Bavaria wore his moustache to conceal a harelip."

"Indeed, Your Majesty! I'd never heard that. But since the King of Bavaria's lip wasn't shaved, then, he needn't have worried about the secret being learned even by his barber; whereas this Irish king, as I was going to mention, had to have his hair cut."

"How dreadful!"

"Ah, but the King was resourceful there, Ma'am. The honour of cutting his locks was decided by lot among all the barbers of his realm, but to win the honour was considered very unlucky. For it was noticed that no barber who cut the King's hair ever was seen again."

The Queen weakly closed her eyes for an instant, as if to shut from them the scene in which some unhappy barber, for reasons of state, unavoidably lost his head.

"One day," Disraeli went on, thoroughly enjoying himself, "an old woman came and threw herself at the King's feet. It seemed she was the widowed mother of the latest member of the Royal Company of Barbers to be chosen; her son was her sole support, and she pleaded so pitiably for his life that the King was moved, and agreed to make an exception. He would spare her son, he said, on one condition: that the young man swear an oath never to reveal whatever he might see while cutting the King's hair. This the young man did, and so was spared. But as time went on, his awful knowledge weighed so heavily upon his mind that he could no longer bear it, and prayed for relief to whatever god was patron of the arts, and hence of barbers. And the god came to him in a dream, telling him to leave the city by the western gate and travel until he came to a fork in the road where stood a great tree; he had only to whisper his secret to the tree and would be relieved of it for ever. So the barber did as he was told, and was relieved. But in after years, Madam, the tree was cut down, and from the wood a harp was made for the King's harper. And the first opportunity the harper had to try the new harp was in the great hall of Tara, with the King on his throne and all the court assembled; and no sooner had the harper touched the strings than they sang out the terrible truth: 'The King has the ears of a horse! The King has the ears of a horse! . . .' The sounds died away and the hall was very still. The horrified musician went and threw himself at the King's feet, and all the rest stood dumbfounded, awaiting what the King would do. And the King was very pale and shaken, and at first was very angry; but to the harper he did nothing, nor to the harp that had given him away. But slowly he reached up and removed his helmet, and bowed his head that all might see."

There was a pause. "That's all, Madam," Disraeli said.

"Oh! Mercy! What a horrid story," said Queen Victoria. "He ought *never* have done it!"

"But I was coming to the moral, Ma'am—not the moral which the Irish would draw, for I don't think that would be one to which Your Majesty or Your Majesty's Government could subscribe. To me, the story serves to clarify a concept that runs through the whole of Irish literature and song, down to that infamous street anthem about —ah—the wearing of a certain colour. And the concept seems to be that under the helmet of Power is the mark of the beast. Ah, but that Irish king was Power in its most primitive form: he was absolutism unenlightened and unrefined. How different from the wise and benevolent Constitutional Monarchy under which the British peoples have attained to the pinnacle of their greatness! And yet it occurs to me that the Irish are still confusing the two. And how natural, Ma'am! Throughout two centuries, the Sovereign has passed less than three weeks in Ireland. Does it not appear that a show of more interest in the country would be politic?"

"What are you suggesting?" asked the Queen, with a qualm.

"I am suggesting, Madam, that seeing is believing; that the personal graciousness of so great a Royal House as reigns in Britain can do more in Ireland than armies or than any doctrine preached by Home Ruler or Disestablishmentarian. I suggest, by Your Majesty's leave, that His Royal Highness, the Prince of Wales, visit Ireland— let us say for the hunting; thus combining public duty with pleasure as becomes a Royal Prince and Heir."

Victoria, who had feared he was going to suggest something worse, hesitated. "Well . . . we shall see. But," she quickly qualified, "the expense must be borne by the Government! It would be wholly for political considerations, and therefore we must not be imposed upon with the bills! No one who wanted rest and relaxation would think of going to Ireland!"

Disraeli bowed. "The Government will gladly undertake the expense, since the Prince will only smooth the path for Your Majesty's ministers."

The bow was modestly returned.

Now! thought Disraeli: now for Manchester! For of course he had not been indulging himself in all that whimsy about the ears of an Irish king for nothing, least of all for Ireland. He had but moved a pawn to gain a queen. Now for the coup.

But when next he raised his eyes to hers, upon the very verge of Manchester, he was surprised to see that she was rigid, her gaze fixed in astonishment upon something just beyond General Ponsonby's shoulder. And turning to make out what it was that ailed her, the Prime Minister was struck into another piece of statuary wearing exactly the same expression.

What both were staring at was a face protruding inexplicably from behind the window hangings: a small, stubby, incredibly dirty face, as of a gnome that had tunnelled up through some forgotten secret passage underground; and the round brown eyes of it, looking unnaturally large and bright amid all that grime, were staring right back at the Queen.

The reputedly giddy Miss Prior saw it, and a little cry escaped her.

Mr. Brown saw it, and roared: he lunged across the room in a swirl of kilts and sporran and pulled it, struggling, into the open.

"Great heavens!" gasped the Queen, at the first sight of the full figure, which in that great flopping coat looked only half a figure.

"Naseby!" commanded Mr. Brown.

"Y-yes! Yes!—Horrible!" trembled Mr. Naseby. His jowls were pumping in and out like a frog's, his stout arms shook back and forth at his sides, and he seemed about to have that apoplexy after all.

"Tak' him out, Naseby!"

The Sergeant Footman charged. He seized the captive by both shoulders. "Out! Out with you! Out!" And the biggest Little Thing ever to disturb his existence was thrust violently off scene in the grip of Mr. Naseby's fists.

"Oh!" breathed the Queen, when it was gone; she refreshed herself from a glass of water, then imperiously rose.

Dinner was over.

And Manchester lay in ruins under the table.

6

Whatever ironies attach to the memory of Charles the First, the gentlest must be this, that of all the laws he decreed by his royal will, those which have endured the longest are to be found not in the lawbooks of his country but in the Servants' Hall of his castle, where still hang the *Twelve Good Rules for Servants* that he handed downstairs from his study:

I	Profane No Divine Ordinance	VII	Repeat No Grievances
II	Touch No State Matters	VIII	Reveal No Secrets
III	Urge No Healths	IX	Make No Comparisons
IV	Pick No Quarrels	X	Keep No Bad Company
V	Maintain No Ill Opinions	XI	Make No Long Meals
VI	Encourage No Vice	XII	Lay No Wagers

These Rules Observed Will Maintain
Thy Peace and Everlasting Gain

And beneath these stern injunctions, Mr. Brown, who customarily broke all of them (with the possible exception of No. VIII if we give him the benefit of the doubt on those evenings when he entertained in his room with a bottle), found the castle-breaking boy again after having seen King Charles's great-great-great-great-great grandniece safely into the White Room.

It was Mr. Brown's policy to hold aloof from Household affairs, save when his sensitive nose caught a whiff of injustice, as in the case of Slattery and the lamp, and then he was capable of laying about him like a Covenanter to set things right again, but anything touching the personal safety of the Queen was a matter in which he yielded province to no one. There had been the famous case of Arthur O'Connor, who had presented a pistol in the Queen's face as she descended from her carriage in front of Buckingham Palace. Mr. Brown had landed upon him heavily, torn the pistol from his grasp, and handed him over to a constable. It had turned out that O'Connor was an Irish Patriot, and that his pistol wasn't loaded. There had been the case of the runaway carriage horses, likewise overpowered by Mr. Brown. There had been the Fenian kidnapping threats, which had caused him for weeks to sleep at night with a pistol under his pillow. He was suspicious of all comers where the Queen was concerned, and in this incident of the dining room thought he smelt the sinister. A clarty sacket hiding in the castle not six feet from the Queen! How had he got there? Something queer about that. To employ children in their businesses was common practice among criminals, and chances were the bairn wasn't in this alone. For all Mr. Brown knew, he might be the instrument of some arch-thief or assassin who, in fact, might be lurking somewhere in the castle himself this minute—he and his whole gang! The gillie's face was bristling as he strode into the Servants' Hall, and he was fingering the haft of his dirk.

He did not immediately see Wheeler, but easily divined his whereabouts by the ring of human forms that was certainly surrounding something, and by the babel of tongues abusing it. There were servants of every kind and degree in various stages of curiosity, indignation, and confusion; on the edge of the throng was Noonan, wringing her hands; beside her, Slattery, stretching his neck to peer over the heads in front of him; and there, with his broad scarlet back, his red face, and his booming voice, was the Sergeant Footman commanding everyone to stand back while he got to the root of the matter. Then from the centre of the throng rose a shrill wail that Mr. Brown recognized as the cry of the underdog, and instantly Noonan was clawing her way to the rescue.

"For shame, for shame to yez all; it's only a poor starved thing it is," she was shrilling.

"Keep out of it, woman," Slattery advised her, greatly agitated. "Keep out of it sure or you'll rue the day."

"And what's it to 'er, I'd like to knaow!" demanded a sister scrubwoman.

"Indeed, let 'er keep 'er plice!"

"Stop pushin', girl!"

"Silence! Stand back!" boomed Mr. Naseby with trembling jowls. "Here! We'll see about this. Stand——"

But a stronger hand than Noonan's was hurling shoulders to right and left; Mr. Naseby himself was stood back violently, and the words died on his lips as he looked up into the considerable countenance of John Brown. At the sudden appearance of the Queen's fierce hulking gillie, sounds died on lips generally, including the wail on Wheeler's; even the two tears on Wheeler's cheeks stood still, and there was silence in the Servants' Hall as Mr. Brown looked him distastefully up and down. But Wheeler was no longer merely frightened. He was overawed, intimidated, and charmed together by the barbaric figure and hairy visage now dominant among them all, and he stood like a boy in front of the lion's cage at the zoo, his whole being gone to his eyes.

It is very flattering to be looked at in this way, as every lion knows, but John Brown was better proof against those ingenuous dark brown eyes than were mere shipmasters and policemen.

"None o' yer greetin' and gowlin', mind!" warned Mr. Brown, towering over the prisoner; and clamping his fist onto a skinny shoulder, he demanded to be informed what Wheeler had been doing at the Queen's dinner party and who had put him there.

But in the expectant hush that followed, Wheeler only dropped his gaze, and gulped.

" 'Twas some man brought ye!" declared Mr. Brown. "What man?"

The ancient chivalry of the London streets laid down but one honourable line of conduct for a boy in Wheeler's position to hold to: defiance, expressed by the impenitent swagger, the curling lip, the jeering tongue. Too late. He had already degraded himself by bawling. He felt this keenly and blinked at the floor, a lost soul.

"D'ye hear, ye skellum! Was it yer father brought ye? Whaur's yer father?"

"Ain't—got un."

The gillie frowned. "Then wha brought ye? Answer, now!"

The prisoner drew a baggy sleeve across his wet eyes and behind it muttered something unintelligible.

"Speak up, man!" charged Mr. Brown, giving the shoulder a shake.

"Arr, I come on a barge."

"Och, a river barge, was it?" For this, which might explain the coal dust, seemed not unreasonable, so far as it went.

Wheeler nodded, his lips resolutely compressed. He wasn't going to do *that* again.

"Frae Lonnon?" For with his appearance and accent, the boy couldn't have passed for hailing from anywhere else.

He nodded.

"And wha smugglt ye into the castle? Answer, lad!"

"I—I——" Wheeler suddenly caught his breath and blurted: "I sneaked in."

"Ah! Sneaked in, did ye? And wha put ye up t'it?"

"I sneaked in, and 'en"—convulsively he caught his breath again —"I falled down the 'ole!" And gouging into his eyes with sooty knuckles, he began to do it after all. He was only seven.

"Hole?" insisted Mr. Brown, tightening his hold on the shoulder. But the sobbing intensified. The shoulder under Mr. Brown's hand was shaking, and of itself his hand relaxed its grip. He looked at the hand disconcertedly. "Ah, blast it, will ye leave off gowlin'?"

Then Noonan flared up at him: "Musha, you'd frighten the day-lights out of a bear!"

"Be still, girl!" snapped Mr. Naseby; but already Noonan's inter-ruption had set off a chorus.

" 'E's frightened, right enough. Dirty little beggar!" . . . "Snivel-ling little area sneak, that's wot 'e is!" . . . "Spying on Her Majesty at her own dinner table! He do be a bold one!" . . . "Meek enough now, 'e is. Oh, they'll make you 'oller now, you young nigger!"

Mr. Brown roared them down. Then he began to go through Wheeler's pockets. Necks craned to see what this search would produce. That capacious-looking coat, which, it was noticed, sagged at one side, seemed to promise nothing less than platters of the royal plate.

Out came a broken handspike, some twine wrapped around a bit of stick, a rusty harness buckle, a throwing dart (from the Water-man's Arms, perhaps), the end of a farthing-dip candle, a flat stone (suitable for skipping), six inches of dirty gold fringe, a sketch from the *Illustrated London News* depicting two Ashantee blacks pros-trate before the plumed Sir Garnet Wolseley, four copper nails (worth 4*d*. a pound), and a small lump of coal.

Amid general disappointment, Mr. Brown began stuffing these articles back into the coat, while Wheeler, who had been somewhat distracted from his lamentations by the necessity for keeping an eye on his property, stood with arms raised clear of the pockets, docilely, though with his lip out, his chest still heaving in little spasms, and saw that he got back all that had been taken from him.

Mr. Brown observed gruffly that apparently the boy had stolen nothing anyhow, at which Noonan folded her hands across her apron and gave a brisk nod as if to say that this only clinched what she could have told them herself to begin with. "Sure not, and look at it, destroyed with starvation."

"Starvation indeed!" sneered a chambermaid.

"Ask it, itself."

Mr. Naseby glared at the intractable woman. "*Will* you mind your place, girl!"

"Sure, sir, I was only thinking——"

"Hold your tongue!"

"Naseby," Mr. Brown said unexpectedly, "ye're a sumph!"

"Eh?" inquired Mr. Naseby, swinging round in a startled way.

"For what kind of a woman d'ye tak' Her Majesty," Mr. Brown confronted him severely, "that ye imagine she'd turn a starving subject frae her door?"

"Why——"

"Haith, are they better Christians in Newgate Prison, where they gie a man his bellyful afore they hang him? Gin the scamp's come thigging or thieving, and he's starving, man, he'll taste o' the Queen's bounty first and her punishment after."

The Hall people exchanged glances, but no one dared cross him, not even Mr. Naseby; so, to Naseby's embarrassment, Wheeler was led to a side table where a sullen potboy set before him a plate of mutton and greens. But no one was half so astonished at this as was Wheeler himself, and he had to be prodded sharply by Mr. Brown before he would touch a morsel. When he did pitch in, it was observed with disgust that he ate with his fingers. But fingers were the least of it. He ate like an animal, rapaciously tearing off hunks of meat with his teeth; he stuffed his mouth full, and the brown juice oozed out between his lips, streamed down over his dirty hands onto the plate, and dripped onto his coat; and when his crammed gullet rebelled, he would disgorge its contents, coughing and belching, tears of pain swelling into his eyes, only to fall to again as ravenously as before. Not that he was especially hungry; he always ate in this way and he supposed that everyone else did too. Only, perhaps, he was eating faster than usual, for his eyes kept darting round at his captors as if he expected them to stop him at any moment.

It was a revolting spectacle. The higher servants who still hovered about, and those lower ones who had been sent back to their tasks but arranged to pass that way from time to time, derived from it a warm inner satisfaction; they shook their heads at one another, whispering that it gave them the fair 'orrors, and Mr. Naseby, being especially gratified, threw up his hands at it. Even the coarse John Brown was revolted. But he was of a different breed. From a long line of Aberdeenshire crofters he had inherited a strange jumble of intolerances in which an antipathy to vagabonds was mixed with an active abhorrence of hunger and a deep resentment against the enemies of the downtrodden. The bairn did appear to be half starved, and so Mr. Brown's revulsion was not unrelieved by another kind of satisfaction, which arose from a consciousness of his own worthy deed in having procured the food for him, so that when Wheeler had emptied his plate, the Christian man ordered it filled again. But this time Mr. Brown denounced the practice of eating with the fingers, and thrust a fork upon Wheeler. From the way Wheeler handled it, it was clear that he knew spoons but not forks, so Mr. Brown took it back again and demonstrated how a bit of meat might be impaled on the tines and conveyed on them to the mouth. Wheeler was urged to try this. He held the ungainly utensil poised in his fist, stabbed suddenly, and skewered his target. He looked up and giggled.

"Now then, now then?" said Mr. Brown. "Eat it, eat it."

Wheeler raised the food awkwardly to his mouth and put out his tongue to bring it in, but succeeded only in disengaging it from the fork, and it plopped back onto his plate.

"Na, na, na," Mr. Brown said, shaking his head at the frustrated boy. "D'ye imagine ye're fishing a salmon, that ye maun gaff it wi' yer tongue? Keep yer tongue out o' the road, man; 'tis like stowing the fish i' the basket after ye've landed him."

Mr. Brown performed again, more slowly, pausing with his hairy jaws stretched wide, the meat suspended between them on the end of the fork—watched fascinatedly by Wheeler, Mr. Naseby, the second steward, two master cooks, and a storekeeper. He pushed the meat back into the cave of his mouth, closed jaws and lips, and, with a magical flourish, withdrew the fork empty.

Mr. Naseby, who had been leaning forward slightly in order to follow the trick, straightened himself with a sigh.

"D'ye see?" asked Mr. Brown.

Wheeler nodded and eagerly essayed the thing again, watched anxiously by all hands. This time he did it.

"Aye!" said Mr. Brown amid murmurs of relief. "Ye've got the hang o'it. Practice, laddie! Practice will mak' ye as handy wi' the fork as the gentles."

His appetite blunted, Wheeler began to enjoy the game as much as any English tourist learning to eat with chopsticks; he thought it very arch. To be sure, thought Mr. Brown, watching him with approval, the young kelpie had only needed to be shown. Mr. Brown felt pleased with himself. He did not fully realize why, and had anyone explained to him the obligation the feeling implied he would have been amazed.

He returned to business. That story about the Hole: what Hole? The facts were drawn from Wheeler in little jerks; in his embarrassment, many of his words were unintelligible, and his allusions were vague, but from what his inquisitors were able to make of the confession among them, they gathered that he meant he had somehow sneaked past a gate and fallen the rest of the way by accident. This brought a hoot from Mr. Naseby, who after all had some reason to be bitter in the matter: wouldn't he personally be called to account for what had happened during dinner? "Hah! Fell in, did he? A pretty story," he said. "Look here, boy, do you see any green in our eyes?"

Mr. Brown turned on the Sergeant Footman irritably: "As I told ye afore, Naseby, you're a sumph."

Mr. Naseby's head went back. "Well! I like that, I'm sure. A—a what, did you say?"

Only the slightest twinkle came into Mr. Brown's eye, but it gave him a friendlier look. "Dinna fash yersel', man. 'Tis quite an opprobrious expression."

"Oh," said Mr. Naseby doubtfully. But the word festered in his self-esteem, and as soon as he could do so with dignity, he walked away. "Sumph," he muttered, "wasn't it?" And in front of all those others, too. Mr. Brown was all too highhanded indeed. Then it occurred to him that the proper authority to deal with a burglar in the castle was the guard. And, as much out of a sense of revenging himself upon Wheeler and Mr. Brown as in the hope of making up for this oversight before it should be noticed, the conscientious Sergeant Footman slipped out to summon the guard in person.

He might have contented himself with notifying the first sentry he came to, but sentries to Mr. Naseby were only bric-a-brac, though largely invisible. He might have ascended the stairs to the Guard Room in the State Apartments, or taken himself to the Guard House at the bottom of the Lower Ward, but he went instead to a mere figurehead of a post off the privy chambers; and the reason his steps rolled that way, instead of towards either of the other two headquarters of the military, as they might more judiciously have done— the reason, in fact, that events now took the turn they did—deserves some slight philosophical consideration. A Sergeant Footman was responsible for seeing that each evening a member of his staff, receiving from a wine steward two bottles of Madeira, took them to this guard room and no other; hence this one had the only practical claim upon Mr. Naseby's attention; he couldn't be bothered with any other.

This one gave the impression of being much the oldest guard roost in the castle, though perhaps it wasn't at all; an impression by far the most striking of having been left over from the Middle Ages, and left over for certain it had been. Left over from the days when there had been better reason for guard rooms situated hard by where the Sovereign lay, left over in any age that could only smile at it respectfully, as at an old soldier's stories. It seemed to sigh for the England of warrior kings, clanking champions, and stout baronial retainers that bore watching. Long ago it had tacitly surrendered its active functions to the room in the State Apartments, and nowadays was without any real justification for existence. Yet here, like their predecessors in earth-girdling succession, officers of the Royal Household Guards as late as Victoria's day continued to keep the vigil, only because no one cared to assume the responsibility of telling them not to, and here continued loyally to drink the health of George the Third in the wine with which his late Majesty's thoughtfulness continued to supply them, since no one ever had presumed to cut it off. And here this evening the vigil was being more or less kept by two young gentlemen of the Grenadiers.

One was the second son of a duke, and he, having been out late the night before, was sound asleep on a sofa.

The other, who was all too painfully awake, was nobody but the only son of the vicar of Appleton Thorn, Cheshire, and therefore, by Guards standards, a gentleman barely. He had connections, however. It was known that he was related to the Hamiltons, and that his sister had married a fortune in the City. But the Hamiltons paid him scant attention, and for all the money he could risk at cards, his sister might as well have married an old-clo' man in Petticoat Lane. No doubt he realized that being in the Guards was more than he deserved, let alone being permitted to keep the vigil in the little sinecure room; but his gratitude had curdled.

He resented the Guards, knowing well that he was over his head in them and would be better off in shallower water. Here he was, he told himself this evening (having no one else to talk to), an obscure, unbattle-tried subaltern in a regiment of his betters; strapped, sure to be passed over in the lists, condemned to idleness in a deadmen's guard room; finished, rotting, and at twenty-five! Buried alive, by God, like the Lady Maud de Braose, whom they said King John had sealed up in these very walls somewhere. As good as mounted in a museum—"*A Royal Household Guardsman. Reign of Victoria the First. Windsor Excavations.*" If only it had been his luck to be in Africa with Wolseley. If only he could arrange to be sent to India. Always some sort of show going on out there. A man might . . . But if she married while he were out there, he might not even know! Well, she *would* marry, of course—some blighter. What could he expect? What had he to offer her? For goaded as he was by an ambition to make his name and fortune, Charles McHatten suffered worse from a more presumptuous passion. He hankered to possess Emily Prior. The Honourable Emily Prior, by some accounts the greatest beauty of the kingdom, daughter of a viscount and granddaughter (on her mother's side) of an earl. Useless to think of it; folly even to dance with her; and as for galloping his horse to catch up when he saw her riding in the Park, that was as dangerous as following a will-o'-the-wisp. Yet he knew that his desire to be near her was what kept him rotting in the Guards. He was a fool.

Whom would she marry? He looked resentfully at the noble Dicky Wetherell, snoring gently on the sofa. No! *He* wouldn't have the sense to ask her; fancied himself a gay dog, going to play the field till he was tottering on for forty. Not Dicky. But whom? Blast it, what should it matter to him anyway?

And McHatten, a tall, lean, dark-faced young officer with a precociously sardonic lip and a backward little moustache that obviously never would come up to Guards' standards; a young man seated behind an antique oaken table scarred by an incalculable number of boots exactly like his own, many of whose wearers doubtless had been as unhappy as he (not that it mattered now), looked bitterly round his tomb; at the pikes and halberds, swords and shields of unknowable Guardsmen; at the faded banners, captured somewhere once; at the casques and breastplates, crusts of lusty bodies long nourishment for primrose and yew—and swore. He raised his glass with a silent toast to India and drank the dead king's wine.

As he set the glass down, a sentry entered with Mr. Naseby in tow. Mr. Naseby was out of breath, and his thick rusty brows were raised in apology for the news he bore. McHatten's impulse was to tell him to go to blazes: this wasn't the place to report anything. But the slightly supercilious look on the face of the sentry stopped him. So he was thinking that too, was he? Impudent bounder. And the part about the boy's having been caught in the Queen's presence alarmed him. That sounded as if there were going to be a row. And soured as he was on the Guards, he felt anger at the realization that the Grenadiers likely would be the butt of the whole Royal Barracks on the morrow. He thought, Shall I wake Dicky? and looked again at his senior officer, blissfully unconscious still. No. It was Dicky that could go to blazes. He buckled on his sword, crowned himself with the intimidating bearskin, the strap hooked smartly under his lower lip, and, bidding the sentry follow, went with the footman.

But when he reached the Servants' Hall, Wheeler had gone. What! had he stole away? No, they told him, he had been marched off by Mr. Brown. Brown? The gillie? The same. Where had Brown taken him? No one knew. The deuce! what business had Brown got——

"Begging your pardon, sir," Mr. Naseby said, "it was Mr. Brown captured him; then I brought him down here, you see, and then Mr. Brown came down and took charge again, as it were, and examined him."

"Examined him? On whose authority?" McHatten had heard tales of the highhandedness of the Queen's gillie; he had visions of a report on a Guards matter being made to Her Majesty by him.

"Why, on his own, sir, I expect."

"So the boy was 'examined' in the Servants' Hall by a gillie. And why wasn't the guard notified until now?"

Consternation suddenly seized Mr. Naseby. He saw trouble only piling up ahead of him. Now it would be charges laid before the Master of the Household by the Captain of the Guard! Negligence; disobedience to the rules; dereliction of duty and disrespect of authority; jeopardizing the security of the Household! He repeated prayerfully that everything had been on the authority of Mr. Brown.

"Nonsense. Brown is a servant. He'll hear of this, I shouldn't wonder. If that little beggar escapes, you'll all hear of it." But what was worrying McHatten was the certainty that the Grenadiers would hear of it. Besides, he was disappointed. In the tedium of his life as a keeper of the vigil, even this had promised excitement. And it might come to something—who could tell? That was why he hadn't wakened his senior. He said, "Do you expect me to call out the troops and hunt the boy through the castle?" but what he meant was, Am I to let them know in the main Guard Room and have the case taken out of my hands already?

"I expect not, sir," Mr. Naseby answered abjectly; and the other servants, who at first had thronged round like hounds avid to pick up the scent of Wheeler's blood, began to slink away.

McHatten had an inspiration. "Look here—*you* find him."

"Me, sir?"

"Why not? You've got troops of your own, haven't you? Send them out to look for him. It will save rousing the whole castle."

The light of this novel suggestion dawning upon the Sergeant Footman illuminated his round face like a lantern. "Why, that's an excellent plan, if I may make so bold, sir!"

And Mr. Naseby began deploying "troops" like a field marshal. He deployed not footmen alone, but pages and maids, porters and gardeners, and other servants not strictly under his command, for he considered that he had been deputed special powers, and so cunning was his deployment that in no case did he send a servant to any part of the castle from which, under the general regulations, a servant of that kind was debarred.

Mr. Brown, meanwhile, had let Wheeler lead him to Outer St. George's Gate and there seen for himself that the pedestrian gate in the fence had been left unlocked. Then he had been led back through the Inner Gate and into the fog of the Great Courtyard for proof of the open coalhole.

"The 'ole!" Wheeler suddenly trumpeted. "The very one, sir!"

And Mr. Brown was in no position to dispute the evidence, having just fallen into it up to half the length of one leg. He climbed out cursing and bent down to examine a gash on one bare knee, extracting gingerly therefrom several small pieces of gravel. Wheeler watched him while he mopped the blood with a handkerchief. "Gawblimy! Do it hurt, sir?" But Mr. Brown only confided to his beard certain maledictions upon the coof that had left the hole uncovered for a man to fall into. He found the cover himself and heaved it into place. Then he took Wheeler to his room in the Clarence Tower and bade him sit by the grate while he ministered to the wound. He applied a brown liquid to a clean handkerchief, the handkerchief to his knee—winced—and, courageously raising the bottle to his lips, took some of the medicine internally also. "Ga-ah!" he said, wincing again, and the sensitive Wheeler winced with him. Mr. Brown dressed the knee, took another draught from the bottle, wiped his mouth with his sleeve, and returned to the inquiry.

Wheeler, by this time, had lost his fear, and if his shyness remained, so did his admiration for his host, whom he earnestly desired to like him. It required therefore little cunning for Mr. Brown to draw from him the facts of his visit, along with several about Wheeler himself, including his place of abode, his orphanhood, and his uncle, in supplying which Wheeler threw in a few extra on the river Thames, Blackwall Stairs, Limehouse Cut and Folly Ditch, the ancient craft of mudlarking, and 'Ooker Morgan, the celebrated Peterboat man. Mr. Brown was capable of making something of all this, he was even impressed, but what impressed him most, if it also amused him, was that this boy who had stowed away on a coal barge and come all the miles from London's docks to see the castle should call it the pilothouse of the ruddy world and seem to fancy that from here the Queen shooed off heavenly bodies that were forever running derelict in a kind of universal sea and driving down upon England to send her to the bottom. Smiling, he asked: "Wha told ye that, laddie?" Bill Grams had told him and he were a bargeman on London river, and Wheeler had seen the Queen—it were the Queen, weren't it?—he knowed it were the Queen. "Aye," Mr. Brown admitted, "it was the Queen." And Wheeler said, "Gaw!"

Some such way as this had the son of Aberdeenshire crofters felt about the Queen once, and with some such awe had entered for the first time the castle of Balmoral. He lit his briar, and his eyes, turning upward with the smoke, showed him the photograph over the mantel. It was a photograph of a painting done twenty years before. Victoria and Albert; she slim and graceful in a riding habit of black velvet, with a Highland cap on her and a Victoria plaid draped from her shoulder, and she was sitting a pony—little Loch-na-gar that was, he kent; and the Prince in full Highland dress with the Balmoral tartan, standing at the animal's head and holding the bridle. The Queen had given Mr. Brown the picture a few years after Albert's death, and at the bottom had written: "To our loyal, good servant and friend, John Brown. Victoria, R." Just so had they looked, he minded, the day they had gone that picnic beside the Dee near Braemer; the day he had handed Her Majesty a cup of tea which she had pronounced the best she had ever tasted, and he had answered, "It should be, Mum, I put a grand nip o' whisky in it." And recalled to himself, as it may have been, by the power of suggestion, he took another pull at the bottle.

"Sae ye've come," he said, wiping his mouth with his sleeve again, "sae ye've come to hae a look at the castle. Waesucks, ye should see Balmoral. Windsor's grander, maybe, but na ways near sae bonny."

Mr. Brown condescended to relate something of his favourite of all the royal residences, situated among the green mountains of his native shire, with magic casements opening upon the Dee; and the more he told, pausing once or twice again to fortify his constitution against infection, the bonnier Balmoral became, until he was wreathing it in all the glamour of a Scotch mist: Balmoral with its hundred-foot tower, its turrets and castellated gables, bothies and pleasances and woods full of red deer, its halls hung and carpeted in tartans, its stag heads looking down from the walls. There was piping, he mentioned, round the table at dinner, and often reels and sword dances after, and when Victoria and Albert first had entered it, an old shoe had been flung after them for luck, and when the news of Sebastopol's capture had arrived in the middle of one memorable night, the Prince had risen from his bed and led all the villagers to the cairn on the top of Craig Gowan and there had been dancing by the wild light of a bonfire of victory and thanksgiving, and whisky had been passed. And again Mr. Brown paid his compliments to the power of suggestion.

And he talked on. If there frequently passed his lips that flagrantly inverted phrase that had shocked so many of his listeners, "Me and the Queen," it was not intentionally impudent, and who could blame him for noticing in the grandeur of his tale the grandeur of himself, who moved so grandly through it? Besides, the large enraptured gaze of Wheeler, whom he perceived now to be a worthy bairn, moved him to pity for all such as knew nothing of court life and were so eager to be informed, and he only wished to oblige.

7

Patiently, in the White Drawing Room, Disraeli had been trying to weave another web in which to consign the Queen to the merchants of Manchester. But the Queen kept breaking all his silken threads as fast as he could spin them.

The ambuscade in the dining room had upset her; her attention wandered, and—not an everyday nuisance for Benjamin Disraeli— she frequently changed the subject. It was growing in her mind that the incident had only gone to show how little security she had, what disrespect there was nowadays, with what shameful negligence she was attended. And she was thinking what a fuss she was going to make—oh, she would let them know. How shocked Albert would have been; Albert, who had so deplored inefficiency in the Household and done so much to correct it. She did need Albert, she would always need him. . . . But the tears that started to her eyes were stoutly ordered not to dare; she requested her Maid of Honour to sing; and Disraeli knew that he was beaten.

Miss Prior asked what Her Majesty would care to hear, and, something of Mendelssohn's or Mozart's being suggested, chose a song that the Queen once had told her that she used to sing herself, in her singing days—"*Schöner und schöner schmuckt sich.*" She sang it in a vibrant contralto, and, being permitted to select her own encore, gave them the coquettish "*Batti, batti,*" from *Don Giovanni.* (Ah! thought the Prime Minister, noting the lively accompaniment of eyes and bosom—that's better.)

Then it was over. Victoria rose and bade them good night. She urged her Minister to come again soon, she cautioned him to take care of his gout and not to overwork himself, promised to send him primroses just as soon as there were any—distant prospect; and then, through the ebony door leading directly to her chambers, vanished. What a disappointing end to an evening that had begun so auspiciously, he thought. He might see her for a few minutes again when he took his leave in the morning, but morning was no time for wheedling a woman. Confound that boy. Yet Disraeli had been surprised at the strong effect the incident had produced upon his Liege. Shocking, yes, but trivial, so far beneath her. And, being annoyed, he permitted his cynicism to penetrate his Tory sentiments: "The sheltered grande dame. This is what comes of having lived barricaded in her tower, shutting out the world." Had she any conception of her own Birnam Wood, which tonight had sent her but one of its saplings; of East End slums, the Shoreditch Nile, the Ratcliffe Tiger Bay? But of course! she had read Mr. Dickens.

Miss Prior politely took her leave; then General Ponsonby, who pleaded dispatches to get off.

"There'll be a gentleman waiting to look after you," the general told him, and, stepping to the door, summoned a bright-eyed, fair young man. "This is Mr. Phipps-Haven, sir. Perhaps you'd like to see some of the things in the Corridor—that's where they keep the Koh-i-noor, you know."

It was the custom for the Queen's guests to be offered a sight-seeing tour of this kind when she had retired; but Disraeli shook his head. "Thank you, no." In his present mood, the celebrated bauble was but an emblem of his own deficiency; a poor consolation prize, he thought, for the philosophers' stone.

"Or the billiard room, sir?" hopefully suggested Mr. Phipps-Haven.

Disraeli turned to him with hooded eyes and faintly smiled. "I hope you won't think me frivolous, but I should be grateful if you'd show me the Library."

"Will you step this way?"

He said good night to the general, and followed. "Do they teach billiards on the playing fields of Eton?"

"I couldn't say, sir. I went to Harrow."

"I beg your pardon."

Phipps-Haven hoped he had not appeared smug. Out of courtesy he inquired: "Where were you educated, sir?" And then, dimly recollecting that the great Dizzy was said to be something of a bounder, wished he hadn't.

But the Sphinx answered only: "Ah, where?"

He was an odd one for a P.M. Phipps-Haven remembered that his father had never trusted the Old Jew, as they called him. "Fancy foreign fellow," his father had said. "Clever, though. Damned clever." An execrating judgment.

A footman stood aside to let them pass. It was a long walk, and the old man leaning on his stick soon began to tire, perceiving which the young one slowed his pace. A hurrying page came bounding out of an intersecting hallway, saw them and stopped, abashed; he bowed himself nearly double, and Disraeli, going by, raised an eyebrow at his guilty head. They went round to the State Apartments and to the far end of that long building, traversing corridors and stairs on a road of red carpet reaching farther into time than into space; passing now another respectful servant, now the inscrutable armour ectype of some outrider of the realm. Disraeli was silent, dreaming how much had passed here of gallantry and lustre, vanity and mischief, rapture and grief—and thinking that the servants seemed uncommonly thick about the place for this hour. They ascended a narrow staircase from the print room, and, having just come from the drawing room of Victoria, entered into the private gallery of Elizabeth. This was now the Library.

A clergyman and a lady were before them, poking about in it; recognizing the Prime Minister, they bowed courteously and the clergyman bent down and whispered to an old man who was poring over something at a littered table above which burned a weak colza flame. Evidently the librarian. He looked up over the tops of his half-spectacles, and beaming vaguely in their direction, ushered them in with a benevolently welcoming gesture, if a slightly oily one, that is common to old keepers of books and dwellers among them everywhere. Disraeli gave him a pleasant nod as of recognition. The man reminded him of his father.

Elizabeth's gallery was of properly royal dimensions, nearly a hundred feet long, he judged; and, through a bust of herself on the superb stone mantel at the far end, Elizabeth, he saw, still presided over it. He paused to admire the great window set in carved stone mullions, the original ceiling decorated with the arms and badges of the House of Tudor, and noted yet hanging from the wall opposite the window an iron ε. Armchairs of ebony and scarlet leather were ranged round the walls in an elongated hollow square guarding the row of ebony tables, inlaid with ivory and topped with glass cabinets, which ran down the middle of the room; and in these cabinets were exhibited some of the Library's choicest items, which Disraeli, raising his glass to his eye, now engaged to examine.

He beheld the Metz Psalter of 1457, the Aldine Virgil of 1505, Elizabeth's prayer book, a copy of Shakespeare——

"Ha!" said a high voice at his shoulder, and he turned to find that he had been followed by the librarian. "That Shakespeare—1632, you see it is, sir; 1632—signed by Charles Stuart just before he went to the scaffold. Fancy! Parting gift to Sir Thomas Herbert—parting gift. *'Ave atque vale!'* Ah! *Ars longa, vita brevis*—eh?" And the old man cackled. "My name is Huish, sir."

Disraeli hated to be dogged about in a library. He thought irritably, Does he suppose I can't read the card for myself? But looking at Mr. Huish, he relented before he spoke. The curator of these treasures had the same peculiar fragility as they. The veins showing under the yellow skin of his forehead were like watermarks in old paper that would go to dust if you touched it; the blue eyes, so pleased and anxious over the concave tops of his spectacles, had the faded look of eyes in an illuminated volume of antique printing, and all about him hung a smell of must. It appeared that someone ought to be appointed curator of him.

"I was just thinking," Disraeli said, "how much my father would have enjoyed seeing this Shakespeare."

"Oh! Of course! Your father. Spelt it with the apostrophe, didn't he? Author, *Curiosities of Literature*. Know it well. Fine scholar. Dead now, I expect?"

"Yes, long dead."

"Too bad, too bad. But . . . *exeunt omnes*, all of us. *Curiosities of Literature*. Remember it well. *Ars longa, vita brevis.*"

"He also wrote a commentary on King Charles," the son suggested.

"Eh? He did? Dear, dear." A frown crossed the sunken face. "Haven't got it here, I regret to say. . . ." He brightened. "Have something of your own, though, sir. Some of those novels of yours. Er . . . *Lothair*, I believe; three volumes . . ."

"Yes," Disraeli said dryly, "I took care you had. I presented that one to Her Majesty myself."

"What? You did? Yes. Recall now. Inscribed too, wasn't it? Three volumes. Blue vellum. Well, you're in good hands at Windsor, Mr. Disraeli, if I . . . do say it. You'll be preserved—preserved. *Ars longa*——"

"True," Disraeli agreed, "and life being so short, I believe if you don't mind I'll just have a look at that handsome chimneypiece before I go."

"What? Oh! Our chimneypiece! Yes indeed. Famous, famous . . ."

Disraeli stumped down the length of the gallery, trailed by the librarian and the Gentleman-in-Waiting; he halted under the mantel. From the middle distance the clergyman and the lady regarded solemnly the tableau of their Prime Minister gazing up into the face of their ancestors' Queen, a tableau of which their Prime Minister was fully as appreciative as they. It flattered the actor in him, but it also submerged the cynic. He might have been asking: "Have you anything to say to me?" Even as he once had dared ask a sphinx in the Egyptian desert. The librarian pointed out, carved in the stone, the date 1583—"Twenty-fifth of her reign, of course," he recited happily; "fiftieth of her life." And there too Elizabeth had caused to be wrought the badge given to Anne Boleyn by Henry the Eighth. But between this and the badges on the ceiling Disraeli divined a spiritual difference. Surely she had not meant this one for mere heraldic display; this one had been a burning commemoration—part of her attempt to restore by an act of sovereign will her mother's honour! Here in this house! What scenes of solitary brooding might not be conjectured from its presence by the bed of her fires!

"Speaking of Shakespeare," Mr. Huish said suddenly, "er . . . it was in this gallery *The Merry Wives* was first given. So they say, at least; so they say. *Merry Wives of Windsor*. . . ." Disraeli had a vision of the room thronging with Elizabethans, the Queen upon a dais ringed round by her courtiers, Essex, Burleigh, young Cecil, Bacon, perhaps, and by the farthest wall a platform on which——But Mr. Huish was shaking his head and admitting regretfully, "Never found any proof of it myself." Gone!—all of them. No proof!

"Tell me," Disraeli asked, nodding up at the bust, "have you ever seen her?"

"Eh? Queen Bess? Herself, you mean?" Mr. Huish cackled and wagged his head. "Oh, now, you've heard the tales, have you? Oh, there are some queer ones, you know. There was a certain young lord, I remember; but that was long ago. And there was a young lady painter; paintin' the view, she was, from the window there . . . Ah, but then! they do say, you know, sir"—and he looked up at Disraeli under his brows—"they do say she . . . walks . . . sometimes."

Phipps-Haven laughed. "Bosh, sir! You don't believe she walks, as they call it?"

"I? Oh!" And the old man cackled again. "There, now; pullin' my leg, are you? But remember—h'm—*Damnant quod non intelligunt*—eh? Young chaps! Have you ever studied the subject? Strong personality like Her Majesty's up there . . . room they say she loved . . ." He paused and chewed ruminatively. "I have been here, my young sir, nearly fifty years, come next Michaelmas. Longer than Her Present Majesty, bless her. And I say to myself—as you should say—*Age quod agis!* Ha! *You* may say, *Aegri somnia!* And yet, though she has never seen fit to . . . show herself to me . . . I tell you . . . she is here. Eh? What do you say to that?"

"Well, if you'll pardon my saying it, sir—sounds a bit thick to me," said Phipps-Haven, grinning.

"Of course! Of course! But you haven't been here fifty years!" And he wagged his head, frowning, and chewed again, doubtless thinking: *"Damnant quod non intelligunt!* Young chaps! Coming up here like this!" For it was plain that he held disbelief in Elizabeth's ghost to be as great a disparagement of the Library as a doubt cast on the authenticity of one of its manuscripts.

Disraeli said: "No doubt Her Late Majesty is a comfort to you here."

"Oh, come, sir!" Phipps-Haven protested. "Surely you don't mean that *you* believe in ghosts."

"If at my time of life I knew of one, I should find it a great comfort, I assure you," answered Benjamin Disraeli.

And as they talked of shades and heaven in the Library, the forces of earthly calamity were gathering in other parts of the castle.

Up in the Clarence Tower, in the imported mist risen like Sinbad's genie from a bottle, Mr. Brown was making the most of an audience such as he had never enjoyed before in his life, and making also marked progress into the woods of psychology. In regaling Wheeler with what was possibly the most luxuriant example of brag that anyone in Windsor had ever listened to, he had succeeded in winning himself completely over to Wheeler's cause, and under that warmly admiring gaze had reached the point of exchanging a prisoner for a protégé. Precisely that point was reached when, coming to the end of a tale and after once more easing his dry throat at the bottle, he repeated, "And sae ye've come to see the castle!" and bethought him, in his generous mood, what a pity it would be should the pilgrim be turned out in the cold night without having seen it at all. "Well, now, I'm minded to show ye a bit o' it mysel'. Aye, I will, man. I'll show ye a bit ye'll ne'er forget." At which piece of magnanimity Wheeler was overwhelmed.

They descended the stairs, Mr. Brown unsteadily lighting the way with an oil lamp with which he had equipped himself in the knowledge that at this hour a great part of the castle would be dark. And as they emerged into the Grand Corridor, they were seen by a large young chambermaid named Munn. Munn scurried with her intelligence to the Servants' Hall, where McHatten yet waited with his field marshal. Having had to come rather a long way, however, she had barely finished her report when Slattery arrived with a fresher one. He had just seen Mr. Brown and the boy abovestairs in the State Apartments, entering the Grand Reception Room.

"What!" said McHatten. "By Jove!" And he set off in pursuit at once with the sentry. Under the circumstances, it was only natural that Mr. Naseby set off too, and that Slattery, being lighter on his feet than Mr. Naseby, was already ahead of him. But Noonan, the scullery maid, though as interested a party as any, knew well enough that the Grand Reception Room was no place for her. For a moment she only stood wringing her hands in the midst of the excitement that the hunt had left behind it, then suddenly she clutched the arm of Munn. "God help me," she declared, "I'm for seeing what they do to him. Will you be coming with me then like a good one?" And pulling Munn after her, she seemed really to leave her no choice. But Munn, being a woman herself, and also a party to the matter now, needed no pulling after the first tug. Discipline in Windsor Castle was being rudely trampled upon tonight, and on the whole there would be the devil to pay in the morning.

But the Grand Reception Room was not Mr. Brown's destination; it merely lay on his royal road. With his torch held high before him in one fist, and Wheeler by the other, he paused not at all in this large and sumptuous chamber, though the lamplight glittered overhead as upon clusters of jewels that might be had for the plucking, gleamed mysteriously in mirrors, on gilded picture frames and the warm limbs of inviting sofas and chairs, and though Wheeler's feet luxuriated in a carpet soft as mud; Mr. Brown led the wondering boy straight through this apartment into the next. And this one was almost as large as the other, but, after it, looked bare and cold as the nave of a church. On the floor there seemed at first glance to be no furniture at all, and the long wall opposite them as they entered let in six chill panels of the night, spaced by five cavernous mirrors in which the tiny lamp flame multiply shone like the eyes of so many watching cats; and now Mr. Brown was leading the way down the middle towards something that began to loom up in the darkness fearsome as a pulpit. Before this he stopped, raising his lamp that Wheeler might see, and Wheeler sucked in his breath sharply. "Aye," said Mr. Brown, not without vanity: "the throne!"

"Crikey!" Wheeler breathed, and hastily uncovered, and standing awe-struck at the foot of the unapproachable vacuity, in the shadows and the silence, clutching his cap in his hands, he respectfully bowed. Mr. Brown smiled down at him benevolently, and belched.

The throne of Her Britannic Majesty stood upon a dais carpeted in crimson Indian velvet; over it hung a velvet tester of Garter blue, and behind it a backdrop of the same noble cloth and colour gloriously emblazoned with the royal arms. And the chair itself was a graceful one, rather small for a throne, and in effect simple, but in fact elaborate; it was all carved and fretted and covered in silver gilt, had crystals and amethysts in it, and its arms were wrought like dragons with silver teeth. But Wheeler was seeing the Queen sitting there in her Crown, with her Sceptre and her Orb, a vision that marvellously improved it—seeing that, as it were, with one eye, while with the other he was seeing them gape at him as he told them about it afterwards on Blackwall Stairs. And the finest sight in the room by far was Wheeler's face.

"Aye," Mr. Brown allowed critically, "it's gey braw and muckle costly, but the Queen owns hantle grander."

He walked over to a French cabinet which, like the few other articles of furniture in the room, was backed deferentially against the wall, and carefully set the lamp on it. Then he reached into his coat for the restorative, which he had brought along against the dangers of drafts and the night air. He removed the cork and accorded to punctilio a fine gesture with the bottle toward the throne. "To Her Majesty!" he said gallantly, and drank a long health. "Ga-ah!" Observing that the bottle now was empty, he was about to part with it on the cabinet, but appeared to reflect that this was no place to leave it, and with admirable propriety returned it instead to his pocket. He reached to take up the lamp again, but, struck by another munificent thought, paused. His eyebrows went up roguishly.

"Haith, now; would ye no like to sit on 't?"

Sit on the throne? Ah, lawks! It was exactly what he had been wishing he could do, only he hadn't dared mention it.

"Pho!" said Mr. Brown amiably. "Thae daffing page boys be aye sitting on 't when there's nane by to catch 'em. Climb up, laddie, climb up; only see you don't soil the cushion."

So, egged on by that stable-bred rascal in his jocose mood, the deluded boy climbed up on the seat of the anointed. He sat caressing with his hands the silver-toothed dragons, and, meeting the eyes of his patron, burst nervously into a giggle. The sight struck Mr. Brown as so good a joke that he too began to laugh, profaning with salvos of merriment that sanctum sanctorum of the realm; and thus it happened that by reason of his own din he did not hear the arrival of McHatten, the sentry, and the candlelighter in the doorway.

"Good God!" McHatten said, and rushed forward to drag the usurper down.

Mr. Brown whirled just in time to meet this surprise attack. "Ha't!" he roared in confusion. "Wha gaes there!"

"Stand aside! I want that boy."

Blocking the way, the gillie focused his eyes upon the intruder and looked him up and down. "Oho! Do ye, now!" Mr. Brown was in high gore at being so rudely set upon. "And aren't ye the bauld sojer o' the Queen, laying siege to a bit laddie wi' yer trusty grenadiers! She'll gie you a medal, na doot!"

The young Guardsman's leathery but sensitive cheeks darkened. "Damn your impudence!" he said.

"My impudence, is it! Damn yer ain, ye menseless coof! And I'll thank ye to tak' tent o' yer cursing tongue in the—the——"

Mr. Brown was going to say, in the presence of the bairn, but he was distracted by the Olympian advent of Mr. Naseby and the two vestal virgins, Noonan and Munn. Mr. Naseby was blowing like a spent bull, and the unthinkable irregularity that met his eyes did for him completely; he collapsed into the nearest chair. For Wheeler, in his terror and bewilderment, still was perched upon the royal eminence behind the rampart of Mr. Brown, though he was poised to bolt as fast as James the Second at the first sign of a breach. But besides, the throne itself, on which she had never before clapped eyes, was enough to abash Noonan. "Sacred Heart o' Jesus!" she said. and dropped a curtsy.

"Ah, losh," said Mr. Brown in disgust. "Is the whole castle to come doon on us noo?" He spat on his palms and rubbed them together under McHatten's nose. "I'm expecting," he averred, "a trup o' horse ony minute."

Perhaps it was the slight lurch to Mr. Brown's body as he said this, or it may have been the wildness of his eye. McHatten looked at him keenly, then took a quick step towards him, hoping to catch a whiff of the circumstantial in support of his suspicion. But just as quickly Mr. Brown fell back, and laid a hand on his dirk.

"Hoolie! Ye slee swaddy! It's but for yer auld mither's sake I'm sweer to send ye hame a ghaist!"

Anyone hearing Mr. Brown now would be little inclined to doubt the testimony of certain former recipients of his hospitality that when conditioned for it he could talk for ten minutes running without employing intelligibly a single English word.

"Drunk as a lord!" McHatten said.

Mr. Brown's eyes flamed; he snapped himself erect. Although in that flickering light he was seeing two McHattens, subtly mingling as if deliberately to confuse him, it was his belief that his aspect and bearing were as respectable as any man's, and he regarded the accusation as a churlish attempt to discredit him on the basis of a mere surmise that he had taken a waught or two maybe. "Ye blethering callant! I'm as sober as a douce dean! But ye maun be sozzled yersel' to mak' sic a brattle in the Throne Room. I'm minded to turn ye in for 't."

McHatten was not by nature a patient young man, but in view of Mr. Brown's condition he was trying to be a forbearing one. "Stand aside, I tell you. You're obstructing the Queen's business."

"Ho! Obstructing, am I? Havers, man! It's yersel' is obstructing the Queen's business—you wi' yer blastit bellum and clishmaclaver! Did I no capture the bairn mysel', and are ye no ob-obstructing my investigation o' the matter?"

"*Your* investigation!"

Noonan had heard and seen enough to know how things stood for Wheeler. "Sure," she reasoned softly, forgetting her place again, "and who's a better right to be investigating it?"

"Aye!" challenged Mr. Brown.

"Investigating it indeed!" McHatten was aware that by some bizarre jest of Fate this Scotch lackey who so defied, flouted, and humiliated him was a royal favourite and a privileged person, a regular Lord Nonesuch of the Household, who, if the case were to be brought to issue, very likely would receive the protection and even the support of the Queen. He also knew that he himself would be subject to censure, however technical, for having taken the case into his own hands instead of notifying the main Guard Room, and that if a row resulted his superiors would be much annoyed with him. "Investigating it indeed! And is that the prisoner's dock where the little brute is sitting?" His lip curled. All the outrageous humour of the situation was apparent to him, absurd and incredible as a scene of opéra bouffe, but his contempt for it went sour in his mouth. "Brown, you're wearing the wrong costume. Your Mistress ought to turn you out in cap and bells. You couldn't have made a droller monarch for a court masque. Look at him. And this court of his. A Footman Pursuivant, I presume; a Duchess of the Scullery, a Chambermaid-in-Waiting. And who am I? Windsor Herald or the Knave of Spades? And the Corporal there? Ah, he's the Royal Executioner, Brown. And who," turning savagely to Slattery, "are you, pray? Crossbones King of Arms?"

Slattery, thus directly addressed, jumped. "Is it me, sir?" he said uncomfortably. "Ah, sure, your honour, I'm only the one lights the candles, now."

"Good! The Royal Magician! That throne used to belong to the King of Kandy, you know there's a nice touch. We ought to have a grand vizier."

There it was—darkly lighted by the oil lamp on the cabinet, shadowy, with highlights picked out by the icy chandeliers, the great mirrors, the giltwork on walls and ceiling, the steel of the sentry's bayonet—that idiotic little harlequinade that was to produce such surprising consequences and at which the historians have never ceased to marvel: the burly, stupidly blinking gillie in his heathenish toggery; the even more grotesque Grenadiers in their red tunics and monstrous bearskin headgear; the portly and periwigged Sergeant Footman in his flaming livery; the tall, skinny candlelighter, all in black; the kitchen slavey and the chambermaid; and presiding over all from his canopied roost of grandeur, that dirty, ragged, frightened child from the mudsill of London. An odd scene for logical historians to puzzle over in after years; but the crowning oddity was yet to come.

"We ought," McHatten had said sarcastically, "to have a grand vizier."

"Will I do?" asked a voice. And there in the doorway was the frail, portentous figure of Benjamin Disraeli.

Disraeli was as interested in thrones as Wheeler was, and had seen not a few in his time, but never before the one upon which Wheeler happened now to be sitting. In his youth, when he had ached to rise in the world, to mingle with dukes and duchesses, be bidden levees, and happily lose the common touch, this and the specimen at Buckingham Palace had been the two he wanted most to see, and tonight, having left the Library and come stumping back through the State Apartments, he had expressed a desire to look in at last upon the glorious loot of Kandy. But really, it was this, and not the Library, that he had been out to see from the first: he had only been dissembling again. Phipps-Haven, who may have felt that he had done his duty by the distinguished sight-seer, had pleaded that at this time of night the Throne Room would be dark, but, receiving no comment upon this objection, had concluded that it was after all not weighty enough to deflect a prime minister; so, taking a candle from a sconce, he had lighted it at a gas jet and resignedly led the way. "Queer!" he had said when it became obvious that a light burned in the Throne Room already. And then they had looked over the threshold. Phipps-Haven had been properly shocked. But the Prime Minister, though amazed enough, had been far from shocked. He had laid a silencing hand on the young man's arm, and, smiling a little, had looked on unobserved as if from the wings of a stage, until, unable to resist so inviting a cue as the one McHatten had thrown into the air, he had responded with his entrance line: "Will I do?"

But he saw from their horror-struck faces that he wouldn't do. One might rise to be a prime minister of Great Britain, but never at one and the same time that and a grand vizier. The young officer, he noticed, looked particularly appalled at the notion; he was snapping the corporal to attention, swinging round and clicking his heels, and now had turned suddenly to bronze. Those servants, after exhibiting the facial expressions with which they would one day receive the Angel Gabriel, had disposed themselves in attitudes of self-abasement, the men with heads bowed, the women sunk completely to the floor. Even Mr. Brown looked distressed in a befuddled kind of way; he was staring glassily, his hairy jaws agape, and he swayed a little. But the boy, taking advantage of the distraction, had slunk off the throne and burrowed into hiding behind it.

"Mr. McHatten, sir!" announced Lieutenant McHatten formally. "Grenadier Guards!"

Benjamin Disraeli only grunted. As a person, he felt that he had a right to resent this kind of treatment, but of course as a personage he knew that he hadn't. He stood fingering in one gaunt hand the eyeglass that hung round his neck on a black ribbon, surveying from the threshold, in his sphinxlike way, the ruins of the comedy, the players like dropped puppets, lifeless and out of shape. What fools people were! What a pity! He came slowly into the room on his stick, looking at them as he passed—behind him young Phipps-Haven, very grim. He stopped in front of the officer.

"What did you say your name was?"

"McHatten, sir!"

"Um. . . . Will you believe me, McHatten, if I tell you that I once knew a real grand vizier—sat on his cushions with him when I was about as old as you are, and smoked a pipe three feet long?"

"Indeed, sir." The Guardsman's face was crimson. He was wondering how much the Prime Minister had seen—and heard—and how, when the matter came up before his superiors, he ever would explain having stood by and allowed that young ragamuffin to occupy the throne. In fact, it appeared that some sort of explanation was called for now. "That—that boy, sir, broke into the castle, I believe. I was just——"

"Quite so; that was a good speech you made, McHatten. You ought to be in Parliament. And the boy," Disraeli said, looking round futilely for the creature; "he, I suppose, ought to be in Newgate, eh? Mr. McHatten, have *you* ever presumed to sit on a throne?"

"I?" McHatten began to fear that this old man was playing with him in some way, and at that moment was ready to believe of his character all the diabolism imputed to it by Mr. Gladstone. "No!" he flung out scornfully.

"No? Well, you see, I have. And there are many who hold that I should have been clapped in Newgate Prison long ago. But with all my experience, McHatten, think what an ornament I might have been to your court."

What this most un-English of prime ministers may have been getting at would be hard to say; but just then the Throne Room was shaken by a thud that momentarily unnerved everyone, and he was deprived of a further hearing. Mr. Brown, in making some clumsy movement, had fallen to the floor, and instantly became the centre of attention.

McHatten saw his opportunity; he signalled the sentry and together they executed an enveloping attack on the throne. Wheeler was hauled out from behind it, fighting hard.

"No 'arm! No 'arm!" he was screaming. "I'll cut it—str'ight, I will. I swears! . . . 'Ere, carst off yer 'ooks, carn't yers? *Aow!* Gaw *blarst* it! . . ."

His fallen champion had managed to get only to his knees, and seemed incapable of rising any higher. "Whoosh!" he was muttering. "Ah, whoosh!"

"Footman," McHatten said to Mr. Naseby. "The Queen's gillie will be obliged to you if you'll assist him to his quarters." He turned to the Prime Minister and clicked his heels again, smartly. "Your servant, sir!"

He marched from the room.

And the last that was seen of Wheeler, he was being dragged through the doorway by the corporal in McHatten's wake, fighting still, cursing, assuring everyone that he had meant no 'arm, and on the whole thinking little of his chances ever to tell his story, after all, on Blackwall Stairs.

"Jesus, Mary, and Joseph!" said Noonan in a dismal tone.

Disraeli, who had stood watching Wheeler's exit with half a smile, lowered the glass from his eye, and sighed. And a few minutes later, as he hobbled off to his bed, he was thinking of the time when he too —or was it really he?—had sat upon a throne.

8

That summer of 1830 there had begun for young Benjamin Disraeli an adventure that he was to carry like a vision through the rest of his life, and to translate in his artistic Oriental way into terms of living destiny for half the world. It was a deeply spiritual adventure, but he went through it in a state of physical excitement, romantic and sensual, and it began for him in the mountains of Spain, in the wild, storybook mountains of Andalusia, haunted by brigands and smugglers and roved by herds of savage bulls bred for tragedy in the ring, of Andalusia with its dazzling sunshine and fragrant airs, its orange trees, pomegranates, figs and olive groves, its walled towns nailed to high shimmering peaks in the distance, and the rude roadside crosses that marked the places where murder had been done lately by the Jose Marias, and the soft church bells, and the little wayside inns where you might sip the tawny wine of Malaga and hear a seguidilla sung by a rustic balladier in a velvet bolero or watch the landlord's daughter dance a rampageous fandango with a rose in her teeth. Or so, at least, were the mountains of Andalusia, of Granada, then, when young Disraeli was there.

Young Disraeli was an impossible dandy modelling himself upon the Byronic, and given to attitudinizing, or perhaps it is only fair to say driven to attitudinizing, for he was possessed of a demon with which he had as yet arrived at no arrangement. It darted quick glances out of his large, black, lustrous eyes, indolently lidded and long-lashed as any girl's; it surprised strangers by speaking with his rather beautiful lips; and while he had been writing his latest novel, only just before leaving England, it had seized hold of his pen.

"Think," it had written, "of unrecognized Caesar, with his wasting youth, weeping over the Macedonian's young career! Could Pharsalia compensate for those withering pangs? View the obscure Napoleon starving in the streets of Paris! What was St. Helena to the bitterness of such dark existence? The visions of past glory might illumine even that dark imprisonment, but to be conscious that his supernatural energies might die away without creating these miracles —can the wheel or the rack rival the torture of such a suspicion?"

Benjamin Disraeli doubted it.

The title of this novel was *The Young Duke*, and it had moved that gentle, skullcapped old scholar, his father, to snort: "Dukes! What does Ben know of dukes!" But what did Ben not know of them —he who had read all about them, and observed them so keenly (if from a certain distance) and imagined what it was like to be one, and determined someday to be a duke himself! As well ask what he did not know of unrecognized Caesar or obscure Napoleon, each with this same demon raging in his breast. Only his beloved, comforting sister, Sarah, understood, but she was troubled by none of the doubts that agonized the champion himself: Sa alone was sure.

Young Disraeli was slim and elegant, wore his thick black hair in ringlets, with a curl pendant on his forehead, and had a fine, long countenance of the most sensitive Semitic type, handsome, and, in repose, already sad. He came armed with a flashing wit, a grandiloquent fancy, and a fantastical taste in costume, and he wrote home in triumph from Gibraltar that he had been pronounced the only being ever to have passed the Straits with two canes—one for day and one for evening: he changed them as the gun fired. He was the delight of the ladies at the Government House and the wonder of the officers' mess. And who was this flamboyant young adventurer, and whence had he come?

In the race-proud, Christian country of England, Disraeli could trace his name no farther back than his grandfather, a Jewish immigrant from Italy who traded in Leghorn hats, Carrara marble, and other commodities of his native land, and was remembered as a lover of music and macaroni, and who by virtue of an advantageous marriage and some prudent business in the Stock Exchange had left his son Isaac amply secured against his own commercial incapacities, free to pass his life among books, in writing and in conversation. Isaac was a disciple of Voltaire, a friend of Byron and Tom Moore, and in the world of letters had achieved a high respect, even a quiet fame. From him, perhaps, young Ben had inherited a good measure of his intellectual powers—but certainly not his demon.

Ben had been sent to a small private school in Blackheath, and it was there one day that he discovered upon himself a deep and ineradicable mark. It was the mark of Israel. He had been reared in the Jewish faith but loosely; his father was too much the Voltairean to practice it himself, and in his own youth had been little encouraged to do so: his haughty, domineering mother, whose family had some claim to an escutcheon, if only a foreign one, had appeared to regard the Star of David as a blot upon it. And now, for the first time, at Blackheath, among these blue-eyed children of Christ, Ben was made to feel his Jewishness like an ugly scar. It set him apart and seemed to render him in their eyes immeasurably inferior. He was at first astounded; and he was intensely hurt. Only now did he feel himself to be a child of an outcast people, driven at one time or another from most of the lands of the earth, even from England, which, though he

CARL A. RUDISILL
LIBRARY
LENOIR RHYNE COLLEGE

loved it, he might love only as a wistful stepchild, for here he was debarred from enfranchisement by his religion, and from social acceptance by the Scar.

Then, in a sudden quarrel with the Elders of the Synagogue, Isaac D'Israeli renounced his religion, and, though never to profess another himself, had his four children transformed into Christians by a Mr. Thimbleby at St. Andrew's, Holborn. Ben was twelve. By way of beginning life anew, he was transferred to a school in Epping Forest. But the water had failed to wash away the mark: he discovered that he was still a Jew. True, he had been baptized not merely a Christian, but an English Citizen to boot; yet he was still also a foreigner. Secretly he was ashamed—for now of course he was really nothing at all; and the demon raged. Why this curse upon him? Did he not have twice the brains of any of these others, thrice the sensibilities, ten times the spirit? Despise him as a Jew, would they? Then he would despise them! But first he took boxing lessons. Schoolboy games bored and physical exercise easily fatigued him, but by force of will he also taught himself to excel on the playing field. And meanwhile, by the exercise of his wits, by his inexhaustible invention, by the tales he could tell on a rainy afternoon, the castles he built out of paper and peopled out of his head like a boy Balzac; by his gift for enduing the familiar with the strange, the ordinary with the romantic; by his very dash and colour, he gained an enviable ascendancy over his mates. And when, inevitably, it befell that he had to fight, Ben knocked the other boy down. After that he was insufferable. But his cockiness over this purely animal triumph, while real enough, was minor: the great thing, he had discovered, was not to knock other boys down but to capture their imaginations! As he grew older he developed this thesis according to his expanding opportunities. And so we behold him in Spain with his hair in ringlets, two novels and a satire behind him, and a fund of debts, flaunting a magnificent air, a glittering facility of epigram, lace at his wrists, and two canes, one for day and one for evening.

He was five-and-twenty. At that age his future rival, Mr. Gladstone, who was now but twenty, would have been in Parliament for nearly two years and be already a member of the Ministry. But Mr. Gladstone came of a Scottish family and was an Old Etonian; and, as would someday be remarked by his biographers, Benjamin had to perform prodigious feats to reach the level where William would only naturally begin. In this seductive summer of 1830 he was still far below it; and yet, at twenty-five, he had three times attempted to carry off at a single spectacular coup the great keys of London.

He had left school at fifteen and taken up his studies under a private tutor. Like the unrecognized Caesar and obscure Napoleon with whom he felt such a sympathy, he already hungered for great emprise, felt himself to be a man of destiny, and for two years he cloistered himself in his books as in a temple, to prepare himself for the nuptial couch with the unknown greatness whose face he ever longed to behold, like a girl on Midsummer Eve. He read twelve hours a day, he turned over almost the whole of his father's library, he read not only the great Greeks and Romans, but the historians, the poets, the philosophers, and the lawgivers of the modern world, preparing, and searching, searching for a glimpse, an outline, of that dazzling form and face. And then? Why, then he was articled to a firm of solicitors in Frederick's Place, Old Jewry.

This dull but instructive existence had lasted for another three years, until, on a short tour with his father on the Continent, he had looked one evening into the waters of the Rhine, and seeing, perhaps, deep down, the gliding shadowy form of a Rhine-daughter, had thrilled again to a presentiment of his romantic destiny; and stripping himself of the vulgar livery of Swain, Stevens, Maples, Pearse, and Hunt, had dived naked to wrest from her the magical golden Ring. It was a deep plunge, and she led him all the way to the malarious Amazon, among palms and parrots and crocodiles, and left him with a sheaf of Spanish-American mining shares, which, as he emerged with bursting lungs, turned to ashes in his hands. And he plunged again, even deeper, and a whale swallowed him and cast him up like the prophet where he belonged, back beside the muddy Thames, with more ashes, infinitely more, only here they called them debts. And he wrote pamphlets to prove to his ignorant countrymen that they were really gold moidores, very instructive pamphlets, designed also to educate the investment interests, the House of Commons and the Chancellor of the Exchequer in the nature of joint stock companies and the business of mining, and dedicated to the Prime Minister; and they served to embarrass the Chancellor fearfully in a cherished legislative project of his, but not to disembarrass the author. He had incurred debts of which he was not to get clear for thirty years, and had achieved this magnificent failure at the trifling age of twenty.

She whom he had taken for a Rhine-daughter had turned out a Lorelei; but he reflected that perhaps his true destiny awaited him here in London. And before he was twenty-one he had conceived a plan for a great newspaper that would force *The Times* to the wall. He conceived that he had been born for high stakes and derring-do, and in this new scheme graciously accepted as partners the head of a publishing house and a general of finance, both of whom conceived that he would put up a quarter of the capital. And so he would, he resolved, somehow, when the time came. He saw himself embarked —or soon to be embarked; as soon as he had the deck of this new dream-argosy under his feet—upon the great adventure of his life, his voyage to capture the imagination of the world! And while the ship was building, he went forth into the world to reconnoiter a bit. He reconnoitered in drawing rooms and at dinner tables, observing, perfecting himself in the ways of fashion, sharpening his wits, developing his charm. And it was now that he blossomed out a dandy, in green trousers and canary-coloured waistcoat, in grey military trousers and bright blue surtout, in a suit of black velvet with ruffles, red clocks on his stockings, and shoes with silver buckles. He cultivated especially the friendship of women, whose company he was always to prefer to men's, and who he sensed could teach him more than men could and would help him higher. Young and old, he delighted them all, and they him, particularly the married ones. True, these were very minor drawing rooms, but he made them do: one had to begin somewhere. And soon he would climb to the great ones, the salons of the powdered footmen, and the finest talk in England, and the greatest ladies. But the preparations for the launching of a newspaper are necessarily complex and hazardous, and in the course of those for this one, a bitter misunderstanding developed between the publisher and the young promoter: suddenly, again, gold turned ashes in Disraeli's hands.

High emprise! Great stakes! Think of unrecognized Caesar, of obscure Napoleon; and view the young Achilles moping in his tent. Was he beginning to doubt his destiny? Never! But he thought perhaps it lay in another direction; he was certain that it lay upon some perfumed couch to which he only had to find his way; but where? Could it be here—close by him—all unseen? Here in his study he thought he saw its shadow move upon the wall!

He had within him a buried vein of quietness, a detachment, an Oriental feeling for the abstract and the absolute, in which, far more deeply than in experience, his sapling cynicism had its roots. It was this, rather than any shallow dishonesty with himself, that brought him now, in recoil from his second assault on El Dorado, to regard the victory that he might have gained with loathing as a transitory, delusive, and empty thing. And besides, the recoil had shaken up an old proclivity of his, an ambition much neglected of late, and he thought he saw a better goal. What should he have been doing in Fleet Street or on 'Change! He possessed a genius that transcended such petty dreams: he possessed the power to make himself immortal! He would put it to the test at once. And so he wrote a novel.

The hero was Vivian Grey, a rash youth to whom Disraeli himself bore a striking resemblance, as to a lesser degree did Disraeli's newspaper experiences to the plot. Those experiences were as heavily cloaked as a kidnappers' chorus, but not heavily enough to deceive the author's recent partner, the publisher, who thought he detected his own face under a villain's mask. It was a tale of ambition, intrigue, and treachery, full of bitter satire and swordplay, of irony, epigram, and moral reflection, and containing also contumelious caricatures of the Chancellor of the Exchequer and the Duke of Wellington. Disraeli was scourging himself with the knout of a fallen nun, but he was drawing and quartering society. He wrote in the character of a gentleman of fashion, anonymously, and the only person privy to his secret was a woman—the clever, attractive, and sympathetic Sarah Austen, wife of a solicitor friend of his family. It was she who encouraged him, gave him advice, and, when the time came, found him a publisher. And perhaps—perhaps it was she who first hinted that the author was a person of such an exalted rank, as likewise were the persons of his drama, that he dared not reveal his name. So, at least, the publisher slyly informed the public—and *Vivian Grey* was an immediate sensation. The author found himself an anonymous celebrity, with a titillated public guessing breathlessly at his identity and at those of the fellow aristocrats whom he had tumbrilled before its malicious gaze. And then somehow it came out: the author was an obscure person for whom nobody cared a straw; he was a mere impudent boy, a lowborn pretender who had hoaxed London by the meanest, most revolting artifices and with total disregard of all honourable feeling. The critics ridiculed his "ludicrous affectations of good breeding," and in their rage added that as a literary performance, *Vivian Grey* was no better than catchpenny trash. He did not know that Goethe liked it; he had not yet heard that the genius of Weimar thought it showed more true originality than any book he had read in years. At the sensitive age of twenty-one, Benjamin Disrael knew only that by the exercise of his greatest energies he had built almost to the stars, and now, for the third time, was tumbling down amid the ruins of a grandiose fiasco, reviled, stigmatized, and laughed to scorn.

And in the depths to which he sank with that enormous titter in his ears, a strange malady laid hold of him. Later, its physical manifestation would be diagnosed as chronic inflammation of the tissues of the brain. His body languished and wretchedness like a prehensile monster seized his spirit. At times he would rouse himself, only to sink back, torpid in mind and limb. He, the eager man of action, buried himself in the old country manor house to which his father had retired in the Chilterns, brooding, bitter, even as the unrecognized Caesar, the obscure Napoleon. The old scholar Isaac D'Israeli, looking at him sadly over the top of a book, saw into his heart: "My boy, you have tried to become a great man too quickly." His sister took him for quiet walks in the woods, comforting, encouraging, striving to restore his confidence. Sarah Austen, too, understood and pitied and tried to help him. She and her husband took him on a holiday to France, Switzerland, and Italy, and under these stimulating changes of scene he appeared to rally: something of his old enthusiasm was evident in his letters; and to the surprise of everyone, he began a Second Part of *Vivian Grey*. His father was led to expect him back cured. But Sa was not fooled. She was not surprised when on his return he relapsed into melancholy, nor that the once-dashing Vivian was become as morose as Werther. "The springiness of my mind is gone!" lamented the hero of Part Two; and the public perceiving that this was all too sadly the case, he was left to weep alone. Ben's father urged him to study for the Bar, and he was entered at Lincoln's Inn, but he seldom attended. He talked of settling down to agriculture. And this period of his life lasted for two years.

But he was a resilient young man, and presently began again to grow restless, to dream, and to see visions. And the first unmistakable symptom of his convalescence was that he wrote a satire on the Utilitarians. Here in a merry fable was the true Disraeli, affirming the majesty of the individual in the teeth of a doctrine that denied it, affirming the imponderable wonder of creation and his contempt for apostates who shook not their fists at Heaven but their pencils in the

ing in the courtyards? In a fine debauch of fancy, he was peopling the Alhambra even as he had the paper castles of Higham Hall: he saw the place swarming with Saracens in glancing mail, with lithe sultanas, concubines, and dancing girls, each a beauty; with bland merchants displaying brocades from Italy, blades from Damascus, jewellery from Egypt, prayer rugs from Persia; with Christian slaves, and eunuchs lazily waving fans, and mellifluous musicians.

"It's like being transported into the middle of the Arabian Nights!" he said.

Young Meredith was amused at his enthusiasm. Disraeli led him prowling through the Court of Lions and the Hall of Ambassadors, down to brimming baths, up to lofty towers and miradors commanding the gorge of the Darro and the fertile plain of Granada. To Disraeli, it was all very romantic, and something more—something for which he had not found a word. And coming into the epical Hall of the Abencerrages, he sat cross-legged with theatrical grandiosity upon the stone bench which in the previous chapter of this chronicle the Prime Minister took the license to call a throne.

No kings were the Abencerrages, but they were the flower of Saracenic chivalry in Spain, warrior barons of the king's right hand, viziers of the royal right ear; and if this wasn't really a throne, it had been the next thing to it when the scimitar ruled in Granada.

The old Spanish woman, their guide, who was the caretaker of all this sublime decay that had been the Palace of the Alhambra, folded her hands and regarded the young man narrowly. Her strange look caused him to suppose that his act had offended her.

"I beg your pardon. Do you object?"

She shook her head quickly back and forth. "No, no, no; but I do not object, of course, *señor*! It is only that I do not see before now. Most times I can tell, but your costume deceive me. Ah, *sí*! You," she said, pointing at him knowingly, "are a Moor!"

Meredith laughed. "She takes us for a couple of Mohammedans!"

"No, *señor*! You, I think, are *inglese*; but he—a Moor. No?"

THE MUDLARK

Disraeli was a little embarrassed. It was his olive skin and Semitic
aspect that had deceived her. But she would not be convinced: now
she understood his ebullient delight over the ruin.

"Many, many Moorish come to the Alhambra, and always it is the
same. You think it belongs to you, no?" She laughed indulgently. "Sí,
sí, I know! All you Moorish who come here, you say that someday
you will return, someday you will rule again in the Alhambra!" And
she shrugged amiably. "Quién sabe [Who knows]?"

It was a most romantic notion, which of course fitted perfectly
into the game he had been playing—even improved it a bit; and
hadn't some of his ancestors come from Spain? Perhaps some of
them had come from this very part—who knew? He drew himself
up regally. "Sí," he said, and improved it a bit more himself: "Es mi
casa [This is my palace]."

Meredith thought the incident immensely droll, and that evening,
after a gay dinner at the posada where they had put up in the city
below, he set it all down in a letter to Sa. But Disraeli, who had retired for the night, found himself launched by it upon a reflective
voyage of exploration and rediscovery, his galleon a deep four-poster,
his binnacle primed with the contents of two bottles of Malaga
shipped at table. He was remembering pleasantly that through his
grandmother he came of two great families of the Sephardim—the
illustrious Villa Reals of Portugal and the noble house of Ibn Xaprut
of Spain; that through his mother he might trace descent from Isaac
Aboab, last Gaon of Castile, who had led his people into exile from
the terror of Torquemada in the fifteenth century. And then dimly
he recalled his grandmother's boast that an Ibn Xaprut had been
vizier to the Caliph of Cordoba! When? Who? In Moorish Spain,
no doubt, the Jews had lived as kinsmen to the conquerors; and he
thought: Quién sabe indeed! Strange that none of this had ever ap
pealed to him much in England, that he had never thought it important or distinguished before. England! In England everything not
English was made to appear a little second-rate; it had taken a

glimpse of Spain to suggest to him the true glory of his heritage. In England the great families deemed their heritages old, yet before the Inquisition there had been Jewish families in Spain that had been old before the coming of Hannibal and Scipio Africanus, before Carthage and Rome were, old when the whale disgorged Jonah at Tarshish! . . . Spain! He lay pillowed on his clasped hands gazing out through a doorway opened upon a balcony: beyond he could see the moonlit roofs of Granada and above and beyond those the dark ragged shape of the Alhambra, for him now an immense riddle flung across the stars. He slept, and in his dream restored the palace to all its olden splendour, and sat surrounded by a magnificent court, glittering, upon the seat of the Abencerrages.

That was the beginning—for Meredith a merry paragraph in a letter home, but for Disraeli, Disraeli of the Childe Harold pilgrimage, the ringlets and the two canes, it was the beginning of an idea that was to seize hold of his mind, first to bedazzle and then to clarify it, to direct his energies and send him spiritually turbaned into the grand arena of his life.

From Spain, having from the outset planned to leave Portugal for the homeward voyage, they sailed to Malta, and there, at Valeta, on the threshold of the East, Disraeli went the canes one better by parading through the streets in the costume of a Greek pirate—red shirt with silver studs as big as shillings, striped blue jacket and trousers, red cap and slippers, and a bright red sash full of daggers and pistols. And from Malta, still playing pirate, out to sea aboard the yacht of another young adventurer, one James Clay, who had beaten the whole Valeta garrison at rackets and billiards and the Russian Legation at cards, and whose valet was a mustachioed ex-gondolier of Venice in whose arms Byron had expired at Missolonghi. Disraeli and Meredith had thought of joining the Turkish Army in the Albanian war, but upon arrival at Corfu found that the war was over, and went instead to congratulate the Grand Vizier at Yanina. In the mountains, in a khan of Ali Pasha as large as a Gothic castle, they were entertained by a young bey, whom they introduced to the delights of brandy and then put to bed on his cushions, rolled up in a sacred carpet, and in the Hall of Audience at Yanina were received by Reschid, an old *mitrailleur* who was reputed to have slaughtered four thousand noncombatants in the past three months, and who offered them narghiles and thick Turkish coffee and assured them that the peace of the world was his holy object, the happiness of mankind his dearest wish.

From Yanina through the Ambracian Gulf to Athens and the plain of Marathon; but Grecian culture was only a distraction for Disraeli now, and they pushed on to Constantinople. Mosques again, muezzins and dervishes and snake charmers, the sparkling Bosporus and the pungent, bubbling ragout of the Bazaar. The East entranced Disraeli, fascinated him with its vivid colours, its romance, its deep-flowing currents of mystery; and perhaps because it did this, because it appealed to him so strongly through his imagination, it stirred him also in a profounder, more personal way. There are some men who cannot look comfortably into the future because they cannot see clearly a fixed point of orientation in the past; of such are many of the children of exiles and of emigrants scattered over the whorls and wrinkles of earth, and of such was he. He who in England had felt himself a stepchild, an orphan in a strange house, his origin hopelessly confused and lost in the darkness behind him, had here an almost preternatural sense of kinship, of sympathy with the ethos of his surroundings: he had found at least the field of his orientation point, and was comforted, not because he was able to recognize it, but because in doing so he was able at last to accept it.

But when he came, by Jaffa, into Palestine, it was not a renascent surge of his fathers' faith that inspired him: it was rather an ardent response to the scenes of ethnogenic experience by which, centuries before he was born, his spirit had been formed and tempered. This was his fathers' home: he was moved as by an ancient tribal chant for the dead, and by an awareness of the hovering genius of his people. And yet—it was strange—when he first looked down from the Mount of Olives and saw Jerusalem like a handful of stones at his feet, it was not of his fathers that he was thinking, but of what old countrymen in England told about the oxen kneeling in their stalls at midnight on Old Christmas Eve. Was he Jew or Christian? He was wholly neither one nor the other, he supposed; and perhaps, wherever he went, he would always be something of a stranger. But now he had his bearings.

Meredith, in a hot archaeological fervor, had gone off alone to search for the ruins of a lost city on the Gulf of Smyrna—"some unheard-of, cock-and-bull city," Disraeli had called it; and the Childe Harold was left to continue his pilgrimage with Clay. The months that followed were to leave upon his memory a kaleidoscopic impression of rich experience, enchanted landscapes, and lustrous horizons: the Holy Sepulchre, the Tomb of the Kings, bathing in the river Jordan, and attempting to steal into the Mosque of Omar disguised as a Mohammedan; the Syrian desert, palms and camel caravans and moments when like Hazlitt's father he conjured glimpses of the patriarchal wanderings at the distance of three thousand years; Egypt, the Pyramids and the Nile, granite colossi of gods and kings, avenues of sphinxes and halls of a thousand columns; mountains of burning sand, and a simoon weathered on a desert beach of Libya.

And then his meeting with Mehemet Ali.

Mehemet Ali of the soft white beard had been an Albanian tobacco merchant impressed into the Turkish Army when Napoleon had set out to conquer Egypt. And conquered Egypt had been, but not of course by Napoleon: by Mehemet Ali. When the presumptuous Corsican had been routed at the Battle of the Nile, Mehemet Ali had scrambled from the wreckage and proceeded to climb to power as a loyal subject of the Turks. He had climbed until his only rivals were the Mamelukes, and them, when the time came, he massacred. Now he was Egypt's Pasha, and a most efficient one he was. Having first prudently expropriated all the land, produce, manufactures, and merchandising privileges to himself, he encouraged farming and commerce of every kind; he encouraged labour also, to the point of enforcing it, and he taxed his subjects abundantly; he had conquered the Sudan, built Khartoum; he had organized a model army on the latest Western lines, and now was on the point of using it in a model rebellion against the Turks. He had attained to a position so much to be respected that he was being eyed with some apprehension by England, France, Germany, and Russia. And it was at this point in his career that kismet arranged his meeting with the young man who one day was to begin the undoing of it all.

Wandering one day in the palace gardens at Shubra, Disraeli came upon Mehemet Ali playing chess with his court fool. The Pasha was surrounded by resplendent viziers and courtiers and by a guard of black slaves in scarlet and gold; and as it was well known that the old man had a curiosity about Englishmen, one of the viziers presented Disraeli. Disraeli and Mehemet Ali talked for a long time. When the audience was over, Mehemet Ali asked Disraeli to return. Disraeli returned several times. Mehemet Ali asked his opinion regarding the institution of an Egyptian Parliament. Disraeli said he didn't think Egypt a congenial atmosphere for successful representative government, and he gave reasons.

"You speak truth," said Mehemet Ali. "But in spite of all, I will have my Parliament. I will have as many Parliaments as the King of England. Behold!" and he displayed two long lists of names. "Here are my Parliaments. To prevent the inconveniences you mention, I have decided to elect them myself."

Disraeli smiled. "That is all very well," he made bold to say, "but were I you, I should not content myself with the governing of desert tribes."

Mehemet Ali was not offended. He too smiled—thinking, one may suppose, of some plans he had. "You are a wise man. But were I the King of England, neither should I content myself with a government of the West."

"Nor I," said Disraeli, a little to his own surprise. From the back of his mind came the conception of an England modelled after old maritime Venice, an England wedding not only sea and shore but West and East. He spoke of this.

"Allah kerim, but you spit pearls! I think it is well that you are not the King of England. But if you were, I should offer you an alliance by which together we might rule the world. For it is I," declared Mehemet Ali, "who hold the key to the world's other side."

"The key to the Far East?"

"You will see," said Mehemet Ali shrewdly. "Some day." But he would say no more.

Someday truly Benjamin Disraeli would see; but in the meantime he saw something else, and Mehemet Ali unwittingly had helped him to see it, had focused the young man's attention upon an idea that had been hovering darkly in his consciousness for months, possibly for much longer; and so vividly did it present itself to him, so forcefully did it strike him, so personally did it make its appeal, that in a subjective sense it was entirely original—it was as if no man in history had ever been vouchsafed such a conception before.

He saw how, in a realm beyond words, beyond clay and paint and sound, life itself might be used as a medium of art. He saw it being used in great coloured masses—plastic, quick, intelligent, aspiring; used on the grand scale, but not in the way Mehemet Ali used it, not with personal power as an end in itself, but only as a means to an end: used for the intellectual and spiritual expression of the artist! Not impiously, but worshipfully, in acts of stewardship performed with a priest's reverence for the material. Used for the creation of masterpieces in the architecture of human society! For the fulfillment of history in living forms! For the building of structures that would stand as universal principles realized and made eloquent! Used to sculpt a frieze of destiny in its own substance!

So, in Egypt, at the pitch of his odyssey, Benjamin Disraeli in the fettle of his youth and at the boiling point of his energies conceived suddenly of the business of statecraft, of the designing of the moulds called nations and empires, polities and constitutions in which mankind is cast into shapes. He saw it then as the highest test of genius, the noblest and most exciting of pursuits, and as that for which he had thrice mistaken mere vapourings in dreams—the vision of the purpose for which he had been born. High emprise! To get his hands into those coloured masses, to model them according to his own concepts, and to carve his name like the signature of a sculptor into the pedestal of the future! Here, it seemed clear to him now, was the emprise for which he had been preparing himself all his life—in school, in his father's library, in the drawing rooms of London, and on this maieutic pilgrimage!

The idea had smote him like revelation, it enflamed him like a first love. Impatient to return to London, he hurried to rejoin Meredith in Cairo. There, on the brink of his grand assault, a famous old journeyman of the art which he had just discovered awaited him with a smile.

Meredith, the affianced husband whom Sa had sent to watch over her brother, had been stricken with smallpox at his archaeological diggings, and been brought to Cairo gravely ill. In the bed where Disraeli found him, he died. He had not found his city.

Ghosts of that time visited the Prime Minister as he limped down the corridor from the Throne Room that night at Windsor. Ghosts out of Spain and the East and the never-again-to-be-reached London of that grand climacteric of his youth, shadows of old enchantments from the world of a man's twenties, with its unrecapturable tang, its priceless, irredeemable promises. He saw Meredith laughing at him again in the Alhambra, and the bereaved, gentle face of Sa. Of Sa, who had never married, who had devoted the rest of her life to her brother, and been so sure for him, and now too was dead. He reached his chambers. He disrobed slowly and stood a moment looking at himself in the cheval glass, remembering how once he had fancied the way his calves would look in court breeches, and what Mr. Brown had said this evening about the kilts. From somewhere in the fog wreathing the great stone pile that had come to stand above the meadows of Saxon goatherds, above the slumbering Thames, a voice reached him, faintly, hoarse with dampness. Eleven o'clock, it said, and all was well.

9

"The truth is," says Arthur Hodge in his *Aspects of the National Psychology*, "that the Wheeler Case was one of those trifles which for reasons afterwards difficult to understand arouse a clamour out of all proportion to their importance. False rumour, we may say, perhaps mere gossip giving rise to alarming reports in an irresponsible press, must be to blame. Often this proves to be true. But sometimes we must look for less obvious factors, embedded perhaps in the psychology of the moment, or buried deep in the childhood of a people. Beware the British trifle. The most exhaustive research disposes one to insist that the Wheeler Case *per se* was of no importance whatever, and yet one must add that it led to mob violence and perhaps nearer than we know to political disaster."

Not that all this came suddenly the next morning. The explosion, as with that other trifle known as the War of Jenkins's Ear, took a bit of time. But on that morning the powder trail is plainly visible and the flame may be clearly perceived as it sputters along to the charge.

10

At half after three that morning, a tall figure wrapped in a cloak appeared upon the North Terrace where Elizabeth used to take her constitutional. It was McHatten. He had been kept almost five hours in the main Guard Room, assisting at the inquisition of Wheeler, not to say being subjected to one himself. He was tired but in no state for sleep; the sentries shivering in the fog noticed that he didn't appear to mind the cold at all, and in fact he welcomed it. He had been subjected to something of an ordeal in that Guard Room.

The Grenadier Guards, as everyone knows, are a proud regiment. They are the First Foot Guards of the Royal Household Troops, and when the initiated speak of "the Guards" they do not mean the Household Cavalry. The Grenadiers are of the blood and tradition of the Cavaliers. At the time of the Commonwealth they went into exile with their princes; they fought in the Spanish Army and returned in glory at the Restoration. They fought also at Waterloo, and some of them in the Crimea, and at the time of the Wheeler Case had been resting gloriously on their laurels ever since. They protected

— 121 —

the Royal Family, performed duties at Court, changed themselves beautifully at the mounting of the guard, and made the British heart swell with pride whenever they sallied out on parade. It was well known that the Coldstreamers were fearfully jealous of them. The miserable Life Guards, of course, jibed at them as nothing but infantry, and bounders in mere line regiments scoffed that they were only for show. And yet—tut, tut, they were the Grenadier Guards. There was really nothing finer, and the lowest ranker in the British Army knew it. It should therefore be clear why the first minds in history to recognize Wheeler as a little disaster were—saving possibly a sergeant footman's—Grenadier Guards minds.

It was not just that some beggar had managed to steal past the sentries and go skylarking in Windsor Castle at night; it was that the beggar was such a little beggar, and actually had gone *Boo!* to the Queen. It was also that he had not been apprehended even then, but hours later had been discovered by the Prime Minister sitting on the throne. No good trying to hush that one up. By tomorrow it would be the joke of every mess in England, and, what was equally terrible to contemplate, of every club in London. There was a general grave nodding of heads when Major Fontoon declared that it was likely to prove the most humiliating thing the Regiment ever had been brought to face up to.

But Fontoon had behaved as if it were all McHatten's fault.

"Damn it, man, why did you let him sit there on the blasted throne? Why didn't . . . Oh, the devil with the gillie! We've heard enough about him. Do you mean to say you let a grubby batman manage the show? What? . . . But you could have pulled the brat off before the Prime Minister came in, couldn't you? That's the devil of it—the Prime Minister! Good God, you might as well have done it before the whole House of Commons. . . . Eh? . . . But you ought to have reported the matter; you had no right taking it on yourself, sir! We'd have known what to do. You presumed, that's what you did—presumed."

Major Fontoon paced up and down the Guard Room, savagely munching at his moustache, while McHatten stood furious and red in the face and the other young officers tried too obviously not to look at him. Wheeler was crouched where they had flung him, in a high Gothic chair beside the armoured equestrian figure of Queen Elizabeth's champion depicted in the act of flinging down the gauntlet to the enemies of the Throne, and opposite to the busts of the first dukes of Marlborough and Wellington, which stared at him stonily. He was as dirty as when he had arisen from the coal car, but as he watched the caged-tiger pacing of the major, one noticed chiefly the whites of his eyes.

"You, boy!" Fontoon suddenly arraigned him, stabbing a finger into his face. Wheeler jumped. "Do you know what you've done? Hey? Stop wriggling! I've seen your kind. Sit still!"

Fontoon and the other officers naturally took the same view that Mr. Brown at first had assumed, that Wheeler was a tool of party or parties unknown, and they held on to it for dear life. Any lesser explanation would have been intolerable to them. For obviously, the less formidable the culprit, the more ridiculous they. On the other hand, should some man-sized conspiracy be turned up, they needn't feel so small themselves; it might even be said that they had nipped it in the bud—the Regiment's disgrace might be turned to its glory! As they grasped this idea, they looked at each other meaningfully, and at Wheeler harder than ever, and grimmer and grimmer grew their efforts to wring a confession out of him. It was going to be either Wheeler or the Grenadier Guards.

But grimly as they tried, they got little out of Wheeler. He, to begin with, was too frightened to make much of a case for himself, and they, in the second place, were too frightened to let him. Whenever he screwed up enough courage to tell them a bit of the truth, the major cut him off in the midst of it.

"Humbug! Don't you try to tarradiddle me, boy! You'll make a clean breast if you know what's good for you, you—you young Guy Fawkes! That's what you are, isn't it!"

They shook him and poked fingers into him and shouted threats at him, and the tears that he could not restrain made trenches through the soot on his face. He was a little hysterical. But to say that the Grenadiers were cruel would be to take an unrealistic view of the situation, because of course they were going on the premise that he was a dangerous criminal, and were only trying to acquit themselves well in the case before sunrise, and as time wore on their proddings and shakings were in fact mainly for the purpose of keeping the exhausted boy awake. Finally they gave up bullying for cajolery. Fontoon, with his moustache in tatters, even promised to put in a word for Wheeler. He outlined briefly the way he supposed the crime might have been committed—that was, at the direction of a gang of clever cracksmen, in the manner of a play he had seen once at the Haymarket—and begged Wheeler to admit that this was a pretty shrewd guess. Useless. For Wheeler, despite their best efforts to prevent it, had escaped rather suddenly into sleep. His head had lurched forward into the lapels of the coat, one arm had slipped off the arm of the big oak chair and hung limply down, the dirty hand half open. And even Fontoon, looking at that hand, hadn't the heart to shake him again.

"Well . . . ah . . . h'm," the major exhaled, gazing down at him wearily. He brought out his large gold watch, sprang open the cover of the hunting case, and saw that it was three in the morning. "Awkward, awkward; but we're not done with him yet. We'll not let him out of our hands till we've got his damned little affidavit. He's not to leave this room. See that he's well guarded." He turned to McHatten. "I want you to make out a report, sir; a full report. You understand? And do it at once."

McHatten wrote the report. Standing afterwards on the terrace, he wished it had been the resignation of his commission. But no; that was exactly what Fontoon would give a Derby winner for, someone to lay the blame on and disown. *"Beastly outsider, you know. Mystery how he ever got in the Guards. It was thought best to let him get out quietly."* That was what they'd all like; or so it seemed to McHatten. But he wasn't going to give it to them. He was going to stay and see it through. He thought with a pang of Emily Prior, dreading what she might hear of the affair. Inwardly he cursed Mr. Brown, and Wheeler, the cause of it all, and himself for being such a fool. He also cursed the Prime Minister. *"Mr. McHatten, have you ever presumed to sit on a throne?"* Now what had been the meaning of that silly question? He wondered uneasily again how much Disraeli had seen and heard. Strange, foreign old man—why hadn't he said plainly what he meant? And then, in his resentful brooding, which was half an examination of conscience, McHatten defiantly faced the thought he had not permitted himself to recognize at the time, that behind the words there had been a suspicion of tameness and prosaism, of mediocrity. Had that been it? Why, damn that old man! What right had he to such an assumption? What could he know of someone he had never seen before? And who was he— Prime Minister or not—who was he? An outsider, even more of an outsider than McHatten. . . .

But perhaps he hadn't meant that at all. How could he have meant that? Perhaps—perhaps this was only Charles McHatten accusing himself!

The anger drained out of him; he felt a sickening emptiness. Was this what he was? Weak, dull, second-rate? Or, if not, why had he permitted himself to be made such a fool of in this affair? But what could he have done—what? How, really, had he been at fault? It was ridiculous. . . .

Attuned now to the stillness, he heard a sound like distant laughter. Water, he told himself, water tumbling over a weir somewhere in the abyss beneath the parapet. The cold penetrated his cloak and he shivered. His face was wet with fog. He turned and groped his way back into the castle.

A royal cock at the Shaw Farm stretched his invisible neck and crowed. No sign of day was visible, but that didn't matter. He was like the old Welsh farmers who, rising before the sun, used to come out into the farmyard and beat on the ground; beating for day, they called it. He crowed again, a solitary, insistent call, and in the sodden darkness another answered him, and he replied.

Pale lights appeared in scattered tower windows of the castle. Water splashed into basins, feet scraped dismally in passages, hands were chafed, coal was shovelled into banked fires, kettles were put to warm: a sickly yellow streaked the gloom to the east. The morning came on painfully.

The porter at the Tradesmen's Entrance leaned back in his chair and stretched his arms as a kitchenmaid entered his cubicle on her way to the cellars. " 'Allo, D'isy," he said. "Going down to meet yer lighty-love so early in the mor-ning?" Daisy tossed up her nose at him and swept by without answer, but he called after her, "Did you 'ear if they nabbed the burglar?"

Daisy stopped as suddenly as if she had run into a wall. "Burglar! 'Eavens, was there a burglar?"

"Was there a burglar! You didn't 'ear nuffing about it?"

"No!"

"Why, bless yer, there was great larks abaht this 'ere burglar. Popped in on 'Er Majesty at 'er dinner table, and then popped off again."

" 'E did!"

" 'E did, straight. I'm surprised you didn't 'ear nuffing abaht it."

"Gawd!" said Daisy, eyeing the cellar door dubiously. "I wonder if they caught 'im."

"I dunno. But a nice dark cellar'd be a likely plice for 'im to 'ide, now, wouldn't it?"

"It might, and I don't see anything so funny, I'm sure. A burglar in the castle indeed! At this rite it won't be long till a body's not sife dead in Westminster Abbey. Well, *I'll* not set foot down there till I know if they caught 'im." And Daisy scurried back the way she had come, followed by the porter's gleeful laughter.

By nine o'clock, news of Wheeler's exploit was current, in one form or another, from Bell Tower to Great Park. Nothing quite so picturesquely shocking had occurred in the castle within the memory of the oldest denizens, and it caused a pleasant excitement. It was handed on to tradespeople arriving with their wares, and so passed out the gates and trickled down Peascod Street in the Royal Borough of Windsor and was heard by a porter at the White Hart Inn and a barman at the Crown and a commercial traveller just arriving at the Ship from Birmingham. It made a great stir. By noon it had been carried over the bridge to Eton by a clergyman of Trinity, had been conveyed to Reading by a bailiff, and was jogging over the Datchet Road to God-knew-where in the van of a gypsy tinker. But the tinker had heard that Wheeler was a dwarf, the bailiff only that he was a thief, and the clergyman that he was a Certain Gentleman's idiot bastard that had been shut up in the Devil's Tower since birth and had escaped after braining his keeper with the butt of an oil lamp. All agreed that he had frightened the Queen at dinner and been captured in the Throne Room, but the tinker thought that the dwarf had tried to stab Her Majesty, the bailiff that the thief had tried to steal the gold plate, and the clergyman that the crazy bastard had claimed the Throne as his birthright. No one was sure what the Prime Minister had been doing in the Throne Room at the time, but it seemed evident that his presence proved the importance of the matter and lent a good deal of weight to the version the clergyman had heard. And in a remarkably short space of time, this version had come home to roost in the castle, where some credulous souls who had never laid eyes on the protagonist of the tale recalled pointedly that certain rooms in the Devil's Tower were kept locked; so that even in the castle there were many who knew not what to think.

The "dispatches" that General Ponsonby had mentioned having

to write when he excused himself from the White Room on the previous evening had turned out to be crisp memoranda directed to the Governor of the Castle, the Captain of the Guard, the Master of the Household, and the two Scotland Yard men on duty at the castle. These notes recited tersely the occurrence at the dinner table and stated that Her Majesty required thorough investigations with a view to fixing blame and insuring against any such disgraceful invasions of her privacy in the future; and the general added that she awaited full reports from all departments concerned.

The two policemen were taken by surprise, for the efficient Ponsonby had been the first to inform them that anything in their line had come up. They hurried to his office to ascertain where they might arrest the criminal, and when the general proved unable to tell them exactly, took up the scent in the Servants' Hall, where Mr. Naseby directed them to the guard. At the Guard House, however, it appeared that no one could tell them anything. They were referred directly to General Lord Frederick Incledon; but the month being November, the trouble was that Lord Frederick was fox hunting in Sussex. The policemen insisted. They were politely informed by an officer who looked far more official than they did that as a matter of fact, by a very old law, police jurisdiction inside Windsor Castle was vested solely in the Governor, so that they really hadn't the authority to insist at all. The policemen waited upon the Governor. He kept them waiting for half an hour and then explained that he was trying to get a message through to Lord Frederick and could not act until he had an answer. The defeated policemen telegraphed a cipher message to the Yard, asking for instructions.

At ten-thirty, under the deferential shaking of a young underfootman, Mr. Brown came awake.

"I'm sorry, sir; I knocked at your door but you didn't hear me. The Queen has sent for you twice, sir."

Mr. Brown sat up at a lunge, flung the footman's hand from his arm, squinted at him, and cleared the phlegm from his throat with a roar.

THE MUDLARK

"Q-queen?" he said thickly, blinking about. "Queen?"

"Yes, sir. I was to say Her Majesty wanted you at once."

"She'll no' see me the day! She kens damn' well I'm fu'!" roared Mr. Brown, and collapsed.

There was nothing for it but to tell Victoria that her gillie was ill. She pursed her lips, but said nothing. She kent well enough that her gillie was full, for she kent her gillie, and in fact had read a preliminary report of the Wheeler Case, sent her by the guard, which had spared Mr. Brown not at all. Her Majesty had sent it back without comment.

At about this time, in another part of the castle, there occurred a conversation which no one would have thought could possibly influence the course of the Wheeler Case, but which was in fact the fount of certain minor events that were to have an astonishing effect upon it later. This conversation was between Noonan and Slattery.

"Did you hear what they done with the little parisheen?" she asked him.

She was standing in the doorway of his work cuddy at the foot of the Prince of Wales's Tower, where she had never stood before, but if he was surprised to see her there, he guessed that she had sought him out on purpose to put the question, there being no one else with whom she felt she might discuss the subject freely; and being sensible that this gave him an advantage over her, he went on trimming the wick of his lighting lamp with the intense care of a man cutting diamonds.

"I did not. But he'd no call to be sneaking in here like a thief in the night. 'As ye sow, so shall ye reap.' It's the way of the world."

"The way of the world!" she echoed contemptuously. "If you'd look at the Good Book with both eyes for once, Slattery, you'd find, Suffer the little childern to come unto Me."

"Would I!" he said, flinging her a glance over his shoulder. "And what of the Queen? Will herself suffer every little hobbledehoy off the river Thames to come unto her, and she eating her dinner?" But

— 129 —

his eye was attracted by the indignant swelling of her handsome bosom, and he softened towards her. "Ah, but I see you've a kind heart, Katie," he said, coming round socially on his stool to face her, and clasping his knees. "And indeed I was thinking when you came in, it'd be a long time before we'd see the beat of it: lo and behold, the ragtag of all May-day gossoons taking his ease on the Royal Throne of Britain!" He chuckled: "He! he! he! he! That young Guardee couldn't make heads or tails of it entirely. 'Would I be the Windsor Herald or the Knave of Spades?' says he. And did you hear what he called you?—'Duchess of the Scullery'!"

"Him, is it? Small heed I paid to what he called me."

Slattery observed the curve of her strong neck as she tossed her head defiantly, her proud, dark eyes, the figure with which even her censorious garments had to compromise a little. Before she had presented herself in his doorway he had been thinking not indeed of Wheeler but of Noonan, and wondering how he might safely approach her on the subject of lifting their workaday acquaintance onto a cosier plane. For a starter he thought he might soother her into walking out with him, maybe, but of course he realized that where Noonan was concerned any such proposal would have to be introduced delicately. He said softly: "Still and all, he wasn't far from the truth there, I'm thinking, with the duchess as plain to be seen as the scullery." But at this she shot him such an umbrageous look that he hastened to reassure her. "Oh, you don't understand me. Wait now. You take me own case." And folding one long leg over the other, he leaned himself upon it while he expounded his meaning. "The Slatterys was great folk onct, so I've heard, but me mother was an O'Rourke, the same that was princes of Breifny in the old times. Royal blood, they had. And the minute I clapped eyes on yourself, says I, There's an Irish girl with good blood in her the same as me, says I. You can't hide the old blood, I says. And tell me, wasn't I right, now?"

Noonan, though she was not unpleased, laughed at him. "Yerra, is it that kind of blather, and don't I know it like I know the sound of an old chimney on a windy night? Me old da, God rest him, would be all times letting on if he'd had his rights he'd-a been High King of Ireland."

"And maybe he would, then; why do you doubt him? What way would you be better informed than himself, and you not knowing your own name till he told you? And besides that, couldn't I tell there was good stuff in you the minute I seen you? Indeed it's low the mighty have fallen, and ourselves the proof of it. Moiling and toiling, toiling and moiling from dawn to the dark of night, us that would be as great as any if we had our rights; for by the hokey I'm as good as any man walks the earth if it's himself of Wales, the same as you're the equal of any woman if she's got a crown on her, and we'd be showing them all if we had the chanct."

She looked at him levelly. "Playing with fire's not the way to be showing them, Slattery."

"Fire, you say! Now before God I never played with fire in me life. There's a thing, is fire!" he hinted darkly. "The great wonder of the natural world they do say was pinched from heaven, with the power to warm or destroy, to cook the grub of an honest man or consume a greedy one in the pits of hell . . ."

"Is it a sermon you're giving us?"

"It is, maybe; or a parable." A new thought smiled behind his eyes. "Have you never looked into the grate, and it burning, the way you'd think to be seeing things in the coals?"

"I have, and who hasn't?"

Suddenly leaning forward, a teasing twinkle in his eye, he asked: "And what did you see there, tell me?"

"Tell you, will I!" she laughed. "I'll not."

"Was it a man, I wonder?"

"It was not. And if it was, you may be certain, he was a long chalk from the spit of you."

"Oh, now," he said gently, "I wouldn't think to be that fortunate.

But they do say there's a power to be seen in the fire if you've the gift in you. I've heard there's fairies in it will tell your fortune if you ask them kindly, and sure when I've a chandelier lighted it's like a ring of them dancing."

She regarded him with a quizzical smile. "Now what kind of a man is it at all will be one minute burning down Windsor Castle and the next one seeing fairies in the fire?"

Slattery raised his eyebrows at her. "You don't believe in them?"

"Believe in them! In God's name, Slattery, talk sensible."

"Well, now, there's scholars believe in them, the same as scholars that don't. What do you think of that, now?"

"And if there is, then?" she asked curiously.

"Well, then, look at the matter logically, Noonan. Isn't it a known fact that the scholars that don't believe in them wouldn't believe in anything anyhow unless they could see it? Small warrant it gives them, I'm thinking, to be passing judgment on a mystery of creation the equal of that one. And as to the priests, girl, isn't it a queer way they have to be exorcizing creatures they'll tell you ben't there anyhow? Oh, if you get a priest in a corner he'll tell you he was chasing devils, but who's to know what he was chasing? Could his reverence see them any more than he could the invisible angels? For he believes in angels, surely? And don't the scholars hold there's no such thing as angels, or devils, or people even, but monkeys only; and don't each side deny the infallibility of the other? 'Faith,' says the Church; 'Reason,' says the scholars, but in the halls of learning of Oxford University the Prime Minister of Britain, a Jewish man, too, rises up in his wisdom and declares for the angels; and isn't the Prime Minister a reasonable man? And what does St. Patrick tell us? St. Patrick tells us some of the angels won't be going to heaven till the Judgment Day, but did you ever hear that from a priest itself? Now I've heard it argued that the Good People are nothing at all but angels doing penance for their venial sins, and St. Patrick meant them. Who's to know, Noonan? Me own mother that was an O'Rourke and an educated woman—housekeeper at the Royal Catholic College of Maynooth she was, and a daily communicant in her last days—she believed in them; and would you call her a pagan?"

"I'd not," said Noonan respectfully. "But could herself see them?"

"She could, and they going by in the fields of an evening; and could talk with them too, but would tell no one what they told her."

"Musha," volunteered Noonan suddenly, "I knew a man ploughed up a Gentle Bush was struck blind from that out. It was what they said anyhow, and sure enough the man was stone blind."

"Now I declare to God," marvelled Slattery. "Well, there's queer tales going and I don't know." He recaptured his knee and looked up at the ceiling thoughtfully, and after a moment he sighed. "Ah," he murmured, "it was a saint she was."

"Is it your mother?"

He nodded. " 'Swear to me, Eugene,' says she to me with her last breath, 'swear to me, Eugene, that you'll not fall away from the Church like your father done, and never miss Mass of a Sunday.' 'I'll swear,' says I. 'And go to confession at least onct a month.' 'I will that too, Ma.' 'Thanks be to God,' says she, and dies with her beads in her hands. But it's a poor sinner I am, and haven't seen the inside of a chapel in a twelvemonth. Is it any wonder me conscience is at me, the way I've broken me sacred oath to a dying woman given? But there's nothing but Protestant services in this place."

"God have mercy on you, Slattery!" Noonan cried. "Isn't there St. Edward's in the town, where you may go to six o'clock any Sunday of the year, or weekday either, and don't they hear confessions of a Saturday night?"

This seemed to amaze him. "Is it the truth you're telling me? And me thinking there wouldn't be a decent church in twenty miles!"

"Sure anyone could have told you; yourself is to blame for not making inquiries. God pity you, man, it would turn the hair of a wild animal to stand before His Almighty Seat in a state of mortal sin the like of what you're in, or the half of it only."

Slattery looked gravely at his hands. "Aye. It's that maybe has been keeping me from inquiring this long time. For I'll confess to you, Noonan, a great fear comes on me with thinking of the blackness of me soul and I've little heart to be entering His Sacred House in that shape."

"Aw, now," she said compassionately, "that's not the way to be talking. You've only to remember what the Gospel tells us: there's more joy in heaven for a repenting sinner than for ninety-nine never sinned at all. Indeed it's glad to see you Our Lord will be, Slattery. And Father Fuller, too. He's the one I always go to confession to when I can get him, a gentle, understanding man he is, and light with the Hail Marys. I had a general out of him a while gone by."

"Will you be going to Mass on Sunday next?"

"I will. And why don't you be? Sure, it's comfort you'll find there. For your mother's sake, go."

"Me mother's sake," whispered Slattery huskily. "Wirra, it's an unfaithful son I've been to her."

"And if it is, make it up to her at last, then; do. Aw, come, man, it's in her name I'm asking you."

The sinner spread his hands and gazed at them thoughtfully. "If I did, maybe," he hazarded after a moment, "would it be possible at all for me to go along with you, then?" He turned his face to her beseechingly. "For if I went it alone I'd be that tortured with guiltiness I'd not get past the holy water."

Noonan lowered her eyes. "Indeed," she replied in a low voice, "if it'll help your mother rest easier in her grave I don't mind. I'll be going to the six o'clock as always."

"Ah, Noonan! She'll bless you at the Foot of God this night. It's all I'm needing is the hand of a good woman to be leading me back to the fold and I'll be a good Catholic man again. Ah, Noonan!" And he reached gratefully for her hand.

"But what am I doing gabbing here the whole day!" she exclaimed irrelevantly, drawing back in embarrassment. "They'll wonder am I dead or whatever. I'll be going now, Slattery. I've the pots to wash out and the floor to scrub. I'll be glad if you'll walk to Mass with me on Sunday."

He was left looking at an empty doorway and a patch of blank wall in the corridor beyond. The light of Christian joy that had illumined his face but a moment before had gone out like a snuffed candle. Then he smiled, as fauns smile when we don't believe in them.

Shortly before noon, a carriage bore the Prime Minister out through St. George's Gate on the way to the railway station. And on the way back to London his train passed another that was bearing home from there a man whose entrance into the Wheeler Case was apprehensively awaited in the castle. That man was the Master of the Household.

Sir Gilpin Jarvey was a white-staffed proctor of the Crown and a member of the august Board of the Green Cloth; and his office, a creation of Albert the Efficient, was of the kind called permanent, which meant that it was above politics. It consolidated certain practical powers formerly divided chiefly among the Lord Steward, the Lord Chamberlain, and the Master of the Horse, and although the peers answering to those lofty titles changed with every Government, it was Sir Gilpin's conviction that the incumbents lived only for the day when something would happen to prove the reorganization a horrible mistake. Thus he was as fearfully haunted an individual as even Mr. Naseby, who, however, having no suspicion of the truth, looked upon him as the Pitiless Absolute. But where the Sergeant Footman's fear manifested itself in a trembling uncertainty, the Master's took the form of a holy aggressiveness, and it was by reason of this that those officers whom he had superseded in responsibilities of which, in fact, they were only too glad to be relieved did wish for his downfall quite as intensely as if they really had been jealous of him.

THE MUDLARK

"Mismanagers is what I call 'em—*mismanagers*," was his theme. "Would you believe the disgraceful conditions that existed when they were in the saddle? Would you believe that the windows were never clean or that the Queen of England couldn't have a fire to warm herself by? It's the truth, sir! When Prince Albert inquired who was responsible for the state of the windows, he was informed that my Lord Chamberlain had charge of the insides of some, and my Lord Steward of the insides of the others, but that the outsides were the business of Woods and Forests, sir. But the trouble was, Woods and Forests never washed at the same time Steward or Chamberlain did, so when a window was clean on one side, it was sure to be a little pea-souper on the other. And when he inquired why there wasn't a fire, he discovered that my Lord Chamberlain had laid one but couldn't light it, because you see the lighting was the traditional prerogative of my Lord Steward, and it seemed that Steward had sent round to do the lighting before Chamberlain had sent to do the laying, and having found nothing to light, the Steward's man could charge the fault to his opposite number in the Chamberlain's department, while the Chamberlain's could point to his tardy laying and charge it right back to his vis-à-vis in the Steward's. And there it was, sir, while the Queen of England froze. But Her Majesty has a fire now, I warrant you. And you may see for yourself, if you'll just notice, that all the windows are clean. I keep things shipshape, if I do say it; ship-*shape*."

And Lord Shipshape was what they called him. He was a little porcupine of a man with one eye; the other he had lost in India as a youth—in battle with the Sikhs, he said, but the gossip was that he had lost it to a pig in a sticking accident; he wore a patch and was pleased if you remarked that he looked a little like Lord Nelson. One of the great passions of his life was bell ringing, and he belonged to that noisiest of civilian companies of England known preposterously as the Ancient Society of College Youth, which met fortnightly for practice in the belfry of St. Paul's Cathedral. There, on the evening of Wheeler's escapade, he and his colleagues had been having at it in deafening devotions, coats off, sweat shining on their happy faces as they yanked away at the ropes, and the twelve great bells of St. Paul's had crashed out of the darkness like a Vulcanic anvil chorus, driving to cover every dog in the City of London; after which the brethren had adjourned to their regular tavern for ale all round and a jolly little go on the hand bells. And so it happened that next morning Sir Gilpin's worried clerk had to apprise him by telegraph of General Ponsonby's memorandum; and so he had the whole railway journey from London to Windsor in which to torment himself with it.

By the time he received Mr. Naseby in the afternoon, he was fairly convinced that the scandal he had dreaded for so long had at last arrived to unhorse him, and the sight of his face easily persuaded Mr. Naseby of the same thing with regard to himself. But really Mr. Naseby had expected nothing else. He had lain awake half the night dreading this interview, and had climbed the stairs to it like a man ascending the scaffold. He was less ruddy than usual, and in his anxiety had developed a twitch in one fat cheek, which caused it ever so slightly to bounce now and then as if it were made of rubber. The Master could not keep his eye from straying over to watch for this phenomenon, which irritated him greatly, nor could Mr. Naseby help waiting self-consciously for the next bounce, and both of them would give a little start every time the thing occurred. Then the Master would tell Mr. Naseby to get on with the story, and Mr. Naseby would do his best. But the Master kept interrupting.

"What! It was the servants found the boy the second time? After Brown had disappeared with him? When the guard didn't know which way to turn? You sent the servants out to search the castle, and they found him and led the guard to him? What? Speak up."

"Yes, Sir Gilpin; that was precisely how it was, sir."

"Eh? By Jove!"

And when Mr. Naseby had told the whole terrible story, no look of fury but rather a cunning smile twisted Sir Gilpin Jarvey's face. "Why, Naseby," he said, "we are not at fault, then. On the contrary, I should say we are to be commended, eh?"

"Sir?" said Mr. Naseby, looking stunned.

"Of course!" the Master said. "Don't you see? Castle grounds— jurisdiction of the Governor; gates and general security—Household Guards; my responsibility is limited to domestic management. Yet my men—servants, mark you—had to do the other chaps' work for 'em! You see that, don't you? Confound it, man, don't sit there looking such a stupid ass; I am congratulating you, Master Sergeant Footman, con-gratulating you."

"Y-yes, sir."

"Go and bring me every servant that had a part in last night's work; I'll interrogate 'em all before preparing my report. My report!" he repeated, thinking how that was going to make certain parties squirm. "Oh, I'll give the general a report—with pleasure! Lively, Naseby—out!"

"Yes, Sir Gilpin."

And having bowed himself out, Mr. Naseby seized his nervous cheek in his fist and gave it a disciplinary pinch. Ah, but the ordeal was over now, and here he was, still pleasantly intact. "Lummy!" he murmured, marvelling that he had indeed been praised, and that through such a scandalous affair as this recognition had come to him at last. He set forth with a reflective smile on his lips, and, arriving belowstairs with the air of the successful major general that he had turned out to be, summoned Slattery, Noonan, Munn, and the four underfootmen who had served the Queen's dinner, marshalled them into a docile rank, and informed them of the mission to headquarters upon which he was about to lead them.

"I may say," he announced, "that for running that young rascal to earth when the guard hadn't a notion where he was, the Master has been pleased to honour me with his compliments." He noted the blank amazement on their faces and beamed at them. "Yes, and as I did that with the help of others belonging to the staff, I am pleased to congratulate them as well, I am indeed. The Hall has distinguished itself this time. But then, when danger threatens, it's our job to rally round Her Majesty, isn't it? Well, then!" His features resumed their official sternness. "Do your duty at all times and I dessay we'll get on better than if you don't."

When Mr. Naseby and his little squad filed into the Master's office, they found him positively smiling. His Cyclopean gaze came to rest upon Munn.

"Well!" he said, amiably enough. "Whom have we here?"

Munn blushed and bobbed clumsily. "Munn, sir."

"Chambermaid, Sir Gilpin," said Mr. Naseby.

"Ah! A new one, hey? Well, Munn, we may as well begin with you. What part did you play in last night's little drama, eh?"

"If you please, sir, I 'ad nothing to do with it."

"Come, come, you must have had something to do with it."

"She was in the Throne Room when—when it happened, Sir Gilpin," Mr. Naseby explained. "And before that, as I recall, she spied him larking through the castle with Mr. Brown."

"So? Good girl, Munn; very sharp of you, I must say," the Master complimented her.

And when he had finished interrogating the whole rank, he was confirmed in his opinion that his creatures had covered him with glory.

"You did well, all of you. Yes indeed," he chortled as the possibilities of the thing grew on him. "Don't know what would have happened if it hadn't been for the servants. Those others didn't know what they were about, eh? Prevented something very nasty, I expect, h'mmmm? Ugly little brute, by all accounts."

"Begging your pardon, your worship," Noonan spoke up, "it was hungry he was."

"Hungry, you say? Aye, no telling how long he'd been sneaking round; days, probably; stealing what he could, too, I'll wager. Sneaking past that great booby of a guard; lying in wait for the Queen—makes me shudder, upon my word!"

"Please, sir," Noonan began again, but, receiving an angry look from Mr. Naseby, stopped short, only to fling out again recklessly, "What will they do to him?"

"To whom?" asked the Master absently.

"The lad, sir."

"Do to him? Let him slip through their clumsy fingers again, I shouldn't wonder. Blessing we're not all such fools in Windsor Castle or they wouldn't have him now, would they? Hey?" he demanded of Munn triumphantly. "What do *you* say?"

"No, sir," said Munn, bobbing again.

"No, by Jove," said the Master, "they wouldn't."

When he had dismissed them, Sir Gilpin Jarvey sat thinking for a while, and his one eye glittered—the eye by which he had more in common with Lord Nelson than was generally supposed. Then he summoned his clerk and carefully dictated his report to the general —a remarkable document, beginning with what was in effect an indictment of the Household Troops and ending on a note not dissimilar to that of Nelson's own account of the Battle of Cape St. Vincent.

Scotland Yard had responded to the call for help from its two representatives at the castle. The response had arrived in the person of Inspector W. P. Ash, whom students of Yard history will recognize as the famous "Busher" Ash, who foiled the attempt of the Moreau brothers to spirit the Rosetta stone out of the British Museum, who brought the jewel thief Van Huyl and the dynamiter Lamb to justice, and who bagged the whole Plummer Gang in a trap at Ipswich. His appearance in the Wheeler Case surprised even his two baffled colleagues and strengthened them in the view that there was more to the matter than met the eye.

Ash was a tall, thin, rather shabby man with intense black eyes

THE MUDLARK

and a pointed Vandyke, who looked like the kind of demon we imagine has marked up the margins of all the heavier books in the public library, and he had got his soubriquet of Busher from a way he had of slowly stroking the underside of his beard with the back of his hand, a mannerism which, when he employed it during the examination of criminals, was said to madden some poor devils to the point of confession.

"I tell you, Inspector," said Sergeant Wotton, "it's my private opinion there's some sort of a skeleton hiding in this 'ere cupboard. Speaking in private, you understand, we've heard some queer tales, we have, haven't we, Dicey?"

"We have," said Dicey.

"We have indeed. Not that we put any faith in 'em, sir; not yet, leastways. You know how people are, Inspector. But if I may say so, this ain't no ordinary case or there wouldn't be so many in high places trying to shield the suspected party." And dropping his voice, he related the rumour of the idiot bastard.

"That, Sergeant Wotton," said Inspector Ash coldly, "is as shocking a bit of chitchat as ever I've heard. I'll remind you that the complaining witness in this case is Her Majesty herself, and that we, Wotton, are in Her Majesty's service."

Sergeant Wotton humbly touched his forehead. "Right, sir," he said.

And Busher Ash, being a methodical man, began at the beginning. Instead of at once tackling Wheeler, who, he reasoned, would keep, he sent for Mr. Naseby.

This was just before Mr. Naseby had been received by the Master of the Household; if he appeared nervous, taciturn, and anxious to get the interview over with, it was only because of his apprehension over the next one on the same subject. But Ash, not knowing this, found his behaviour suspicious: indeed it was not inconsistent with what Wotton had said. Not that Ash took any stock in that twaddle—not for a minute he didn't; but reflecting

— 141 —

that in certain circumstances a queen's sergeant footman might conscientiously hesitate to tell everything he knew, he decided not to press matters just at present. He turned to the next witness on his list. And this, unfortunately, was Mr. Brown.

Being informed that the Queen's gillie was ill in his room, he went there and knocked on the door. But the voice that answered him sounded as if a huffy bull might be penned up inside.

"Hauld yer clatter, man! Swith aff and tell her I'm ramfeezled."

"It's the police, Brown," the detective called through the door. "I'm coming in"—for of course he didn't want to get a sick man out of bed. But he found the sick man standing at a table, kilted, shirted, and shod, and pouring from a pitcher a large mug of beer. Ash stopped on the threshold with an exclamation of apology.

The surprised Highlander blinked at him. "Po-police?" he inquired.

"Yes. Ash is my name—Inspector Ash, from the Yard."

The announcement as usual had its effect, but this time not of the usual kind. Mr. Brown banged mug and pitcher down on the table and faced him indignantly. "Ye refer t' *Scotland* Yard, I pr'soom. An' sin' ye've borrowed the name wi' the property, then borrow the manners, an' dinna bre'k in a mon's costle withoot his pairmission!"

"Oh, look here," Ash said easily, closing the door and coming into the room. "I could have sent for you, you know."

"Ye could," the gillie blazed. "Ye could ha' sent till the seas gaed dry."

The hard eyes of Busher Ash glinted. But looking at this great ape who, servant or not, was said to order the Queen about like a drill-sergeant; measuring him, and taking thought that tact was the thing in a case involving royalty, he returned a soft answer: "Come, now. They told me you were under the weather; I only let myself in so you needn't disturb yourself to open the door. It's about that little game last night."

"Game?"

It may have been that Mr. Brown, so startled at first, and then so angry, and not being very sharp today anyhow, had not previously connected the inspector's visit with anything in particular. Now he looked rather shocked.

"Last—last nicht?" he repeated.

"That's it. You don't mind a little chat about it, I hope?"

A sudden fit of coughing racked Mr. Brown. "Ah, as ye see, I'm a sick mon," he explained apologetically.

"What's the matter with you?"

"Weel, there's a queer weakness comes ower me at times, an' ma head gaes a' tapsalteerie. I dinna think——"

"It won't take long; just make yourself comfortable," Ash said hospitably, offering Mr. Brown's own armchair; and meeting the policeman's knowing eyes, Mr. Brown saw no alternative but to totter into it like an invalid.

But if the change in him was unconvincing, so was his testimony. He pictured a little vagrant gaining access to one of the best guarded citadels in the world by a succession of accidents that was all too pat on the face of it; he was absurdly vague about what had happened afterwards, and many of his answers to direct questions conflicted with Mr. Naseby's story. His coughing spasms obviously were feigned for the purpose of evasion. Then he grew irritable, and finally lost his temper again.

The truth was, of course, that the evening was largely a blank in Mr. Brown's mind. He had no recollection of anything that had happened after he and Wheeler had come up to this room together from the coalhole in the courtyard, but he had a dim impression that something disastrous had occurred, and in this dilemma was too canny to speak freely. Besides, he disliked policemen on principle, and in particular disliked the way this one kept brushing his beard at him. But his malingering, his blunders and his quarrelsomeness gave a different impression. Ash, though again he thought he'd better not insist just yet, came away with sharpened suspicions.

The great detective went directly to General Ponsonby, who armed him with a firm request upon the guard for Wheeler's delivery, and this the inspector presented at the Guard House, where it was gravely studied by the officer in charge.

"Just a moment, Inspector," the officer said, and left the room. Ten minutes later he returned with two other officers.

"Be patient, Inspector," one of them said. "The boy will turn up, I'm sure."

"Turn up?" said Inspector Ash.

"Oh, don't fret. The colonel has taken the boy in charge; he's looking into the case personally for General Incledon. But just at the moment, you see, we don't know where they are. It's all right, though. Just sit down again, won't you? You don't mind being patient for a little longer?"

Inspector Ash resumed his chair.

The fog had lifted. Boats were moving on the river again. They had brought tales of the Queen's burglar as far as Staines and Maidenhead. But long since the Great Western and South Western railways had carried them to London, where already they were common gossip from the Skin Market to the Inns of Court. . . .

Sergeant Wotton entered the Guard House to hand Inspector Ash a telegraph message which, when the inspector had deciphered it, became his latest instructions from the Yard:

YOU ARE TO INSIST UPON CUSTODY OF SUSPECT. IF DENIED COMMUNICATE IMMEDIATELY. UTMOST IMPORTANCE.

The message came from old Q himself.

"Odd," the inspector thought. "Of course I'd insist on custody! Unless . . . There, now! there's something behind this. And I don't like it; I don't like it at all!"

As usual, Ash was perfectly right, there *was* something behind it; and this was what it was:

Early that morning Major Fontoon, dispatched by Colonel Coggeshall, had left the castle for Sussex; there he had laid the matter directly before General Lord Frederick Incledon, whose strategical brain had commenced at once to devise a plan.

Lord Frederick agreed that this was the kind of thing one could not easily hush up. But then if he hadn't believed in making the effort against whatever the odds, he wouldn't have been a British soldier. Also, he said, it might be wise for the guard at the castle to be doubled against the possibility of another thrust by the gang, if there was a gang, for in a show like this one never knew what there was; and come what might, the Regiment should hang onto the scoundrel till it had discovered the facts. Nor did he fail to anticipate that the police would come poking their noses into the case; he personally would attend to them, he said; and in the meantime it might be convenient if the prisoner were—ah—mislaid for a time.

Fontoon cheered up. Old Inky had known what to do, right enough; he might yet save the day. Fontoon went back to buttress the ramparts of Windsor while his stout commander sallied forth to London upon a one-man holding attack.

The general went directly to the office of Commissioner Sir Joseph Kew in Great Scotland Yard. He chatted for a few minutes about little enough, because he wished it to appear that the reason for his call, when finally he got round to mentioning it, was of such slight moment that Sir Joseph need never dream of refusing his request. But in the course of this tactical small talk he happened to mention the weather, and the weather being now quite clear, it reminded him that he had missed his hunting, and led him into the easy error of grumbling about this. The shrewd, wrinkled face of Old Joe Kew betrayed nothing, but he was sufficiently acquainted with his visitor to be sure that if it had meant giving up a day with the hounds, only the most pressing business could possibly have got Lord Frederick out of Sussex. And when that business turned out to be the case of the Queen's burglar, of which Scotland Yard as yet knew almost nothing, Kew reflected that if it could play this kind of havoc with the life of a major general, it must be a very important case indeed—and he politely declined to stay out of it.

"Stubborn old fool!" the general inwardly stormed as he left the building. "Afraid—that's his trouble. Trouble with all underlings. Never should have gone to him at all."

And he went round to see the Home Secretary.

The incumbent successor to the great Peel, founder of the Metropolitan Police, was Sir Richard Cross, one of the most astute gentlemen ever to occupy the Home Office. He had high principles and was not likely to interfere with the duty of Scotland Yard even to oblige a commander of the Guards who was also the heir to a dukedom, a Knight Commander of the Bath and Master of Hounds—not, especially, when that duty involved the punishment of an offence against the Queen. But he was interested, greatly interested; the more so because Incledon, abandoning the line that there was really nothing to the case, implied that it was too important to be left to the thick thumbs of policemen.

"And as you know," the general explained, "the protection of Her Majesty is the Guards' first responsibility."

The secretary replied: "I believe it is also the responsibility of the Yard's Special Branch."

"Well, I suppose it is, in a way, but this is a castle matter; it occurred in the castle, and the castle, after all, is Guards' territory. Besides, you know, provost authority inside the castle is traditionally vested in the Governor; that's the law, Mr. Secretary, a very old law."

The secretary smiled.

"But," said the general, "we'll turn the case over to you in due

time, of course! Dash it all, we're not going to try it by court martial
and settle it with a firing squad, if that's what you're thinking. But
first let us get to the bottom of it. Let us proceed quietly, with no
meddling by those noisy bobbies of yours. They'd blow it to pieces,
scatter it to the winds. Oh, I grant you they're well enough for their
own sort of thing; very good at it, I hear. But don't you agree that
this is a bit out of their line? Her Majesty's safety is above all other
considerations. That is why I have doubled the guard at the castle
and——"

"Doubled the guard, Lord Frederick?" asked the secretary.

"Yes, sir, and I'll triple it if necessary; I'll call out the whole
Brigade. So you see, we really don't need——"

"Whole Brigade?" said the secretary, sitting up.

"I say, if necessary, sir," said General Incledon, who was glad to
see that he had made an impression. "I mean, of course, that we're
ready for all comers. So you may call off your dogs, if you—don't
mind the expression; and if that's against regulations, what of it?
Break 'em, sir, break 'em! I've broken hundreds in my time. This is
a serious matter."

"It must be," the secretary seriously agreed. And he sent down
the street for Commissioner Kew.

A while later General Incledon had been reduced to pleading
rather wildly before both officials for what he called a sporting
chance. But the more he talked, the more he only convinced them
that what he was asking was out of all reason. And at last he had
to retire from the field. He set out for the Horse Guards but suddenly
stopped, debated with himself, and changed his mind. Better not go
letting Headquarters know about this—it might only make matters
worse. Better to withdraw and regroup. But the holding attack had
failed.

"What do you think of all this, Kew?" asked Secretary Cross
when the general had gone.

The stooped. squint-eyed old man rubbed his nose. "Shouldn't care to say—yet. I've sent one of our best men to Windsor to take charge of the case; haven't heard from him yet. But I'll admit to you, I'm becoming more interested every minute."

"So am I. I should really like to hear what your man makes of it."

"You'll have a report, I promise you. I bid you good day, sir."

"Good day, Sir Joseph. And good luck."

It was on his return to his office from this disturbing interview that Kew sent the cipher message to Inspector Ash.

. . . And having finished his report to the Queen's Secretary and dismissed his clerk, the Master of the Household sat back in his chair. He sat with the fingertips of one hand pressing thoughtfully against the fingertips of the other, and his eye was glittering again. A full minute passed. He rose and began pacing the floor. He stood at the window awhile, seeing nothing that was visible from there. Then he popped into his antechamber and sent for Munn. He sent for Munn separately and by name, which was singular, because the Master never dealt separately with any of the lesser servants except through their immediate superiors, nor for that matter generally remembered for more than a minute the names of any beneath the rank of underbutler. So as Munn emerges this time from the amorphous swarm belowstairs, it behooves us at last to look at her.

Yet who shall say what she looks like? For the object Munn offers a curious study in human perspective. To Slattery, a tall man, whose eyes are on a level with her own, she is a great doorful of a woman with a head of hair on her like a rick of hay after a blow. Noonan, whose point of view is a foot lower, thinks it a pity that so pretty a face has to be mounted at so impractical a height. But Sir Gilpin Jarvey, whose Nelsonian eye looks out at about the same level as Noonan's two, thinks the whole arrangement enormously practical, even the hair; and he is a practical man.

11

In the main Guard Room, as in the town of Jericho when events were closing in on it, time had stopped. The knight leaning from his horse in the act of flinging down the gauntlet to the enemies of the Throne remained the picture of suspended animation, Marlborough and Wellington kept their inscrutable watch without blinking, and Wheeler was as abstract a factor as the square root of things, asleep in the big oaken chair.

It was cold in the Guard Room in the early morning and no one threw a cover over him, but being used to the doorways of London he huddled up like an old campaigner and slept on dreamlessly. In those bleak hours when his fate was being decided elsewhere in a way he did not apprehend, it was as if he huddled there in counterpoise between one phase of his existence and the next. But there would be no going back up that coal chute.

Seven o'clock, and over his breakfast in another part of the castle Colonel Coggeshall was apprised of the night's happenings; eight o'clock, and the tireless Fontoon had departed on his mission to Sussex; eight-thirty, and Coggeshall himself, flanked by half a dozen officers nearly as indignant as he, confronted the oblivious prisoner.

"This is the young whelp, is it? Not very clean, I must say. Wake him up!"

The prisoner was given a shake by one limp arm. But it failed to rouse him. He was seized by both shoulders and shaken briskly. But he only whimpered and sank back into his void. Wheeler was exhausted.

"Here!" Colonel Coggeshall said impatiently, and bending down he took hold of the lapels of Wheeler's coat. In that instant a pungent reek befouled his civilized nostrils, a racy and complex reek, in which he could not have been expected to recognize the brusque seasoning of kelp and tar smoke, fish, hides, and the multifarious ingredients of tidal mud into which a city has long emptied its drains, the reek of life and work and time on London river; but then he couldn't have been expected to like it if he had.

"My word!" the colonel said, in recoil. "He's filthy. He *stinks!*" And without apology for having used the right word, he speedily dusted his hands. "Full of lice too, I expect—crawling with all kind o' things! What's that on his face?—the Black Plague for all I know! We can't let vermin like he's got go trotting round the castle. Give him a bath!"

Wheeler came to with a gasp: he was the naked prey of cold water.

"Ay! Aow! Avarst!" he screamed. "Daon't—daon't, I *begs* yer! Avarst! Avarst!"

But there was no appeal. Before the whole Guard Room, the fighting, yelling, cursing child was being held upright in a portable receptacle that looked roughly like a large coal scuttle but that was in fact a simple device for mortifying the flesh on cold mornings, known as a hip bath. He was being doused and sponged with water that had been lukewarm when it left the kitchen but that had played a ghastly trick on him while being lugged upstairs in pails. He was also being vigorously scrubbed with soap, then topped off in the best military fashion with a strong disinfectant; and these things were being done to him by three soldiers who were tall even for Grenadiers.

He would always remember his baptism of sanitation as one of the most degrading experiences of his life.

Rubbed dry with a barracks towel, he stood snivelling in a circle of soldiers—up for inspection; his thin shoulders and buttocks trembling with the cold, while they turned him round and round, peering into his ears, probing his scalp, making him lift each foot to show the bottom; and he was mortified.

"He'll do," an officer said. "They're not born this clean; not his lot."

Wheeler's hands were two fig leaves in front of him; he looked up, the gameness of his outthrust underlip betrayed by eyes that were on the verge of tears again, and said apologetically, "I s'y, if aw *am* done ter tyste, sir, waon't yer just give a chap 'is hinexpressibles?"

"Eh? What's that?"

"Maw bags, sir." For although he might endure the cold on the rest of him, he was of course unmanned without his trousers.

But by Coggeshall's order all his clothes had been taken out and burned. He was thrown a bundle from the housekeeper's charity bin. In this he found a boy's black trousers (patched) and stockings (heavily darned) which pretty well fitted him, a cambric shirt somewhat too large, a pair of shoes, battered but still serviceable and approximately the right size, a short jacket only slightly too long at the wrists, and an old cap. There was also a novel garment that delighted him. It was made of wool and had long arms and legs, and he had intended to put this on last as a sort of coverall, but the soldiers stopped him and made him put it on first. It felt pleasantly snug and warm, but it irritated his skin and he was not at all satisfied with the arrangement. But he did not dare to argue, and besides, he could not wait to put on the other garments too. He was thrilled with all these new clothes, the finest he had ever had in his life, and when he stood up in them before one of the long mirrors he thought with a giggle that they made him look a proper toff. But after a moment he wondered what had become of his own, particularly his coat. He would have liked to keep his coat. The new jacket wasn't so warm as it, he perceived now, and he wouldn't be able to get a quarter so much into the pockets: that was important in his business. And he began to examine the jacket more critically now, feeling somehow that he had given his coat for it; and in the midst of his good fortune he had a dim sense of loss.

He was given a dish of gruel for his breakfast, and was just scraping the bottom when Coggeshall returned, trailed by his dutiful staff and also by the harassed McHatten, whom the colonel had been having at in the meantime.

"That's better!" the colonel said, surveying the transformed prisoner, and he walked around him on a tour of inspection, breathing freely now, for the boy who had reeked of the primal fall of man now smelt like nothing human but as safe as a base hospital.

The inquisition resumed. All that need be said of it is that it went very like the other session, with about the same damage to the nerves of both parties; that it adjourned promptly at one, reconvened at two-thirty, and ended two and a half hours later—in a sudden, bitter defeat for the Grenadier Guards. The Governor had signed a paper forcing them to yield up the prisoner to Scotland Yard.

And so, at five o'clock, Wheeler passed into the hands of the relentless Busher Ash.

Then it began all over again, in a much more efficient way; but little need be said about that either, just yet. Other things were about to happen elsewhere, things far more important to the Wheeler Case than the police inquiry, more important to it, in fact, than Wheeler.

But it may be told how the inspector probed into him for hours that evening while Wheeler sat fascinated by the measured brushing of the beard; how Wheeler slept that night under guard of Wooton and Dicey in a cell-like chamber of the Round Tower, the stones of which still bore the initials of more illustrious prisoners who likewise had waited upon Fortune there, and who probably had lost their heads; how next morning he led Ash over the route from St. George's Gate to the coalhole that was no longer open, and went with his captor that day to London—his first train ride—to be lodged privately, as befitted an enemy of the Throne, in a tight little upper room of the Clerkenwell House of Detention, there to languish an unconscionable time till the inquiry should be over.

No, there would be no going back up that coalhole, and he feared just then that there would be no going much of anywhere else either, not perhaps ever again; he knew not what was to become of him; but all at once there came over him a need that he had never felt before in his life, and in that moment the dark loft over Ah Fook's dispensary of *kaif* and oblivion in Dolphin Lane achieved the saddest glory of human architecture, being the place for which a child was homesick.

He climbed up on his bunk to the iron-grilled window, hoping that over the roofs of Clerkenwell he could see Poplar, but he couldn't; nor Limehouse, nor Stepney, not even the river. London lay under the familiar haze of all her chimneypots, old and dirty, in the waning afternoon, but wherever the clouds above the haze had left a cranny, feeble rays descended slantwise, like ropes of gossamer—the sun's backstays they were called in those days of sail and poetry, and Bill Grams, once, calling his attention to the sight, had told him that was the sun drawing water.

Drawing water after her as she went, water from the river; and he knew that now the ebb would be running, and ships leaving, and he could see the mudlarks gathering on the stairs. For the scene was all there in his head, of course: the ancient thoroughfare of sprits and rigging and gaunt cranes, the gulls, the puffing tugs, barges with brown sails, ponderous lighters, and a ship just making down the fairway, her men flinging back a chantey from the halliards. *What ship?*—for it was a matter of pride with him to be knowledgeable of ships; and he recognized her right off—*Cutty Sark!* That smart black hull with the yellow trim was a clipper hull, that was, but he knew her by the cut of her and her shrouds inside her bulwarks and the white woman at her prow and all that goldwork round her trailboards. He wouldn't just like to be aboard of her now, would he? Go where she was going, see the world, and all that? And the larks they'd have and all the singing and the things they'd have to tell when they came back! Sailing on the tide as the sun went down, *Cutty Sark*, for China and a cargo of tea. . . .

Making for the mists whence his father came, whither his father vanished before ever he was born.

12

From *The Times*, two days after
Wheeler's arrest:

A shocking experience is understood to have befallen the Queen at Windsor the other evening. While Her Majesty was dining with a company of distinguished guests, of whom the Prime Minister made one, a shabby prowler was discovered lurking behind an arras only a few feet from Her Majesty's chair. To the consternation of Her Majesty's attendants, before he could be apprehended, he fled, and there ensued a search of the castle that was not rewarded until some time later, when he was taken in the throne room. The Queen, by all accounts, remained calm, and when the intruder had bolted her presence, coolly signified to her guests that the dinner was to proceed as if nothing had happened. The guilty wretch is described as being of deformed body, swarthy complexion and a most forbidding mien. Little is known of him, and what he was doing in the castle is not clear, but Her Majesty's subjects may rest assured that a thorough inquiry is in progress.

From the same newspaper, next day:

It appears that considerable anxiety is entertained for the safety of the Queen. The guard at Windsor Castle, where the Court is now in residence, has been strongly reenforced in consequence of the cowardly attempt made against our Sovereign Lady as she sat at dinner this week. The police are reluctant to discuss the affair, but it is now known that they have in charge a youth of disreputable character named Wheeler, who burglariously broke into and entered the castle, concealed himself behind an arras, and lunged out at Her Majesty during a royal Banquet. Foiled in his assault, he nonetheless made good his escape amidst a scene of wild confusion, in which several peers, the Prime Minister and other members of the Government were engaged. The swarthy, squat young ruffian, said by some to be a dwarf, led Her Majesty's guard a furious chase through the castle, and after several hours during which he eluded his pursuers by wily ruses known only to the most practised of criminals, barricaded himself in the throne room. He then had the impudence to sit on the throne till the guard had smashed the door and dragged him down to face the consequences of his actions. It is said that at the time of his arrest he was not armed, but a systematic search of the castle is being made to ascertain whether he disposed of a weapon in the course of his flight. In the meantime, some mystery attaches to the whole affair. How the depraved dwarf, if such he is, managed to enter the castle and make his way into the royal apartments has not been explained, but a report that he had been a prisoner there even before the assault and had escaped by murdering his keeper is discredited by Scotland Yard. However, the police do not overlook the possibility that before he shewed himself at the Banquet, he may have been skulking about the premises for some time, and the extraordinary measures now being taken to ensure Her Majesty's safety may be regarded as grim evidence that he was not without accomplices. . . .

One thing that may strike the reader as curious about these two reports by the same newspaper, the greatest newspaper in the world, at that, with certainly as good a claim to confidence as any other newspaper, is the disparity between their two accounts of the original incident, the first within reach of the truth anyhow, but the second out of all hail of it. At a guess, this is what happened:

The Times's correspondent at Windsor, having heard of the Queen's burglar next morning, notified Printing House Square, for which Scotland Yard confirmed as much of the story as at the moment it could; but the next day, with the guard at the castle mysteriously doubled, with the Grenadiers in a bafflingly hostile mood, with all kinds of rumour coming down from Windsor and the public already showing signs of uneasiness about it all, the Yard cautiously held its tongue. This alone was enough to arouse what a newspaper calls its instinct. And the re-enforcement of the guard was a fact that seemed to speak for itself. In those days *The Times* did not enjoy the same confidential position that British officialdom accords it now; it was as much in the dark as its rivals, and with them thrown back upon reason and ingenuity. It found other sources of information, some of which flowed only too freely, and some not freely enough.

But by comparison with the reports of other newspapers, *The Times's* reports were conservative, which is the reason they have been given here—so that without having to wade through the reports of the other papers as well, the busy reader may say to himself, "Conservative! If these were conservative, what must the others have been like?"—and be able to conceive of them quite as well for the purpose as if he had. But there is also another reason. Even then *The Times* was thought of as "authoritative." In some of the best bow windows in London, its alarming second report of the business only substantiated for many of its readers what they already had heard but hesitated to believe, while others searched knowingly between the lines and were convinced of even worse.

It was the same with one newspaper or another all over England, in taverns and restaurants, inns and dwelling houses, on 'Change and street corners and village greens; the same with hearsay; and the false rumours to which Professor Hodge attributes in part the great phenomenon of the case were in full career.

That phenomenon, to him, was of course the disproportion between the trifling thing that Wheeler did and the whopping public fuss that was to come of it, but the rumours were a bit of a phenomenon themselves, and it is interesting to read that he connects them to some degree with the psychological "conditioning" of the public by previous national experience. What he means by this, I think, is that the public mind, schooled to some reverence of the Sovereign's person and to a nice regard for the rules of place, could not readily comprehend a gutter boy violating the Queen's privacy for any but the most monstrous reasons: it could not possibly imagine the truth on its own hook, and in the absence of calming explanations it naturally imagined everything else. But here Hodge retreats into a mystic cloud. "Beware the British trifle," he says, at which we can only nod with the same opaque conviction that we accord the oracles of the atom bomb, though that trifle be mostly American—remembering that what killed William the Third was quite literally a British molehill. (What disaster when they explode a *British* atom!) The riddles left begging are: why the calming explanations of such a simple matter were not immediately forthcoming, and why, when they did come, they acted not at all like oil on water but like oil on flame; why the public at first refused to have anything to do with them and the hotheads burned all the hotter. And the answer is respectfully suggested: Because there were forces working at cross-purposes to the firemen. Victoria's domestics and her Grenadier Guards were certainly working against them all the way from Pudding Lane to Pie Corner; not forgetting that puissant body, the Ancient Society of College Youth.

Who will believe the reassuring public verbiage of a lady's solicitors when her cook is whispering a better story out the back door? But Her Majesty's servants were only going loyally on the black hints of the Master of her Household, who was the genius of the whole particular movement, and he, perhaps, was only the tool of what a psychologist nowadays would call a "defence mechanism." The aggressive Sir Gilpin Jarvey was comforted by the view that his vassals had prevented something dreadful, and he propagated his opinion not only through the castle but among all the bell ringers of St. Paul's Cathedral. What allies were there! Think of those doughty Youths, many of them with snow-white locks but as spry as monkeys, apple-cheeked, taut-bellied, tough of thew and bright of eye, ready at a moment's notice to call London to arms or to worship, to peal out the tidings of history, come death or *Te Deum*. Think how they walked with beadles and sextons, vicars and vergers, deacons and archdeacons, prebendaries and canons, and drank their ale fortnightly in the Amen Tavern, at the corner of Paternoster Row and Ave Maria Lane, not far from Fleet Street; and how in the course of their daily living they must have penetrated into banks and exchanges, the Inns of Court, Parliament, and probably into the British Museum, the Bible Society, the Royal Academy, Guildhall and the Abbey, country houses and bell foundries and musical teas, and kept running down to Oxford, if only to see how Great Tom was holding up and haply give him a clang.

And the servants read volumes in the dark attitude of Mr. Naseby, who accepted Sir Gilpin's view as gospel and throve on it, though what had been prevented he hadn't a notion and he discouraged inquiries. It was to be assumed that if anybody knew the truth, the Master of the Household did, and as for the Sergeant Footman, who was thought to be in the Master's confidence anyhow, hadn't he been in on the whole thing? But it was recalled what Mr. Naseby had said about it being the servants' duty to rally round Her Majesty in a pinch, and it was allowed that although Mr. Naseby knew all right, he would never, never tell.

"There he goes," they would say as he went waddling down a corridor, "—mum. He'll carry that story to the grave with him, Naseby will. Aye, and that's not all he'll carry." For in their curiosity over what they thought he knew about the Wheeler incident, it had occurred to them that he probably knew a good deal else besides. "His father was in his place before him, and his grandfather before that; there's a bushel of royal secrets that man could tell if he was minded, but they'll bury them all with him. He could write a book,

I tell you. A regular walking archives, that's what he is; and there he goes—mum."

As national interest in the case grew, it followed that interest grew somewhat more than proportionately in the town of Windsor, which siphoned all the latest privy comment over the castle walls and piped it to London, which distributed it to the rest of Britain. Yet on the national scale, no one version of the story at first gained any measurable headway over the others, for although most of the servants leaned towards the Boy in the Iron Mask myth, as the canard of the Devil's Tower came to be called by its Tory depreciators, the Grenadier Guards kept hinting privately at some kind of criminal plot, about the nature of which they were fascinatingly vague. Impartial thinkers in the public houses pointed out that the Household Troops would be as likely to know the truth as anyone, and a lot likelier too, while on the whole women and radicals preferred the other story. But in fact the influence of the Grenadiers was at its weightiest upon upper levels of society, so that for a time it appeared that the national division of opinion would be drawn on lines of class as well as politics.

Benjamin Disraeli was mildly astonished at all this ado, but, whether from some ironic humour, he refrained from returning frank answers to persons who inquired of him exactly what had happened. To Randolph Churchill he said reflectively:

"The English are really a romantic people; sometimes I forget that, and then something like this comes along to remind me of it. I do believe they regard Her Majesty rather like the heroine of a novel."
—*The pot*, thought Lord Randolph, *calling the kettle romantic!*—
"They complain of her withdrawal from public affairs, they accuse her of neglecting her duty to Trade, and they make a terrible fuss about the burden of the Civil List. It's all mostly fraud; all to cloak a case of childlike pique at the royal lady for concealing herself from them. But then, you know, I find it charming."

"Dizzi-ben-Dizzi," muttered Lord Randolph to himself when the

Prime Minister had passed on with a pleasant nod. He took it that Disraeli had dissembled in order to refrain from speaking of what was a very serious matter; and that day he indited to Her Majesty a letter expressing his deep sympathy and concern, but, bethinking what some of the rumours were, he did not send it.

Disraeli is on record as having made some quizzical remarks about the English at this period of his career, but for that he must be forgiven, because at the time he was understandably annoyed with them. For years he had tried to do something to alleviate slum conditions, to awaken the land to the dreadful hazards of bad drainage and fetid rivers, rat-infested rookeries and oppressive working conditions; he had fought these things even in his novels, and now that he had come to power he was determined to write them out of existence in the laws. But it was hard going. "*Sanitas, sanitatum, omnia sanitas,*" he had said, trying to relieve a dull subject, but even members of his own Party only harrumphed back at him that this was not the business of Parliament, but of plumbers—a policy of sewage. He had spoken of "Two Englands," the rich and the poor, pleaded as reasonably and as eloquently as he could for a bridge across the gulf between; but the Old Gang, whom he had thought almost converted to his own new conception of Toryism, had muttered that this only proved what they had always known, that this damned foreigner was dangerous; and at the grand climax of his career all the old mistrust had come out of the past to plague him—a foreigner still. Yes, he was a foreigner, but he thought he understood the English better than the English understood themselves; and perhaps, in his satiric mood, the confusion into which they had been thrown by the East End sapling gone to Dunsinane amused him.

To his secretary, Darcy Hammond, in Downing Street, he made what the young man thought a very odd comment indeed:

"Have you read your nursery rhymes lately, Hammond? No, I dare say you haven't. Only children and old people appreciate nursery rhymes; everyone else thinks they're nonsense." And he recited softly:

> " 'How many miles to Babylon?'
> 'Three score and ten.'
> 'Can I get there by candlelight?'
> 'Aye—and back again!'

"How old are you, Hammond?"

"Thirty," Hammond smiled. "Why? Don't you think I'm old enough to understand it?"

"Oh yes, to understand it, but not to appreciate it, not to appreciate it. One has to be"—he shook his head—"three score and ten."

Before Hammond could inquire what this had to do with the Wheeler Case, the Prime Minister had turned to affairs of state. "Well, about this Canal business. You are familiar with it, and I should like you to call personally on Baron Rothschild and make the situation clear to him. Also, to anticipate his own agents in Cairo, who will be sure to advise him that the Khedive is talking about only mortgaging the shares—tell him that's all nonsense: a forced sale by any other name smells sweeter."

"I understand, sir."

"Two millions sterling by the first of the month and the other two guaranteed by the first of the year—unreasonable, I know," Disraeli went on, "but a little better than the first demand; and say that if we don't meet Ismael's terms I greatly fear De Lesseps will. There is scarcely breathing time. God knows, Rothschild won't like having to raise two millions in that kind of hurry, but God and the Baron both know what will happen in the money market if I have to go to the Bank of England, provided I can get it from the Bank of England. I'll ask Parliament for a commission of 2½ per centum, as he requires. It will bring cries of anguish from the other side of the House, but I agree that in the circumstances it's a fair price—and I will get it. Say that I must have his absolute assurances on these terms. And impress on him this particularly: that the Government will commit itself on his spoken word, but that he has only my spoken word that Parliament, when it meets, will accept the debt. I pledge him as security the British Government."

Within an hour Hammond had returned with the reply:

" 'Tell Dizzy he shall have it.' "

With such great schemes in his head, what man would interest himself in the plight of a mudlark named Wheeler?

"There was another message, sir."

"Eh?"

"Lord Rothschild said, 'And since we're buying the key to India, as he calls it, tell him I'd be obliged if he didn't send my niece-in-law's brother there.' "

"Niece-in-law's brother? Where?"

"To India, sir. It seems he's in the Guards." Hammond consulted a slip of paper. "A Lieutenant McHatten."

"Oh, a soldier. The poor-knights of our everlasting chess game." His brow contracted. "What name did you say?"

"Mc——" Hammond had to look again. "McHatten."

"M'm. Not exactly a common name. I wonder if that's the young man who—— Is he at Windsor?"

"Yes; in the Grenadiers."

"Ha! And he's connected with the Rothschilds, is he? Lucky dog."

"Excuse me, sir. Are they sending the Grenadiers out to India?"

"I don't know, Hammond; but if they are, it will be rather a shock to the Grenadiers, don't you think? Dear, dear; there'll be dozens of McHattens besieging Whitehall, won't there? Well, I leave this one to you, my boy. India did without Brummell; now it will have to manage without Baron de Rothschild's niece's brother. See to it." The Prime Minister dismissed the subject with a wave of his hand. "What is the time in Egypt?"

Hammond said it was three o'clock.

"And the Cabinet is called for two. The message to Stanton will have to wait . . ."

India was to be secured without McHatten, though not without Rothschild: one of the great dreams of Disraeli's political and artistic life was about to come true; and that evening after dinner, in the study of his residence at No. 2 Whitehall Gardens, there recurred to him sweetly the words dropped into his ear so long ago by Mehemet Ali of the soft white beard:

> It is I who hold the key to the world's other side.
> The Key to the Far East?
> You will see—some day.

And the words of Rothschild, only today: Since we're buying the key to India . . .

He was a man to savour that kind of thing; but he thought: The key to India is London. He sat slumped before the fire, an attenuated empire-maker indeed, looking rather like some old pasha or khedive himself, in the red Turkish fez that he affected to keep his head warm, and a long, quilted red silk dressing gown. Then another recollection lifted slightly one of his drooping lids. He could not resist going to the bookcase and taking down the novel in which, thirty years before, he had written some of the ideas that had begun to float round in his skull fifteen years before that, in his conversation with the Khedive Ismael's grandfather. The book was Tancred, or the New Crusade. And, turning over the leaves, he reread this:

" 'If I were an Arab in race as well as religion,' said Tancred, 'I would not pass my life in schemes to govern some mountain tribes.'

" 'I'll tell you,' said the Emir, springing up from his divan and flinging the tube of his nargilly to the other side of the tent; 'the game is in our hands if we have energy. There is a combination that would entirely change the face of the whole world, and bring back empire to the East. Though you are not brother of the Queen of the English, you are nevertheless a great English prince, and the Queen will listen to what you say; especially if you talk to her as you talk to me, and say such fine things in such a beautiful voice. Nobody ever opened my mind like you. You will magnetise the Queen as you have magnetised me. Go back to England and arrange this. You must . . . quit a petty and exhausted position for a vast and prolific empire. Let the Queen of the English collect a great fleet, let her stow away all her treasure, bullion, gold plate, and precious arms; be accompanied by all her court and chief people, and transfer the seat of her empire from London to Delhi. There she will find an immense empire ready made, a firstrate army, and a large revenue. In the meantime, I will arrange with Mehemet Ali. He shall have Bagdad and Mesopotamia, and pour the Bedoueen cavalry into Persia. I will take care of Syria and Asia Minor. The only way to manage the Affghans is by Persia and the Arabs. We will acknowledge the Empress of India as our suzerain, and secure for her the Levantine coast. If she like, she shall have Alexandria as she now has Malta: it could be arranged. Your Queen is young: she has an *avenir*. Aberdeen and Sir Peel will never give her this advice; their habits are formed. They are too old, too *rusés*. But, you see! the greatest empire that ever existed; besides which she gets rid of the embarrassment of her Chambers! And quite practicable; for the only difficult part, the conquest of India, which baffled Alexander, is all done!' "

The words of the Unrecognized Caesar, the Obscure Napoleon; and the Prime Minister smiled. The wild dream of a day when anything was possible. And yet, not all for nothing. In '58, at some pains, he had helped to wrest from the Honourable John Company the last vestige of its historic Monopoly, and present India intact to the Crown. There was satisfaction in that. But in those days there had been no Canal. The next step! As he had forced India upon Parliament then, he would force upon it now the security of India—and the first foothold in Egypt! That great desert ditch to the Red Sea had to be kept out of the hands of Bismarck and the Czar: it had to be made a bastion of Britain's Mediterranean power, which alone could preserve Turkey as a bulwark against Russia and maintain the equilibrium of a bellicose and uneasy Europe. For romance was always rational with him, usually even practical—that was his saving grace. And he thought India to be of more consequence to Britain than was generally realized. In the future the "tight little isle" (tighter than ever now, he noticed, with its agriculture ruined, its industrialized economy dependent on foreign markets, and its population fast outgrowing it) would need such vast dominions for its own maintenance. That, he would have said, was realism. But in attending to these practical matters, in bringing true his concept of Britain's bread-and-butter destiny as a great maritime power, as a greater Venice, lording it East and West, he fed on the food of high romance and artistic achievement that his spirit craved. He looked again at *Tancred*: "Empress of India"—the first mention of such a title; and Her Majesty thought it her own idea! Well, it was time to force that upon Parliament too. He could already hear the objections: "Too showy! Really a little vulgar, don't you think?" Nonsense. When would the English learn that to rule in the East one had to appeal to the imagination? And he rather thought that perhaps the Prince of Wales hadn't better go to Ireland after all, just yet; perhaps he'd better go to Delhi, and accept as heir apparent of the new empire the fealty of the Indian princes, amid elephants, in a magnificent Imperial Durbar. . . .

What was the time in Egypt then? The white moon, it is reasonable to suppose, was shining on the pyramids, while in Cairo the sensible man devoted himself to his harem. In Delhi it was a few hours before dawn; minarets rising black against a glittering sky; Brahmin and Untouchable asleep. And that evening, in London, Patti was singing in Covent Garden; Sothern was back from America, tugging at his Dundrearies again, just as if there never had been a Mr. Lincoln. And London dined in Soho, amused itself at the stereopticon, pressed seaweed, or read Lost for Love *by the author of* Lady Audley. *And there sat one old man in his dressing gown, alone, in his hand the lever of which Archimedes dreamed, that could move the world; scheming to make things somewhat different for the lover in Egypt, and for the child that tonight would be conceived; for the sleepers in India and their descendants; imagining a proposition by which generations of Englishmen would be committed to adventures in the desert for their own good. And for good or ill, it would come to pass.*

There was a knock at the door. The image in the chair did not move. The door opened: an apologetic cough on the threshold.

The head slowly turned.

"Beg pardon, I feared you were asleep, sir. This just came. Lady Chesterfield sent it round."

"Lady Chesterfield?" The face had come to life. "Let me see it, Phillips."

The butler came forward and put into his master's hands a large pasteboard box, under the string of which was a blank envelope.

"May I bring you anything else, sir?"

"Nothing, thank you. Mr. Hammond is coming in later. I should like you to wait up for him if you will be so kind. And show him in directly."

"Very good, sir."

As the butler withdrew, Disraeli was opening the envelope eagerly, the destinies of nations forgotten. The note was in a large, graceful hand:

My dear D.:

You really must forgive me this, but someone must look after you, and when Selina told me you were bent on going to Lady Norborough's masque as Marco Polo I simply could not bear it! We are such old and good friends, and you do know my feeling for you, so please do let me be your counsellor in this. Marco Polo forsooth! Permit me to say that you have not yet lived down those utterly fantastic waistcoats you once wore—and all those jingling gold chains! For my part—but only for your own dear sake—I should prefer not to see the Premier at the ball at all, but if the rt. hon. gentleman must go, do let him be sensible and go in the costume he finds herewith. For I swear, I will not speak to a single Marco Polo all evening!

Your devoted A.

With a slight smile discernible on his lips, he turned his attention to the box, fussed impatiently with the string, and after some difficulty got the cover off. He took out a frivolous thing of shimmering blue silk and held it out before him in the lamplight—a blue domino. Hmph! He got up, stood blinking at it a moment, and then, holding it against his gaunt frame, over his red silk dressing gown, walked to a small wall mirror, tilted downward, in which he endeavoured by moving backward and forward to survey himself full length. Pallid! Hackneyed! There would be dozens of people in dominos. Always were. And what was the matter with Marco Polo? There was a role with character—with Idea! What could Anne have been thinking of? Ah, of his legs, no doubt! But how could she know what his legs looked like? "I shall have to tell her that she presumes!" he thought, and the tassel on the fez wagged. He returned slowly across the room, sank back into his chair with the domino on his knee, and sighed, knowing that he would wear it to please her. Dear Anne! And there arose before him the vision of her, not as she was now, but as she had looked at another masque ball forty years before, dressed as Cleopatra, the most brilliant figure in a brilliant room! And Lady Londonderry, a sultana, all emeralds and diamonds; and the beautiful Caroline Norton, a Greek—dead now, both dead! And Castlereagh there, and the Duke of Wellington; and himself, the young blade who that year had challenged the great Daniel O'Connell to a duel (but O'Connell had given up duelling after killing a man, and had declined to meet him)—himself as a Spanish cavalier. He had good legs then, Lady Ches might have remembered!

Anne, Countess of Chesterfield, was a widow, two years older than Disraeli, and a grandmother. Her sister, Selina, was the wife of the Earl of Bradford, whom the Prime Minister recently had appointed Master of the Horse; Selina was seventeen years younger than Anne, but she also was a grandmother. And these two were presently the reigning beauties in Disraeli's gallery of women. Theirs was the company he most eagerly sought—one's rather more than the other's; they were his chief confidantes, and he told them everything, even what went on in the Cabinet; they understood, encouraged and admired him; he paid them gallant court—one especially; he wore their gloves invisibly into battle—one's a bit nearer his heart; he wrote ardent letters to both of them—but the Earl of Bradford's wife began to find hers a little embarrassing. For at three score years and ten, the widower Benjamin Disraeli fancied himself in love again! In love with a married woman, with an old friend, with the wife of his Master of the Horse! Was it ridiculous? Selina told him it was, but he replied that unfortunately for him his imagination had not deserted him with his youth, a fact too sad to be ridiculous, and he wrote her somewhat bleakly: "I have lived to know that the twilight of love has its splendour and its richness." Twilight of love? He filled his letters rather with its heat, grandeur, and despair, until she became frightened and threatened to break off with him entirely, and he, begging her not to inflict such a punishment, pledged himself to more restraint, in a sentence whose very rhetoric tended to disguise and mitigate its own terrible, unrepentant metaphor: "I awake from a dream of baffled sympathy, and pour forth my feelings, however precious, from a golden goblet, on the sand."

What was she like, Selina, that she could do this to such a man, do it to the Prime Minister of Britain, mover and shaker of empires, who was called a Sphinx? Once he had described her to herself: "A sweet simplicity, blended with high breeding; an intellect not over-drilled, but lively, acute, and picturesque; a seraphic temper, and a disposition infinitely sympathetic." She was a little above the medium height and of a light complexion, with grey streaks appearing in the dark blonde hair that she wore parted plainly in the middle; she had a prominent nose and hardly any upper lip, a wonderful placement of neck on shoulders, a fine carriage, wore her clothes with an air; and she was full-bodied and brimming with energy—not a beautiful woman, but by all means a likely one. She was gay, coquettish, an indefatigible goer to balls and race meetings, but a good wife and mother for all that, with two handsome daughters to marry off, and she commenced to find the Prime Minister's constant attendance in Belgrave Square neither proper nor convenient, yet— pleasant. As a lady she was compelled to be a little cruel to him, and as a woman she healthily enjoyed it.

Disraeli needed women, he always had and he knew that he always would, if more spiritually now than otherwise. As a young man, on parting with a mistress once, he had undertaken a novel as a catharsis and at the same time a celebration of the passion she had inspired in him, and on one of its quieter philosophical pages had written: "A female friend, amiable, clever, and devoted, is a possession more valuable than parks and palaces; and without such a muse, few men can succeed in life, none be content." He had indeed confessed to Selina recently that to women he owed everything, including the fact that his heart would not grow old along with his body. He needed the inspiration of women, enchanted by them even while performing wonders for their delight—at once the exalter and the exalted; he needed their warmth, their sympathy, their applause, and their solace. The death of his wife two years before had left him desolate.

People had thought Mary Anne a strange wife for Benjamin Disraeli: a scatterbrained magpie of a woman, a prodigy of tactlessness, bad taste, and miseducation, who never could remember which came first, the Greeks or the Romans, and who once had shattered a conversation about Grecian sculpture by exclaiming, "Oh, but you ought to see my Dizzy in his bath!" A Member of Parliament, tactless himself, had remarked to her husband that he must be a man of remarkable qualities to be able to endure her foolish chatter; to which the husband replied, "Not at all. I possess only one quality in which most men are deficient—gratitude." She had in fact been his patroness before she became his wife. Disraeli had been a neophyte in Parliament then, and she the wife of Wyndham Lewis, his elder colleague for Maidstone; she had taken him under her wing, counselled him, gone to a good deal of trouble to see that he moved advantageously in society, praised him to great men, and once had interceded for him with Peel. "She believed in me when men despised me." He had married her seventeen months after Lewis's death. He did not think her foolish. She had a native shrewdness that he respected—and he thought her judgment of men excellent. But gratitude and respect were only a little of what he felt for Mary Anne. She was as warm and tender as she was artless; she was mistress and mother to him; and puzzling though it was, it came to be recognized that their romance was rather beautiful. She had filled his great need.

Tonight, in his loneliness, his heart went out to her. Reaching into the table drawer at his side, he took out a small jewel case and a golden key with which he unlocked it. Inside was the last letter he had ever received from Mary Anne—found among her effects after she was dead:

"My own dear Husband, If I should depart this life before you, leave orders that we may be buried in the same grave at whatever distance you may die from England. And now, God bless you, my kindest, dearest! You have been a perfect husband to me. Be put by my side in the same grave. And now, farewell, my dear Dizzy. Do not live alone, dearest. Someone I earnestly hope you will find as attached to you as your own devoted—Mary Anne."

An artless, repetitious note, setting forth in the familiar hand the sweet spontaneity of the woman between the genteel conventionalisms of the schoolgirl; and out of it he felt her love sweep over him again—remembering that even while she wrote, she had known that she was dying. Known it and kept it from him, and kept from him as long as she could even the fact that she was ill, and suffering—all that time! "If I should depart this life before you"—trying to spare him even now the pain of knowing she had known! How like her that was. Never thinking of herself, always of him: "Farewell," and then,

"Do not live alone." Of him, even dying! His head went back against the cushion. Mary Anne! Mary Anne!

And a little later, as Egypt slept, as India awoke, as the theatres of London stood empty, and Wheeler, perhaps, on a Clerkenwell mattress, was beating up the China Sea, Darcy Hammond found the Prime Minister asleep in his chair, with his mouth fallen open, the tassel of the fez lopping over one cheek, his dead wife's letter slipped to the floor, and on his lap the costume for a masquerade.

13

Next day at No. 10 Downing Street, having discussed Suez, Herzegovina, Russia, the Berlin Dispatches, rates, endowed schools, a proposed Artisans' Dwelling Act, and the Mercantile Marine, the Cabinet rose.

"Now," said Mr. Gathorne Hardy to the Prime Minister as they walked from the room together, "touching on Lieutenant McHatten——"

Disraeli stopped and turned his weary face to him with a pained expression. "You too?" he said.

He scarcely had expected such a small Army matter to reach the attention of the Secretary for War.

The secretary went on: "May I ask what your personal interest is in the young man?"

"I have no personal interest in the young man."

"No? I'm glad to hear it."

"Why?"

"Because it seems the Missus has."

THE MUDLARK

Disraeli looked at him for a moment without speaking. Then he said, "I must hear more of this," and, linking his arm through Hardy's, led him slowly into the Prime Minister's Room. He carefully closed the double doors, walked to his desk, and let himself down behind it, motioning Hardy to a chair in front. He clasped his hands on the desk top, and said: "Well? What is Her Majesty's interest in Lieutenant McIatten?"

"She's the one that wants him transferred."

"Transferred? You mean out of the Guards?"

"What she said was, out of England—as far away from England as possible; and she mentioned India. So India is where he's being sent, and of course that means out of the Guards."

"I see. That seems rather severe."

"It is, rather. Shouldn't think his Army career would be especially promising with a mark like that against him."

"A mark like what?"

"Transfer at Her Majesty's desire, of course. Too bad, but do you see a way out? You know those letters the Missus writes. Three pages this time."

"Three pages on Lieutenant McHatten!" Disraeli said. "Whatever did he do?"

Hardy hesitated. "Officially, I don't know that. That was the one thing she left out, and I take for granted it was no oversight. But I had some discreet inquiries made, in a roundabout way—because, frankly, that memorandum from your office on McHatten made it seem advisable for me to know." Hardy chuckled. "He wants to make off with her Maid of Honour."

Disraeli lifted his brows. "So that's it. Which one? Not Emily Prior?"

"Yes. Lord Stithian's daughter. A great beauty, they say. Know her?"

"I do. And I can quite understand the lieutenant's wanting to make off with her. But what about Emily? Is she—'willin' '?"

— 174 —

"She must be. They say she's being guarded like Helen of Troy."
Hardy laughed. "Her mother thinks it's no sort of match for the girl
at all. And the Queen is furious. So there you are. But I'm a little
surprised you didn't know. Well, at any rate, now you understand
my position."

Disraeli nodded thoughtfully, studying his outstretched hands on
the desk in front of him. He said: "But there happens to be Baron
Rothschild to consider."

"Rothschild?"

"At the same time he agreed to purchase the Canal for us, he
asked us not to send his niece's something-or-other to India."

"Niece's someth—— McHatten?" The Secretary for War pursed
his lips in a silent whistle. "But surely you don't think—— Surely it
wouldn't affect the Loan? Not such a slight thing?"

"No, hardly that. But 'slight' is the very word that occurred to
me. To refuse a man like Rothschild a small favour is often worse
than to refuse him a great one."

"Yes, but of course he'll have to understand."

"Understand? The Queen, Hardy, has not always been as kind to
the Rothschilds as she might have been. The name has been submitted to her for the Birthday List and has not appeared on it. They
know why it hasn't appeared: the Rothschilds always know everything; and as you're aware, their information often has been as useful to us as their money—in the matter of Prince Bismarck's present
reduction of his army, for example. They understand too well already. They've been very patient and very generous. But it's never
wise to pique them, Hardy. And there's another difficulty."

Disraeli leaned back, the hands folded neatly across his waist. "It's
true that I have no personal interest in Lieutenant McHatten, but I
have some personal interest in Baron Rothschild. He's one of my
dearest friends. He has also been my benefactor. He helped me when
I was young, when I was nothing; and he's helped me since. Could I
in conscience explain the circumstances to him so he wouldn't blame

me, and let him blame my Sovereign? I could never explain. But I shouldn't like him to think me either ungracious or ungrateful—least of all, paltry. As you say, it's such a 'slight' thing."

Hardy wore a troubled, stubborn look; one finger was rising and falling a little irritably on his knee. "Well, it's an unpleasant business, I see that. But where's the alternative? Are you asking me to refuse the Queen?"

"Suppose for a moment that I were."

"Well? Are you?"

"One of Her Majesty's closest friends is Lady Margaret Prior—has been ever since they were girls; and Her Majesty is much attached to Emily herself. Now for Her Majesty to assist Lady Margaret in saving Emily from a marriage they both think would be a mistake is a very kind and gracious thing for Her Majesty to do. But Her Majesty has a kind and gracious nature, and I seem to recall that in the same circumstances she also tried to save Georgina Osborne and Gussie Hyssop, but they both went off and left her anyway—and she never forgave them. In fact, whenever any of Her Majesty's women leaves her for some worthless fellow, she is always distressed; and why shouldn't she be? It's a form of treason. A Minister can't let himself be associated in that kind of thing, can he? But do you remember the Great Bedchamber Crisis?" The Prime Minister shook his head. "Hardy, Hardy, I have much to learn from the career of Sir Robert Peel, but I think you may trust me not to emulate him there."

Hardy had no patience with this kind of talk, which seemed to him only the longest way round to the obvious. He said bluntly: "Personally, I never intended to emulate him there. But that settles it, then. McHatten goes to India."

With his hands on his knees, on the point of rising, he looked to the Chief for confirmation of this decision, but the Chief only shook his head again.

"It settles nothing. That is merely our dilemma."

"But—— Yes, I *see* the dilemma. But what else is there to do?"

It was the Chief who rose. He paced meditatively to the grate, his hands behind his back, and did not answer. He asked: "Why doesn't McHatten resign?"

"I don't know. Perhaps he will, since Rothschild can't help him."

"Too late for us; the mischief will have been done." He stared at the fire for a moment. "Is he still at Windsor?"

"No. In barracks here in London. He'll stay there without leave till his ship sails."

"And when will that be?"

"A week—a fortnight; I'm not sure."

"H'm." The Prime Minister turned and paced to the window. He stood there with his back turned. "I wish," he said to his reflection in the pane "that I'd never heard of Lieutenant McHatten."

14

In those days society still was se-
lect, and relatively impregnable. Its perimeters were defended by
fierce old dowagers demanding to see the colour of one's blood
rather than one's money, and within that circle young ladies of the
upper class were shut in yet another circle defended by their moth-
ers. As children they were handed from nursery maids to governesses
in great, grave houses heavy with mahogany and damask, where a
fly buzzing in a red shaft of sunlight from a stained-glass window
could be an object of hellish fascination on a monotonous afternoon.
Emily often killed flies then. And frequently, of course, the little girls
were taken to their parents' country houses, which was a joy;
searched for primroses with their everlasting Miss Babbidges, went
for rides and picnics, and were catechized by beaming vicars who
confronted them on hearthrugs at tea. Once, while her family was at
New Park, in Cheshire, when she was eight, Emily eluded her Miss
Babbidge during an expedition to the village of Appleton Thorn, and

several hours later was found dancing with the children of her father's tenants, round the old thorn tree from which the village takes its name, in the ancient yearly bawming ceremony of pagan memory. She was suitably punished. Emilys were taught never to forget who —whom! they were.

The pillars of their education were the Bible and *The Fairchild Family*; they read *Pilgrim's Progress*, *Alice in Wonderland*, and *Little Women*. They had music teachers and dancing masters and French mam'selles; they learned also to embroider and to paint neat water colours. And as they grew up they read Sir Walter Scott and Mr. Tennyson, *The Ingoldsby Legends* and the *Ladies' Gazette of Fashion*, though on Sundays, of course, *Paradise Lost* was the limit of their frivolity. And on Sundays they went to church and listened to long sermons, and afterwards there were long family prayers. They brushed their hair a hundred strokes before they went to bed.

They played at croquet and archery on the lawn, and at whist in the parlour; they rode; they observed the ritual of the afternoon drive through the Park, always accompanied by Mamma or Miss Babbidge and with a liveried footman on the box, and they went to the selectest of balls in the Assembly Rooms. But they went there, as it were, under armed guard. If a young man danced a quadrille or a Roger de Coverley with a young lady he fancied, he always felt Mamma's sights trained on the back of his neck. And if he called at the young lady's house, she and Mamma received him together in the parlour. Mamma embroidered vigilantly in a corner while her daughter discussed Ruskin or Matthew Arnold with him or went to the piano and played him Tosti. And if the young lady rather fancied the young man too, there was little she was permitted to do about it under the rules, only smile and look demure and hope that Mamma would approve and catch him for her. And if Mamma did, she could hope to spend the greater part of each year in the family way till she was provided with the fashionable number of children, which was the exact number Her Majesty had, which was nine.

This was the life planned for Lord Stithian Prior's daughter, except that while she was still in her cradle, the Queen one day leaned over it and whispered to her mother that the child should become a Maid of Honour. This was to render her education more intense, if not much fuller, the limits of her freedom narrower still.

A Maid of Honour had to be a sort of world's champion young lady, the model of good breeding, of modesty, neatness, punctuality, and industry. She had to know polite French and German almost as well as English and be able to read beautifully aloud in any of the three; she also had to know a little Latin, and to write a legible, *ladylike* hand. She had to be able to play or sing any kind of music at sight, do it well, and if necessary for hours at a time. She had to be a good dancer, and good at games, had to sit a horse well, be accomplished with the needle, and no more accomplished with the pencil than she should be. She had to know how to talk, and when not to. She had to dress with propriety and taste, be amiable and discreet, pious and sensible. She was to deprecate all High Church frills, do her duty to God and to the Queen.

Nature, in her distribution of babies, you must have observed, is not always above whimsy, but she abhors imbalance, and probably left a prim, sedate little tot with some theatrical family after having dropped Emily off at the Priors'.

Emily from the beginning was the healthiest little animal in her set. She was vigorous of limb and exuberant of personality; she was selfish, capricious, headstrong, and impatient. She told extravagant lies. She domineered over other children, and was apt to play Red Indian with too fine a gift for it. She squirmed during prayers. She resisted education, and as for Mr. Fairchild, that avatar of Jehovah in the *Swiss Family Robinson* of her world, she abominated him. She much preferred the bloodthirsty sepoys of that old soldier Jugiez, their gardener at New Park, though sometimes in the midst of a tale of battle she would shriek and cover her ears—just enough so she could still hear. And somehow she had come by a verse of one of

Tom Jugiez's songs, the words of which may not be quoted without violating the Devil's copyright, and one day was discovered by Miss Babbidge tenderly singing her doll to sleep with it. Altogether, she was about as fine a bit of raw material as any parents had a right to expect. But the Priors grew seriously alarmed.

Miss Babbidge, it is to be feared, was a loving and indulgent old soul, but Lady Margaret, that bosom friend of Victoria's, while loving enough too in her own way, was a woman of strong will and no nonsense, and Lord Stithian was an old colonel of the Lancers whose concept of parental duty fell somewhere between the principles of courts-martial and the way to curb a frisky filly. Miss Babbidge, all in her best bonnet and cape one day, kissed Emily tearfully; she was boosted up into the fly, and her box beside her, and was whisked off down the drive never to return. Her place was taken by a tall, beaky woman called Mrs. Hummingly, whose mild voice and melancholy eyes were extenuated by references from the Gladstone family. And the correction of Emily began. But that is a story for another evening.

Firmly, and at times not gently, she was brought to face up to her destiny, and became at last as docile as any other little girl in her uncompromising world. Emily accepted the inevitable, if with reservations. She had put away her tomahawk, cunningly, it is true, meaning to leave it there only until she should grow up to be her own mistress and might come back and play Red Indian as much as she liked; but in time she forgot her tomahawk. And secretly she retreated at first into a world that no one else knew anything about, which was invisible and where she had friends her parents would never have approved and had adventures they would not have believed; but in time all that was forgotten too. As the twig was bent in Victorian England it generally inclined. But the running sap has started the same old impulses in twigs since twigs began. If Emily's secret world faded with her childhood, a new vision shone ahead— one that would have shocked her parents more.

She had grown into a splendid specimen of maidenhood, juiceful and resilient, and though she was rather tall for the ideal of her day, she was of such harmonious parts as to suggest no idea of dimensions. She was already one of the recognized beauties of the realm. She had what is often called the true Celtic face, and in fact is not that at all, but never mind; she was nonetheless a type, and her face with its striking contrast of light and dark reflected something of the violence that must have attended the fusion of bloods in the Celtic invasion of Britain. She had straight hair that was almost black and that she wore in ropes round her exquisite skull; a pale forehead; straight dark brows and long blue-black lashes that heightened the impact of the grey brilliance of her eyes; a straight nose; high cheekbones under which her fair skin faintly bloomed; a rich, tender mouth; a fine chin that she carried slightly upward; a full, graceful throat. She had superb shoulders and arms that by candlelight neither men nor women could look upon with indifference, and she knew both when to display them and when not.

She was not noted for her wit, but that, anyway, did not become young ladies, and she was a brilliant listener: Emily could be charming. She read French and German with ease, spoke them as well as English girls ever can, and had a good grounding in Latin. She had a lively and cultivated speaking voice, sang sweetly; it could be said that she played the piano with a shade too much expression and danced with too much enjoyment, but only a captious hag would have said so. She sewed well and sketched poorly enough to escape censure. She was an admirable horsewoman, and a fearless. She did as her parents told her. She said her prayers. Altogether, Lord and Lady Prior told themselves modestly, she was an exemplary young lady. Secretly she read Ouida.

Her vigour had by no means deserted her, but she kept it in bounds when the occasion demanded, which in her case was saying a good deal, but she was not always able to contain her high spirits, which accounted for the bubbles of laughter that burst singly upon her lovely lips from time to time without much apparent provocation and that had so startled Mr. Gladstone. Aesthetically, this detracted from her somewhat. But she could be as sad as gay, and with no greater outward reason. Not many knew that—partly, no doubt, because she had learned her lessons well and did not inflict her moods upon others. But her sadnesses were of a kind not rare among girls of her age and circumstances, and then they were not really to be enjoyed except in private anyhow. Privily she read Swinburne.

Like many real beauties, she was no more vain of her looks than most women, and not a whit less. It was for their practical romantic value that she appraised them in the glass. But balls always brought out the proof of their beauty, and if at such times she rejoiced in them, her joy at any rate was not so sinful as the emotions of less fortunate maidens who beheld her triumphs from chairs ranged among the potted palms. Some young ladies, indeed, thought her rather a flirt, and blamed her for it or not, according to their natures and their own opportunities; and some young men thought her so too, but they were the bitter ones. It was a fatuous charge. The truth was that when she exulted in her charms, she did so because of the romantic probabilities with which they endowed her as a woman; and what beauty worth her salt could have helped it? There were stirrings in her that she scarcely understood. There was a feeling of abundance that she could scarcely contain; a gallant need, a reckless drive; and there was a delicious apprehension. She was at the season when the very air is aglow and the flowers are full of honey, the sweetest and most painful time, of parted lips and racing pulse, listening, under the wings of the descending swan.

When she went off to Court, her mother said to herself with satisfaction that Emily certainly would get a duke. But Emily did not think of the matter in quite the same terms. She wanted—she knew not what she wanted. But there were some lines of Goethe's that in her heart she recited in flawless German and that could move her close to tears:

Knowest thou the land where the citron grows?
In dark leaves the golden orange glows. . . .

Would she ever find it? She thought she might. Would she know it when she saw it? She was sure she would. But it was with a vague uneasiness that she contemplated the future towards which her whole life had been directed—not that in any definite or even conscious way she criticized it: in her inexperience she would not have been capable of doing so. She did not think of it as narrow, and indeed it needn't be. She thought of it only as fixed, inescapable, final; and perhaps, as she looked forward to the great adventure of her life, she asked herself if afterwards that would be all. Life as it is lived is never enough for Twenty-one. Beyond experience, and only on the threshold of awareness, inevitably she measured it against her own surging capacities, against her troubling intimations of mystery and wonder. And in the meantime the jealous regimen of her life as a royal companion weighed heavily on her—

> *Knowest thou the mountains where the cloud-bridge spreads?*
> *High through the mist the wary mule treads,*
> *The ancient dragons dwell in cavern halls,*
> *The crag drops sheer, and over it the falls.*
> *Knowest thou it all? . . .*

Emily remembered Charles McHatten from her childhood at New Park: the Vicar's son, a tall, weedy boy several years older than she, and almost as dark as a gypsy. The McHattens had been small landed gentry in the Wirrel hundred, but the Vicar had been ruined in the great Cheshire cattle plague of '65. She remembered hearing when Charles went back to school that it was a wonder the family could bear the expense. But she never would have suspected that from his demeanour. He was terribly superior then, treating her at best with the lofty tolerance of his greater age, wisdom, and his nobler sex. It was an attitude that as a child she was wont to disparage with catcalls accompanied by the most telling grimaces and distortions of her posture that she could manage, for which she was whipped once by her frightened father. McHatten developed into a stripling cricket hero of the county. It was predicted he would play for England one day. And then she heard that he had gone into the Army. Three years passed. Emily went on the grand tour with her maiden aunt Adelaide and knew no more of him until a day at Lord's shortly after her return.

"Emily Prior, isn't it?" said a resonant voice.

And turning on her father's arm, she saw him—over six feet, lithe, and with the same intensity in his face as in the voice that had startled her. But not playing for England yet, she saw by his clothes: they looked as smart and finely made as any that ever came out of Savile Row, and the grey colour went well with his face, which looked darker than ever. He said he was in the Grenadier Guards. Fancy that, she said—perhaps they'd be at Windsor together one of these days; and she told him she was soon to be a Maid of Honour. Was she! That was a piece of luck; he was at Windsor already; they'd have some times when she came; he'd take her riding in the Park; and the river, as she knew, was fine just there. She remembered that he had rowed for his school: he had the look of tensile strength that the rower has, and with it gave an impression of pitched energies and of a temperament tinctured with quicksilver. But he seemed a very earnest young man, and he looked at Emily very earnestly indeed. And all the time she was thinking how pleasant it was that they had met again now—because now she was beautiful. There was a pleasure in that with a man who had looked down his nose at one when one had been an ugly little girl; and sinful or not, she couldn't help hoping afterwards that he had been properly dazzled.

But dozens of young men were dazzled by Emily Prior, and she gave this one not another thought until months later, when he turned up at a ball at the Wetherells' in Park Lane. She saw him standing alone by the wall, staring into the midst of the dancers and looking rather out of it. She was not surprised to see him out of it in a house like the Wetherells', but she was a little surprised to see him there at all, though of course he was in the Guards now and she supposed he must be a friend of Dicky's; and being the sort of girl she was, she broke through the ring of her admirers to go and greet him.

"Charles! How nice to see you! Whatever is the matter? Have you lost your partner?"

"No!"—a bit roughly, she thought, and without seeming at all dazzled. "Isn't your mother here?"

"Yes! Come and speak to her. She'll be so——"

"Thank you; I won't trouble her just yet." His dark young face was a shade darker than it should have been, and he was looking at her angrily. "I hardly thought she could be here."

"Well?" she said, taken aback.

"You might—you might at least——"

"What?"

"Not make a spectacle of yourself!"

All her breath went out in a single exclamation of shock and outrage: "Oh!" The blood rushed into her cheeks, and whirling in a sudden crash of silk, she left him. She swept round the room, through the door to the terrace, back again, looking for her father. What a beastly thing to have said! What incredible presumption! And what had she done—what? Could she help it if—— She stopped suddenly, wondering if anyone else could have thought the same as he. Oh no, surely—no! But when she found Lord Stithian, she did not tell him. That would not have helped matters. And lying in bed that night, her cheeks burned again with the shame of it. She stared into the dark, reviewing her behaviour, trying to see herself as he and others had seen her; and there were hot tears in her eyes.

Some things were hard for a girl like Emily to understand. If it had crossed her mind that he was jealous, she would not have entertained the notion—Emily was not that sure of herself. But on the contrary, she thought that he disliked her; and youth cannot bear to be disliked by anyone. Along with her humiliation and anger, Emily was hurt. He didn't like her. Why? Did she seem too frivolous, not sincere enough? It was a question that sometimes worried Emily. And there was another thing. She felt that she had not dealt very well with that small crisis. She had shown her feelings, had bared her wound to him, when what the situation had called for was—savoirfaire. Then she thought what she might have said, how she might have laughed; and, in her mind, sailed laughing from the field, leaving him crushed by the consequences of his own uncouthness, or, as Emily put it to herself, hoist by his own petard.

Two weeks later, having begun her first wait as a Maid of Honour, she was riding one early morning in Windsor Park, riding one of Her Majesty's own spirited greys decorously sidesaddle in a flowing black habit ordered especially for these decorous paths—it was quite suitable to them, she thought, without being unflattering to herself—when she heard hoofs beating up behind her. She turned, expecting to see her groom coming alongside, and saw instead Lieutenant McHatten again, in riding clothes, on a tall bay.

He reined the animal into pace with hers, with a slightly sardonic "May I?"

Emily did not cut him dead. She looked at him with what he was intended to take for amusement, and did. All the grimness he had mustered for the ordeal of apologizing without humbling himself melted away in a sense of being made a little absurd. But fixing his gaze straight between his horse's ears, he said: "I suppose you thought me rude the other evening."

"I thought you—crude," she said maliciously.

He flushed. "I suppose I deserve that. I suppose I was crude. But I suppose I felt—responsible."

"You?"—with delectable incredulity that made him flush a little deeper. "Why?"

He admitted uncomfortably: "I don't know."

A deer bolted across the green meadow in front of them and vanished with a crash into Windsor Forest. Only the horses mentioned it to each other.

Emily began to be pleased with herself, conscious that this time she had definitely the upper hand. And perceiving in him the almost sullen contrition of a small boy, she began to be amused in fact. She did not wish to be cruel, but she was determined to put him in his place, so that his prodigious male vanity should not lead him any further into presumption. And without having the thought concretely before her, she knew that here was a practical exercise in the woman's business of managing men: she felt that she was learning how.

"Really," she protested. "Were you looking on me as a child?"

"No! As a woman."

Emily liked the way he had said that. But she was glad he was not looking at her. It made her conscious of her body.

She gave a gay laugh, from pleasure and a sense of power. "Yet you said you felt 'responsible.' Surely you don't think me"—she used a reckless word—"giddy?"

McHatten knew the word that the supporters of her rivals used against her, the judgment attributed to Mr. Gladstone, and in the arrogant way she used it following upon that laugh he inferred a mockery of himself, almost a contempt. McHatten did not enjoy being trifled with. He set his jaw. "Are you sensitive about that?"

He had not merely avoided a polite disclaimer, but he had brought the Gladstone charge into the open and counter-challenged her with that: it was as if he had flung it in her face. And it appeared that Emily was sensitive about that. She reined up her horse on the instant, fully as angry as she had been at the Wetherells'. "You— Whig!" she said. It was a word without political reality in that day, but only a suffragette would have cared about that—besides, in old Tory families it was still a pretty strong epithet; and spurring ahead, she left him at a gallop. It was clear that he was not to follow, but he had no intention of following. He thought she had said "pig."

Whenever she saw him after that, she ignored him. But she noticed that he equally ignored her. She did not know how many times he waited for her near that same path in the Park, nor that whenever she appeared only his pride kept him from riding out to overtake her.

And that was the extent of McHatten's acquaintance with the maiden whose hopeless lover he took himself to be. It has happened on less at his age.

McHatten sank into the frame of mind in which we found him toasting India that evening in Farmer George's wine. The Honourable Emily Prior, daughter of a viscount and granddaughter of an earl! Folly to think of her. He thought of her hair, her lips, her eyes, her arms, her white throat. (Giddy? The fox that said the grapes were sour lied in his teeth, but at least he did not becloud the issue.) He thought with bitter pride of that remote connexion of his—at least his aunt Lucy always claimed him as a connexion—that Colonel Careless who had held the fugitive King Charles sleeping in his arms in an oak tree while Cromwell's soldiers searched the wood for him: might not Charles McHatten therefore hold a mere viscount's daughter in his arms? Twice in his wretchedness he very nearly attempted to speak to her again—once in the nave of St. George's, and once meeting her face to face in the Great Courtyard. Each time she quickly turned her back on him, and then he (though she could not know it) turned his upon her. And each time that they pointedly ignored each other, the gulf between them was widening. Useless to accost her now. And why attempt it anyway? The Vicar's son! She would laugh at him for a skipjack, a grovelling fortune hunter. Not for him, that tender grape. For him rather some country squire's daughter, plump and stolid and smelling of the hedgerows. Or some frock-coated City man's, whose charms were to be weighed with her dowry.

It would have surprised him to know that he had attracted her. But it would have hurt him to know just how. With his dark good looks and his intensity, she had thought him a romantic figure; but then a gamekeeper once had impressed her in much the same way.

And McHatten, with his fierce restraint, his scowls, his tactlessness, and the deep vibrancy of his voice, generated an atmosphere of turbulence and compression, and she was a little afraid of him. Altogether an odd sort to set up for a young English gentleman. She thought of him as "tramontane." It could have applied to a Corsican bandit.

Suddenly Emily had an experience that must have been unique for a Maid of Honour in Victoria's Court. Late one evening, having left the Queen cosily retired for the night, she went as usual (and according to the rules) straight to her room, but as she pushed the door shut behind her she saw that this time she was not alone. He stood in full uniform, somewhat melodramatically, in the centre of the floor, his figure sharply outlined by the moonlight streaming in through the window behind him, and although his face was in blackness she knew at once who it was. She caught her breath.

He said: "Scream, if you want to."

But until driven to it, a young lady thinking of her reputation seldom does. The rage in Emily's throat burst forth in a savage whisper: *"How dare you come here!"*

A good question, though indeed to his superiors an almost equally interesting one might have been *how* had he come here; for, officer of the guard or not, had it been known that he was anywhere in this part of the castle, let alone in the room of one of the Queen's Maids, it would have caused nearly as much consternation as if he'd been Wheeler.

"You have nothing to fear," he said in a low voice, nobly.

Just through the door on the right was the sitting room that Emily shared with the other Maid of Honour, Harriet Villing; beyond that was Harriet's bedroom, and just down the corridor were the apartments of Lady Kuno, the Lady in Waiting and ex-officio Mother of the Maids.

"Leave at once!" Emily hissed at him across the floor.

"When I've said what I've come to say."

"*Now! This instant!*" She pointed straight-armed at the door.
He did not move.

"*Leave, I say!* . . . *Do you hear?* . . . *Get out!*"

McHatten turned his back.

She sprang across the room and faced him, her arms rigidly at her sides, hands clenched, her lovely mouth distorted with virulence. "*My father would kill you for this!*"

He towered over her. The moon seemed to have washed all the colour out of his face, and all the youth: it looked sallow and strained, almost haggard; and for the first time she was afraid of him. She saw his precocious lip curl.

"Yes, your father would kill me. And if you call the guard, I think I could be shot. Or sent to prison. Stripped of this uniform. Disgraced. And my father too." The words shot out at her in a fusillade, each one like a pellet. "I know. And I came. But you're not the one who's in danger. Did you think I came for that—sneaking in here like a coward? No. That wasn't the way I came. That's not the way I want you."

Emily fell back a step.

"Yes!" he said. His voice was a rushing force; she could feel it. "I came to declare myself—now—this way—when you have it in your power to destroy me. And I shan't touch you. Do you think that's nothing? A poor country vicar's son! A nobody! Was that what you thought? But you see what I am; you see what risk I take for you. My life—my honour—everything. Only to tell you. Only to let you see. No, this is not nothing. It's something to be wanted like this, even by the Vicar's son."

And they faced each other in the moonlight, and the moment was also a force, a thing they could feel, a thing created out of energy, like a leaping current between two poles. Emily's hand had gone to her throat; her eyes were bewildered. They stood taut, looking at each other. Then McHatten moved; it was like a withdrawal. The current broke.

He said quietly: "Will you call the guard now?"

"How—how did you find my room?"

"There is a plan of the castle in the Guard House."

"In the Guard House? But—but then anyone—might—come here."

"If another man came," McHatten said, "I would kill him."

All at once the tautness left her, she seemed to wilt; her head drooped forward and she covered her face with her hands. He looked at her in astonishment. He saw her shoulders tremble and heard her sob.

"Go—go now. . . . Please. . . ."

McHatten crossed the room and went out without a word. The door closed soundlessly behind him.

Then the little gold clock on her night table absurdly tinkled.

It was the night after the arrest of Wheeler.

When McHatten reached his billet he was shivering. His underclothes were cold with sweat. He slept that night from exhaustion. But the next night he slept scarcely at all.

In reaction from his rash act, he was more miserable than before, tortured by a cruelly clear view of the ludicrousness of what he had done, and of the tremendous gravity of it; by an exaggerated idea of the lowness of his station and the highness of hers; by a growing conviction that she would never forgive him. And his mind kept reverting to the picture of her crying, to the sound of her sobs. The effect upon her appalled him.

But even now he did not see the selfishness of what he had done. Yet he had clearly thought out the deed beforehand. He had rationally approved of it, not barrenly for its desperate grandeur, but practically, as a way of enforcing her serious attention and of showing her at once his sincerity and his mettle; as a deed in keeping with the policy upon which he was determined, which was to overcome by bold strokes the handicaps he had been born with and to achieve by force of demand the pre-eminence he thought he deserved. Now the deed appeared to him the greatest piece of folly of his life. And yet he was resolved to brave it through—if he could. For the policy remained. It was on the whole a muddled and uncomfortable position for a young man to be in. And with it, his position in the Guards since Wheeler had turned up was unhappier than it had been before.

He ranged the Park on horseback, attended the daily services in St. George's, kept popping in and out of the Library until Mr. Huish began to wonder at his sudden and so fitful interest, visited the garden of the Round Tower Moat where ladies were wont to take the air, the terraces, slunk about the Grand Corridor, where again he had no right to be—in vain. He began to fear that Emily had left the castle. And all his other fears gnawed at him.

Emily was greatly shaken. She avoided the decorous paths of Windsor Park, she avoided St. George's; she confined herself to the Royal Apartments, went down corridors quickly, and at night not only locked her door but put a chair against it to give warning of intrusion; she had another chair sent up and put it under the knob of the door to the sitting room. The Queen one morning noticed that her eyes were red and inquired if she had been crying; Emily denied it, and really she hadn't; she was emotionally upset and had been sleeping badly. It was not that she lacked courage, but that her courage was overwhelmed. Her feelings would not resolve themselves, and in that state she had no will. This thing that had happened to her was in tumultuous conflict with everything she had been taught. And McHatten was a wild man. Who else would have done what he had done? What might he not do next?

One midnight a week after his visit to her room she came awake with a start; she was sitting taut upright in the bed. Something had happened—what? She was in terror, all her senses suddenly alert. There was no moon; the room was in blackness. She listened, hearing nothing but the beating of her own heart and the idiotic obbligato of the clock. Then a door opening, feet shuffling rapidly across the floor—the floor of the sitting room! Urgent knocking at the door.

"Emily! Emily! Are you all right, Emily?"

"Oh! Harriet! Hattie! is that you?"

"Yes. Are you all right?"

"Yes; yes, I think so. Wait a moment."

Emily leapt out of bed, tore the chair away from the door, and admitted her colleague, Miss Hattie Villing, a small, blonde, round-blue-eyed young lady in a long white flannel nightgown almost exactly like Emily's own.

"Emily! What's the matter?"

"Matter? I—I don't know."

"You screamed!"

"I?"

"Yes; I heard you! I was reading in bed. I'm sure it must have been you. What is it? You look so—funny."

Emily did look distraught; her eyes were still a little wild, her loose black hair was tumbled. "Do I? It's nothing. I . . . Did I really scream? I suppose I must have been dreaming. Something horrid. Isn't that silly? I'm awfully sorry."

Now there were sounds in the corridor. There was a knock on the outer door of the sitting room; it opened and in came Lady Kuno, saying to someone behind her: "Just wait, please. I'll call you if you're needed." She sailed in, a commanding woman in a long quilted robe, her face shining greasily.

"Well! What is it, my dears? Was it one of you that cried out like that?"

"It was Emily," Hattie said. "She had the nightmare, Lady Kuno."

"Oh. Poor dear." Lady Kuno took Emily's hands in hers and looked at her.

"I'm so sorry, Lady Kuno. I'm very much ashamed."

"Nonsense. It must have been a very bad dream. What could it have been?"

"I don't know. I can't even remember. But it must have been that
—a dream."

"And you don't remember it? That's strange, Emily."

"Yes—yes, isn't it? Perhaps I'll remember it tomorrow."

Lady Kuno, a widow for twenty years, looked into Emily's eyes
as if she would probe through them into her soul. "Very strange,"
she said. She put her hand on Emily's forehead and felt that it was
hot. "Are you ill, dear?"

"Oh no. I'm sure I have no fever. It was just the nightmare."

"You could have had a pain," Hattie suggested. "Did you have a
pain here?" And she clutched her side.

"No. Just the nightmare," Emily said, embarrassed. Then she saw
with a new fright that Lady Kuno was staring perplexedly at the
chair against the door to the corridor. "Oh, the chair!" she said. "I
always do that, you see. I—I'm really an awful coward, I suppose."

"Such a silly girl," said Lady Kuno. "Really, Emily, no one is
going to harm us here. In Windsor Castle?"

"I know. Awfully silly of me."

"Of course it is," agreed Lady Kuno, who always put a chair
against her door. "Would you like to come and stay the rest of the
night with me, Emily?"

"Oh no. No, thank you, Lady Kuno. I'm quite all right now. But
it's so sweet of you to ask me."

"Very well, then. Go to bed, both of you. Good night."

"Good night, Lady Kuno," they chorused, and standing in their
long folds of flannel, their hair down their backs, the two Maids
dropped their curtsies.

Lady Kuno sailed out.

"Good night, Emily," Hattie said doubtfully.

"Good night, Hattie. Thank you so much."

"Emily?"

"Yes?"

"Would you like to come and sleep with me tonight?"
"Oh yes, Hattie! Yes!" And Emily rushed to get her pillow.

It was Emily's duty to present herself in the Private Sitting Room
each morning at eleven. But the next morning she was summoned
there at ten. She was surprised to find her mother there with the
Queen.

Victoria was enthroned in her erect manner in the centre of the
many-cushioned couch, in a black dress and shawl, a white tulle veil
falling from her head to her shoulders, looking like a plump mother
owl. Lady Margaret Prior, a tall, rawboned woman, sat straight-
backed on a chair on the Queen's right, her mouth set in a grim
line; and quite as rigidly on a chair on the royal left sat Lady Kuno.

They gazed at Emily like the Three Fates.

"Come and sit here by me," Victoria directed her, indicating a
footstool in front of the couch.

"Very well, Ma'am," Emily said, and wonderingly did as she had
been told.

"Your mother," Victoria informed her, "has asked us to let her
take you home."

"Home? . . . Now? But my wait isn't finished till next week."

"I know, and I certainly should not like to let her take you away
from me, Emmy. But your mother has brought us some distressing
news. Most distressing. It concerns this Lieutenant McHatten."

"Lieutenant McHatten!" A red tide swept up Emily's neck and
covered her face. "But Mamma—Your Majesty——" Her frightened eyes turned from one to the other. "I don't understand. . . ."

From under the shawl ends on her lap Victoria withdrew one
dimpled hand that held the open pages of a letter. "He has written
this to your father," she said, holding the letter out; and Emily
seized it.

"Excuse me, Ma'am," she said.

"Read it, child."

Emily read:

MY DEAR LORD STITHIAN:

You will wonder at my speaking of this matter in a letter. I have this day asked leave from my Regiment in order to wait upon you in Cheshire. It has been denied for the present, but you may be sure, sir, that when it is granted I will go and speak to you in person. Until then I can take no other means of informing you of my feeling towards your daughter, Miss Emily Prior, and asking your consent——

Emily looked up, wild-eyed. "Oh! He had no right. Truthfully, Mamma—Your Majesty—I have given him no right! Oh, I don't know what to say. . . ."

Victoria turned to Lady Margaret and nodded. "There! You see? Emily is not such a little goose. This is all his doing."

"I hope so, Ma'am," Lady Margaret said without conviction.

"Of course it is! Do you wish to speak to her, Margaret? Do, by all means. This is no time to stand upon etiquette."

"By your leave, Ma'am," said Lady Margaret, and fixed her daughter with a matriarchal eye. "Have you given this man any encouragement?"

"No, Mamma!"

"Has he asked you for his hand?"

"No!"

"He hasn't asked you? But surely you knew he was thinking of you in that way?"

"I—I suppose I knew."

"How? Has he made any advances?"

Emily was painfully embarrassed by all this, and resentful; resentful of McHatten's presumption, but also of being subjected to what she considered a public inquiry into the matter, here before the Queen.

"Has he?" her mother insisted.

She dropped her eyes. "He said he w-wanted me."

"Wanted you! In marriage?"

"Of course! He meant that. Though he didn't just say it that way."

"Then how did he say it?"

Emily hesitated. She put her hand to her forehead. "Oh, Mamma! Don't ask me that, please! He's very honourable, if that's what you mean."

"But," stipulated Victoria, "you have given him no encouragement?"

"No, Your Majesty! I hardly think I could have."

"And you would never dream of accepting such a man, would you?"

"No. Oh, I don't think so. I don't know him very well." Emily had never been an intimately confidential daughter, and though she had always been a dutiful one, ever submissive to her mother's authority, she felt that this was a field into which no one had any business prying—not her mother, and certainly not the Queen. "Oh, Your Majesty—and Mamma—don't ask me any more, please! I really don't know what to say."

The three ladies exchanged glances.

"But we are concerned for you, child," the Queen told her. (Child! She was not a child.) "And think of your dear mamma, how worried she must be. Now tell us, what is he like, this impudent fellow?"

"He's not really impudent, Ma'am. I don't know; what shall I tell you?"

"Is he," the Queen asked, "a handsome young man?"

"Well, yes, I suppose so. In a dark way. Everyone thinks he is. I think so, rather. Papa's seen him. But that's nothing. He had no right doing this. He's—he's impetuous, that's all."

"Impetuous!" said Lady Margaret.

And Lady Kuno echoed: "All!"

"It's just his way; his nature, I think. He's very—tramontane. But

THE MUDLARK

I've said I haven't encouraged him. You needn't be alarmed. Please, Mamma. We mustn't bother Her Majesty with such things."

"Tut, tut," Victoria said. "It's my duty to be concerned about the welfare of my little Maids. And your mamma and I are very old friends, my dear. And I do hope you are not serious about this foolish young lieutenant, because I am going to forbid you to see him any more."

"Forbid, Your Majesty?" Emily said. "But I've told you——"

"Never mind. Your mother knows what's best for you, Emily, and so do I. We both have your welfare at heart. You come of a fine family, and you are also a very pretty young lady. I shouldn't be surprised if Lieutenant McHatten weren't the only young man who had lost his head over you. But remember that you must keep your own. Keep it until the *proper* young man comes along, child, and then one day you will make a fine marriage and live happily ever after. And frankly, my dear, in your case, I should forbid any marriage that was not absolutely to the best advantage, as I know Lady Margaret would wish me to do."

"Forbid?" said Emily again, and leaped up. "But Your Majesty, that's not fair!"

Victoria stared at her coldly.

"Emily!" said her mother.

"Emily is upset," Victoria said, "I fear."

"That's no excuse," said Lady Margaret.

Emily said: "I beg Your Majesty's pardon."

Her Majesty inclined her head.

"My daughter is not herself, Ma'am," said Lady Margaret. "She doesn't look very well either, I must say. I noticed that directly she came in. I really should like to take her home."

"We shall see," the Queen said.

"Last night," volunteered Lady Kuno, "she had the nightmare."

"It was nothing, Ma'am," Emily assured the Queen.

"She screamed," said Lady Kuno. "In the middle of the night."

"Screamed?" said the Queen.

"Yes, Ma'am. She said she'd had a dream. But then she couldn't remember what it was. Or do you remember now, Emily?"

"No," Emily said almost violently, her hands clenched in front of her. "I don't remember. It was just a dream. What does it matter? I don't remember."

There was a pause. The ladies looked at her gravely. It was obvious to them that Emily was beside herself.

"Well," said the Queen, and turned to Lady Margaret. "You needn't worry, Margaret. I'm sure Emily is not, as I have said, a goose. She is going to be sensible. And we will do all in our power to help her. We will see that this Lieutenant McHatten is removed, Margaret. Yes. He shall certainly be sent away."

"Sent away?" Emily said. "Where?"

"Never you mind, my dear. He is not the sort of young man for you. But don't you worry. He will merely be transferred to some other station. Away from England, I think; that will be safest, and so much pleasanter for everyone—himself included; for we must spare his feelings too, Emily. He need never know the reason. There. You see how simple it is?"

"No!" Emily burst out. "That's not fair either! It's not fair to him! You mustn't do such a thing to him on my account!"

Again they stared at her. Her mother blushed furiously and snapped again: "Emily!"

"Well, it *isn't* fair! Oh, Your Majesty, I am not being rude; I don't mean to be rude. I am Your Majesty's loyal subject, but as that Mr. Greville says—yes, that scribbling old gossip whom we all so despise; as he says, it's the misfortune of princes never to hear the language of truth; it's true, and I will speak out—I will! Mr. Mc-Hatten may wish to marry me, but that is not a crime! Is he to be punished for asking Papa? And by what right? This is not the Middle Ages. And Your Majesty is not an absolute monarch. No, Your Majesty is not! And yet you speak of forbidding any marriage of mine that you do not approve, Ma'am! By what right? I am a loyal subject of my Queen, but I am a freeborn English girl! I will marry as I wish, and not as I am told! I will make my own life! And —and again," said Emily, standing very straight before the couch and shaking with emotion, "I beg Your Majesty's pardon!"

Whether anyone else ever spoke to Victoria in such a fashion is not apparent from the record, but it is extremely doubtful. One of the sons of the Duke of Abercorn, however, being presented to her, had the reckless courage to stand on his head, a deed for which he was admired all his life, though he had taken the advantage of being a child at the time.

Except for the one scandalized pronunciation of her name by Lady Margaret, none of the three ladies had made any effort to stop her. They were about equally stunned. And in the dead silence that followed as their dilated eyes contracted and their mouths arranged themselves in creases of doom, the full sense of what she had done nearly overcame Emily. Her face was white. Her mother's was flaming, but Lady Margaret was having some difficulty with her vocal cords. Victoria's face was almost as purple as George the Fourth's.

The Queen commanded: "Go to your room, miss! Go to your room and pray God to forgive you! Go to your room and remain there until you are sent for!"

Emily fled. She fled to the door, fumbling in her pocket for her handkerchief; at the door turned to make a hasty curtsy, and fled into the corridor. She almost ran, the handkerchief pressed against her mouth, and in the corridor passed Mr. Brown, leaving him agape; turned a corner—and beheld coming towards her the guilty, the ubiquitous Lieutenant McHatten, flagrantly off limits again. She stopped. He stopped, taken aback as much as she, lifted a hand towards her as if begging her to wait.

"Emily!"

She did not wait, but to his astonishment was hurrying to meet him.

"Charles! Charles, they're going to——"

"Emily! What is it?"

She must not tell him! Her training throttled the impulse. The Queen was going to banish him from England, and she could not tell him. "Oh, Charles, you shouldn't have! You shouldn't!" And she held out his letter still clutched in one hand.

"What! How did you get that? But I would have told you, Emily. I couldn't find you. I thought you'd left Windsor. Why are you crying? What's happened to you?"

"My mother has come to take me home!"

"Home!"

She read the thought in his eyes. "Oh no; no, I didn't tell her, I haven't told her anything. It was your letter. Don't you see? She never would consent. Oh, I'm sorry, Charles."

"Never consent," he repeated heavily. "And you, Emily? You would never consent either. Would you, Emily?"

"I don't know, Charles; I don't know. What does it matter now? It's all to be arranged. It isn't going to matter what I want. It isn't even going to matter!"

"Not going to matter? If you should want me, Emily—if you should want me, it would matter. I'd make it matter. But everything I've done has been wrong. I know, I know. But if I gave you time; perhaps if I gave you time, Emily?"

"No, no; I don't know, I don't know, Charles. How can I know? What's the difference!" She pressed her face into the handkerchief. "What's the difference!"

He was silent, at a loss before her trembling emotion. He raised his hand as if to touch her shoulder, as if to comfort her, but he did not dare. He wanted too much to take her in his arms.

"I love you, Emily. That's the difference. And if you should want me, it would make all the difference. If you should want me, Emily! And if you should, would it be such a sacrifice?"

She did not answer.

"You can't marry a great name or a great fortune," he said gently; "not really. You can only marry a man. But most of the men who made the great names and fortunes of England are dead, you know. I can make both for myself—for you; and I will. I swear to you that I will. But it's you I want, you more than all else, you to love, and to love me. Don't let your mother make the choice. Don't let her tell you I haven't the right because I have no name and no fortune. . . . Emily! Do you remember the oak sprigs we used to gather in Cheshire? Tell them there was another poor soldier once who held a king in his arms, held him sleeping in Boscobel Oak while the Roundheads searched the wood for him, and every year since then children have gathered sprigs of English oak in commemoration of it, Emily! Emily, do you remember? Do you remember the oaks sprigs of Cheshire? Look at me, Emily."

Gently he drew her hands away from her face and turned it up to him. Her grey eyes were full of tears, and her lip quivered, and in a rush of feeling suddenly he did have her in his arms. For the merest instant he felt the softness of her, the warmth of her breasts, the fragrance of her hair, her breath upon his lips; and then she stiffened and tried to pull away.

"Don't! No, Charles, please; please. . . ."

He could not have let her go then; his arms tightened; he pressed her to him; she turned her face away; his lips crushed into the flesh of her throat. All at once the vitality seemed to go out of her; she was without stiffening, passive, almost inert; and he drew back, shocked, relaxing his arms.

"Emily!"

Great globes of water stood in her eyes. "It's all right, Charles; but you mustn't, please. You must give me time. You must—give me time. . . ."

And then she was hurrying down the corridor away from him.

Next day McHatten was ordered to London. He had to go without seeing her. He did not know then that it was a transfer, and even when two days later he learned that it was, and that he was to be sent to India, he did not guess the reason. He thought it was because of Wheeler. With all his quick sensitivity to his position, it never occurred to him that the Queen of England knew of his existence. But desperately he asked for the first time in his life, through his sister, the powerful assistance of the Rothschilds.

Emily's mother did not take her home after all. The Queen decreed that until McHatten was safely out of the way Emily would be better off at Windsor; and so she stayed on, beyond her time, doing her duty as a Maid, in all but name a prisoner. She knew that McHatten had gone; else he would have come to see her; she knew that he had not been given the opportunity. She felt very sorry for him, and resentful of the Queen; but the training was strong in her and she had apologized to Her Majesty for her outburst, though she had done so without conviction in her voice; and Victoria in such a matter was graciously pleased to be lenient.

"You mustn't take things so hard, my child. We know what is best for you; you will see. But sometimes, I know, it is very hard to be young, dear. Yes, and I know you think I am only a meddlesome old woman and do not understand; but I do. And now I am going to tell you something. There was a time when I too thought I was in love with a young officer. Yes, Emily, I thought I must be very much in love. But I was a queen, you see, and not allowed to be in love with a young officer. I was not allowed to love anyone but a prince. And I thought that nowhere in the world could there be a prince so fine and handsome as that young officer. . . . Dear me, I wonder what ever became of him. . . . And I was very sad, Emily. But then"— Victoria spread her hands, as if to say, There it was!—"then one day I met my cousin Albert. And I forgot that young officer. I knew at once that it was Prince Albert I loved. Such a handsome man he was, my dear, and so distinguished! And so good, so *very* good. And——"

But Victoria could not go on. She returned to her sewing. "You will see," she said. "You will see."

Were they right, after all? Was it true, as she had heard, that when the right man came along, one knew at once—instantly—like that? That was what she had always hoped it would be like. And was it true, as her mother said (though it sounded so horribly snobbish!), that one ought never marry except in "one's own sphere"? Emily had heard tales about some who had done otherwise. But if she did that, what then? That alone was not happiness. And if she did as she was told, if she married as she was told—— But she couldn't do that, she wouldn't; not just to be doing as she was told; not unless she were truly in love! Truly, truly. But would she ever be, so truly that there couldn't possibly be a mistake? And how would she know?

Lying in bed, with the moon once more streaming into her room, almost unconsciously she touched with one finger the spot on her throat where McHatten's lips had been; and her eyes glistened.

Knowest thou the house? . . .

> (. . . WHITE PILLARS HOLD THE BEAMS,
> THE CHAMBER SHIMMERS AND THE HALLWAY GLEAMS,
> AND MARBLE FIGURES STAND AND LOOK AT ME.
> O MY POOR CHILD, WHAT HAVE THEY DONE TO THEE?)

15

Busher Ash was that common garden paradox, the logical but unromantic man. In all his wide experience with criminals it had been enough, and that was why he had no patience with journalists, whom he considered to be just the opposite. His professional attitude was a little cynical, as policemen's generally are, their experience inclining them that way. He knew the types, ways, and tracks of the underworld as a trapper knows those of the forest; he listed robbery, love, drink, and revenge, in that order, as the chief motives for crime, and if you had told him that drink was not a motive he would have stared you down. It would have been equally naïve of you to argue that mudlarks were not a type, a criminal type. He had them on his list, just under costermongers.

Mudlarks were without visible means, which was reason enough to distrust them. They were starvelings and scavangers. They were foot-loose, filthy, and sly as rats. The river police would tell you that when they saw their chance they would sweep a coal barge, climb up the mooring lines of ships, and steal anything they could carry, and that the young ones would grow up to be smugglers or river pirates. But the young ones often ran in thieving gangs ashore, many became sawney-hunters, dead-lurkers, till-friskers, area-sneaks, and shallow coves, or, with their quickness and their animal cunning, made apt pupils for cracksmen, prop-nailers, thimble-riggers, and charley-pitchers. Sometimes Ash thought he ought to list them above costermongers.

He did not for a moment doubt that Wheeler was potentially a dangerous character, and was prepared to believe that he was one already. By having broken into "and entered" the castle, he was in the inspector's eyes certainly a criminal, and a mighty bold one at that. It was possible that he was some cracksman's devil—it was possible; but the inspector was too old a bird to think so for long. After his second interview with Wheeler, he came in the main to believe him—to believe, at least, that he had played a lone hand, for he could not believe that robbery had not been the motive. What puzzled him was the same thing that has puzzled Hodge since, the great public fuss. He saw the case in its proper perspective, as a remarkable trifle and nothing more. He so described it to Commissioner Kew, adding:

"But I must say, Sir Joseph, it does have all London agog, if you've noticed. These newspapers have got it all wrong, you know, and the public's excited. I don't like that. Now I'd like your permission to make a statement—or better yet, if I may suggest, sir, perhaps you'd better make one yourself."

Ash was a lover of order. That was why he voted with the Conservatives, who, however, were not nearly Conservative enough for him, and in fact he doubted their wisdom in permitting people to vote at all. He was too coldly rational to be much of a snob, but at the same time he was too cynical to trust the country to everybody. It was a natural view in a guardian of the public peace who had won his spurs in Houndsditch and fought in the riot squads of the fifties. He knew the mob and feared it. And in the present case he saw cause for alarm.

For one thing, the republicans (regarded by Ash in much the same way as the modern policeman regards Communists) had seized upon it to inflame the voters, declaring it to be glaring evidence of mismanagement in the Royal Household, and on this slender peg they were hanging new tirades against the expenditure of public funds to support a leftover Royal Family.

But at the same time a different interpretation was turning the case against these agitators. The pubs were ablaze with rumours that at the back of it was a plot to assassinate the Queen. There was said to be a whole gang in the offing—by some said to be Fenian, by some Popish, by others republican; a gang which, according to one cloudy version, had sent Wheeler into the castle with some false keys. And the innate loyalty of Britons to the Crown was beginning to get the better of them again.

A Hyde Park orator, delivering his customary harangue against the Monarchy, had been torn from his box by the crowd, which yesterday had only entered into academic dispute with him or derisively cheered him on. Irishmen had been stoned in the streets of Liverpool for the first time in almost seven years. A man had been arrested in front of No. 10 Downing Street with a placard demanding "WAR ON THE POPE." And not since the death of Albert had so much sympathy gone out to Victoria. Everybody was demanding a public inquiry, and everybody wanted Wheeler's head.

Commissioner Kew was as much alive to these danger signs as Ash was, but instead of being relieved when Ash told him the case was a trifle, he became only more uneasy. If the case was a trifle, then he did not understand the hysteria any more than Ash did, and when he did not understand such things he liked them less. This was because he was directly responsible to the Home Secretary, upon whom any public explosion set off by the case might have political repercussions. And if it was a trifle, why had Major General Lord

Frederick Incledon, K.C.B., behaved as if it were a calamity and tried to keep Scotland Yard out of it? Why was the guard at the castle doubled? Why, as he had heard, had all leaves been cancelled; why was the whole Brigade being held in readiness, as Secretary Cross had told him, and for what? And what was it Sir Gilpin Jarvey knew that he had discreetly declined to tell old Humphrey Alcock (a Youth and a member also of Sir Joseph's club)? Scotland Yard, whose authority to act in the case the Home Secretary had upheld and whose competence he had defended, could ill afford to blunder now. If the case was a trifle, the Yard had better make bloody sure of it before saying so.

And there was another consideration that gave the commissioner pause; a more personal one. People were saying that he was getting old—oh, he knew what they were saying. They were hinting that he'd better retire. Let him botch a case like this and they'd say he was in his dotage. He'd be forced out. "They," he thought, were only waiting their chance. He knew them: the fools!

"Don't think there's anything in it, eh?" he said to Ash. "Want to close the case? So soon? Sure there's nothing else you want to look into? H'm? No loose ends? No little details that may look a bit too innocent? Eh? What's the matter, Ash? Getting old?"

"Old? Why, no, Sir Joseph. I'm only fifty-one."

"Fifty-one, eh? Had a mind like a whip at your age. Still have. Look at the Prime Minister; he's not so much younger, eh?"

"The Prime Minister? No, I shouldn't say so very much."

"No. Seventy-five if he's a day. And still in his full powers, mind you. There's a lesson for you, my boy. Never let down; never. Why, at your age I'd have gone at this case night and day. *I'd* have got to the bottom of it."

"Well, as to that, sir, I've gone at it pretty hard myself, and I think I *have* got to the bottom of it. It's as I'm telling you, nothing much in it; and that's my considered opinion."

"Nonsense. You've worked on hard cases before. Why, in that

Plummer Case you were like a bulldog. How old were you then, eh?"

"Then? I was forty-three then. I remember I passed most of my birthday lying on my stomach in Ipswich."

"Ah, you were hard as nails then. But I advise you not to let down now—or you'll spend your next birthday sitting in your garden. Mustn't let that young whippersnapper pull the wool over your eyes. Don't overlook anything. There may be more in this than you think, Ash. Remember, the Queen is in this case. Eyes of the whole country are on us. You've got to be thorough. Got to be brilliant, Ash, brilliant. Suppose I told the secretary there was nothing in it and then it turned out there was, eh? You understand? Go at it hammer and tongs, Ash, tooth and nail. Perhaps I'd better put Gowdy on to help you."

Gowdy! Inspector Ambrose Gowdy, that was, of the Green Park Murder Case, of the Tumbleton Priory Murders, of the famous Royal Mint Shortages Scandal, and the celebrated affair of the Witch of the Helston Furry—Ash's only rival!

"Not necessary at all, Sir Joseph," Ash said with admirable calm. "I'm sure I'm quite capable of going it alone. If there's anything in it, I'll turn it up yet, I give you my word!"

"That's the ticket. Back to work, then. Let me have daily reports of your progress. And put some ginger in it, Ash, put some ginger in it," said Sir Joseph Kew with an inspiriting cock of his jaw.

Having, as he thought, already solved the Wheeler Case, however, there was little else but ginger that Inspector Ash *could* put into it; so he put in plenty of that. On that day and the next, all the acquaintances Wheeler had mentioned in even the most digressive way since the beginning of the inquiry were rounded up by Ash's men, placed separately on the griddle, and then herded together and suddenly confronted with Wheeler himself.

There they were, a whole roomful of them—his uncle, Mr. 'Erbert Wheeler, the well-known bargeman; Mr. Bill Grams, his uncle's mate; a boy known as the Sparrer, after the bird, little Petey Stingo and old Mrs. Dawkins, all mudlarks; Meg Bownes, of the Waterman's Arms; Ben Fox, the tosher; Iron George, the swag-barrow man; Mrs. Feeney, the hurdy-gurdy woman of Trafalgar Square; Dandy Fitch, the one-legged rat-catcher; Ah Fook, the prosperous merchant of Dolphin Lane; and, to his utter bedazzlement, 'Ooker Morgan, the distinguished dredger, himself.

"Blimy!" Wheeler gasped, his face lighting up with joy at the sight of them all. He thought they had come to visit him, and was charmed by the tribute. But suddenly he hardly knew whether to be glad or sorry.

From all sides their eyes converged on him, angry, sullen, accusing, questioning, innocent, or inscrutable. Inspector Ash stood watchfully in the doorway, clutching his beard. Beside him stood a stout matron of the detention home wearing a superior sneer. And a tall constable was posted in each corner of the room. But of all things in that room Wheeler was most conscious of the eyes of the 'Ooker, at whom in his embarrassment he dared not look again. He therefore directed his gaze at his uncle and offered brightly:

" 'Owjer like me new duds?"

From somewhere deep in his uncle's chest a growl was heard. "Duds!" he repeated. "Duds, says 'e!" And the aggrieved man addressed the room at large. "Wot abaht gratytude, that's wot I'd like to know! 'Ere I've cared for 'im like me own, toiled for 'im, spent me 'ard-earned money on the little barstid, trying to do me dooty by his maw! Why, when 'e was a tot, I uster do without me beer to buy 'im 'Mother's Blessing,' so I did. And 'ere's the thanks. Slips 'is cable, prigs them 'ere fancy duds and is took up 'ousebreaking in Windsor Carstle—Windsor Carstle, if you please! Strike me dead if it ain't disgriceful! I wash me 'ands on 'im, that's wot I do. I bin a honest man all me life—poor, may be, but honest, I swear, honest as the d'y, and I serves notice 'ere and now, I disowns 'im. Dis-owns 'im, that's wot. I tell yer, Inspector, 'e's broke me 'eart!"

"Ar," sighed Bill Grams, and dolefully shook his head.

"Wull," spoke up the 'Ooker in a peevish bass, "he ain't my kid. Why, I never clapped me blinkers on 'im afore, so 'elp me. Wot's more, sir, I ain't never see none o' this 'ere lot afore, 'cept Meg 'ere, and 'er's the barmaid at the Waterman's Arms, to be seen by one and all in lawful hours; a decent 'ouse it is, sir, ain't that so, Meg gell?"

"Aye!" said Meg Bownes emphatically. "A 'ard-working barmaid in a decent 'ouse, that's wot I am. Wotjer bring me 'ere for? I ain't done nothink."

"You ain't done nothink!" shrilled Mrs. Feeney, the hurdy-gurdy woman. "Wot abaht me? Ain't I a hones' woman? This 'ere ain't my kid, me doxy. I ain't got no kid. A poor lone woman is wot I am, Inspector, a poor, lone, hones'——" But the others would not wait their turn and Mrs. Feeney's bellow was lost in a chorus.

Ash, the lover of order, raised his hands; the four constables intervened; the clamour ceased. And coming into notice again, the little barstid was observed to be standing abashed and crestfallen, looking ruefully down at his new shoes.

Then for the first time little Petey Stingo spoke, privately, in a startling bass like a coal-whipper's, to the Sparrer: "Lawks! 'E ain't arf a stunner, wot?" And Wheeler, recognizing this as a compliment to his appearance in the new duds, looked up at Petey gratefully under his lashes and tried to smile.

"'Ush yer jaw!" wheezed Mrs. Dawkins, shaking Petey by the elbow, and unctiously bent one creaky knee to the inspector.

Ash signalled to the matron; the matron seized Wheeler by the shoulders, whirled him around, and pushed him into the next room. Ash followed, closing the door behind him. He seated himself on a corner of the table and narrowed his eyes at the prisoner, pulling on his beard.

"Now, then," he said. "It's no good, you see. We've got them all in charge. And we've got sworn statements out of all of them. You understand what I mean? They've narked."

Nark was an everyday word to Wheeler: it meant to peach to the police. But he only looked away, and swallowed. He did not understand at all.

"Come, come, they're no friends of yours. You heard what they said, even there in front of you. Threw you over in a minute to save their own skins. Scoundrels, the pack of them. Now you're young, my lad; you've got your whole life ahead of you. You don't want to spend it all in prison, do you? Because that's where you'll rot if you don't speak up now and tell the truth. Oh, you're going over the stile, you know; it's like to go hard with you if you don't let me help you."

Wheeler, having just been so cruelly rejected by his own, was feeling deeply just then the bitterness of life. He was doubly tempted to do a bit of narking himself. But he really couldn't think of anything to nark about, save that the 'Ooker had got rich by fleecing drowned people and selling their bodies to the hospitals, as he had heard—but this was something that he could not bring himself to mention. Anyone else, perhaps—but nark on the 'Ooker? It would have been to betray the whole set of values held dear on the stairs. Besides, when he had rotted in the bridewell for the 'Ooker's sake, it would be reported: "And 'e never narked on yer, 'Ooker; 'e never narked!"

When at last Wheeler was sent back to the little grilled room in the top storey, Ash was only the better satisfied in his mind that the boy had told him the truth in the first place. But this was scarcely comforting to Ash. Commissioner Kew already had rejected Wheeler's simple tale and was holding Gowdy in readiness to find a better. *What's the matter, Ash? Getting old? . . . You'll spend your next birthday sitting in your garden.* Policemen finding themselves in this dilemma have been known to manufacture evidence to suit the emergency, and with Wheeler and his friends this would have been easy. Ash, therefore, was in a fair way to do some wrestling with his conscience. In the meantime only the burden of that conscience kept him burrowing into the facts a little deeper in the dismal hope of finding his own opinion wrong.

Wheeler's uncle, Bill Grams, Ah Fook, Iron George (a known duffer), Petey Stingo, and the Sparrer were detained for a bit at Her Majesty's pleasure, the others being released, and that evening Ash played another card. He had the Sparrer suddenly thrust into the same room with Wheeler, and remained outside the door with a police clerk to listen.

The Sparrer was a quick, delicate-looking child of about Wheeler's own age and height, and he was dressed much as Wheeler had been, in an oversize coat reaching to his ankles, under which his ragged trousers were held up by a single brace, but he had no shoes and his feet looked like rough little models in mud.

After a short pause occasioned by the mutual surprise and embarrassment of the prisoners, the officers heard:

" 'Ullo, Sparrer."

"Dirty bugger! Yer tipped me lay."

"Me? I din't! Not me, Sparrer."

"Hookey you din't!"

"I din't! I takes me dyin' oath!"

"Yar! Oo put the coppers on me?"

" 'Ow should I know? Wotjer do?"

"I ain't did nuffink!"

Another pause, and again the Sparrer's voice. "Wot *jew* do?"

"Sneaked inter Windsor Carstle."

"Windsor Carstle!"

"Ya-as, I did, so 'elp me—str'ight! *J* seed the Queen."

"Yer a liar!"

"I ain't a liar! Arsk the slops, they'll tell yer. Sat on the bleedin' throne, too, that's wot. Jes arsk!"

"G'arn. She's kilt."

"Oo?"

"The Queen, that's oo."

"Yer a liar!"

"I ain't a liar! She's a stiff 'un, I tell yer. They done 'er in."

"Oo done 'er in?"

"Murdrers."

"Wen?"

"Donno. Yesty, I 'eerd."

"Wy'd they do that for?"

"Ya-ar, she's rich, ain't she? Wotjer think? 7 lay they got a 'aul! Sixty bob, may be. And crowns! And finnufs! Ar!"

" 'Ow'd they do 'er in?"

"Bashed 'er 'ead in."

"*Crikey!*"

16

But the Queen's head, by God preserved, was full of indignant thoughts concerning the Wheeler Case, and that morning she had been busy making some of them known in the proper quarters.

Far from being touched by the general concern that almost overnight had lifted her out of her unpopularity and endeared her to the hearts of her subjects, the Widow at Windsor had been moved to wrath by all this clamour at her gates. Everyone was demanding a public inquiry, and this she considered to be perfectly ridiculous. It had been disgraceful enough for that little arab to come trespassing into her dining room (What could parents be thinking of nowadays? There was no respect any more!), but now it appeared that the rest of Britain was to come tagging in after him! It was nothing but an attempt to drag her quiet life and her household affairs into the open, inspired by the republicans and the cheap press.

Mr. Delane, the editor of *The Times*, received from General Ponsonby a letter of rebuke for having been duped into publishing such a disagreeable suggestion, while Mr. Cross, the Home Secretary, received one stipulating that on the contrary Her Majesty desired the inquiry to be private. Cross dispatched a note to this effect to Commissioner Kew, who showed it to Ash with the observation that a public statement now would be out of the question.

But Cross was worried, and he mentioned the matter to the Chief.

"Kew seems to be having his difficulties with this case. Whether we ought to continue to be guided by Her Majesty's wish for a private inquiry remains to be seen. The people's temper is rising. Don't you think they have a right to some kind of reassurance now?"

"Pish!" Disraeli said. But instead of elucidating the meaning of Pish, he suddenly gazed off into space, and in that attitude appeared by the gleam in his eye to receive an inspiration from the Devil. "I'm glad you spoke of it," he said. "You know, there may be something in it."

"You think so?" Cross asked, with wrinkling brow, for he remembered that the Chief himself, in some mysterious way, had been involved in the case, and wondered what on earth he meant.

"Will you be good enough to send me whatever facts have come to light, or permit Sir Joseph to do so?"

"Of course!"

Perhaps, Cross thought, there was something to these rumours one kept hearing, after all. He certainly wished the Chief would take him into his confidence.

"Thank you," Disraeli said. "I'll let you know."

Later he said to his secretary: "Do you remember that fellow McHatten? I should like to know something more about him, Hammond—privately. And when we've got a report on him, perhaps we'd better send for Mr. McHatten. Mr. Secretary Cross today presented me with an excellent excuse."

When McHatten was informed that he was wanted in Downing Street, he thought his reprieve from India was at hand. But why the

Prime Minister should send for him he could not imagine. Disraeli, he knew from his sister, was a friend of the Rothschild family, but he hardly thought the Rothschilds would have bothered the head of the Government with such trivial Army business. And anyway, these things were not done for a man by sending for him; they were done quietly, by written orders. But this old Dizzy, everyone said, was an Oriental, and could not do things in the ordinary way; he was bizarre in everything, and when he did a man a service, McHatten fancied, he probably made a parade of it. Yes, McHatten could well believe that. He did not like this Dr. Fell.

Across his desk, as McHatten was ushered in, Disraeli saw, if not a truculent young man, at least a proud and rather scornful one; but this was an attitude that of itself did not displease him in the young, provided a brain went with it. And in his eye, as he half rose, painfully, a smile flashed, like a trout in still water. "Very good of you to come, Mr. McHatten." He motioned to a chair and sank back into his own. "A good deal has happened since you and I last met. It seems now we were in at the beginning of something. I had no idea then."

"Neither had I," McHatten said a shade bitterly.

"No? I thought perhaps you could explain it to me."

McHatten glanced at the Prime Minister sharply. "I don't profess to be a sage, sir; I should have said it was the other way round."

It came to the Prime Minister that somehow he had been suspected of irony again; a bad beginning; but inwardly again he smiled. A good retort, considering the mistake, and a lovely rash one. Not many men in London would choose to match wits with him like that. "I fear I deserved that for a very clumsy remark. But of course I meant that you are familiar with the case and I am not." And as McHatten reddened: "Oh, don't apologize; I brought it on myself. I'd rather you told me something about this little ogre Wheeler."

"Wheeler?" McHatten said, and thought, What the devil has Wheeler to do with it; why doesn't he come to the point?

"Yes. Don't you know that's why I asked you to come here?"

"*Wheeler?*" McHatten repeated incredulously, his hopes dashed; and suddenly became alarmed. Wheeler, to the best of his knowledge, was the cause of his present trouble in the Guards; now he could imagine only that Wheeler was going to cause him further trouble, or why had the Prime Minister sent for him in the case? The Prime Minister! He thought wildly of the raging public scandal, the silly rumours of a plot to assassinate the Queen, and wondered if now he was being suspected of treason! Wheeler seemed to have becomes his nemesis. He said uneasily, "No, sir."

"Then perhaps I'd better explain. The boy Wheeler is something of a popular villain now, you know. In fact, this extraordinary homunculus whom you and I dreamt we saw sitting on Her Majesty's throne has made more of a sensation in one night than Springheel Jack did in his whole career of nights. There's a notion abroad, as you may have heard, that he's involved in some regicide conspiracy—and all sorts of things, none of which I can believe. But the difficulty is—I ask you to consider this a confidence; the difficulty is, Lieutenant, that the police as yet have not been able to reassure us. Here on my desk you see—a dossier on the case, brought to my attention by the Home Secretary. He conceives of Wheeler as a political *enfant terrible*. And as always there are the radicals, making capital out of another aspect of the business. So, strange as it may seem to you, Lieutenant, the homunculus threatens to become an embarrassment to Her Majesty's Government. Politics teaches a man to be prepared when he can. That's why I'd like you to give me your opinion."

McHatten was relieved but also a little puzzled. "*My* opinion, Mr. Disraeli? But I——"

"You arrested the boy, and I dare say you were privy to the examination of him afterwards, weren't you?"

"Yes, that's true."

"Well?"

"Well . . . the guard damned well turned him inside out that
night and back again next day. They seemed to think it was another
Gunpowder Plot." McHatten grinned. "I remember the major calling him 'a little Guy Fawkes.' "

"And what do you think?"

He shook his head. "I think he told the truth."

"You don't believe he had accomplices?"

"Not a bit of it. Poor little devil. He's a London mudlark. Said
he came to Windsor on a coal barge to take in the castle. Managed
to get past a sentry post and found himself in the Quadrangle. Well,
it was dark, and that night there was a thick fog. There are coalholes
in the Quadrangle, you see, and it was just his luck that some fool
had left one open. Well, he fell into it—into the cellars. Then he
climbed upstairs and hid in the Private Dining Room. That's all."

"All?" said Disraeli in an incredulous tone. "And you can believe
that?"

"Yes, I can believe it. Though I don't suppose anyone else can."

"You're wrong, Lieutenant. I can."

"You, sir?"

"I can believe much more improbable things than that, Lieutenant.
But when I can't prove or explain them, I'm careful where I say so.
And I may have to explain this. But I don't say I do believe it either
—yet. I shall have to know something more about the case, or about
the boy."

"Oh well, he's a vagabond, you know. A wild little brat. And,
after all, a boy. That makes it credible enough for me."

"But a London mudlark, you say—and he went to Windsor to
see the castle? Precious few London mudlarks have ever been out
of London in their lives—or as far into it as Finsbury Circus or
Clapham Common. And going all the way to Windsor to see the
castle! Why should he do that? What do mudlarks know about
castles—or care? I think, Lieutenant, that the ignorance of our mudlarks would surprise you. The master of a ragged school once told

me that he had examined a mudlark to see how far his common knowledge went. The boy thought England was in London, Lieutenant. And he wasn't sure who Jesus was, but thought He was King of England. Unfortunately, the new Education Laws, such as they are, haven't been in force long enough—and aren't strong enough—to do much for the mudlarks. Trying to drive them all to school is like trying to round up all the rats in the sewers. It would take the Pied Piper of Hamelin."

"Well," McHatten said, "this one may not know who Jesus was, but he knew Wellington—recognized the bust of him in the Guard Room, called him "the Arn Juke." And he knew the Queen right enough, and knew he'd sat on the throne. And he asked a lot of questions when we gave him a sporting chance. I admit I was surprised—and rather struck, you know. I think he's intelligent. But Lord, he speaks the worst Cockney I've ever heard, and smells like an outfall, and I don't suppose he has the least idea of right and wrong—not as the rest of us have, anyway; and damned if I don't think that gives him a kind of advantage over the rest of us. Almost as if he'd been born without original sin. I'm surprised he didn't steal anything at Windsor; perhaps he hadn't the chance. I should have thought that if he'd seen something he liked, something shiny, you know, and strangely shaped, he'd have lifted it without a qualm. I feel rather sorry for him, but, by God, I envy him a little too."

Men seldom surprised Disraeli, but McHatten had. McHatten had surprised himself, and had broken off with the feeling that what he'd been saying sounded like rot; he scarcely knew what he meant, or if he meant it at all. But Disraeli, who had been studying him, knew what he meant, and thought: Better and better.

"So do I," he said; "so do I."

"Do you, sir?"

"Youth," Disraeli said; "I always envy youth. But I don't often pity it. What will he be like in forty years—in twenty—in ten?"

"God knows!" McHatten said with a laugh.

Disraeli was toying with a pencil. "Sometimes I used to go prowling London at night; on foot, you know; I was a real Londoner then. And one night under the gas lamp in front of the National Gallery, I came on an old friend. 'Friend' may surprise you when I describe her to you and tell you what she was. She was one of those old drabs one sees shuffling along, with grey hair straggling down under battered straw bonnets, half toothless, and with a fondness for gin; and she was what they call a 'follower.' A follower, as I hope you do not know, is the duenna of the underworld, the watchdog sent by the brothel keeper to follow the streetwalker and be sure she doesn't sell her finery in the first rag shop or waste her time in some public house. Ah, I seem to have had a reprehensible education! But I had known this woman before. There had been a time when she'd been one of the handsomest demimondaines in London. She'd been an actress once; I remember her at Astley's forty years ago, as Venus in one of those equestrian dramas they used to give, called, I believe, *The Charioteers*. And I remember her at the Cremorne Gardens, on the arm of a certain young dandy who sits now in the House of Lords; and later at Kate Hamilton's. And here she was, a hag, 'following' a poor strumpet she called Sal, who wouldn't have been in it with her in her young days. And she turned her face up to me in the ghastly light of that street lamp and I didn't know her; she had to tell me who she was. I was shocked, as you may imagine, and of course embarrassed, and I suppose she knew, though I tried not to show it. She told me she'd 'come down awful'—she was a Cockney; she said she got nothing for 'following' the girl, barring her bed and board and a shilling or two when she asked for it to buy a little gin—'white satin,' she called it. 'Come down awful,' she said. And yet, she said, it wasn't awful. Sometimes she tried to think it was, but she couldn't believe it entirely. 'The fact is,' she said, 'life's sweet, and I don't care how you live. It's as sweet to the 'ore as it is to the hempress, and maybe it's as sweet to me as it is to you.' Well, I don't know that life's as sweet to the 'ore as it is to the hempress;

it depends on the 'ore and depends on the hempress; but I'm sure it was as sweet to that particular grand beldame of the night as to our gracious Queen, and only because something in herself had kept it so. She was brutalized, yes, but she still had the most precious of earthly things. And I took off my hat to her in front of the National Gallery."

He did not explain what this had to do with Wheeler, but only looked at McHatten with a queer twist to his lips, and McHatten vaguely understood that it clarified and extended a thought in what he himself had been saying a moment before; and although he had listened with a grin, he shuddered. "But good God, the depths, the emptiness! No hope; not even courage. Only a sodden last look round. And she called that life!"

"You can understand Wheeler better, can't you?"

"Yes!" McHatten laughed. "He's a bit more in my line. He likes to see and do things, that kid, or I miss my guess. And strictly between us, sir, he's embarrassed the Grenadiers no end. They'd give their buttons to make him six feet tall and an experienced burglar."

The door opened and Darcy Hammond came into the room. With an apologetic word to the visitor, he handed a slip of paper to the Prime Minister, who glanced at it and said, "Let him wait."

McHatten rose, sensible that he had been taking the time of a busy man. But Disraeli motioned him down again. "No, no, not yet; it's all right." McHatten reluctantly obeyed, resuming, however, only the edge of his chair. The secretary withdrew, and McHatten was at the same time embarrassed and flattered to see the busy man upon whose attention the affairs of the nation waited settle back like a man at his club, as if he had nothing better to do than talk to him.

"I've been wondering," Disraeli said; "could you possibly be related to old Robert McHatten?"

"He was my grandfather, sir."

"Was?"

"He died some years ago. Did you know him?"

"I remember him well. He sat in Parliament for—for——"

"The Cheshire Wirrel, sir—for fifty years; and he and his father between them sat for it for nearly a hundred."

"Indeed? A family constituency?"

"Used to be."

"Then I suppose you'll be standing for it yourself someday."

"No, we're out of it now. Dad's in the Church—Vicar of Appleton Thorn; and I'm not much for politics either."

"M'm. As I recall, your grandfather was a Tory."

"Yes, we've always been Tories."

"In that case, I should think you owe it to the Party, as well as to your family."

"Sir?" said McHatten in surprise.

"I mean that with all the industrializing you've had up there in recent years, the Party's weak in Cheshire now. You have an old Cheshire name. Very valuable. You're intelligent, educated, you know the Army, and I take it that, being in the Guards, you're well acquainted in other circles. You have wit—I saw that when you floored me for my clumsy remark directly you came in; and I remember you made a very good little speech in the Throne Room that evening. I think you'd be good in debate. I should say the Party needs you. But then, I suppose that for the present you're pretty keen on a career in the Army, eh?"

For a moment McHatten could say nothing. He was bowled over. The truth was that he was as well qualified for politics as many young men of his acquaintance who went into it as a matter of course, and, in his own opinion, much better qualified. The idea had never appealed to him before, but suddenly it appealed to him now. In a flash he saw it as a release from the position in which he was mired as a soldier, and at the same time as a way in which he might sooner, he was sure, cut his mark in the world and prove his mettle to Emily and her stick of a mother. For an Army career was a slow process in these dull days, whereas in the House of Commons a man might show what he was made of any day in the week and achieve pre-eminence almost at once, as it seemed to McHatten. And here was the Prime Minister, the Leader of the House, the Chief of the Party, actually inviting him in!

"By Jove!" he said. Then a cloud came over his face, and he said, "No, not now, sir."

"Not now?"

"Oh, I don't say no. I think it might be the very thing. Politics, the House, and all that. I'm really not so keen on the Army. I might —I might——"

"Yes," Disraeli smiled, remembering what he had told Melbourne once, "you might become prime minister."

"Well, hang it," McHatten said with a laugh, "I might!"

The Sphinx leaned back in his chair and did something few of his friends had seen him do for thirty years—*he* laughed: a shocking sight, as grim as a gargoyle. "If you do," he said "it will serve you right."

"But I'll have to wait a bit, sir."

"Why?"

McHatten was thinking of the vague cloud hanging over him in the Grenadiers. Being under the impression that his superiors were for getting him out of the way in order to make him the scapegoat in the Wheeler Case, he was determined not only to await the re-scinder of his transfer, which he was confident the Rothschilds could obtain for him, but to remain in the Regiment until either he was vindicated or the affair blew over. Wheeler again—his nemesis.

He answered: "Personal reasons."

"I see. How long?"

"I can't say. Six months, perhaps, or a year."

"A year!" The Chief naturally fastened upon the round figure, though for the defeat of his object anything longer than eight days would suffice. What he wanted was McHatten's resignation from the Army before that ship sailed. And he began to lift himself out of his chair, assuming almost mechanically the position of debate. He walked to the grate and returned. "Naturally I'm disappointed," he said.

Again McHatten was surprised. What could it possibly matter to the Prime Minister what a young nobody did?

"I don't pretend," Disraeli explained, "that my suggestion was made in any altruism towards yourself, McHatten. It was made in plain, objective Party interest."

"But really, sir——"

"We are weak in Cheshire," Disraeli went on, disregarding this protest. "You come along and appear to be ready-made to our purpose. Our weakness happens to be your good fortune. But don't imagine that we'll wait for you. We must begin to act at once in order to correct as many of our weaknesses as possible at the next elections. At once, McHatten."

"Yes, of course. And I thank you for your offer. I'm really a little overwhelmed, you know. And I think I'd like to accept, but just at present that's impossible. As I say, there are reasons."

"H'm. A pity, a great pity. I think you might do well in politics. And whatever your reasons may be, I hope you'll weigh them carefully. You're a young man, and, I judge, full of energy and enterprise, full of confidence. I know. I remember. Casting your eyes round at a world full of treasure that's to be had for the lifting. And you may think, Oh, the time's not ripe yet, I can lift that whenever I choose. But I counsel you out of my own experience, an opportunity like this seldom if ever befalls a man. Listen to me, McHatten. I would have given a year of my life for it at your age."

"I do appreciate the opportunity, sir, but it's impossible." McHatten stood up to leave. No use prolonging it. He had taken enough of the busy man's time. "Besides, I've heard it takes money to launch a political career, and I haven't got the ready."

Disraeli grunted. Young fool's sister was married to a Rothschild, wasn't she? He said, "Money can be raised, it can be raised if a fellow has his head about him. But there." He wouldn't urge the young fool. "If you won't, there's an end to it." He held out his hand. "When you're ready, come and see me. Perhaps we can find you something."

"Thank you, sir. That's very good of you, I must say!" And McHatten warmly shook the Prime Minister's cold, prehensile hand.

He left, and, seeing no one but Darcy Hammond in the anteroom, concluded guiltily that the caller kept waiting during the interview had lost patience and taken himself off.

Strange man, the P.M., but not at all like his first impression. Not like what one heard he was, either—not at all. An affable old man, and surprisingly garrulous. Too garrulous for a statesman, and much too careless of his confidences. Lord, that story he'd told about his "friend," the old trull. Good thing he hadn't told *that* to the wrong man!

"And they say he's so devilishly clever," McHatten reflected as he emerged into Downing Street. "I don't think he's a clever man. But, hang it, I do think he's a very good one!"

17

The good man Benjamin Disraeli, when McHatten had gone, stood scowling at the empty air. He felt as if he had suffered a political defeat, and at the hands of a young fool. And yet—there was the pity of it—McHatten had a brain, and spirit; he might have made excellent raw material; and with an old Cheshire name, and with the Party so weak in Cheshire. But he was a fool all the same; all the best young men were fools. And the "reasons" he had mentioned, the infernal "reasons" that might not be pried into—probably absurd. Disraeli wondered what they might be; he opened a drawer of his desk and took out Darcy Hammond's report:

McHatten, Charles Edward. Only son Rev. Hugh McHatten, Vicar Appleton Thorn, Cheshire, and Caroline Smith McHatten, daughter Rev. Charles D. Smith, late Rector Little Waltham, Essex; grandson Robert McHatten, M.P. for Cheshire Wirrel (1818–68), deceased. Educated . . .

He scanned down the page. Nothing. Nothing that would have deterred Benjamin Disraeli had he been McHatten. Had he known what the "reasons" were he might have been able to get round them. But it was always hard for an old man to deal with a young one in such situations; and Disraeli suffered a small pang, having been made to feel his age. He had gone to a good deal of trouble for that young man, all to extricate himself from a false position with a friend; and stuffing the paper back into his desk, he wondered what he could say to Rothschild. A small matter, perhaps, but to Disraeli a humiliating one. He felt almost as if he had taken money under false pretences. And to think that he'd been trying to play Cupid for that young idiot, and for the Honourable Emily Prior; a new role for him, who till now had always played the suitor. Selina would enjoy that one. And then he remembered that this was the night of Lady Norborough's ball and that Selina would be there! And Anne!

Except at the Bradford or Chesterfield house, or that of a Rothschild, a Manners, or some other dear friend, he seldom dined out any more, being, for one thing, too busy, and for another, not disposed to be "exhibited," as he called it, and expected to "perform." And he hated clubs. More often than not he dined alone these evenings in the big house in Whitehall Gardens, sitting like some emaciated Buddha at the head of the long board of polished mahogany, attended only by Phillips, to whom he seldom said a word. He ate slowly, absently, without relish, often pausing with a spoonful of soup half raised to his mouth and staring thoughtfully at the wall, to Phillips's half-pitying exasperation, and often leaving the meal half finished, because the loneliness of it was more than he could bear.

But tonight he ate quickly, though even more sparingly than usual, and quite startled Phillips by making an epigram about the cheese. He took his coffee in the study, skimming over some papers Lord Derby had sent round from the Foreign Office. But he could not keep his mind on them, and, locking them up, began to chew his coffee, giving last thoughts to a decision that he meant this evening to put to the touch. This, he fancied, was going to be one of the most important evenings of his life.

He went into his dressing room and stood uncertainly before the two costumes—the blue domino and the Marco Polo—like a girl torn between modesty and décolletage. But it was not a genuine hesitation, only a reluctance, and submissively the Prime Minister took down the domino and put it on. The tyranny of women! He had dismissed his valet for the evening, thinking, "True, no man can be a hero to his valet, but he'd better not be a clown to him either." And he stood before the glass in the thing, turning this way and that, trying it with the hood and without, in each case raising the small black mask to his face. *With* the hood, of course; that at least gave it a dash of mystery. But he looked at the Marco Polo slippers with their graceful, upcurled toes, and put them on instead of the ones Lady Chesterfield had sent, explaining to himself that they would be more comfortable.

The windows of Lady Norborough's house blazed invitingly into Great Stanhope Street. Two footmen in scarlet and powder stood at the door, a policeman with them and a porter at the kerb. And from kerb to entrance the pavement was a gauntlet of watchers, curious and for the most part silent, a few derisive, with here and there a vocal one to welcome each arrival the moment the officer happened to be looking the other way.

"Wayo, guvnor! Going to 'ave a trot, are yer? Wot! at your age?"

And as the officer turned wrathfully upon that one, another would pipe up behind him:

"That the missus with yer? Ah, she's led a dog's life, ain't she?"

In the privacy of his closed carriage, the Prime Minister discreetly divested himself of the long black overcoat whose snugness defined the thin, bent frame so familiar to Londoners, and of the tall black hat, adjusted the mask across his nose, pulled the hood over his head.

And there descended upon the pavement a figure that might have stepped from the stage of Covent Garden.

" 'Ullo! 'ere *is* a larky 'un. Come aht from be'ind that marsk, guvnor; let's 'ave a look at yer fice."

"Ah, 'e's a grand old ruin, 'e is."

"Blow me if he ain't forgot 'is old gel!"

"Not 'im! 'E knows wot 'c's abaht."

"Come on, cocky, give us a darnce."

"Wot! W'y, bless 'is 'eart, 'e's orl ready fer bed!"

The unknown marched calmly down the gauntlet, mounted the steps, turned, gravely bowed, and vanished into the house. A cheer went up behind him.

He gave up his invitation, strolled to the ballroom, and, on the verge of making his entrance, glimpsed through the portieres another domino that appeared to him exactly like his own. There, hadn't he known it? There probably were dozens of them prancing round. Women and their notions of propriety! But Anne was right, he supposed. Seeing their Prime Minister turned out in the stockings of a Venetian adventurer would horrify the English—or it would in a prime minister of his age. But think of young Pitt—youth and power at the same time! Pitt could have come as Marco Polo; he could if he had good legs. And entering the ballroom, Benjamin Disraeli was wondering if Pitt the Younger had.

The loose folds of the domino disguised his frame, the hood altered the line of the well-known stoop and, with the mask, concealed his features. But it must have been that the English hardly expected to see their Prime Minister in a domino either, because it appeared that no one recognized him. The orchestra was in the midst of a sprightly waltz from *Die Fledermaus*. The warm light of the many candles was reflected on the polished floor. Round and round swung the couples of a gay and motley company out of Romance and History. And his spirit expanded as he stood there, beneath his costume almost as incongruous a figure on the fringe of that assembly as the stranger at the masque of Poe.

A hand touched his arm and a woman's voice said:

"My dear Mr. Disraeli! Is it really you?"

He turned and saw Lady Norborough, large, robust, and trailing yards of voile.

"Alas, no, madam, only part of me, but all I had left to bring at your kind invitation."

"Pooh! I always say you're the youngest man I know. Didn't you bring a partner?"

"To tell the truth, I begged to escort Lady Chesterfield, but she feared my loose ways in a carriage and preferred to meet me here in the light. May I compliment you on a delightful party, and on looking a right noble vestal virgin?"

"Vestal virgin! Heavens, dear man, don't you recognize me?" And she held up a ridiculous little silver bow. "Diana the Huntress!"

"But Diana was a virgin goddess," answered Disraeli, nothing daunted. "In yourself, Lady Norborough, I think that's making too much of a good thing."

"Naughty man. Don't despair. There's Ninon de Lenclos right over there."

Ninon he had no difficulty in recognizing as Lady Chesterfield. He thanked his hostess and went to her.

Anne, the widowed grandmother, seventeen years older than Selina, and two years older than he, was of a grave and quiet nature and wore her age with grace and distinction. Her back was still almost straight, her face little wrinkled, her blue eyes were clear and kind, her smile and her voice gentle; and drawing her arm through his, the Prime Minister said: "I'm glad you came as Ninon this evening."

"Are you? Why?"

"I should have said, as the older Ninon. You were never like the young one. But they say the older one was everything to all men, and at your age, may I remind you, had a lover."

She blushed, looking up at him chidingly. "Diz-zy! How can you

— 233 —

speak that way to me? What would my—daughters say if they heard you?" She had a way of catching her breath in the midst of a sentence that he found charming.

"They would say I was a wicked old man for corrupting your mind with things you oughtn't to know anything about," he answered, leading her through the door to the conservatory.

"Nonsense. Where are you—taking me?"

"Don't you know when you are being kidnapped? I want you all to myself for a little while."

"Oh, such foolishness," she said, but seated herself in the chair which he offered her and, folding her hands in her lap, looked up at him again with a mild question in her eyes. "What is it, Dizzy?"

He regarded her silently for a moment. "Forgive me, but sitting that way you remind me of someone."

"Do I? Of whom?"

"Cleopatra."

"Bosh!"

"Don't you remember going to a ball as Cleopatra?"

"Oh—that; of course. But what a long time ago it was, and what a memory you must have."

"I was thinking of it only the other evening. You were the handsomest woman in the room."

"Diz-zy."

"You were. Don't you know that you were a handsome woman?"

"I was; of course I was. And I used to think you"—she bowed—"a very dashing young man."

"Thank you, madam. But now I come to consider it, I can't decide which I like better—your Cleopatra or your Ninon."

"Oh! stop being silly."

"I was never more serious."

"Indeed! Then all I can say—poor man—is that your eyesight must be failing. And if you think I'll say that *you* are as handsome as you once were—then you underestimate mine."

"What, when you haven't even noticed this silly costume I wore to please you?"

"What's silly about it? It does you very nicely, I think. Turn round. There. Yes. Now back. Ver-y nicely indeed. Mercy, when I think you almost came as Marco Polo. You would have been the talk of London, you poor Dizzy. You do need someone to look after you."

"Yes, my dear," he said. "And don't you?"

"I?"

"Think of the old friends, our contemporaries, who were at that ball with us. Your sister, Mrs. Anson. Caroline Norton. Lady Blessington and Count D'Orsay. Lady Londonderry. Lyndhurst. And now Bulwer-Lytton. Dead, Anne, all of them. And you and I are left. Both widowed; both growing old. But such old friends; so fond of each other. I do need you, Anne——"

"You're not proposing to me!"

"I am. That is why I came here this evening."

"You can't be serious!" But she saw from his eyes that he was serious; and catching her lower lip in her teeth, she looked up at him, her head a little on one side, her eyes suddenly brimming. "Oh, Dizzy! I'm so sorry."

"I'm lonely, Anne. Aren't you?"

"A little—sometimes very. But not so lonely as you, I know. I have my children, and my grandchildren. But my life is finished; I've had it. I couldn't begin again. At my age?"

"Why not?"

"You don't love me, Dizzy . . . Oh yes," she said, "I should want love, of a kind; and I could brook no rivals. I am not that old. But you would always think you loved Selina."

"Selina? No," he protested, but at this penetrating accusation his gallantry had gone lame; "but I confess, 'I could be happy with either dear charmer with t'other dear charmer away.' "

She shook her head at him slowly, showing plainly that she knew;

— 235 —

and, rising, took one of his gaunt hands in hers and held it to her cheek. "My poor, dear friend."

So it was no use. After a moment he said: "You're very wise, Anne, and very kind. Will you forgive me?"

"Diz-zy!—you have paid me a lovely compliment."

With a rueful smile he said: "Shall I take you back to the party?"

She patted the gaunt hand. "If you like."

Arm in arm they entered the ballroom, and found their way to a sofa by the wall. She was sorry for him, and in an interval of the dancing called his attention to her sister on the other side of the room.

"There's Selina. How handsome she looks! But she'll think you're ignoring her, sitting with me all evening."

"Ah," he said with a false sigh, "how easily each charmer relinquishes me to the other!"

But he took his leave. As he went round to the other side of the room, Lady Doughton stopped him to introduce her son, and then the Duke of Richmond came up, and when he got free the orchestra had struck up again; he arrived just in time to see Selina whirled out on the floor in the arms of a prancing Spanish grandee whom he recognized as her husband. Fortunate man! But the Earl of Bradford and Master of the Horse ought never to exhibit his legs either, Benjamin Disraeli thought he might add. And now they were waltzing past him—Selina in a flaring dress of bright red, with a high comb in her hair and a mantilla falling over her bare shoulders, a pendant ruby flashing at her throat, and beneath the mask her lips parted in a merry laugh that reached him with the music as she went by, unaware of his presence. But the sweet thrill that her nearness and the sound of her laughter gave him was turned painful by the sense of her remoteness, by the knowledge that her blithe spirit, so different from his own, never would warm the house in Whitehall Gardens, or the great, vacant country seat at Hughenden. Out of his reach for ever! And his loneliness descended upon him there on the edge of the ring of dancers. He felt his age, and his ugliness. Marco Polo indeed! And Lady Chesterfield saw him pull the hood round his cheeks, as if he were cold; saw him turn and go slowly out of the room. The Prime Minister was leaving the party: he would send his apologies to his hostess in the morning. And outside the house he walked the gauntlet once more in his ridiculous domino.

"Wot's up now, guvnor? Wouldn't they darnce with yer?"

"Try the 'Aymarket, guvnor. There's some life dahn there."

"That's the ticket, driver, take 'im to the 'Aymarket. 'E wants ter mike a night of it."

"Nao 'e don't. 'E's got to 'ave 'is sleep. Jest tike 'im 'ome and tuck 'im in."

He was in the carriage, rattling over the stones, pulling off his mask, going back to No. 2 Whitehall Gardens.

There only a feeble yellow glow shone through the fanlight to beacon him. He let himself into the empty foyer, remembering how once upon a time, on nights when Parliament was sitting late, Mary Anne had kept every window blazing with light to welcome him, knowing how he hated the dark.

The dark!

And he groped his way blindly up the stairs.

18

The free evenings of that walking archives, Mr. Naseby, had been passed in the same way, barring accidents, for fifteen years. On Tuesday evenings he would dress himself in his best clothes, brush and put on his tall hat, take his stick, and wend his way into the Borough, to the sign of the Nag and Cart.

This respectable house had stood here for nearly two hundred years, succeeding another that had been burned by the Jacobites, and its name was said to be a corruption of Magna Charta, so that Mr. Naseby could well believe the landlord's boast that de Montfort himself had once quaffed wine on this very spot. It gave him a solid feeling.

Mr. Simms, the present host, would come forward in person to greet the magisterial-looking patron, and with suitable deference escort him into a private room off the saloon bar, where they would be joined by Mrs. Simms and three pints. And seated at a little table covered with a clean white cloth, they would talk what Mr. Naseby called "shop" for two hours every Tuesday evening.

But the shoptalk was all too one-sided to suit Mrs. Simms. It was well known that Mr. Naseby was a closemouthed gentleman, and that from principle, too, and she was too polite to pry, but she wished he would tell them a little something sometimes about goings-on in the castle. Instead he would talk nothing but innkeeping, a topic that after a hard week always refreshed him, for he meant to have a little inn someday himself, of course, and fancied that from the Simmses he was prying trade secrets that would prove invaluable to him later. But until this particular Tuesday evening it had never occurred to Mr. Naseby that on his part he had anything much to tell.

It was true that he was a bigger man now than formerly, but this, he thought, was true only in the Servants' Hall. There certain things had been said, hints dropped, that had set him wondering. He had seen that somehow he had won a new respect there, and when he thought about this he was not surprised. He connected it with the congratulations he had received from the Master of the Household for his excellent generalship in bringing about the capture of Wheeler. But he did not know that he was now supposed to be a walking archives, nor suspect that his fame extended beyond the castle walls. It had not indeed ever dawned on Mr. Naseby that life in the castle was of greater general interest beyond its walls than behind them. So he was not prepared for what Mrs. Simms said this evening when she appeared with the pints.

She said cheerfully: "And how's the book coming along?"

Mrs. Simms knew perfectly well that there wasn't any book. What she had heard was that Mr. Naseby could write a book if he chose, but that of course he wouldn't, preferring to carry his fascinating knowledge to the grave with him. But she was a woman with the bit in her teeth, determined to go as far as she possibly could with what she had. The Wheeler Case was at its height; it was the principal topic of conversation in Windsor Town. All *she* knew about it was what she would hear from the barman, or a tradesman, or from one of the other merry wives. And yet each Tuesday evening she was serving up beer to a man who, if he only would, could tell the whole authentic tale and all the latest that had come of it, not to speak of a lot of other tales a great deal more surprising, if *she* knew anything about it. It was time, Mrs. Simms thought, that some gentle hints were passed to the Closemouthed Man.

"Now, Ethel," said her husband as Mr. Naseby looked at her blankly.

"Book?" said Mr. Naseby.

"Oh, it isn't that I meant to pry," she said, beaming at Mr. Naseby as she removed her apron and seated herself at the table. "But I do think it's nice to be an author."

"Author?" said Mr. Naseby. "Book?" and he boomed forth two separate and distinct reports of laughter. "Me an author? Now whatever put that into your head?"

"Then you're not writing a book?" she asked disappointedly.

"Of course he isn't writing a book," said her husband irritably. "Whatever put that into your head?"

Simms set great store by the friendship and patronage of the Sergeant Footman of the castle and did not like his wife's hinting to Mr. Naseby's face that he was a frivolous kind of gentleman.

His wife sighed. "Well, it isn't true, then. Ah, the things one does hear. But of course I didn't believe it. If you've not the gift you've not the gift, I always say. But we're all cut out for something, and a good thing too. Now honestly I didn't really think he could anyhow."

"Didn't think he could!" said her husband, who felt that his distinguished guest was being insulted. "Of course he could! He could if he wanted, only he isn't likely to want, see?"

"Heavens, you needn't bite my head off, William Simms. I don't mean he couldn't if he had something to write about, but what in the world would *he* write about?"

"What would *he* write about! That's a nice question, that is. Did you hear that, Mr. Naseby? What would *you* write about! Wouldn't she just like to read the book *you'd* write if you'd a mind, eh?"

"Well——" said Mr. Naseby.

"Not half, she wouldn't!" said Simms. "There you are in the castle, day in and day out, year in and year out, eh? There you are serving the Queen, showing in the dukes and the duchesses and the ministers, and a-hearing of every word they say. And she asks what you'd write about! Let me tell you, old girl, the *London Illustrated'd* give a pretty sum for what Mr. Naseby here could write if he'd set pen to paper."

"Why, Will," said Mrs. Simms looking positively astonished, "I do believe you're right. Mr. Naseby's such a quiet gentleman, I never thought of it that way before. He never says a word, does he? Why, you wouldn't think he knew anything, if you see what I mean. My goodness, Mr. Naseby, do you?"

Mr. Naseby, who had listened with opened eyes, recovered himself and chuckled modestly. "Ah, now, Mrs. Simms. I know a thing or two more than I let on, you may be sure."

Before he left the Nag and Cart that evening, he had told all he knew about the Wheeler Case and hinted at a good deal that he didn't know. He had answered all Mrs. Simms's questions about the Queen's tastes in food, had dropped a confidential hint that His Royal Highness might be going to Ireland soon, and been reminded of a story. It seemed that Her Majesty had heard that the Prince of Wales, during a recent visit to the castle, had been lingering over his cigar in the smoking room till past midnight. The Queen hated smoke and had given orders that the smoking room was to be closed at eleven, and, Prince or no Prince, was determined that her orders be carried out. Henceforth, if His Highness lingered, he was to be told to leave. But in order that punctilio might be preserved, this delicate office was to be performed only by a Privy Councillor. Mr. Naseby told this story over his third pint, and it was so well received that he would have liked to tell another. At the moment, however, he could not think of another that he considered worth the telling. But the Simmses had set his mind going, and, walking homeward, he thought of several. He reached his room, disrobed to his undergarments and tall hat, and, sitting on the edge of his bed, conjured up pleasantly the scene at the table. Never before had he been listened to so avidly. But then never before had he essayed the raconteur. Suddenly he let one of his boots drop with a thud. "By Jove!" he thought. "I wonder if I *might* write a book. I wonder if I might dash off me memoirs!"

And in his heart, from that evening forward, Mr. Naseby was a changed man.

Other changes had begun to occur in the castle. There was Munn, the mountainous young chambermaid, who one evening seized Noonan in her arms and kissed her, and when Noonan inquired what that had been for, only laughed and skipped ponderously away. The next day Munn was impudent to Mrs. Buckins, but, being reduced to tears for it by that formidable old termagant, saw her error and promised to be good. But then she began to neglect her duties, and when Mrs. Buckins scolded her for this, she flew into a pet and threw up her place. Noonan, going to help her pack, was prepared to be consoling, but discovered that Munn, if one might believe her, did not need consolation. She was gayer than Noonan had ever seen her. She seized Noonan and kissed her again, and announced that she was going to London and never would be in service again. And sure enough, in the following weeks Noonan began to receive the most triumphant letters from Munn, written from Bloomsbury and telling of a grand flat she had there; telling of new clothes and of the nobs she had met and of going to the music halls, of taking lessons from a schoolmaster in writing and speaking and deportment, and, strangest of all, of taking up the study of bell-ringing!

And a great change had begun in the life of Slattery, the faun. He had gone to Mass with Noonan that Sunday, and the next, and the next, and on the second Sunday had walked her down by the riverside, and on the third Sunday walked her to the Old Weir, where she had permitted him chastely to kiss her. This was more than Slattery had hoped for with Noonan in so short a time and he was greatly encouraged. But it was Christianity that ruined fauns in the first place, and many a faun since then has been subverted by a good Christian woman. Noonan, the moment she had become seriously interested in Slattery, had set out to domesticate him, and, having got him to church first, she turned resolutely upon his joyous proclivity towards arson. At first this availed her nothing; indeed, the more she remonstrated, the more he pranced about on his cloven hoofs, flaunting it in her face; and so, being full of genuine anxiety for Slattery's own good, she took the case to Father Fuller.

The Reverend Ignatius Fuller, though light with the Hail Marys on the Noonans of his parish, was so only because he had a fine sense of justice and never made the penance larger than the sin. But he knew a real sin when he heard one, and was equal to them all with the penances. He was, as Noonan had said, a gentle, understanding man, but he was a conscientious one too, with a sublime faith and a deep sense of his responsibility as a steward of the Lord. He stood ready to dash out into a howling night to attend the sick. He would unashamedly beg from or shamelessly browbeat the rich in order to succour the poor. He would rise from his bed at any hour to counsel or comfort anyone in trouble. And, to disembarrass a hesitant sinner in the confessional, it was his gentle boast that nothing could shock a priest, because priests had heard everything; but what Noonan told him this time nearly shocked him out of his chair.

"Burn down Windsor Castle? Oh, look here, my child, are you sure?"

"It's what he's always saying, Father, and I'm feared he'll do it if he gets the chanct. I'm that crazy wondering what am I to do with him at all."

"Is the man a Catholic?"

"He is."

Father Fuller sent for Slattery.

This, taken merely in the abstract, was the kind of sin he despised, a sin not of commission—not yet, praise God!—but of evil intention, a design for vengeance "deliberately flung," as he put it to himself, "in God's teeth." For this alone he would have sentenced a man to his knees for a week. But burn down Windsor Castle!—the thing in the concrete was appalling; for besides being a crime against property, against culture, perhaps even against life, it involved an ancient feud between peoples. Worse: if a Catholic were to burn down the castle it might bring repercussions upon the Church. It must not be; he certainly must prevent it. Yet he could not report the man to the police, he could not even warn the castle. And falling on his knees, Ignatius Fuller prayed God to guide him.

The full brunt of his afflatus was let loose next day upon Slattery himself, who sat through it very pale, on a chair in the priest's house, wondering if Noonan had betrayed him here or in the confessional —an important point—and filled with dread lest, if it had been here she told him, his English reverence should pass the word to the police. He denied, and with a clear conscience, that he ever would have done such a deed. He swore his solemn oath never to do it. But Father Fuller was not appeased.

"You think yourself an Irish patriot, you are obsessed with ancient wrongs done your country, and you are employed—mercy me!—in Windsor Castle in the service of our English Queen. What is more, you are the candlelighter of the Royal Apartments. Every day the temptation will be before you, and in the evening, as you go round with your burning taper, the heinous urge will be at its strongest: you will have the means in your hands. Oh, my! You must leave Windsor Castle at once—leave or I will never give you absolution. Do not suppose that you may go to another priest and get it, for although you conceal my refusal from him, God Himself will refuse it you! I say to you, Repent of your unholy scheme, and remove yourself from the way of temptation. Leave Windsor. Leave the castle before another evening falls. And pray God to forgive you!"

Slattery, with these terrible words ringing in his ears, and with the fear of the police in his heart, crept back to the castle, packed his belongings, and, without daring to speak a word to Mr. Naseby, left the castle that very day. But of Noonan he took a furious and bitter farewell:

"So it's an informer you are! A female tergiversator! Ah! You with your pretty face and your holy ways, buttering me up with your gra! And wasn't I the fool to be letting you walk up me sleeve—renegade of an Irish crawthumper that you are, thick as thieves with the English clergy, with never the least taste in life of a heart in you, and a tongue that could clip a hedge; letting you lead me to Mass, moryah!—to the slaughter, I'm thinking!"

"Aw, now, Slattery," she protested earnestly, "it wasn't that way I done it. I wanted to save you from yourself, just. All in the world I said to Father Fuller——"

"Father Fuller! There's another able dealer! I'll go bail he gave you an indulgence for this job, in place of thirty pieces of silver. Aye, a great pair are you and Father Fuller, and me trapped 'twixt the two of you. No! I'll not stop to hear another word. It's leaving and done with you I am from this day, may your two eyes be put out by the first whitethorn tree you meet in the dark and in God's time a halter be the death of all such! I'm off, that would have laid diamonds and rubies at your feet, and may the Devil dower you to an English boar!"

And Slattery went to the city of Liverpool.

There he had a brother, Aloysius, in a small way of business; and a few evenings later, with him and a few cronies in Joe Claflin's snug, he fell to relating the defeat of his great design at the hands of a woman.

"There I was," he said, "in Windsor Castle, and me the candle-lighter of the Royal Apartments; there I was, I'm saying, with me plans matured and the tinder only waiting for me to set the spark to it; there I was, only waiting me chance to strike a blow for Erin that would echo down the halls of time—and the Woman's a traitor! A smiling little clashbag of an Irish tergiversator she was, and the first thing I knew, she'd turned me in, turned me in to the English Catholic clergy! Oh, by the holy powers, I had to leave in a blazing hurry, I can tell you; I only got out of that castle by the back of me nail. And that's why Windsor Castle's standing tonight and not a heap of black ruins. And now you see me, lads, cowering in a Liverpool cellar, for I'm on the run, I am, and they scouring the cursed English countryside from here to Dover, blocking every highroad and boreen, searching the trains, aye, and searching cellars like this one, to be hanging me for a holy Irish martyr!"

There was a solemn hush when he had finished, and a wagging of heads, for they were all good men in that cellar, and someone brought Slattery another glass. He was pressed for details, which he forthrightly gave, and they shook his hand all round and there were toasts to him and reminiscences of other patriots, such as Smith O'Brien, Gavan Duffy, and O'Donovan Rossa, and the evening ended upon a passionate chorus of "The Dark Rosaleen."

But the next evening, as Eugene and Aloysius Slattery left the same house, two men accosted them with drawn revolvers, blindfolded them, and hustled them into a carriage. And when the blindfold was removed from Eugene Slattery's eyes, his brother no longer was with him. Blinking into the light cast by a single candle, Eugene Slattery saw that he was in another cellar, not a snug this time but a wine cellar, by the look of it, for back in the shadows were great barrels ranged upon racks, and there was a pungent smell as of old wine-soaked wood. In the centre of the room stood a plain wooden table, upon which the lone candle burned in the neck of a bottle, and at the table sat three men looking grimly at Slattery. Slattery had been pushed into a squeaky chair, his hands were still bound behind him, and close by stood his two abductors like sentries, their faces half concealed in the upturned collars of their ulsters.

Slattery said breathlessly: "What have you done with Aloysius?"

One of the men at the table, the one in the middle, a tall, thin man with a long brown beard and eyes like an eagle's, answered him: "Your brother is known to us, and so long as he holds his peace you need have no fear for him. But you are not known to us. Who was it sent you here? Is it a spy or a decoy you are?" The man's voice was as Irish as his own.

"A spy!" Slattery gasped. "A decoy, is it! I'm not, I swear. Before God, I'm not like to be either of them things!" He cast his eyes from one to the other of the men at the table, but they came back to the one with the beard. It might be John O'Leary himself; for he did not doubt in whose hands he was: Liverpool was a Fenian stronghold. Claflin's whisky still was warm in his veins, and the realization that he was in a nest of Irish rebels stirred his imagination. He flung out boldly: "And God forgive yez for an unworthy welcome to a man on the run, for amn't I just after nearly putting the torch to Windsor Castle?"

"You are not known to us as one of the Brotherhood," said the Beard, unemotionally.

"And how would I be, that did it all on me own hook? But by the Man above, I'm as true a patriot as any!"

"Then you will acquaint us with all circumstances, leaving out nothing and telling no lies, or it will cost you dear. And what have you to say of the boy Wheeler?"

"The boy Wheeler! What has that one to do with it? Oh, now, you didn't believe I was in it with that black-faced young chimney climber!"

"It's said he was out to murder the Queen of the English and grown men put him up to it. What would you say to that, now?"

"Yerra, I wouldn't believe it. It's nothing but old woman's tattle you do be hearing about that little clergyman. Didn't I push him behind the hangings with these two hands, only to save him from the Royal English Guards? It was perishing hungry he was, and no more; but I'd nothing to do with him save out of the kindness of me heart."

The men at the table put their heads together and consulted for some minutes, after which the interrogation was resumed. Slattery told them all he knew and guessed about Wheeler, and all he thought proper to tell about himself, finishing with a diatribe upon the treachery of women.

"Did she tell it under the seal of Confession, man?" demanded the little pinched-faced judge at the Beard's right hand.

"Ah, God, if I knew that!" But then Slattery bethought himself and qualified this damaging admission, leaving as it did an impression that he might not be in danger of his life after all. "But if she did, why would they be after me, I'd like to know? For it's a known fact there's a price on me head as I sit here before you and they're for hanging me like a dog if they catch me or it isn't day yet. And there stands Windsor Castle under double guard, or triple by this time if you go to that of it, and no way to destroy it at all short of a siege itself with soldiers and roaring cannon."

Again the men at the table conferred, and then the Beard said: "You'll be as safe where you are as any place in Liverpool. Sleep here tonight then, till we know what's to be done with you."

The three men went out and left the prisoner alone with his guards. He slept on a pile of rags on the floor; and waking next morning with a foul taste in his mouth and his heart shrivelled to the size of a rabbit's, he began to take stock of his position. How, after all, did he know his captors were Fenians? They might be traitors, themselves spies or decoys in the pay of the English. And it dawned on him that if they were, then he had provided them with a confession that could hang him. His guards were surly and scarcely spoke a word to him, and their manner seemed to confirm his fears. Slattery passed the most miserable day of his life.

Late that night the pinched-faced man returned.

"Young man, you're a blundering fool. This is a great disservice you've done your country. In Windsor Castle you might have been of use to us; here you're of no use at all—you're a great embarrassment. By God, you've placed all of our plans in jeopardy, do you know that? You deserve to be taken by the police. Aye; but we can't risk that. And now I'll tell you what's to be done with you. You're to be smuggled quietly out of the country. Not to Ireland; you could be captured there as easily as here. To America is where you're going. Ah, save your breath; the choice is not left to you. You'll go to America and remain in exile till permitted to return, if that day ever comes. There's your sentence, young man, and be damned to you; for I don't mind telling you, if the say was mine, we'd be dropping you in the river Mersey and be done with you for ever!"

Slattery was never to understand quite how this thing had happened to him; but the facts behind it were these:

A great influx of Irish harvest hands, flooding the country at a time when England's collapsing agriculture could not provide sufficient work for the hands at home, had inspired widespread anti-Irish agitation in a land where the Fenian outrages of the late sixties still were fresh in the minds of the people, and this had provided a congenial atmosphere for one strong rumour that suddenly had flared out of the Wheeler Case. This was the rumour that explained the case as a Fenian plot to assassinate the Queen—the rumour that had caused the stoning of Irishmen in Liverpool, riots against them in London, and a popular wave of "informing" against practically all Irishmen caught in the act of not singing "Rule, Britannia."

The Fenians were forced to lie low, and as the storm raged over their bewildered heads word was passed to them from the leaders of the Irish Party in London that the political situation had become inimical to any legislation friendly to their country. Both within the law and outside it, the Irish Cause was at a standstill. And at this awkward moment, Eugene Slattery had opened his mouth in Claflin's snug.

There was nothing for it but to put him beyond the reach of the police, the Fenians reasoned, or if the police caught him and showed that he had tried to burn down Windsor Castle, it might indeed be a sad day for Ireland.

Considering all the circumstances, it could be argued that Slattery's sentence was not so much the result of his own folly as of Wheeler's. But if Slattery owed anything to Wheeler, Wheeler, as it turned out, owed as much to Slattery. For it was this misadventure of Slattery's that brought the Wheeler Case to its remarkable climax.

19

God again had rested gentlemen, and others. The Queen He had rested at Osborne House, her private estate on the Isle of Wight, and Emily Prior with her; the Prime Minister at Hughenden Manor, Bucks, with a few other poor strays of the season as his guests; and God's bounty had reached into workhouses and prisons. But Wheeler, still locked in the little grilled room over Clerkenwell, might never have known it was Christmas at all, if it hadn't been for the carollers croaking "Good King Wenceslas" under his window in the snow, and for a hunk of plum pudding that had reached him by post. This dainty was his only remembrance, and he never knew who the sender was. But it was Mr. Brown.

And then in St. James's Chapel Royal the Lord Chamberlain once more had dispensed three purses to the poor in commemoration of the gifts of the Magi. The apple trees of Devon had been wassailed in cider to wheedle a good crop out of them. God again had blessed the nets of Tweed as His salmon began to run. And it was the middle of another February.

The Queen now had removed to London, taking Emily along. Mc-Hatten had sailed for India, disillusioned about the Rothschilds, to whom Disraeli sent a note regretting that the case had been beyond his control. And if the Rothschilds were disillusioned about Disraeli, they kept that to themselves and paid over the four millions sterling as if they had amassed so many niece-in-law's brothers that one wasn't even missed.

Busher Ash had wrestled with his conscience and won, and paid for it when Ambrose Gowdy was assigned to the case with him. The East End was seined daily for suspicious characters; crime in London had sunk into a sad depression. And over London river had come a subtle change. Puzzled Londoners stood on the bridges at sunset and asked themselves what it was that made the old scene so different. It was that as far as the eye could follow that thorough-fare of human destiny there wasn't a single mudlark. The mudlarks were staying clear of the river now, knowing that the coppers were on them. It was as if suddenly all the gulls were gone.

Inspector Gowdy could only conclude as Inspector Ash had con-cluded—that there simply wasn't anything in the case or else he would have turned it up. But if this convinced Commissioner Kew he was not yet willing to admit it. He was waiting for people to lose interest in Wheeler. But although the clamour had waned at Christ-mas time, it had risen again under the goads of agitators with the new year, and this phenomenal exhibition of staying power in the fickle public perplexed and alarmed Sir Joseph more than ever and shook his faith in human nature.

Everyone directly or indirectly connected with the case was thor-oughly dissatisfied with it.

And then from Liverpool the leaders of the Irish Party in London were secretly informed by the Fenians that if the Wheeler Case in-volved a plot against the Queen, that plot was at any rate not an

Irish one. They were provided with the facts of Wheeler's visit to the castle, his capture and his first interrogation, as related by one of Her Majesty's servants. And while it was confessed that this servant was an Irishman with certain aspirations of his own, it was men- tioned that steps were being taken to prevent the police from ever producing him and proving anything anyhow.

Till now a fear of Irish guilt had lain upon the Irish statesmen like an incubus and they had been careful to hold their breath. Now they breathed freely again: they inhaled righteous wrath by the lungful and made ready to exhale it in a blast against those who were wrongfully accusing Irishmen of mischief.

And this they did in the House of Commons.

The chamber in which the curious scene took place is gone now, but the first thing people used to remark about it was its smallness. It was a surprisingly small chamber for such a great one, scarcely seventy feet long and as narrow as a chapel.

Empty, it did appear to be the chapel of some austere sect; full, it looked like a chapel let for a cockfight. And cockfights being the main sport of this exclusive club, they were the reason its cantanker- ous Members had browbeaten the architect into keeping it small. But with the growth of Parliamentary representation, it was even smaller now than it had been, and when on extraordinary occasions nearly all the Members turned up at once, some two hundred fifty had to stand.

A cold and stately little chamber in the Tudor Gothic style, elabo- rately panelled in dark wood, and in those days lit by gas.

Down each side of it ran five long benches rising in tiers, one behind another, and upholstered in green leather. These two banks of benches faced each other, and upon the benches Members sat, without desks or tables in front of them, without armrests, sat as men sit on benches in the park, or at a cockfight, many with their hats on. On each long wall above them hung a long, shallow gallery where other Members sat on other benches and looked down into the cockpit. And at each end of the room hung another gallery, looking like a choir loft, for the grudging accommodation of "strangers."

Between the two banks of benches ran an aisle, a thin strip of no man's land across which the champions of opposing parties did battle. At the far end of this aisle, as if put there entirely by improvisation, stood a raised, thronelike wooden chair in which the Speaker sat, wigged and gowned like a judge. Just below him and pushed up against him sat the three Clerks, also wigged and gowned. Below them was the Table of the House—nothing indeed but a sturdy table to put things on. One of the things was the great Mace, symbol of the Speaker's authority from the Crown—literally an intimidating medieval club. And from the Table a narrow carpet stretched down the aisle to the Bar, the boundary within which no non-Member might advance, and to which the House might summon any British citizen to judgment. The Bar had given its name to the whole tribe of barristers, and was nothing else than a bar of metal which might be stretched across the aisle to mark the boundary by drawing it out of a hollow railing at one side of the room to meet another railing at the other.

Indeed the literalness of all these hallowed terms was staggering, but together with the dimensions and arrangement of the room, it told you more about the character of the House of Commons than all the books ever written.

And the aspect of the place was something to ponder.

It was almost midnight on the third day of the debate on the Address in answer to the Queen's Speech.

The Queen's Speech had been written by Mr. Disraeli and read in this instance by the Lord Chamberlain in the Queen's name. It had been a general statement of the policy which the Government intended to pursue, and this debate on what answer to return to it was in effect a test of that policy in the House.

It was conceivable that the policy would be rejected, and when that happens to a policy there is nothing for the Government to do but resign. No one seriously expected that to happen now. The Government was at present too young and strong to suffer a defeat upon such general policy lines as had been laid down in the Queen's Speech, always provided it had the support of its own Party, which was to be assumed. But the debate on the Address was a fair barometer of what might happen when the component parts of the policy were presented later in specific bills; and there were signs of impending hurricanes.

On the first day the formidable Mr. Gladstone had thundered against the Suez Canal announcement. He had as good as said that British imperialism in Egypt was not compatible with the plans communicated to him by God, and he had indicated that at four million pounds sterling the ninny of a Government had been swindled anyhow. But it was known that he was saving his heaviest bolts to attack the authorizing bill itself at its most vulnerable point, the 2½ per cent promised to the Rothschilds.

Now the debate had reached that portion of the Queen's Speech touching on the Condition of the People, and the signs were only gloomier.

The domestic policy outlined by the Conservative Government sounded more like something the two Labour Members would have offered. It advocated the elevation of servants to equal rights with their masters before the law. Relief of trades-unions from criminal liability for strikes in restraint of trade. Slum clearance and public housing. It proposed to compel manufacturers to purge waste matter of impurities before emptying it into the rivers. It wanted expensive safety regulations for factories and merchant ships. It would extend education at public expense, forbid the enclosure of common lands by private interests, and preserve the commons as public playgrounds.

The Liberals, who represented the great manufacturing interests of the country, looked upon this program with horror. But many of the Conservatives were equally shocked by it. It was the boldest departure from Adam Smith and the doctrine of laissez faire to which any British Government yet had committed itself. It smacked of Socialism. There was doubt that with this sort of policy Mr. Disraeli could hold even his own party together.

The Old Guard of the Conservative Party, that party of the aristocrats and old landed gentry, was the nucleus round which the rebels were rallying. And at the centre of the Old Guard, or very close to it, was the Member for Saffron Walden, Essex.

This gentleman was descended from a Frenchman who had come to England from Germany with George the First, and who, having a bit of money, had purchased broad lands whereon he and his heirs had prospered. The family name then had been Godchaux, but after its first hundred years in the mouths of English squires, had become Gadshaw, and now, in the mouths of mocking Members a quarter century its present holder's junior, it sometimes became "Gad Sir." For Sir John Gadshaw (whose great-grandfather had purchased a baronetcy from George the Third) was usually the most indignant, warlike, and explosive bit of old England in the room. He was a large man with a face like two raw beefsteaks rampant to either side of a giblet; and all night while lesser spirits had wandered out of the House from weariness or boredom, he had maintained his bulk on the front bench of the Conservative Gallery, mentally turning down thumbs upon the gladiators below. For if he had lost faith in the Conservatives, he liked Liberals and Irishmen less, Irishmen least of all. And at the moment he had also lost faith in the Speaker, for the Speaker had just recognized the Member for Limerick, the Hon. F. X. Devoy.

Mr. Devoy said that on behalf of his colleagues and of the people of Ireland he wished to express regret for the distress suffered by Her Majesty in the Wheeler Case, as reported in the public press. However, he said, and cleared his throat. It had come to his ears, he roared, that in this connexion certain rogues and reptiles had circulated a report that this same boy Wheeler had been in the pay of Irishmen whose purpose had been the fell crime of regicide.

A sudden hush had fallen over the House.

He said he wished here and now, once for all, categorically and unequivocally, to give the lie to these liars. He said it was a cowardly attempt to blacken the name of the Irish People, perpetrated by unscrupulous bigots and backbiters hiding behind the foul skirts of Rumour. He said he hereby challenged any man in the House to stand up and prove or defend this nasty little story. He said he noticed that no man stood up. And so, he said, he would call upon the Honourable Secretary of State for Home Affairs to give the House the truth about the case, and he would move an amendment to the Address stipulating that Irishmen had nothing to do with it. He sat down amid the cheers of his colleagues.

The Speaker said the gentleman was out of order.

But Devoy had made a sensation. That pregnant phrase, the Wheeler Case, pronounced upon the floor of the House, had quickened the benches like a trumpet blast. Tired gentlemen lolling in their seats had come alert, whispered conversations had ceased, Members in the act of passing out into the lobby had stopped, turned to listen. And at the Speaker's rejection of Devoy's remarks the House began to grumble.

The Speaker called for order, said that if the Home Secretary wished to make a statement on the subject it might be introduced in the proper form.

Obviously taken off guard, Secretary Cross said he did not wish to make a statement at this time.

More grumbling. For a few moments it had seemed that the Members might be privileged to hear the suppressed facts of the most widely discussed case of the day, the greatest mystery of the day, and now they were being put off again.

The dewlap of Sir John Gadshaw hung quivering over the rail of the Conservative Gallery. As secretary of the Essex Society for the Protection of Young Females and chairman of the Metropolitan Free Drinking Fountain Association, he had participated in two indignation meetings inspired by the Wheeler Case, as well as in two resolutions insisting upon the country's right to be informed in a crisis; he had also written personally two letters to *The Times* about it, and so was deemed by his friends to be an authority in the subject. He was also a staunch defender of the Throne and a believer in the dictum that Englishmen ought to settle their own affairs, and he considered Devoy nothing but a meddling foreigner.

"Damned cheek, I call it! Why don't Cross put him in his place?"

On the floor of the House sat another Member who also looked upon the Wheeler Case as more or less his property. This was William Robinson, the radical, known to his admirers as the "Brummagem Harrier." He was one of those who, outside the House, had tried to use it as a pry to open the whole Royal Household to critical examination. He had also considered doing so in the House, during the Question hour, but being as much in the dark about it as anyone else, he had not cared to risk challenging the Government with it. Now this had been done for him by someone else, and he saw that he had the Irish Party at his back. He rushed into the breach and moved adjournment of the debate under Standing Order No. 10 for discussion of the case "as a matter of definite and urgent public importance."

This was drastic procedure, often used as a method of obtaining censure of the Government in an emergency, and its employment now created another sensation.

"Damn him!" said Sir John Gadshaw, his Tory sentiments rising.

But the Chair declined to receive Robinson's motion, saying that a matter under police jurisdiction could not be raised under this rule, nor should a matter that might lead to reflections upon the Sovereign, as the Member for Birmingham very well ought to know.

"Hear, hear!" said Gadshaw loudly.

In the impasse, the only man on his feet was the Hon. Cornelius
Lynch, of Dublin, and catching the Speaker's eye, Mr. Lynch said
he wished to point out that no English Sovereign had ever been murdered by the Irish so the Irish were without precedent for the deed,
whereas he might point to the case of Charles the First, of sacred
memory, might he rest in peace—murdered by the English themselves, and that after a trial by the House of Commons. (Laughter.)
And as for raising a matter that might lead to reflections on the
Sovereign, what about that case, he wanted to know. Wherefore he
moved a question of breach of privilege, to wit, denial of access by
the House to the Sovereign's person.

The Chair said it was clear that the Member did not understand
either the intent or application of the privilege raised, and declined
the motion.

The House stopped laughing and growled.

That sane old Parliamentarian, the Speaker, in his solemn canoni-
cals, was not shocked at this childish behaviour of the House. It was
an aggregation of individualists, the main body of them not much
different at bottom from the bluff and often peevish ealdormen of
the Saxon Witan—lords of the country's natural resources and private energies, crusty country magistrates, old soldiers; and with
these, a little camp of unappeasables waging a war of attrition in a
cause lost seven hundred years. For all the practical nonsense of the
wigs and robes, the Mace and the Bar, this was still a council of
shires and parishes, tribes and families and individuals, with many
things in common and many differences, old feuds, and here and
there an ancient grievance, an open wound. The Members kept a
virile grasp of their representative responsibilities and privileges, and
for a principle could fight like heroes, or when their interests clashed,
bicker like farmers across a boundary stone. But sometimes in what
seemed their pettiest polemics one could catch the echo of some tremendous avowal, a right wrung from a Lancastrian king, a guarantee
from a Stuart, a freedom asserted in defeat since the time of Strong-

bow. Even in this, a continuity, a reaffirmation, a handing on. But sometimes it was confoundedly annoying; and the Speaker called loudly for order.

All this time the Prime Minister and Leader of the House, Benjamin Disraeli, had been sitting as if detached from the proceedings, sunk into himself in a characteristic half-somnolent attitude, on the front bench by the Table, one leg hanging over the other, arms folded, his tall hat tipped over his brows, his heavy eyelids drooping of their own weight. Now the hanging leg lifted itself and fell into place beside the other, one hand removed the hat, placed it gently, top down, upon the floor, and it was seen that the eyes were open: it was seen by many, for these unobtrusive signs of life had in them the quality of phenomena, as if manifested by stone. And now he was rising. It was this, more than the remonstrances of the Speaker, that restored order.

In a low voice that somehow penetrated to all corners of the chamber, the Prime Minister said the Government did not wish to leave the impression that it was unwilling to make public the facts of the Wheeler Case or to debate them. On the contrary, in deference to the wishes of the House, the Government itself would move adjournment to examine the case at whatever time the Speaker might deem proper. But he wished to suggest to Mr. Speaker, he said, that Mr. Speaker, having no information on the case, might suppose that as a matter under police jurisdiction it had nothing to do with the questions now before the House. He respectfully suggested that it did. There were certain aspects of the case that were so closely bound up with the Government's policies that in order to discuss them, he submitted, it was hardly necessary to change the subject. If, therefore, Mr. Speaker would accept the Government's assurances in this regard, Mr. Disraeli would enlighten the House upon the Wheeler Case during the debate on the Address. And he sat down.

It had made eyebrows shoot up like window blinds. Not a man

THE MUDLARK

present but itched to hear about Wheeler, but this was presenting the opportunity in a way none had expected and all considered reckless. It meant that the Government offered its own precious time for discussion of a very touchy question, in such a way that a defeat upon the question could have serious repercussions upon its policies, and although Disraeli might be very sure of himself, he could be too sure. Risky tactics. But the Brummagem Harrier scrutinized the Prime Minister through narrowed lids, seeing in this courteous acquiescence to his wishes nothing but treachery. F. X. Devoy, on the contrary, grinned like a man who has outwitted a leprechaun. The Liberals were puzzled but hopeful. Uneasiness rumbled over the Conservative benches and erupted in the gallery.

"Jehoshephat! What's this?" said Gadshaw. "Another leap in the dark? Head in the lion's mouth? Angels wouldn't do it, sir! Always said he wasn't fit. Piece of damned nonsense!"

Secretary Cross himself was dumbfounded, and although the Prime Minister leaned over and whispered a word to him, he did not look reassured. Even the Speaker seemed to deprecate the idea. But he accepted the Government's assurances. He pursed his lips doubtfully, gave his head a shake, and again recognized Mr. Disraeli.

Word of what was passing had circulated in the lobby, and the half-empty House began to fill up again. Returning Members like late-comers to a church service moved awkwardly to their places amid the irritated "sh!-ing" of their colleagues as that oddly exotic figure that looked like Hammurabi in a frock coat slowly regained its full height and softly pronounced the antique formula:

"Mr. Speaker, sir——"

20

The Speaker remembered the first speech Benjamin Disraeli had ever made in that exclusive debating club almost forty years before—a spectacular failure. The Young Jew had just come in for Maidstone, and what a strange theatrical figure he had made, his hair all curls, his fine hands sparkling with rings, his magnificent waistcoat glittering with gold chains. The Speaker remembered with what curiosity the House had turned to look at him as he rose, that notorious stripling who had engaged in such a violent public controversy with Daniel O'Connell and challenged him to a duel. "We shall meet at Philippi," he had said when O'Connell refused; and now, they had all supposed, this was Philippi, for here he was in Parliament at last, and O'Connell had just sat down. The Speaker remembered how he had lashed out at O'Connell over the snarls of the Irish champion's colleagues, and then launched into such high-blown rhetoric that the whole House had begun to laugh and jeer at him, and how finally he had gone down in a gale of hostility, but with his tattered pennant flying:

"Though you won't hear me now, the time will come when I will make you hear me!"

Sometimes the Speaker wondered if the Prime Minister had ever recovered from the wounds of that famous rebuff. But he remembered that some few Members had admired his courage, his readiness, his beautiful voice, his command of language, and had discerned in them the seeds of triumph.

"But first," they had counselled him, according to the stories one heard, "you must learn to understand the House. They thought you too forward, and much too brilliant. And they resented that rhetoric. Speak plainly and to the point. Don't reason too well, or they'll think you're trying to be witty. Try to be a little dull. Astonish them with figures and dates; then they'll think you sound. Bore them, and after a while they'll begin to yearn for the wit and eloquence they know are in you; because in spite of all, they do like a good show."

Well, Benjamin Disraeli understood the House now—no man better; and in this the Speaker felt a bond with him. The Speaker enjoyed listening to Disraeli, not so much for the evident talents that dazzled the others, but for the less evident ones—for his thorough comprehension of the House's mind, his extreme sensitivity to its moods, his mastery of the instrument of procedure, and for the subtle way he bent all three to his purposes. Among the Prime Minister's admirers it was not unusual now to hear him called a great man; the Speaker might have his doubts there, but those of Benjamin Disraeli's detractors who questioned his fitness to lead the Commons the Speaker despised: he thought the Old Jew, if nothing else, a great Parliamentarian. He hoped he had not put his foot in it this time.

Mr. Disraeli informed the House that any suspicion of an Irish conspiracy against the Queen in the Wheeler Case must be deprecated by Her Majesty's Government, since the most exhaustive police inquiry had uncovered no ground for suspecting anything of the kind.

The quiet words, which in a moment had dispelled the cloud that had hung over Irishmen for months, were greeted with jubilant cheers from the Irish benches, and he waited patiently till the Speaker had persuaded them to subside.

He said that so far as could be ascertained—and the police had left no clue unexplored—Wheeler had been quite alone in his actions and would have to bear censure and punishment alone.

More cheers from the Irish, and a hearty clap on the back from Mr. Lynch to Mr. Devoy. For them it was a valuable victory. But over Mr. Disraeli's head, the frown of Sir John Gadshaw deepened. What did the man want to whitewash the Irish for? Everyone knew they were rebels, and if they weren't mixed up in this it was ten to one they were hatching some other mischief. For the Government to deprecate the country's healthy suspicion of them was nothing but nonsense.

Disraeli went on to recite the overt facts of the Wheeler Case. The boy was a Thames mudlark who had stepped ashore at Windsor from a coal barge; he had entered the castle through an open gate, and in the courtyard had fallen through an open coalhole into the cellars; from there he had found his way up to the Queen's dining room, where he had been seized before Her Majesty's eyes; then he had been interrogated by the servants, and one of them, a kindly man if in this instance a misguided one, believing the boy's story that he had only meant to sight-see, had permitted him to sit on the throne.

"It is an extraordinary story," Disraeli conceded, "and one that the police hesitated to accept. For indeed from the series of fortuitous circumstances by which the boy Wheeler got into the castle, it appeared that the way must have been prepared for him. The police have not been able to discover that it had. They find that the gate had been left open by a trusted porter and the coalhole by a tradesman; that a dense fog blinded the sentries to the boy and the boy to the coalhole. But the House may judge of the matter for itself when it has heard me out, for there is something more to tell. But I confess that I am as puzzled as anyone.

"It happened that I was present in the castle on the evening in question, and I was puzzled enough at the time to see the boy in the Queen's dining room; I was more puzzled later to find him sitting on the throne; but I am most puzzled now to encounter him at the Bar of this House. And yet," he continued without pausing, as the eyes of the whole House mechanically followed his to the Bar as if Wheeler actually had been standing there, "and yet, when I consider the larger aspects of the case, it seems that this must have been his destination from the beginning." The House, having stared for an instant at empty air, self-consciously looked back at him. "Now the House of Commons," he went on, "is a strange place to try a mudlark. But it is the best of all places to discuss those aspects of the case that I have mentioned, for they concern the nation. They offer us here a practical study in the business of government, and it is in the light of them that I shall hold up the Wheeler Case to the inquest of the House. I shall speak of various things. Of London, of Parliament, of theories and policies of government, of nations and the wealth of nations, of children, and perhaps of politics. And if these subjects appear irrelevant to the Wheeler Case, I will remind the House that it is not of the Wheeler Case we are speaking, save only as it sheds light upon these subjects, since indeed Mr. Speaker has not given us leave to adjourn the debate; and yet, I submit, they are all bound up with the story of this mudlark."

The Speaker, gazing upon the Prime Minister with an entirely judicial expression as became so impartial an officer, thought, Ah, why did I doubt him? But the Brummagem Harrier divined here only the insinuative tactics he had expected and thought to himself that the man was a snake. And on the front Opposition bench directly across the aisle, Benjamin Disraeli's great antagonist, William Ewart Gladstone, grew uneasy. He had nothing but loathing for the devious methods of Benjamin Disraeli, and when he sensed one commencing to operate he was always uneasy. He began to be especially so now, because he had no notion what Disraeli could be getting at. How could he? The Wheeler Case was the Government's property: how could he tell what it contained? And now he felt that his disadvantage was growing, for what Disraeli was saying now seemed to have no bearing on the case, and where it might be leading baffled him.

"There is a sensitive plant," Disraeli was saying in his gentlest and most dulcet tone, "called the Brazilian mimosa, which is so delicate that if you touch it, its stalk will droop and its leaves close tight; and we have the word of the learned doctors, Adam Smith, Malthus, Bentham, and the elder Mill, that it is the same with the wealth of nations. The wealth of a nation, they tell us, consists in the aggregate material wealth of its individuals, and it withers at the touch of Government; it cannot be cultivated, it must be left to nature; by which I take it that it does not like civilization. But the mimosa grows in greenhouses and is a harmless plant, and is very beautiful, while the wealth of nations, these scholars teach, thrives only in a jungle, and kills many other plants around it. That it does so, say Smith, Malthus, Bentham, and Mill, does not matter so long as it grows. And this has long puzzled me, because the pictures they draw of it are very ugly. And I should be inclined to regard the wealth of nations as a plant better done without, did I not suspect that the learned doctors, being, I hope, human, have erred, and that what they take for the wealth of nations is not the wealth of nations at all."

Mr. Gladstone shifted his weight from one sturdy ham to the other, crossed his knees, and tugged irritably at one muttonchop whisker.

"Then what shall I say is the true wealth of nations?" went on Mr. Disraeli easily in his beautiful voice. "What shall I call the grand capital of Britain? The faces of the Honourable Members on the Liberal benches opposite warn me that they think I go too far. Adam

Smith is their prophet; that one of the laity should presume to deny his first canon and offer another in its place seems to them the height of impudence and of rashness. But I think I may repeat to the Liberal gentlemen in perfect safety an immortal British platitude of which their own faces are shining examples, and say that the true wealth of Britain is British character. They dare not deny this, nor do they wish to; the private fortunes which they and their fathers have amassed in commerce are founded upon it; and since this self-won power was the shibboleth by which they came up into this House, it may be said with equal truth, No character, no Liberals.''

A chuckle ran over the Conservative benches, but the Liberals looked to appreciate neither the joke nor the compliment.

"But character, being a word so often loosely used, may be an ambiguous one in this connexion, and I may be understood to mean the enterprise of the British, their power of will, their resourcefulness, their common sense. I include other qualities with these. I mean their gusto, for example, and their imagination, their boldness, their fortitude, and their probity, their doggedness and their chivalry, their deep humility and their inborn pride. I mean what it is that makes them so formidable in war, courageous in adversity, and generous in victory, makes them good farmers and honest merchants, and inspires them to sail the seas, conquer deserts of sand and ice, explore with the same intelligent wonder the infinities of the firmament and of a flower, see in the majestic procession of the equinoxes a confutation of all the profound babble of the laboratory, and what it is that can bring tears to their eyes when they look upon the beauty of their fathers' fields. This is a spiritual fund, not a material one, and it is the true wealth of Britain. It too is a tender plant— not so tender as the mimosa, I agree, for it does not thrive in greenhouses, but it is even less like the wild orchid of Dr. Smith, for it wants cultivation, and a foul soil will poison it.''

The Speaker began to catch the drift, and again was reassured; he placed one long finger against his cheek and listened. Sir John

— 270 —

Gadshaw, too, began to feel a little better, not because he caught the drift, though he felt immensely flattered, but because he noticed the discomfiture of the Liberals.

"Perhaps," Disraeli said, "there are some Britons in the House who do not believe this. To them the British character is indestructible; it is imparted to the babe by the climate, by the limestone in our water, and is bred into him by the glorious history of his fathers. It may be that they have never seen what prison or poverty can do, even to a Briton, and have forgotten the history of Rome.

"Now it must have been observed before that Messers Smith, Malthus, Bentham, and Mill have a good deal in common with Mr. Darwin, for they believe in the law of natural selection—survival of the fittest; indeed, Messers Malthus and Bentham have been acknowledged by Mr. Darwin. . . ."

"Darwin!" thought Gladstone irritably; what in heaven's name had Darwin to do with it?

"I am aware," Disraeli was saying, "that to many honourable Members, Mr. Darwin's name is anathema, or so they would have us believe; and I should spare their feelings did it not appear that while condemning his theory of natural selection in biology, they openly profess it in social philosophy. Here, Mr. Speaker, is a glaring inconsistency which may suggest that although these Members condemn the estimable Josiah Wedgwood's grandson as a heretic, they are in reality worse than he is. For Mr. Darwin merely reports what seems to him to be a law of nature, a law for which he in no way can be held responsible, while these gentlemen have not only accepted for years the same primitive principle in its cruelest form, but they have long been its apologists in this House, and whether it be a true law or not, they have certainly laboured to make it one. So if Mr. Darwin in his diligent researches into the mysteries of the flora and fauna of the earth, has found out nothing else, I should say that he has found out these gentlemen."

Another chuckle from the Conservatives grouped behind their

Chief; but from his seat only a few feet under Mr. Disraeli's nose in that intimate chamber, Mr. Gladstone glared at him, abominating with all the passionate sincerity of his soul the sophistry by which he felt that his Party was being placed in a false position by this unscrupulous politician, and mentally he began to gather thunder-bolts to annihilate him in reply. But angry as he was now, he was calm by comparison with what he felt a moment later as his arch-enemy touched him in his religion:

"By the same token, it appears that in the great controversy now raging between Revelation and Science, these same paladins of the Church, to whom Mr. Darwin's name is anathema, have been paying the Church no more than lip service. I trust that they are in the minority here, for I think that on this question the time has come for an examination of conscience by the House."

Mr. Gladstone's celebrated muttonchops seemed to stand straight out from his face and give off sparks.

"Parliament," said Disraeli calmly, "is the Palladium of the Es-tablished Church, but it also has something in common with Mr. Darwin, because it too is concerned with the evolution of Man; and now it must decide whether it will subscribe to his principle of natural selection. But let us view the question clearly, in its applica-tion to the purpose for which we are assembled, keeping in mind that Mr. Darwin himself holds out to us another possibility, which he calls 'man's power of selection.' And what is this? Why, it is the art of improving the breed, and we see the results of it all round our British countrysides—in our foxhounds, bred for speed, stamina, and perspicacity; in our sheep dogs, bred for intelligence, gentle-ness, and heart; and in our bulldogs, bred not alone for their strong jaws but for their proverbial courage and tenacity. These are the descendants of the wolf, the jackal, and possibly other species of monster long extinct. And how were they evolved? Not like the pariah dog of India, or the cringing mongrel of East End London— by cuffs and kicks, in privation and filth—but through the intelligent care of their masters. If I inquired whether this had been worth it, I should make myself ridiculous and draw down upon my head the wrath of every sportsman in the House. But permit me to inquire whether it be either right or reasonable to go on improving our breeds of dog and not our breed of man? Let me present to the House the principle of natural selection as the alternative to the principle of civilization. Then let us make the choice.

"But if you believe natural selection to be a true law governing the struggle for existence, and whether or not you approve of it and would impose it upon your countrymen as part of the Constitution, do not imagine that we have it in Britain now. What we have is in fact a system of unnatural selection, for we have unnatural conditions and cannot postulate an equitable struggle. What we have is a perversion of man's power of selection, since the great inequities of the struggle are of our own making. Britons never would permit such outrageous handicapping as this in a horse race, for when it comes to horse racing Britons are true sportsmen; but somewhere in the character I have just been extolling there must be an ignoble flaw, or they would not condone it in the human race.

"The gentlemen opposite need not fear that for my part I would indulge the faint of heart or coddle mediocrity. I would only forbid the unfair conditions of the struggle for existence and broaden the struggle for the fruits of it. The infant mortality rate among our urban poor is appalling; yet many deaths are never even registered. Many infants each year are drowned in the Thames by their parents. Were they all gathered into some great Stoke Poges, what sad elegies might they inspire to shame us with thoughts of what their country might have done for them and they for their country? For who shall say there were no Hampdens among them, or Miltons? Ah, but one of them might easily have been Wheeler, and then we should have been spared the bother of trying him in this august and busy House of Commons.

"How ever did Wheeler escape? For only think how hard society tried to kill him. It laid an ambush for him at his birth, surrounding his cradle with rats and vermin. It sent off gasses from foul drains to pollute the air he breathed. It tried to poison his mother's milk through her drinking water, but succeeded only in poisoning his mother. She died of typhus before he could walk. It was not necessary to poison his father also, because he had never known a father. He seemed now to be entirely at the mercy of his country. It cut off the light from him, and the proper food. It sent him into the Thames to be a mudlark, barefoot and clothed in the merest rags, exposed to cold and damp and fever. But nothing touched this child. If we assume that he was unfit for survival in the first place, then he must have been an exception to Mr. Darwin's law. Or was he, on the contrary, exceptionally fit for survival?

"His country did not stop at attacking his physical being. It also attacked his spirit, and his soul. It taught him nothing. It withheld the word of God from him. It did not tell him of his English heritage, for it never occurred to his countrymen that he had a heritage. And in the lanes and warrens of the river front, it exposed him to the worst influences of immorality and evil. It cast him out; it denied hope to him.

"But somewhere it failed.

"For one day he raised his head and looked about him, and he walked out of the mud, and he went to see the Queen. Had the way been prepared for him? Windsor Castle's walls are high, but they were no let to Wheeler. The Household Guards, I am told, are the finest soldiers in England, but he passed them as if they had not been there. And he saw the Queen, as you have heard. And sat on the throne, as charged.

"And so," said Disraeli, "he comes to stand tonight at the Bar of the House of Commons.

"We cannot have every boy in Britain attempting to emulate Wheeler, as I am sure they would all like to do, nor countenance actions which do not accord with the respect owed to the Sovereign.

Wheeler must be punished. And I caution the House not to look upon his actions in the light of a mere boyish adventure. True, he is only seven; but was it simply that as he stood in the mud that day he heard, as children do, as young Dick Whittington heard, the high bells of Cockaigne? Partly so, I do not doubt. But the bells of Cockaigne have made criminals no less than lord mayors of London; and in quest of another motive our efficient police have explored every phase of Wheeler's life, his character, even his ideas.

"To begin with, it would be a mistake to suppose him an ordinary mudlark. Somewhere he has picked up stray bits of knowledge which in themselves stamp him an extraordinary one. For example, he has heard of at least two of his country's greatest heroes—Wellington and Nelson; and though it shock the House, I must say that among mudlarks this is most unusual. Then he exhibits an unnatural attitude towards England; unnatural because in spite of all it has done to him, he seems to love it. Now some sailor told him that Her Majesty the Queen was the Mother of England. We have all heard this expression, and of course we do not take it literally, but this unenlightened little orphan did. And that, too, was why he turned to her, and went trailing mud into Windsor Castle. And that is why I say that what he did was no mere boyish adventure. But it seems to me that no duke or admiral has ever paid the Queen of the United Kingdom a handsomer compliment."

The House waited attentively for his next words, but across the aisle William E. Gladstone sat adamant with folded arms, seeing through the whole performance. He saw Disraeli attempting to make Wheeler into a symbol of Liberal Oppression in order to secure a sympathetic reception for the Government's policies. What charlatanism! Disraeli knew perfectly well that the Liberal Party was as much interested in improving the people's lot as the Conservatives were—more so; the only disagreement there was as to method. What a Pharisee the man was! But Gladstone, with all his courage and his hot indignation, could be a tactician too, and he began to question the wisdom of replying after all—at least for the present. Let Disraeli bait him into attacking the Government's policies through the Wheeler Case? Stand up and lay into that pitiful figure of a child that this sorcerer had created for his own design? That would be just what the sorcerer wished him to do. Better, perhaps, to let the Wheeler Case pass for the trifle it was, to wait and attack the real issues in an atmosphere unclouded by ectoplasm. Gladstone, too, could sense the temper of the House.

In that small pause, Disraeli's eyes had rested on his rival's face, and as if reading his thoughts, he said: "Some may have wondered at my motives when I rose here to air the Wheeler Case in this House; but I could not fail to see that in this the whole faith of Tory democracy was involved. Tory democracy conceives that government exists in Parliament for the good of all the governed, and that it should be administered through the great institutions of the country; and it conceives that of these institutions, the patron and guardian of all is that avatar of our continuity, the Sovereign. By what a felicitous turn of events has it come to pass, therefore, that through the Queen, this small Briton makes his appeal to us. He seems to appeal not for himself alone, but for all British children who are as he is. And as Leader of the Conservative Government, I am bound to give him a hearing. But the House is entitled to hear both sides.

"In defence of the treatment that Wheeler has received from his country, the doctrine of Mr. Malthus may be adduced. It is a doctrine that still exerts a strong influence over the minds of practical Christians, for it seems to demonstrate that Christianity is not good arithmetic. By this doctrine the country is overpopulated in relation to the food supply. I do not deny this. In all sorrow I remember that I predicted it when Parliament repealed the Corn Duties. But the Malthusians say there is nothing to do now but leave the surplus population to its fate under the law of survival of the fittest. I say there is nothing to do but get more food. But Mr. Malthus proved mathematically that the population of a country, if unchecked, would double itself every twenty-five years and soon outstrip the capacity of its lands to feed it, and by projecting this theorem he proved that in time the human race would outstrip the capacity of all the lands of the earth. I am not a born mathematician; I make no attack on this abstraction. But to meet such a condition, if indeed it ever arises, I place my faith in the ingenuity of Man, which I doubt that even Mr. Malthus could have calculated to its ultimate extent; and I place my faith, if the House please, in that which confounds all mathematics—the Divine Providence of the Loaves and Fishes. In the meantime I propose to exert my own ingenuity towards feeding the British, so that if it comes to the worst, they at least may not be the first people to go under. But I do not insult the House by urging this policy as a reasonable one. I only say it is the honourable one. I say that we cannot in conscience take any other. And if to take it is to set ourselves like pygmies against the juggernaut of economic law, I invite the House to join me in doing so."

"Hear, hear!" cried an old Protectionist behind him. And a shipping magnate in the midst of the Liberals dared to echo, "Hear, hear!"

Mr. Disraeli ignored them both. He dropped his voice to a tone of simple exposition: "The Government's foreign policy——"

"Hah!" thought Gladstone, and looked around at the naïve rebel who had echoed, "Hear, hear!"

"The Government's foreign policy," Disraeli was saying, "which some have called imperialism, is in its simplest terms a policy of securing food for our population, bastions to secure the supply, now and in the future. The Government's domestic policy, which some have called socialism, is a policy of improving the breed. Together they make a national policy of survival. It is Christian because it embraces the ethic of Charity. It is honourable because it keeps faith with the public trust. Whether it be mathematical I have not inquired. But it is amenable to the assumption that if the theory of survival of the fittest applies among individuals, it must also apply among nations. So though it be contrary to Malthus, it confutes Malthus with Darwin."

"More of his sophistry!" muttered Gladstone.

"But," pursued Disraeli softly, "pardon me, I have never heard overpopulation complained of in time of war. I never heard that there were too many Britons at Lucknow or Sebastopol. I never heard there were too many at Waterloo—but after Waterloo, that was the first time I heard it. His Grace's troops had returned to our islands and been mustered out, and suddenly we discovered that they made too many. There was not enough food or work to go round, and I remember that when some sixty thousand Britons assembled in St. Peter's Fields, Manchester, to demand relief from their distress, the soldiery effected a small reduction in the population on the spot. And history calls that battle—Peterloo. It is a painful memory to us all. Yet the dragoons and yeomanry were more humane than their masters. They did it with swords and muskets.

"Gentlemen never say that the Battle of Peterloo was won on the playing fields of Eton. But taking His Grace no more literally than he intended, they have a notion that Waterloo was won there. Undoubtedly there is some truth in saying so, but only some truth, for I think part of the credit must go to the village commons, to the mines and mills and factories that gave us coal and cloth and gunpowder—and Liberals—and to the many hearths round which His Grace's men heard as children the tales of Hereward and Drake and Magna Charta. I should say that the idea of entrusting a country's battles to its upper classes was better suited to the days of knights and chivalry—yet historians tell us that the Battle of Agincourt was won by English bowmen. I should not say that it was. There is a strong case for the view that it was won by Welsh bowmen. But I should say only that it was won by Britons. And as I should make no distinction between Celt and Anglo-Norman in speaking of that victory, so should I make none between knight and peasant. I should remember:

> " 'For he today that sheds his blood with me
> Shall be my brother, be he ne'er so vile
> This day shall gentle his condition.'

"Yes, it may be the King never said that. But Shakespeare thought it worthy of the King. And in the end there may be some question which is better fit to speak for England—the King or the glover's son.

" 'We few,' runs the speech, 'we happy few!' So there were not too many Britons at Agincourt either. And if it was not by their numbers that Britons made memorable that St. Crispin's Day, then it must have been by their quality."

"Hear, hear!" a voice from the heavens was heard exclaiming emotionally, and it was the voice of Sir John Gadshaw.

"It was the same at Waterloo, at Lucknow, and at Sebastopol; it was the same off Finisterre and Gravelines; indeed, it is a striking thing how often quality alone has saved us. And although I doubt that we need ever worry about outnumbering our enemies, I think from this that we had better take care to preserve our quality.

"Let us consider whether we are in any danger of losing it.

"Mr. Darwin holds that a degeneration of species is caused by changed conditions of life and by the disuse of parts. Obviously we have created these causes in Britain, and obviously if Mr. Darwin is right we must expect the same effect.

"Before the Napoleonic Wars, this was an agricultural country. The only great city was London, which had less than a million souls, and on the average only about a dozen to an acre. Glasgow, Liverpool, Manchester, and Birmingham had each of them a population of considerably less than a hundred thousand. That was the Britain of yeomen and craftsmen, of benevolent paternalism and noblesse oblige. Today we have an industrial country. Our agriculture is undone, our yeomen are a vanishing race; and craftsmanship has been replaced by machinery. To feed the machines half a million Britons upwards from the age of ten are engaged in burrowing into the earth for coal, without sunlight or fresh air, in oppressive heat, and amid hazards that each year take the lives of more than a thousand. To serve the machines, millions of Britons from the age of ten are confined in factories through all the hours of daylight, at tasks that require little skill and that discourage ingenuity. We have an urban society now, and under the smoke that denies it the beauty of the sky, multitudes dwell in sinks of rottenness and degradation. Benevolent paternalism is out of date; we live now by laissez faire—or die of it; and the 'pure reason' of survival of the fittest has superseded that quaint injunction—noblesse oblige. Thus have the conditions of life changed in these islands. But there have also been some less obvious changes. For in some parts of the East End of London, the tales of Hereward and Drake and Magna Charta that His Grace's men heard as children—and even the tales of Waterloo that they left us dying—are becoming as unfamiliar as nursery rhymes are there.

"And what of the disuse of parts? Do you suppose that in a large percentage of our population we are not atrophying intellect? Stunting imagination? Murdering morality? Breaking pride on the wheel and smothering gusto in the cradle? Are we not breeding for physical infirmity, mental disease, and spiritual prostration, engendering hate and social disunion, and so cultivating the destruction of the British nation?

"Mr. Darwin, it is true, tells us that nature takes ages to effect any marked changes in species. But he also tells us that man, by his power of selection, can do it in a few generations, and we know this to be a fact, for it bears out our own experiments with animals. If we think that man cannot do it with man, we have only to compare the factory slave of today with his grandsire, the cottage craftsman; then it may occur to us to wonder what his grandson will be like. If we think that man cannot do it with man, let us trace for ourselves the ugly changes produced in but a single generation by a few years in any prison.

"We are told in *The Origin of Species* that the greatest anomaly in nature is a bird that cannot fly. I should have thought it was a human spirit that could not soar, but these are common in Britain now, and perhaps are no more than a paradox of the times. Mr. Darwin cites for us a freak of nature called the logger-headed duck, of South America, which he says can only flap along the surface of the water. But I will cite you an English mudlark, and say it is a greater anomaly, not because it cannot raise itself above the mud, but because it did—because from the mud of Thames it climbed into the highest air of the Kingdom; for not by any physical laws did it do this, but in spite of them. It was as if the principles of biology, gravity, and even chance had been suspended for the sake of this small bird, and perhaps for our astonishment. It was as if that sublime power of aspiration which in the beginning was vouchsafed to the whole flock, and which we have done so much to destroy in so many, here by some phenomenon had been preserved in full vigour and suddenly commissioned to execute a marvel as a rebuke to us. And since there is nothing in Mr. Darwin's book to explain this, perhaps we should go back to the book of Genesis. For surely the spirit of God moved upon the face of the waters."

For an instant the gaunt figure of Mr. Disraeli stood immobile, the fingers of one hand resting upon the table; then it seemed to relax, and the eyes ran lightly over the silent benches. The voice proceeded in a milder key.

"But the House must not suppose that I rose here to defend Wheeler. I have said that the true wealth of Britain is British character, and by drawing attention to one facet of that character which seems to shine through the deed that Wheeler has done, I have only sought to advance the case of British children, among whom he is but a ha'penny bit of our great capital investment in the future. But nothing I have said can alter the fact that Wheeler has broken the law; nor must it be supposed that the Government commends him to his country's mercy.

"Had I been so careless of my duty as to rise here for that purpose, Mr. Speaker, I should have made a different speech—though indeed I should have had little heart for it after the first glance round these benches, bristling with whiskers and cordoned with watch-chains. I should have dwelt less upon Darwin and more upon Whittington, and tried to evoke in this redoubtable tribunal some memory, if one still lingers, of those bells I mentioned, which get so many children into trouble. But that would have been dangerous, for then it would have been supposed that I intended a comparison between Wheeler and his betters, and I should have had to explain that I intended no such thing, and that truly I have never believed those rumours that at Eton and at Harrow birch rods ply.

"And then I probably should have cited the old English law that a cat may look at a Queen—but there I should have been completely routed; for the Right Honourable Member opposite—my predecessor in office, that very Gabriel of the Opposition whose sword has routed so many casuists before—would have shown in a trice that in the House of Commons no cat was on trial, and that the law does not say a boy may look at anyone.

"I should then have been left without a single argument with which to defend the boy—save only one," and again the voice became grave and penetrating: "that if in this case a conspiracy did exist as charged, then that conspiracy was not against the Queen, but against the boy. But I should not have appealed to his country's mercy. I should have appealed only to its justice."

And Mr. Disraeli sat down.

21

          A strange speech. Sound or specious, honest or merely astute, it had been, and it remains, a regular curiosity of a speech, and one that only the inapprehensible Dizzy could have made.

He had sat down to the applause of both sides of the House, for it was true, the House did like a good show, and by incarnating the Condition of the Poor in the figure of a boy on trial, and that boy one that had captured the imagination of the country, he had deftly touched with melodrama the last hour of the sitting. In the lobby afterwards even Gadshaw congratulated him, but objected:

"What was that bit about 'bells of Cockaigne,' eh? Thought it was Bow Bells Whittington heard?"

"An error," the Prime Minister said, though he didn't say whose.

But as there echoed through the halls of Westminster Palace the archaic cry of "Who goes home?" gentlemen agreed that the speech had been mainly wasted eloquence. "Showy, but signifying nothing," was the way Gladstone described it later to his wife, who as usual had waited up for him; "I did not give him the satisfaction of a reply." But although it is easy enough to say so now, he might have done better if he had replied, and in fact Catherine Gladstone, who understood trifles much better than her husband did and always tried to protect him from them, secretly thought so at the time, and gave him a hint when she protested, "Oh, but, William! think of that poor little boy."

Sound asleep in his room over Clerkenwell, the poor little boy whom a wizard's wand had touched that night wore on his brow the mark of England's immortals, junior grade, the same as Dick Whittington and his cat.

For since in those days the newspapers reported the doings of Parliament with the same thoroughness that today they devote to those of cricketers and actresses, the Prime Minister's utterances, containing as they did the first explanation of the boy's case, were published in full, and they made a much greater impression upon the people than they seemed to have made upon the House. Wheeler, as pictured by Disraeli, became at once a cynosure for their chivalry, their strong sense of fair play, and oddly enough even for their pride of race. He became the image of the Downtrodden Poor like the figure in an alms poster, but at the same time a symbol of British enterprise, stamina, what not; transformed overnight from a little Guy Fawkes into a bloody little hero, the everlasting Briton in miniature. And seizing upon a happy phrase that the Prime Minister had used in passing, they named him in epitome of the wealth of his country—"the Ha'penny Bit."

"The Ha'penny Bit?" they said over their pints in the pubs when the name was mentioned. "Oh, aye. You may take your davy *he'll* get on." And they wagged their heads over him affectionately, calling him "a plucky little barstid."

They wrote letters in his behalf to the Government, the police and the newspapers, even to *The Times*; though the law was the law and there was no getting round the fact that the Ha'penny Bit had broken it. And resolutions expressing sympathy for him and condemning the social conditions under which they felt that he had not had a chance were passed by public bodies, including the Metropolitan Free Drinking Fountain Association and the Essex Society for the Protection of Young Females, and even by the Ancient Society of College Youth, meeting after bell practice in the Amen Tavern. Not that British Justice was likely to truckle to resolutions either; but the point was that instead of dissipating like ectoplasm, as Mr. Gladstone had expected, the figure of Wheeler only gained substance and grew larger and larger at Mr. Disraeli's back. And while a Liberal might hack away at the Government's policies as best he could, it was now too late to hack away at Wheeler, who had become their most formidable advocate. Nor under that pitiful but manly little stare was it possible any more to persuade people that the Liberal Party was as much interested in the welfare of the poor as the Party of British gentlemen was. So it was clear that even while putting nothing past his oily rival, Mr. Gladstone had underestimated him. For Mr. Disraeli, while pretending to address the House, actually had been talking round the House's shoulder and addressing the gullible people. This thing that had happened was incredible, it was unfair, it was positively wicked—but there it was. And it is in relation to its effects that the "wasted eloquence" must now be examined.

That session the Government put through with astonishing ease its program of social legislation, repudiating laissez faire and setting the pattern, historians tell us, for the whole reformation by which Britain was to adapt its gothic polity to a modern world; yet this was a Government of aristocrats. It was the beginning of a revolution so subtly accomplished that, says Arthur Bryant, "The great individualists rode to the guillotine in their own private coaches attended by the Benthamite livery."

But to say that all this came out of the Wheeler Case would be a very incautious thing to do, and in fact it would be hard to say just how far Wheeler's influence went, which may be one reason historians avoid the point and relate Wheeler's story separately in a noncommittal footnote. Perhaps they find the story, recent as it is, hard to believe at all. But then what do you find when you consult the historians on Whittington? That sure enough, in the fifteenth century, Richard Whittington was Lord Mayor of London, that he supplied cloth of gold for the wedding of the King's daughter, lent the King money, built a church, a college, a prison—all these entirely reasonable facts about a dead man the rest of us have never heard of—but that not for a minute do the historians believe the story that made Dick, the boy, immortal! Why they do not believe it they do not say, so it may be simply that they cannot believe it. But historians are honest if exasperating men, and they have to record that during the excavation of old Sir Richard's house in 1862, there was unearthed a stone of fifteenth-century workmanship on which were carved the figures of a boy and his cat. They also mention that on the prison he built there was a statue of a boy and his cat. Scholars have stood baffled before these figures, as before the great stone faces of Easter Island. And so whenever they exhume in their libraries the strange speech that Benjamin Disraeli made in the House of Commons that night, it must trouble them too, and set them wondering, for one weak moment before they go up to bed, whether the same Hand that wrote history could have written a fairy tale.

In Buckingham Palace next day, the proceedings of that sitting of Parliament were duly reported to Victoria by a Privy Councillor. When he came to Devoy's mention of the Wheeler Case, she gave a little start of shock and annoyance. As he went on to relate the wrangling over the matter, she frowned a little harder and twice clucked her tongue. But when he began to read the Prime Minister's remarks, she dropped her needlework and listened with growing horror.

Standing at her right, Emily Prior saw an ominous flush appear on the fat little neck. Mr. Brown, from his post behind Her Majesty's couch, could read as much in the mere set of the shoulders. And General Ponsonby, standing beside the Privy Councillor, could feel the air become charged with unpleasantness.

"Outrageous!" Victoria interrupted. "Was not the Prime Minister informed that we had insisted on privacy in this?"

The general answered: "I informed the Home Secretary, Ma'am."

"But the Prime Minister—wasn't he informed?"

"I can't say, Ma'am. I hardly thought——"

"He should have been informed! The Prime Minister should have been informed!"

The general bowed regretfully.

Victoria turned to the councillor. "Mr. Disraeli ought never to have made such a speech—he ought never to have made it!"

The councillor also bowed.

"We are very much displeased!" Victoria said with a sharp upward shake of the head that made her cheeks bounce. There was a pause. "Continue," she said.

The councillor continued: " 'How ever did Wheeler escape? For only think how hard society tried to kill him. . . .' "

Why, Mr. Disraeli actually had excused the boy, justified him in the eyes of the country! And to think it was he who had done this to her—Mr. Disraeli, whom she had come to regard as such a good friend, sympathetic and considerate, one of the few people in the world who understood her and on whom she had thought she could rely in her trials and her loneliness. Oh, it was cruel. Even if the boy wasn't so bad as they had all made out—that wasn't the point. . . .

The councillor read on: " 'His country did not stop at attacking his physical being. It also attacked his spirit, and his soul. It taught him nothing. It withheld the word of God from him. . . .' "

Not the point; but of course it wasn't the boy's fault entirely. No training. What could one expect? Heaven knew she had tried to set the country an example in rearing her own nine. . . .

" 'And in the lanes and warrens of the river front, it exposed him to the worst influences of immorality and evil. It cast him out; it denied hope to him. But somewhere it failed. For one day he raised his head and looked about him, and he walked out of the mud, and he went to see the Queen. . . .' "

Behind Her Majesty's back, Mr. Brown surreptitiously raised a hairy hand to his eye.

" 'We cannot have every boy in Britain attempting to emulate Wheeler, as I am sure they would all like to do, nor countenance actions which do not accord with the respect owed to the Sovereign. Wheeler must be punished. And I caution the House not to look upon his actions in the light of a mere boyish adventure. True, he is only seven; but was it simply that as he stood in the mud that day he heard, as children do, as young Dick Whittington heard, the high bells of Cockaigne?' "

The Queen had picked up her knitting again and begun to knit and purl as if by second nature, the way she did when Emily read aloud to her out of a book. Poor boy. Such a dirty little boy, she remembered.

" '. . . Some sailor told him that Her Majesty the Queen was the Mother of England. We have all heard this expression, and of course we do not take it literally, but this unenlightened little orphan did. And that, too, was why he turned to her, and went trailing mud into Windsor Castle.' "

Wasn't that rather impudent of Mr. Disraeli? Why, it was almost as if he were blaming her for the child's condition! The needles had stopped again, and Victoria frowned.

The Privy Councillor's voice droned on. He was really, she thought, a very bad reader.

" '. . . And it conceives that of these institutions, the patron and guardian of all is that avatar of our continuity, the Sovereign. By what a felicitous turn of events has it come to pass, therefore, that through the Queen, this small Briton makes his appeal to us. He seems to appeal not for himself alone, but for all British children . . .' "

No, Mr. Disraeli would never be impudent, not intentionally, of course; and what he said was quite true, in a way. . . . The needles had resumed their activity. But as the speech continued, they gathered speed and the red spot on the Queen's neck began to flame again, and from time to time her lips worked, though she heard the councillor to the end without any further comment. When the audience was over she merely signified that the speech was to be left with her so she might study it at her leisure; but her tone was not reassuring. The Privy Councillor hoped she did not blame *him*.

It reached the Prime Minister that he had incurred the Queen's displeasure. But this did not come entirely as a surprise to him; it was what he had been dreading. The people had not been the only audience he had been secretly addressing with that queer speech. But the surprise came later; for he never knew what had happened in the palace on that very night, in a little scene between the Queen and Mr. Brown.

When Mr. Brown arrived in Her Majesty's sitting room with her nightcap—a wee whitter mixed with Apollonaris water—he found her sitting alone on the couch, the speech in her lap, staring into the fire, and she was thinking of all the babies that the speech said parents drowned each year in the Thames.

Mr. Brown silently extended the drink, and silently she took it, turning her eyes on him with the sad, almost unseeing look that she gave him sometimes, and when she looked at him that way he knew that she was seeing the Prince. John Brown had been Albert's gillie first; Albert had liked and trusted him, and no man had ever had a more devoted servant. And that was the bond between Victoria and Brown, the bond that mystified so many observers who could not understand why the imperious lady put up with his uncouth ways and his drill-sergeant orders. But the bond was stronger than that. Young R. J. Lees, the celebrated medium, through whom the Queen had tried to communicate with her Consort's spirit, had told her that Brown, like many peasants, had the psychic gift, and she felt this to be true; sometimes when John Brown was present she had a sense that her husband was there too, extending his protection through the faithful Highlander.

Mr. Brown hovered over her as she sipped the whisky, noting the speech in her lap, the abstracted expression, and smiled down at her, an understanding, affectionate smile. He recited gently: " 'There was an auld woman wha lived in a shoe . . .' "

A cloud came over the Queen's face.

"It's true, aye," he nodded, "ye've mony childer."

She reproved him irritably: "You forget yourself."

"It's a sma' thing to forget, Mum. I was thinking of the bairns— highnesses and mudlarks thegither, and the laird's Jock and the wee bit mole of a thing in the coalpits——"

"That," the Queen said more sharply, "will do."

But he shook his head and contradicted her: " 'Twill no do. Woman, woman, do ye no mind yer anointed hands and what's written i' the Beuk o' Kings—'Is it weel wi' the chield?' " He spoke as sternly, as accusingly as John Knox to Mary Stuart: "Britannia, auld chuckie, ye maun answer for yer brood!"

Victoria put her glass down hard on the table. She stood up, her face white, her loose cheeks trembling with anger. "You may go, Brown!"

It was the tone she never used with him, and he looked as if she had slapped him. He seemed on the point of an angry reply, but after a moment his face softened, he bowed his head, and left the room.

First Mr. Disraeli, and now Brown—Brown too! she thought, standing there, feeling more lonely and misunderstood than ever; and crushing the speech violently in her hands, she flung it into the fire. She put her hand on the mantel and leaned her forehead against it, watching the flames consume the paper, but in her mind's eye they only illumined one phrase of that speech: "Mother of England." She turned away from the fire, crossed the room, and flung herself down at her desk, as before an altar, her beseeching eyes upon the supercilious picture of Albert—and heard again the words of John Brown: "Ye maun answer for yer brood!" And suddenly she broke down.

That night the royal widow, who with a shriek like any hausfrau's had virtually renounced the world at the deathbed of her husband, spent in Gethsemane among her images and her keepsakes. But it was not until two days later that Disraeli received from her the letter that so surprised him, the longest letter he had ever received from her—fourteen and a half pages this time; a febrile document underlined to the point of defacement and to the utter destruction of emphasis. It said in part:

It will ever be a *disgrace* to the Nation that it has not properly respected the terrible AGONY of the Queen on her pinnacle of solitary grandeur since the death of her beloved husband—that in *criticizing, importuning,* and *besieging* her with its DEMANDS, it has denied her the common *rights* of a *Woman!* In her grief she has long felt unequal to these demands and might long ago have ABDICATED the Throne had she not been *unalterably dedicated* to maintaining those principles which *he* in his wisdom laid down for her guidance and for the welfare of her dear People. No one will ever know what trials she has endured for THEIR sake. Her own life is *finished,* but she labours on for them alone, as she knows the noble Prince would expect her to do, and, in *sacrifice* of her own *feelings* and comforts as a *woman,* is resolved henceforth to assume an even *greater share* of their burdens and enter more fully into their affairs. She wishes them to feel that she is not only their Queen, but as Mr. Disraeli was pleased to put it, the MOTHER of them ALL! She therefore begs Mr. Disraeli to spare her *nothing* of her ordained task, but ever to *exhort* and *counsel* her in the discharge of it.

Disraeli stopped to read that paragraph again. In the circumstances, his speech alone surely could not have brought her round to this decision; there must be some other explanation! He read on with rising brows, struck by the sacrificial tone, the frequency of eulogistic references to Albert, and, when he had finished, exclaimed loudly enough to startle Darcy Hammond at the other side of the room: "Suttee!"

He told her afterwards that he put the letter down with the thought that he had just read the happiest proclamation of her reign.

And so it happened that the Queen came out of the seclusion of almost fifteen years, into the sight of her people again; nor did she wait for the spring and the Manchester Exhibition of Scientific Industry, but on the 26th February sallied forth from Buckingham Palace to visit the Foundling Hospital.

Of late years, on rare occasions that were understood to be exceptions to her rule, Her Majesty had made ceremonial forays in the State Coach with an escort of Yeomen and plumed Life Guards; this was an informal call and she went in a carriage, but the news that she was emerging into public life had preceded her, and it became, to her amazement, a triumphal journey. Her carriage, with its escort of but two outriders and with the stalwart figure of John Brown on the box, was recognized, people flocked to the kerb to cheer, small boys ran alongside on the pavement, and the portly little woman on the cushions bowed and fluttered her uncertain handkerchief. It had been a long time since she had been cheered like this; usually of late they had been silent, men had not even removed their hats as she went by, and sometimes there had been jeers.

She tried to smile at them.

The Foundling greatly interested her. It was true, she elicited, that babies were drowned in the Thames; their parents did not want them; and had it not been for this hospital, many of these that she saw now very likely would be dead too. Victoria went round the cribs of the youngest, leaning over this one and that one to look, and once she paused to take a baby's finger from its mouth. "You must always do that," she admonished the sister. "It spoils the shape of their mouths." Hadn't she had nine? She also "inspected" the older children, the buildings, the famous pictures—Hogarth's "Finding of Moses," Raphael's "Massacre of the Innocents," West's altarpiece of Christ blessing children; the manuscript copy of "The Messiah" that Handel had bequeathed, the organ he had given for the chapel. And last she listened to a rendition of "God Save the Queen" by the boys' band that had supplied so many musicians to her Army and Navy.

When she left, she found that a small crowd awaited her in the street. A cheer greeted her; she waved her handkerchief again, stood bowing for a moment, and then descended to her carriage. She saw that she had stayed much longer than she had intended; she hoped she hadn't kept the children from their supper. It was evening now; shops and offices were spilling their denizens into the dusk, the streets were filled with hurrying people, omnibuses careened by; she had scarcely realized that London was such a busy place. To Victoria it was a little terrifying. But again her carriage was recognized all along the route. "Way for the Queen!" someone would shout, and the hurrying people would stop, look, cheer, and make way for her. "Way for the Queen!" Hats came off, hands waved; and how warmly they smiled! The tired woman leaned forward to smile back at them out the windows and to wave the handkerchief. At this hour, with its bustle and clatter, she had the feeling that she was really among them, in the midst of their life—London life! "Mother of England," she told herself—"Of the United Kingdom, I mean!" And then a boy shouted: " 'Ello, Mother of England! Welcome to London! Welcome 'ome!" The carriage pulled through the palace gates; Her Majesty was assisted to descend. And as she walked through the door that a footman held open for her, it was remarked that Queen Victoria, whom no servant had ever seen other than austerely self-contained, was gently weeping into her little lace handkerchief.

With the strange turn that events had given the Wheeler Case, it was some time before the Grenadier Guards realized quite how it

Lord Stithian broke off and tweaked his moustache. "Do. eh?" He made a distasteful face. "Dear me."

"My family——"

"I don't care a rap about your family."

"With your permission, sir, I think you do. The McHattens have been gentry in this country for three hundred years. There was a McHatten in the Long Parliament, there was one taught James First of Scotland how to use the claymore—and there was one hanged at Execution Dock. My mother was a grandniece of the Marquess of Abercorn, so I am related, though distantly, to the present Duke, and to Lord George Hamilton——"

Lord Stithian cut in impatiently: "Well. well, you're not a duke yourself, are you?"

"No. . . ."

"Nor a marquess, I suppose? Nor an earl?"

"Not yet."

"Not yet!"

"I daresay all the peers of England have not been made yet, sir."

"Pfa!"

McHatten, with his wild, youthful mixture of self-esteem and self-doubt, bitterness and romance, reacted from the sting of that negating middle-aged lip sound so sharply, so defiantly, and with such extravagant claims for himself that the father for a moment was taken aback. "You have no right to sneer at me, sir! What do you know about me? That I was not born a peer as you were—that I'm the Vicar's son; but you don't know what I have in me—you've no way of knowing. But I know, and I don't think it's absurd to say I may yet be a peer; I think peers have been made from a good deal less. The Prime Minister didn't sneer at me, sir. He invited me to stand for Parliament for Cheshire, sir; did you know that? The Prime Minister thought I had a future, sir."

"Indeed?"

"Yes! And do you know what I told the Prime Minister? I said that if I decided to accept his invitation, I might someday be prime minister myself! He laughed but he didn't sneer. He was once less than I am, yet there he sits. So may I. And one day you, sir, may sit below me at dinner. Oh, I intend no impudence. But if I may say so, sir, a viscount's not very much. I shall aim a bit higher myself. There on the walls, the pictures of your noble ancestors; that cavalier over the mantel—you must be proud of him. Well, I venture to hope that when England's a bit older, I'll be looking down from a mantel as fine as that one—or finer."

"Very commendable," said the ninth viscount, and eyed him with a dry smile. He was not offended. It was one of the times in the life of an older man when a young one suddenly opens his mind to him and gives him a glimpse of the foolish vanity that is there, and the avidity, and the overweening hope, and for an instant the topic of conversation becomes for the older man secondary, and one part of him wants to sneer and another to weep. Emily's father paced back to the mantel. "And you expect Lady Margaret to take you on trust?"

"I hadn't thought of Lady Margaret taking me at all."

Lord Stithian Prior, tweaking his moustache again and looking at the impassioned boy under his brows, and half remembering something, suddenly grinned at him. He said, "You talk like a cavalryman."

"Sir?"

"Bah! but you're not one. Compare yourself with that chap Lochinvar—a cavalryman, sir! He didn't go slogging it over the moors to beg the girl's father."

Disbelief and joy struggled on the young man's face. "Am I to understand——"

"There you go—talking like a Foot Guard again. If you'd come to see me, I'd have shown you the door at once, sir. And, by God, if I hadn't, my wife jolly well would have shown it to me. Good job you didn't come, eh? But it'll make no difference. If my daughter has the sense I think she has, she'll show you the door herself."

All the fire had gone out of McHatten, but the joy went too. "I see," he said.

A chill descended upon the older man as he met the young one's gaze, and he regretted his impulse. Where in the world had it come from? "H'm," he said in the uncomfortable silence. But shouldn't it be up to Emily, after all? Wouldn't she have to marry someone, and didn't he want her to be happy? And the boy did seem to have good stuff in him. Yet Lord Stithian could not encourage such a match by his consent. It was a wonder, he thought, that the insulting blighter didn't ask him if Pontius Pilate had been a cavalryman. But he said: "By the way, I see by the Court Circular the Queen's at Balmoral." And now he had done it.

Up to Emily. And it is doubtful that a better way could have been found to persuade Emily to look with favour on McHatten's suit than the one that had been devised by Her Majesty and Lady Margaret. Emily for six months now had been the Queen's prisoner—a prisoner for love, she had told herself over and over, until finally she had come to believe it, and no romantic young woman ever had felt more sorry for herself. Then, for love of her, McHatten had been sent into exile, and for this she was bound to be grateful to him. All that remained was for his love to bring him back again, swimming, as it were, the deepest ocean, and, wet or dry, he might reasonably have expected Emily to fall into his arms.

But month had followed month, and he had not come, nor had she heard a word from him. His letters, she surmised, were being intercepted; but then she began to wonder if they really were. There he was, in India, probably surrounded by the daughters of his senior officers: was he likely, after all, to pine away of his hopeless love? This became a real worry to Emily. At the same time she contrasted his many opportunities with her own lack of them in her protracted attendance upon the Queen—a lack, she clearly saw, which had

THE MUDLARK

been imposed on her entirely through his fault. When she thought
of that, she felt as if he had left her in the lurch, and was bitter
toward McHatten. She considered the future and found it gloomy.
She had heard of cases in which ladies lurched like herself had lost
their looks and died old maids; and she would rush to look at herself
in the glass. She often told herself that she wished she had never
known McHatten. But then, she never meant it. Frequently in her
room she cried.

And then one evening at Balmoral Castle she received a note from
this errant suitor, smuggled in by an officer of the Scots Guards;
and that night slipped out and went to meet him at the appointed
place. The place was a spot in the West Gardens, and above it, happily, through the mist, a moon was sailing. McHatten had scarcely
expected her to come; he had been waiting for an hour when he saw
her figure, wrapped in a heavy cloak, come stealing round a bank
of flowers. He rushed to meet her.

"Emily! I didn't think you'd come!"

"Charles! Dear Charles!" Her voice was charged with emotion,
the hand that he held was trembling, and he saw that her eyes were
wet. And "Dear Charles!" Such a reception staggered him. But how
could he have been expected to follow the complicated female psychology that had prepared it for him? A lesser man might have been
terrified by it; but in another instant she was in his arms, and he was
engulfed and swept away by a passion as fierce as his own.

She never even returned indoors—as she was to put it later, "for
a toothbrush." In a feat the reverse of Wheeler's, McHatten smuggled her past the sentries, left her in the heather while he went back
for his horse, and, taking her up behind him, carried her off in the
authentic Lochinvar style, so that when Mr. Disraeli heard of it
later, he exclaimed: "We really must get that young traitor to stand
for Parliament. If the electorate ever hears of this his career is made!"
In the early hours of the morning they boarded a train at Ballater,
were married at Aberdeen, and, with the hue and cry behind them,

— 299 —

travelled the length of Britain to Dover, where they embarked for France in a fishing boat. That is how the Maid of Honour eloped in the night with the young ex-Guardsman, who had won (if you were not of the Moncreiffe Party) the greatest beauty of the Kingdom. It is told as an anecdote—a little inaccurately as to the little things—in *Forty Years in the Queen's Household*, by William Wellington Nasehy.

Wheeler?

He was let off with three months in the Middlesex Industrial School—"let off" because when orphans of his age were found to be without suitable homes, and happened to get into trouble, it was customary to commit them till they were old enough to be apprenticed out, but Wheeler's uncle informed the magistrate that he had lately married Miss Margaret Bownes of Poplar Parish and promised that he and his wife would send the boy to school and look after him proper. Mr. Wheeler was sincere: he shone in his nephew's reflected glory and wished to continue to do so, and besides, he had been offered a bit of a charter fee for Wheeler by a London music hall. Alas, when the Ha'penny Bit was released in his uncle's charge, the school board refused to permit him to be exhibited, and his uncle had to send him to school anyhow.

He went to school for nearly four years. Then he ran away. No more was heard of him for several months, which brings his story to 1880. And then——

But a good deal had happened elsewhere by that time.

By that time Mr. Disraeli was Prime Minister no longer, but Leader of the Loyal Opposition, and he had passed from the House of Commons to the House of Lords, for now he was the Earl of Beaconsfield. It was a title that must have given him a particular satisfaction, being one he had invented long ago and filed away in the magical hope chest of his novels. But the Commons had viewed his elevation gloomily. "All the real chivalry and delight of party politics have departed," one Member had said; and another: "The days of the giants are over. Ichabod! Ichabod!" As for himself, "I am dead," said the Old Jew, looking round him as he sat among the peers of the realm; "dead, but in the Elysian Fields!"

He had set Britain on the path of social reform, along which his successor, Mr. Gladstone, was to lead her a little farther. He had bought into the Suez Canal for her, and given her the Transvaal; in consequence, Khartoum and Majuba were in the making, and abroad she was embarked on the Imperial Way, along which Mr. Gladstone in spite of himself was to lead her a considerable distance.

And Victoria was Empress of India now, and put "R.&I." after her name at the bottom of all her letters, and she was entering on the golden period of her reign.

And the McHattens had returned from France, to be forgiven in time by both Lord and Lady Prior, but never by the Queen. McHatten had spent a year in an unobtrusive post in the War Office, and then, with the encouragement of Disraeli and the assistance of the Rothschilds, had stood for Parliament for his family's old constituency, and been elected. In a few years more he was to buy back the family estate, and from time to time to add to it; and he was destined, the records show, for a surprising career. He remained a rebel to the end, but it seemed that the more substantial a citizen he became, the more old-fashioned grew his notions of government, so that the course of his thinking was backwards and he became a rebel in reverse. This hindered him for a while. But then a curious thing happened. It began to be said that such a man was good for the country—his constant and forceful opposition to progress acted as a brake on the socialists and helped to keep change gradual. And since in foreign affairs he was for preserving the honour of England at any cost, his personal popularity increased with his years, even among those who usually voted against him. In the pubs, his name was seldom mentioned without the adjectives "good old" before it, until at the age of seventy he came to be looked upon as Old England in the flesh, and the story of his courtship being still remembered, everyone loved him. He died a baron at seventy-five, leaving his widow with the old-fashioned number of children, which was nine; and Emily had never regretted her choice.

Slattery had been shipped all the way to San Francisco. There, having mentioned his story, he had been taken up by an Irish-American society, which regarded him as a valuable exhibit; his oratory became a feature of its St. Patrick's Day dinners, and he was conspicuous at all Home Rule rallies: he was The Man that had Damned Near Burned Down Windsor Castle. His new friends therefore found him a job as a fireman; and his reputation so impressed his superiors that within three years he was a battalion chief. He married the daughter of a Supervisor of the City and County, with whose help he soon rose to be chief of the whole department. "San Francisco," says a local biographer, "had taken him to its heart." One of the great sights of the city was said to be Slattery charging through the streets in his red juggernaut behind the fine spirited bays presented to him by Lily Hitchcock, though it was whispered that his keeping the fire bell by his bedside had caused his wife several miscarriages in their first few years, till finally she became used to it and gave birth to three more firemen. Even for Slattery, in time, the excitement proved too much, until at the peak of a famous career he had to retire on his doctor's orders. And shortly afterwards he died of excitement, died with the city itself on the morning of 18th April, 1906, having seen as fine a conflagration as any man since Nero; and it was said when he was laid out afterwards that no corpse had ever looked happier.

Noonan had consoled herself with a steadier man, a gatekeeper of the castle, whose wages she collected with her own; they had two children and in twenty years' time retired on their savings to go and keep a small tobacco shop in Newington Butts.

Munn, the Junoesque chambermaid, was to make history of a sort. Under the aegis of Sir Gilpin Jarvey she had acquired three valuable assets—a certain worldly wisdom, a semblance of education, and a proficiency on the hand bells. But a woman of her nature could not have been happy for long with so old a bird, and after a few years she had left him for a charming young Bloomsbury hack. This unfortunately had involved a stoppage of the allowance with which she had been supplying the young man out of the old one's pocket, which so annoyed the young one that he threw her over for a more wieldy lass. In this extremity, Munn joined a troupe of Swiss bell ringers with which she toured the provinces. The head of this troupe seems to have been a born impresario. He saw that bell ringing, as a form of popular entertainment, left something to be desired, and that what was needed to give their turn distinction was a novel and spectacular finish. He therefore devised one. And a year later we find the troupe appearing as a feature attraction in a large London music hall. The finish is nothing less than a dramatization of *Curfew Shall Not Ring Tonight*, in which a great church bell is lowered from the top of the proscenium arch and the scantily draped figure of Munn is discovered swinging back and forth upon the clapper. There is no escaping it: she has a magnificent figure. And in this breath-taking exhibition, she swings into the ken of Lord George Couples. "Gad!" he says hoarsely. "Who's that?" And consults the program. "Mademoiselle Genevieve," it informs him. And so begin the palmy days of Jenny Munn, afterwards one of the most celebrated courtesans of London, and certainly the biggest.

And then——

In September of 1880 there appeared in the London newspapers an item to the effect that the famous Boy Wheeler, also known as the Ha'penny Bit, was said to have been rescued from the Straits of Gibraltar after falling overboard from the barque *Elizabeth P. Summers*, of which he was cabin boy.

A month later another item relating to the same incident appeared in the letter column of *The Times*. This letter had been written by James Summers, owner and master of the vessel, who denied that the Boy Wheeler had fallen overboard. The captain declared he had deliberately jumped, and, when fished out again and asked why, explained that he had done so in order to have a look at the buoy light burning, because it could not be seen from the ship.

Sitting at his desk outside the Leader of the Opposition's room in the Houses of Parliament, Darcy Hammond read this letter and laughed. The Boy Wheeler, he thought, must be a bit touched. And he showed the letter to Mr. Disraeli. But Mr. Disraeli did not laugh. "Remarkable!" he said. "Jumped in so he could see the buoy light, did he? What imagination, Hammond; what gusto!" Then, almost wistfully: "What a life that boy will have. Things will happen where he is. Has the bells of Cockaigne in his ears, you know," said Mr. Disraeli, recalling his own phrase pleasantly; and he smiled.

It was the end of what had been a tiring day. Hammond helped the old man into his greatcoat and lent him an arm out to his carriage. Darcy Hammond felt almost like a son towards Mr. Disraeli, though sometimes he felt more like a father.

"Home," Disraeli said to the coachman; and suddenly Hammond was filled with pity for him, knowing that he had no home. Not in London, anyhow. Not anywhere. He had given up the house in Whitehall Gardens, and was going back to a suite of rooms placed at his disposal by the Rothschilds whenever he was in town. And down in Berkshire there was only a lot of other rooms in that great, cold, empty manor. But the coachman knew where to take him, and as the carriage clattered out of the courtyard of Westminster Palace, Hammond looked after it and shook his head. "Gusto indeed! Imagination indeed!" And there recurred to him that bit of the wisdom of the nursery that the Chief once had told him he was too young to appreciate:

"How many miles to Babylon?"
"Three score and ten."
"Can I get there by candlelight?"
"Aye—and back again!"

In the carriage, the Earl of Beaconsfield had settled back into the cushions. His lids drooped, his chin was buried in the folds of his muffler: one might have thought he had fallen asleep. Far from it. Mudlark, he was thinking—what a wonderful name for it! . . . Bells of Cockaigne! A good speech, that one. But Gadshaw had missed the point. A lot of 'em had missed the point, he was sure of it. The high golden bells—and *they* had thought he meant Bow Bells! The corners of his mouth twitched slightly. He was thinking of all the gaffers hidden behind their blinds in the London evening who could not or would not remember the sound they had not had the courage to follow and might as well never have heard.